Nighttown

Also by Timothy Hallinan

The Poke Rafferty Series
A Nail Through the Heart
The Fourth Watcher
Breathing Water
The Queen of Patpong
The Fear Artist
For the Dead
The Hot Countries
Fools' River

The Junior Bender Series
Crashed
Little Elvises
The Fame Thief
Herbie's Game
King Maybe
Fields Where They Lay

The Simeon Grist Series
The Four Last Things
Everything but the Squeal
Skin Deep
Incinerator
The Man With No Time
The Bone Polisher
Pulped

Nighttown

A Junior Bender Mystery

TIMOTHY HALLINAN

SOHO
CRIME

Published by Soho Press, Inc.
227 W 17th Street Broadway
New York, NY 10011

Library of Congress Cataloging-in-Publication Data

Hallinan, Timothy, author.
Nighttown / Timothy Hallinan.
Series: A Junior Bender mystery; 7

ISBN 978-1-64129-091-3
eISBN 978-1-61695-749-0

1. Thieves—Fiction. 2. Private investigators—California—Los
Angeles—Fiction. I. Title
PS3558.A3923 N54 2018 813'.54—dc23 2018016747

Interior design by Janine Agro, Soho Press, Inc.

Printed in the United States of America

10 9 8 7 6 5 4 3 2 1

To the one I've held hands with all these years.
Munyin Choy

PART ONE

The Night

. . . and darkness was upon the face of the deep.
—*The Scholars of the King James Version*

1

WEEEoooooo

By way of a prelude, a few words about the dark.

In the entire, staggering length of the Bible—Old and New Testaments combined, a total of 783,137 words—darkness is mentioned only about one hundred times, and it gets slagged almost every time. It's identified with ignorance, hell, evil, exile, the absence of God, and other conditions to which few of us aspire. The only *positive* mention of darkness in the whole Book is when the Lord speaks to Moses after dimming the day to protect the Israelites from the sight of Him, and that *good* darkness, the one and only good darkness, is called by a completely different word, *araphel*, which will never be used again. Just that once. For God's personal and merciful darkness.

It gets its own damn *word* to distinguish it from, you know, ordinary every-night darkness, which is Not Good.

According to the King James Bible, translated from a bunch of older languages by forty-seven of Shakespeare's contemporaries, the Lord gets right down to business with the very first line he speaks: *Let there be light*, He says. And then . . .

And God saw the light, that it was good: and God divided the light from the darkness.

And God called the light Day, and the darkness he called Night.

Night is just what's left over after the big chop: over *here*, light, which is good; and over *there*, dark, which is definitely not good and which will be thrown at us, regular as clockwork, every sunset through eternity to lay claim to half of our lives, whether we like it or not. And we're not supposed to like it.

As you can probably tell, I have a problem with this outlook.

I make my living, ninety percent of the time, in the dark. Burglars tend to *prefer* the dark because, while some of us are pretty dumb, there aren't many of us stupid enough to begin a job by turning on the lights. One iron-clad rule of burglary is to avoid unexpected interactions with others, and darkness helps to prevent them. That was taught to me at the age of seventeen by my mentor, the late, great Herbie Mott, and he had the game down cold. Thanks to Herbie's guidance, I've been at this game very successfully for more than twenty years and I don't even have an arrest record, much less a conviction. I'm *good* at this, and I resent the way my old ally darkness is slandered.

It's not that light is *useless*. I'm as fond of a sunny day as anyone who isn't prone to melanoma, but I can't help thinking that giving the sun the night off is one of creation's better ideas. It rests the eyes, it allows plants a chance to take a break from making sugar. It clears the landscape for a lot of very interesting animal life. Most love is made at night, at least by people older than, say, seventeen. Many of the world's most fragrant flowers bloom at night. In place of the monochrome blue of the daytime sky, night offers us the moon's waxing and waning face, set off against the infinite jewelry of the stars.

If it seems to you that I've given this a lot of thought, you're right. Nighttime, in a manner of speaking, is my zip code. It's an undiscriminating neighborhood, one I share with disk jockeys, cops, ambulance drivers, insomniacs, air traffic controllers, French bakers, peeping toms, recovering drunks, speed freaks, the terrified, the bereaved, the guilt ridden, and those with the medical condition photophobia. Sure, it's a mixed batch, but night also evens the odds for the blind and extends a hand of mercy to the odd-looking, the ones who draw stares in the glare of noon. It softens the edges of even our ugliest cities.

But there actually *can* be too much of a good thing.

I had never really subscribed to that idea, but as I stood in the entry hall of Horton House, holding my breath and listening—which is always the first thing I do when I enter a house—I was revising my opinion. Horton House was *too dark*. For the first time in my perhaps four hundred burglaries, it seemed like a good idea to just blow it off and go back out into the comparative glare of a moonless night.

And it wasn't just the dark, which was so close to absolute that I might as well call it that. The house was *noisy*, in the way only an all-wooden house that's more than a century old can be. Horton House had been built by a briefly prominent family in 1908, and every join, plank, beam, and nail was feeling its age and complaining about it. It was almost as loud as a sailboat, which (the claims of their owners notwithstanding) *never* stops creaking and moaning and sloshing. Horton House made so much noise that I was having trouble listening around and through all of it for the sound of something human: movement, breathing, snores, whatever. The place was supposed to be empty; in fact, a sign outside confirmed that the house was due for demolition in three days. Still, I waited and listened, as I always do, in recognition of the perpetual gulf between what I think I know and what's actually happening.

The most off-putting of the house's trinity of disquieting characteristics—the one I found even more disagreeable than the darkness and the noise—was its *smell*. One component was a sharp-edged stink that could only be really, *really* old paper, and I was willing to bet that my little penlight, when I felt secure enough that I was alone to turn it on, would show me the original wallpaper, more than a century old, clinging for dear life to the walls. And running just beneath the sharp wallpaper smell, like a large but muted string section supporting a snare drum, was a pervasive, over-sweet scent with an almost physical heaviness that I first guessed as long-dead flowers, maybe tuberose or narcissus or some kind of lily. It took me a full minute to realize what it really was.

Baby powder.

If what I'd learned about the house was true, there hadn't been a newborn baby here since 1921, and the thought of the smells that baby powder might have been intended to disguise in these latter days was more than a little unsettling. The "baby"—Miss Daisy, the last of the Hortons—had died upstairs, almost exactly a month earlier, at the age of ninety-six after spending almost fifty years confined to a bed on the second floor.

Put it all together, and what it came down to was that

Horton House had a certain WEEEooooWEEEoooo factor. The place absolutely hummed with malice. Miss Daisy,
who had spent eighty years or so alone here, except for a
skeleton staff of servants and a long and apparently unsat-
isfying succession of daytime caregivers, was semi-famous
for hating everything. In her thirties, before the fall on the
stairs that had almost severed her spinal cord, she'd been
nicknamed "the Witch of Windsor Street" for her skill
at terrifying children who dared to play on the sidewalk
in front of Horton House. Her animus remained evident
even after she gave up hoping for a cure and took to her
bed: her response to the changes in her neighborhood, as
the old houses went down and stucco went up to welcome
an influx of new occupants whose native languages were
more likely to be Spanish and Korean than English, was
to put the evolving world literally out of sight and out of
mind. First, she had her gardeners install the thick ficus
hedge that surrounded the property and over-fertilize it
until it was higher than the streetlights and the windows
of the houses on either side. Second, when the home on
her left was demolished to make way for a three-story
apartment house with vaguely French Provincial preten-
sions, she covered the inside of every window in her own
house with two layers of the heavy brown paper used for
supermarket shopping bags. Dark as it was at night, in the
daytime, the light in here in mid-afternoon must have been
the rich color of caramel. I knew much of this because
Miss Daisy had long been the Cruella de Vil of fading Los
Angeles gentility, and as such, she'd gotten her share of
newspaper space and, much later, TV time, although she
was never seen on-screen.

Apparently, one of the more enduring marks she'd left

on Horton House was the odor of that damn baby powder, a kind of cloying sweetness that bordered on decay. I
hated it all the way to the back of my neck, which is a part
of my body I've learned to pay attention to. Everybody
gets the prickles in different places, I guess, but I get them
on the back of the neck, and my neck had essentially been
calling my name from the moment I opened the gate in the
center of that towering hedge.

Which I had done with a *key*, by the way. The key
alone should have told me from the beginning that something was off about the whole enterprise. I hadn't even
turned my penlight on, and I was already having second
thoughts.

Still, I'd just hidden more than $25,000 in hundreds
in my chimney at home and there was another $25,000
waiting for me when this errand was complete. I focused
on that. Large sums of money create a powerful reality-
distortion field, and in my experience it had rarely been
harder to overcome. I was facing a problem that only
money would solve, and the problem involved not only me
but a person I loved.

So. All the creaks, shudders, and groans were just old
wood, nothing that couldn't be explained by the contrac-
tion of an arthritic old house. The smells, awful as they
were, were just smells. Now that I'd forced myself not to
go all fizzy because of the baby powder, I also smelled
tobacco—not fresh, but the indelible nicotine funk given
off by walls, rugs, and furniture that have been marinated
in cigarette smoke for years. The place was dark and noisy
and it reeked, but I seemed to be alone.

I flicked on the little penlight and played it around,
startled for a second by a bulky shape right beside me, an

authentic elephant's-foot umbrella holder, probably from the 1920s: dark, wrinkled, gray skin that was thicker than any leather I'd ever seen, all hollowed out, with four huge toenails in a deeply unwholesome yellow, the whole thing almost hip-high on me. I stepped away from its potent creepiness, did a quick sweep for four-foot spiders and other unwelcome surprises, and embarked on my usual internal preview of the house I was about to explore.

Quite a bit had been written about Horton House since it was built, and as far as I had been able to see from the outside, it still had the original 1908 floor plan I'd read about. The entrance hall, stretching about thirty feet from the front door to the grand stairway, had broad arched openings on either side, the one on the right leading to the enormous living room and the study behind it, and the one on the left affording access to the dining room and the kitchen. This confirmation that I was right about *something* was a relief, because even though I needed the money so badly, I'd been unnerved by how much of it I'd been handed to pay this visit. In my line of work, too much almost always turns out to be not enough.

I tabled the thought and went back to my mental map. Assuming the second floor was as intact as the ground floor seemed to be, I basically knew my way around. The blind spot, if I had one, would be the servants' quarters, which hadn't made the cut for the society pages. Still, I expected to find at least one small bedroom, probably beyond the kitchen. Almost certainly there would be nothing important back there, but it's always a good idea to get a quick look at the spaces you're not sure about before exploring the ones you are.

The curved, darkly carpeted stairway at the hall's end

was wide enough to allow an entire barbershop quartet to sing their way down it, side by side. It led, I knew, to three upstairs bedrooms, two baths, the nursery, and the sitting room, where, I supposed, people once sat. In front of me at the end of the hall, in a recess just to the right of the stairway, was a small nook with a door in it. My guess was that it opened onto stairs leading down to the basement.

I was *not* going down to the basement.

Not believing in the supernatural doesn't necessarily protect you from the heebie-jeebies. Reason lives in one room, and *yes*, I'll concede that it's a nicely lighted room, while unreasoning, primal, bogeyman fear lives in another. The door between the rooms is usually locked, which meant that my comforting, no-woo-woo belief system was not currently accessible. I stood absolutely still, four feet from the scooped-out elephant's foot, with my back pressed against the front door, beaming that pathetic little finger of light around and asking myself why the hell I was there, even though I knew it was plain old money.

Look around. Looking around would divert me.

The penlight put out a yellowish beam that intensified the yellow of the ancient wallpaper on either side of the hall. As anyone who owns an old print knows, blue is the first color that light leaches away, and paper yellows naturally as it ages, so eventually you end up with a narrow chromatic scale that's heavy on yellows, not so much a color wheel as a color semicircle. Wallpaper is no exception, and what had once been peacock plumes now looked like fancy fans and feather dusters made of straw. The hallway's white ceiling was arched, like the doorways and the openings to the other rooms. The effect was beautiful in a slightly churchy manner. Builders used to care about the houses they built.

Dangling above me was a delicately angular wrought-iron chandelier. To my surprise, it was just perceptibly moving, although I could only see the motion in the magnified shadow thrown on the wall by my little light. Somehow, despite the nailed-shut windows and their brown-paper coverings, a draft had tiptoed in. I closed my eyes and tried to sense the moving air on my face. If I felt anything, it came from in front of me and, possibly, to the left.

Since the thought of an open door on the ground floor wasn't reassuring, I decided to locate the source of the draft before I went upstairs. So I took a couple of steps and stopped, fighting the impulse to put my fingers in my ears. The floor beneath me yielded up an extraordinarily varied assortment of creaks and pops. I edged, just sliding my feet, to the left; floors creak less where their beams are joined at the wall. It was a little quieter, but by the time I'd reached the archway to the dining room I'd figured out that a movie company could have recorded an entire film's worth of ominous groans, squawks, creaks, and pops in Horton House without even going upstairs.

Just before I made the left into the dining room, heading toward the kitchen area, I realized why the carpet on the stairway had caught my eye. The hallway floor, by contrast, was *bare*, but not, I thought, to show off the quality of the flooring. To confirm my hunch, I turned around and played the little flashlight's beam over the juncture of walls and floor on either side of the long entrance hall. No question: the ten to twelve inches of wood closest to the wall had been bleached by decades of indirect sunlight,

scarred and scratched by generations of feet, while the
strip down the center, although dusty, was as lustrous as
the soundboard on a fine guitar. It wasn't hard to visu-
alize the missing carpet: a fine old custom-made runner,
thirty feet in length and a good five feet wide. Literally an
antique, the label US Customs reserves for artifacts manu-
factured a century or more ago. If it hadn't been ripped up
because it was worn through or was in tatters, it had been
worth a small fortune.

I turned into the dining room and angled my way relatively quietly along the walls, the windows not admitting
a candle's worth of light through their thick brown paper
masks. The parts of the room I could see seemed oddly
empty—I'd been told the house was still furnished—but I
wanted to locate the source of the draft before I checked
anything else. The temperature had dropped a little as I
neared the kitchen, so I figured I was going in the right
direction.

The dining room was so dark that I was completely
unprepared for the chest-high flare of reflected light as I
turned through the doorway into the kitchen. The glass in
the windows above the sink and counter had been uncovered, undoubtedly the work of a cook, who needed more
light to do his or her stuff and who knew that the mistress of the house was upstairs being sprinkled with that
awful baby powder and wouldn't be dropping in anytime
soon. I snapped off the penlight and tried to blink away
the black negative the reflection had printed on my retina.
I couldn't see much of anything but I could feel the draft
more directly now, and it came from my right. When I
could focus, I saw that the window directly above the end
of the counter was open by about four inches.

Leaving the light off, I went to the open window and got the best look at it I could under the circumstances. Neither on the sill nor on the counter beneath it did I see any dirt or grass or other bits of the outside world someone might have brought in on his or her shoes. When I slipped my hand beneath the window, my gloved fingertips hit a screen, which appeared to be tightly in place. In the interest of thoroughness, always prudent when committing a felony, I passed my palm over the counter, which was greasy but not sandy or littered with shoe crap, and then I got down on my hands and knees and aimed my penlight at the floor. There were no footprints. I stood up and turned off both the light and my mind for a moment, simply not thinking about it. It's a mental version of looking to the side of something you want to see when it's dark.

With my light off, the world on the other side of the windowpanes had the wavy, somewhat watery appearance that's the hallmark of old cylinder glass from the late nineteenth and early twentieth century, a process developed to create a sheet of glass big enough for larger windows. It was blown in the form of a long tube that was slit down one side and opened while still pliable and then put into an extremely hot furnace where it melted and flattened into a smooth but slightly rippled sheet. This was obviously the glass that came with the house, not a later replacement. When I got closer, though, I saw that I had been right in thinking that it had once been covered: The edges of the panes were a remarkably ugly brown where years' worth of dust particles and cooking oil had adhered to the sticky imprint of the tape that once held the heavy paper in place.

Okay, I decided, at some point the cook had simply cracked open the window to provide an escape route for the heat and the odors of cooking. It was a small kitchen, and perhaps she'd been instructed to keep the door to the dining room closed to spare the house's inhabitants the smells of cabbage or cruciferous vegetables, the smoke of broiling meat. I can't say the explanation made me completely happy, but I allowed it, combined with the money in hand and the money yet to come, to keep me from going straight out through the front door and across Koreatown to the apartment I shared with my girlfriend of more than a year now, Ronnie Bigelow. Ronnie and I needed the money. We were planning an operation to kidnap her two-year-old son from his father, a New Jersey mob doctor, and it was an expensive proposition.

The house chose that moment to creak, and I said to it silently, *the hell with you. I'm in, and I'll finish up and get out again.* Twenty-five thousand bucks can muffle a lot of creaks.

The door at the far end of the kitchen opened, as expected, into a cramped servant's bedroom with bare floors—concrete, not wood—and only one narrow window, placed so high by the room's designers that it suggested they'd been afraid someone might escape through it. The room was empty except for a single bed, bare but for a thin, graying mattress and a couple of misshapen pillows. Sheets, none too clean, were neatly folded at the foot of the bed. The closet contained nothing but a tangle of coat hangers and a sharp smell of mouse urine, and when I checked the bathroom I found the barest of minimums: a sink, a claustrophobic shower, and a toilet containing water that would probably give me nightmares for weeks.

The bathroom had neither a window nor a vent, which seemed like the cruelest economy of all.

Keeping the uncovered window in mind, I turned off the penlight as I moved through the kitchen, opening drawers and cupboards until I came upon a cupboard that was jammed solid with brown paper supermarket bags, undoubtedly to replace the ones masking the windows as they aged and tore. This had all the symptoms, I thought, of a full-blown mania. I closed everything and headed back into the dining room, staying close to the wall. I was most of the way to the hallway, when I was brought up short once again by the *carpeting*, or, rather, the lack of it. The dining room *should* have been carpeted. Since the windows in here were covered, I flicked on the light and played it around the room, and on the bare floor was a sparse huddle of junk: a Formica table on aluminum legs, three banged-up folding director's chairs. Total value, maybe eighty-five bucks. Just to confirm my budding suspicion, I crossed the hall and took a look at the living room.

More rubbish furniture on the bare floor, and now I also saw the rectangles on the walls, slightly darker than the wallpaper, the ghosts of paintings that had hung there for decades. The only framed art pieces remaining in the room were a couple of gauzy sepia photographs, one on each side of the fireplace, at about eye level. They did not call out to me to take a closer look. Even the bookcases had apparently been ransacked, creating spaces on the shelves, the books on either side tilting left and right, looking depressed at having been left behind in the methodical disappearance of items of value.

So, unlike the window glass, unlike the house itself, the

carpets, furnishings, and decorations had departed, to be replaced with crap—modern, cheap, and even a little battered. Much of it looked like the rag ends of yard sales, which is to say that it was not just used, but *hard* used. Some items might have sat outside in bad weather. And yet the house had never been rented out, as far as I knew, and the Hortons had never gone broke. The place was going to be razed presumably because the lot was worth more without the house on top of it, and none of the living Horton cousins wanted to live in it.

The missing carpets and the vanished furniture, with its bargain-basement replacements, suggested an appalling little playlet. Rich old woman immobilized upstairs. Downstairs, slow-motion, wholesale theft: sell a piece here, sell a piece there, and there, replace it with crap, knowing the next time Miss Daisy would come down the stairs and into these rooms, she'd be carried through them feet first. One immobilized woman, dependent on others for everything, a woman who had been born into a world where servants were seen as faithful retainers, practically "members of the family." Living in service, dying in service, drawing satisfaction from their positions close to the rich and the near-rich, loving the family's children like their own, taking pride in being part of a great house.

Had that *ever* been true? Couldn't have been. At the very least, I supposed, it had been a notion that reassured the rich that the people who moved through the rooms while the family slept were unlikely to murder them in their beds. Despite that awful, airless little bedroom, that dire bathroom.

If I was reading the ground floor correctly, Miss Daisy had, for at least her last few years, lived upstairs from a

skeleton crew of thieves who cashed in one Horton possession after another, possibly even working their way up
the stairs and into the unoccupied rooms on the second
floor as Miss Daisy's world grew smaller until, at last,
she'd been sentenced to spend the rest of her days in bed,
the cradle waiting at the bad end of life, being turned and
baby-powdered and, one hoped, comforted occasionally,
while pieces of her life walked out the front door. She
might have been an awful old rag—her reputation when
she was younger, and the cold, closed nature of her house
suggested that the solitude in which she lived had been
well earned—but it was hard to imagine that she, or anyone, deserved *that*.

If the original things in these rooms had been the kind
of quality appropriate to the house and the Hortons' place
in society, there had probably been more than a couple
hundred thousand bucks' worth on the first floor alone.
And who knew what the pictures had been? Even if the
people who sold the items had no sense of what they were
worth, they'd still be thirty, forty thousand to the good.

And that thought stopped me with one foot on the bottom stair. If all those fine things had been stolen and sold,
why in the world would the thing I was after still be here?

2
Happy Meal

Five days earlier, when I'd gotten caught up in the events that ultimately took me to Horton House, I hadn't actually been *told* what I was after.

I only knew two things about it. First, I was dead certain that it wasn't what my client said it was. What she sent me to find was a doll, which she described just before she gave me the key and the twenty-five thou. It was French, she'd said, with a hand-painted porcelain face. From about 1860, give or take. A girl of ten or eleven with blonde hair, wearing a yellow dress and a cloak with lace and ribbons. In so-so shape.

She must have seen the doubt in my face, because she added, "Pretty little thing, though."

I'd smiled and nodded as though it made sense. The object she described sounded to me like a Jumeau *bébé*, an antique child's doll. The company Maison Jumeau opened for business in Paris in the 1840s as one of Europe's most exclusive dollmakers. It started out with "fashion dolls" that depicted young women dressed in the height of style, but in the 1860s it segued into dolls for, and depicting, children. *Rich* children. Many of them were quite beautiful in a fussy, slightly vapid, and over-precious way, but the most

I'd ever seen offered for one at auction was about thirty K—less than the fee she was offering me to steal the one she described. And the doll that brought that price was in absolutely mint shape, miraculously in its original box.

So the second thing I knew was that what I was being sent to get was *inside* the doll.

I'd almost said *no* right then, despite the threats she mixed in with the payment. The too-large sum of money was only one of the problems. The other was that she was a new client. New clients make me nervous.

Until five days ago, I'd never met, seen, or heard of the person who sent me into Horton House, nor did I know her name. I met her in response to a call from my primary fence, Stinky Tetweiler. After thirty or forty seconds of painfully stilted small talk—Stinky has no interest in other human beings but his shrink advises him to behave as though does—he told me I was going to meet someone in a McDonald's on Western Avenue. I was to wear a yellow shirt and be reading a book.

I said, "Why would I do that? I don't even like yellow."

"A *job*, obviously," he said. "A profitable job."

"Who is it?"

"I have no idea."

"So," I said, "you're arranging for me to meet someone you don't know, which probably means you also don't know what kind of a job he has in mind."

Stinky said, "She."

I said, "No."

"If you're worried about security, the person who called me to set this up is someone I trust completely."

"So that's a minimum of three people who are already involved. Tell you what. *You* meet her."

"All you have to do is listen," he said. "She'll give you twenty-five hundred just to talk, whether you decide to move forward or not."

"How much are you getting for calling me?"

A pause. Stinky really, really hates to talk about money. "The same," he said.

"I want all of it."

"Why would I—"

"The person who set this up, you said, is someone you trust completely. You don't trust anyone completely, so how that translates to me is that it's someone you need to keep happy. I'm helping you keep him or her happy."

A pause. "But *all* of it?"

"All of twenty-five hundred," I said. "We both know you cut it in half because you always do. You told me she paid you twenty-five hundred, but you wouldn't scratch your own back for twenty-five hundred, so let's say she paid you five. I want twenty-five hundred. I think I'm being nice."

"Doesn't have to be you." If I'd been there, I'd have seen Stinky take a swipe at his infinitesimal nose, the bit that's left to him after a lifetime of enthusiastic plastic surgery. Rubbing his nose is Stinky's tell, and I'll kill the person who breaks the news to him. He said, "I can give this to someone else."

"Do it."

The pause was so long I thought he might have hung up. Then he said, "Have I ever told you that you're unbearable?"

"Yes, thanks. So. Twenty-five hundred from you before I go, and the same from her, in cash when we meet, and I'm not committed to anything. When *do* I go?"

"Tomorrow. Noon."

"I'll be right over," I said. "Small bills, okay?"

Of all the big cities I know none is more visually improved by the arrival of night than Los Angeles. Anyone making a top ten list of the world's ugliest urban stretches would be hard-pressed to include fewer than half a dozen of LA's tens of thousands of eyesores, all of which look better when the sun has made its nightly exit.

There has never been a blueprint for Los Angeles, which is one reason so many people here salivate at the term *planned community*. LA was built in any old order out of anything that happened to be at hand and in any old style (although there are a few nice buildings left over from the '20s and '30s), and absolutely no money-saving shortcuts were overlooked. The city was built, most of it, with the short term in view: a developer simply bought a big hunk of cheap land, cleared away the barley or spinach or citrus, built a few soda-cracker buildings with boulevard frontage, bribed the city to put a couple more streets along his property's boundaries, named the streets after his wife and daughters, folded up his money, and left town. Take a bunch of these and put them together and you've got Los Angeles.

The block on Western that housed the McDonald's where I was to receive my second $2,500 was awful even in comparison with the blocks on either side: two-story buildings as devoid of ornamentation as shoe boxes, made from thinly layered plaster, all covered by a coat of dirt-colored paint that must have been enormously inexpensive, since hundreds and hundreds of gallons of the stuff had instilled the street with a staggering chromatic monotony. Plumped down in the middle of it all, on the east side of Western Avenue, ugly in its corporate, cash-for-calories way, was McDonald's.

I'd forgotten about the yellow shirt until I was halfway there, so I had to make a quick detour into one of Kore-atown's less fancy malls. In the first little store I visited I saw a T-shirt in the eye-itching yellow of a suspect urine sample. It said *Ballet dancers do it on their toes* in a sort of free-hand, tee-hee font across the chest. The T-shirt got me some attention in the restaurant which, like most McDon-ald's, was firmly in baseball cap territory.

It was 10:30 on a cold, cloudy February morning when I got there, ninety minutes early, but even at that hour the place was in overflow mode. I stood watching my food cool in front of the station with the drink machines and the packaged condiments, dodging ketchup junkies, until a booth for four opened up at the front, where I could see everyone who came and went. I slid in, facing Western Avenue across a small asphalt parking lot, and checked the time on my phone. Then I pushed the food toward the empty seats opposite me and opened an enormous paper-back, one of a set containing the razor-sharp mystery novels of Margaret Millar, a woman who was remarkably tough on members of her own gender and wrote like a heavily armed avenging angel. The book was big enough to spot from the street.

The average height of the restaurant's patrons that day was roughly three feet, eight inches, and it didn't take me long to lose all interest. So I wasn't paying attention when a harried-looking mom towing three over-caffeinated kids staked claim to the booth behind me. I heard a few min-utes of desultory, full-mouth chatter that inevitably turned into a squabble over the toys in the Happy Meals; one of the boys got Fashionista Barbie and the girl had a Hot Wheels car, a clear violation of the traditional natural order of childhood. Harried Mom slapped a palm down on the table with a noise like a pistol shot and said, "That's enough. Go out and wait with Eddie."

"I don't wanna go wait with—"

"*Donald*," Harried Mom said in a tone you could have used to sand a banister, "do I give a shit?"

"I'm Danny," Donald said, and I closed the book to give the conversation one hundred percent of my attention.

"You're whoever I say you are. Get your prepubescent butt out there and wait with Eddie. I'll be out when I'm out. And Dorothy, or whatever your name is, give him that fucking car. *Now*."

Dorothy, if that was her name, said, "You shouldn't use words like—" and Harried Mom cleared her throat with enough menace to empty the restaurant.

"ThenIwantBarbie," Dorothy said very quickly. Mom said, "Do you know how to get home?"

"No."

"Well, you'll be working that out in about three minutes if you don't give him that car and get out there with Eddie."

"Sheesh," said a kid whose voice I hadn't heard yet but who had a keen sense of injustice.

Mom said, "You, too, John Doe. You think you're *special*?"

Then there was a sound-effects track of soprano grumbling and kids getting up with much resentful shoe-scuffing, and a minute later the three of them were on the other side of the window, grievance visible in every inch of their bodies, standing around a man in the parking lot who had his back to me and wore his hair in an Afro like a mid-size mushroom cloud.

"He's not gonna turn around," said Harried Mom, sliding into the other side of my booth. "You might as well look at me."

I looked at her. She was plump and heavily made up, wearing bright green plastic-framed dark glasses from the 1950s that angled up into sharp points like a little set of facial elbows, enough lipstick for three women, and more rouge than a marionette. Her round face, its features oddly sharp in such plump terrain, was framed by the worst wig I'd ever seen, a bright orange parody of the whole notion of hair. And, in fact, it wasn't hair; it was a Union Carbide plastic product called Dynel that can be extruded in extremely fine strands, maybe three or four times the diameter of a human hair and that takes dye very well. The new product met its market, and boom! the Dynel wig industry was born. The advantages—that it was cheap and could be thrown into the dishwasher—were offset by the facts that it was hot on the head and it looked a lot like plastic. Still, it worked for department store mannequins designed to be seen from a distance, Japanese cosplay enthusiasts, Halloween costumes, and ironic transvestites.

I said, "Where'd you get the kids?"

"Casting agency. All kids are a blight, but kid actors should be run over the day they get their AFTRA cards." She sat back, cocked her head, pushed the bright glasses down on her nose, and subjected me to a gaze that peeled me and looked straight through me to the wall behind. I did not sense unreserved approval. "They think they're in a reality series with hidden cameras."

I turned to look out the window again, but she tapped the back of my wrist. "You might want to count this," she said.

The envelope was a thick little pillow, and I have to admit that I was flipping through an impressive stack of twenties before I had to resist the impulse to slap my forehead like one of the Three Stooges. I marked my place in the stack with an index finger and looked back out through the window, and sure enough, Eddie, his Afro, and the Mouseketeers were gone. On the other hand, an attractive young woman was coming in. She eyed me for a second, but then her gaze dropped to my shirt, and she shook her head. When I looked back at Harried Mom, she was shaking her head, too, so that made it unanimous.

Her eyes were the odd off-green you sometimes see in olives, but not as warm. "That was test number one," she said, "the distraction test. You flunked."

I said, "Gee."

"Can't imagine why Stinky is so high on you."

"I could have told you not to listen to Stinky." I stopped counting, slipped the envelope into the pocket of my jeans, and scooted across the bench. "Well," I said, "thanks for the chat." She leaned toward me quickly, and something about the movement got my attention. It shoved in my direction a little splash of chilled air that surrounded me completely and ran straight down my spine. It's difficult for me to explain why—in such a brightly lighted, resolutely ordinary restaurant, jammed to the exits with potential witnesses—the gesture packed as much threat as it did. I stopped scooting and looked at the plastic sheen of her hair because I didn't want to look at her eyes, which she hadn't taken off me.

"That's a little tiny bit better," she said. "You paid *attention* to me." She sat back by about an inch, and I resisted the urge to sit back myself. She said, "Look, I have to make a snap judgment here." Her eyes were bouncing around the restaurant until they snagged on someone, but then they kept going. "You're not ideal for me, and obviously you're not thrilled with me, either. We can't all be Romeo and Juliet."

"They had their own problems," I said. I checked out the restaurant, trying to figure who had engaged her attention, and found myself looking at the attractive young woman who had just come in and who was waiting in line to order something she would regret in a few hours. A rap of knuckles on the table brought me back to the issue at hand.

"So we're not matched by fate," she said, tapping a tangerine fingernail on each of the last three syllables. "But time is an issue, as usual, and I doubt I'll find anyone better. And that's why business always involves money, isn't it? Because otherwise we'd never hang around with the people who pay us."

I said, "Really." It was just a bookmark. She'd stopped talking, and that should have been my cue to do what I'd planned to do ever since Stinky called me and told me how many people already knew something about the job: pocket the $2,500, say thanks, and walk out of the place. But walking away would have required me to turn my back on her, and the very idea made the skin over my spine pucker.

"Of course." She spread her hands, the telltale gesture of someone who's making a gift to the thick, an explanation that shouldn't be required. "A salary is what they give you because you'd rather be somewhere else." She tilted her head to the right, the restaurant's fluorescents chasing orange highlights over her curls. "Don't you think?"

I was looking around the restaurant, thinking there might be other Eddies on hand. "I have no idea. Except for two weeks as a busboy in a restaurant when I was sixteen, I've never earned a salary."

"I know, you found your life's work at sixteen, seventeen. That's a lot of break-ins, and Stinky says you've never been arrested."

I said, "Stinky should keep his mouth shut."

"Never even questioned," she said.

I put my elbow on the table and my chin in my hand. It's a posture that expresses patience without being offensive. I waited.

She nodded her head, eyebrows raised: a prompt. "Is that right? You've never been questioned?"

I said, "Do you know the answer?"

She brought her lips together into a poisonous little air kiss.

"Okay, just for the record," I said. "Once. But it was bullshit, a cop's way of forcing me to do him a favor. If I'd said no, he was going to charge me with a job I didn't do."

"But if you didn't do it—"

"The victim was an elderly judge," I said. "What the police think of as a *cop judge*, someone who believes there's no such thing as an innocent defendant, and during the robbery he and his wife were pistol-whipped. Even if I'd only been in jail for an hour I would have come out with my thumbs on backward and a note saying I'd slipped in the shower. So if that counts as being questioned, I've been questioned." I stopped and drew a breath. "But here's the thing. I'm not inclined to work with you."

She patted the absurd hair into place despite the fact that it hadn't moved. "You might want to reconsider that."

I said, "Well, this is how good I don't feel about it. Here." I put the envelope back on the table, pushed it toward her.

"Exactly *one minute*," she said, flicking the envelope aside. "Let me talk for one minute, and you can take the money with you, whatever you decide to do. Twenty-five hundred a minute, okay?"

"You're not going to persuade me."

"I have no intention of persuading you."

"Well, then," I said, starting to get up.

"I'm threatening you."

"With what?"

"Since the moment Stinky mentioned your name, I've been learning everything I could about you. People do talk, you know, even those who aren't supposed to. About the only thing I didn't have was your license plate number, and you took care of that when you drove in here." She looked down at her hands on the table and put them in her lap. "I don't *want* to threaten you, but I do need to talk to you. One minute for twenty-five hundred bucks. How often do you make that kind of money?"

I shook my head, but I didn't get up. It was worth staying, at least long enough to try to figure out how much she actually knew.

"No one lives in the house I want you to hit," she said. "It's going to be torn down in a few days. It's empty. It's secluded. I have the key you'll need to get in. How am I doing?"

"Forty-two seconds to go."

"I won't need it. No one will see you because the

windows are covered on the inside so you can use an arc light if you want to. I can tell you what room it's in. It weighs less than three pounds. You can tuck it under your arm and go."

"Why don't you do it?"

She tightened her mouth, not enjoying the challenge. "That has nothing to do with you. Listen, you can sit here making guesses all day, and all we'll do is waste time." She glanced at a cheap running watch that I would have bet was bought just for this meeting. "It's obviously important to me that you do this. That means I need you to get in and then get out again and *stay alive* at least long enough to meet me for the handover, and you can do that anywhere you want, in front of as many people as you want, on *America's Got Talent* or whatever it's called, if you want. Is the minute up?"

"Yes." I put a hand on the table to push myself up.

She reached out and rested her fingertips on the back of my hand. The orange nails matched the hair perfectly. She pushed them into my skin just a little, and I resisted yanking my hand back. "I've told you it's urgently important to me that you get in and out in one piece and that you can make the delivery anywhere you choose. What I haven't told you is how much I'll pay you and how much of that you can walk away with in exchange for about five minute's worth of work."

"Why the nonsense with the kids?"

"Obviously, so I could get up and leave without being noticed if anything smelled bad."

My phone gave out the little xylophone tremolo that announces a text.

I said, "How much?" I glanced down at the phone and

saw a nice, sharp picture of my would-be employer taken by someone who had a good clear angle from behind me.

She said, "When I have your attention, you'll find out."

I pocketed the phone and looked over at her in time to see her reach into her purse and pull out a large manila envelope about two inches thick. "First payment." She dropped the envelope on the table, and I could hear the *plop* even over the noise level in the restaurant. "Twenty-five thousand. Add it to what you've already got. Do you seriously think I'd let you walk out of here with this much money if I didn't think you were going to make it out of the house and bring me the thing I want?"

I said, "*First* payment?"

"Another twenty-five on delivery."

"Thousand."

"If you want me to say it out loud. Thousand."

"Who else wants it?"

She said, "Excuse me?"

"You're willing to pay me, as you say, very well, to go get something. That means one of two things: either it belongs to someone who won't intentionally give it up and knows how to defend it, or there's someone else who wants it. In either case, you're afraid of that someone."

"There's no one I'm afraid of, not in this world or the next."

"Then go get it yourself."

She sat back in the booth and gave me an eye that lowered the temperature in the whole restaurant. The earlier chill was Miami by comparison; this one was so thick it felt viscous. "Yes or no. Right now, in the next five seconds." She put her hand, fingers splayed and flat, on the manila envelope and the smaller envelope beside it. "*Yes,* and you walk out of here a lot richer. *No*, and you'd better keep your eye on the rearview mirror. For the foreseeable future." She pushed both envelopes to my edge of the table and smiled. "Maybe both eyes."

Twenty-five K. Another twenty-five K to come. Versus looking over my shoulder for however long it might be, worried not just about me but also Ronnie. I slid the envelope off the table and into my lap and said, "Fine. Have it your way."

Dismal as Horton House was, the sight of the books that remained on the living room shelves had cheered me slightly. Books, I think, exude a kind of airborne tranquilizer. The percentage of the world's murder victims who are killed in libraries is statistically negligible. I could feel the soothing waves of silent words, sort of an imaginal massage, loosen the muscles in my back and shoulders. From the bottom step, I looked back through the living room archway, beaming the penlight at the shelves, and promised myself a stop there on the way out.

It says something about the priorities of the age in which we live that I've never known a burglar who stole books. The sole exceptions to the rule are when the target has essentially ceased, economically, to be a "book" and become, instead, a *valuable object*, a category that says nothing about the items it includes except that they're in extremely short supply. It's certainly not about merit; a battered copy of *Don Quixote* is in the same sale bin, at the same markdown, as a paperback of *Fifty Shades of Grey*. It's about scarcity. As someone once observed, if the ground were littered with rubies, we wouldn't bend down to pick them up.

The more somebody else wants something, the more we have to have it.

But *these* shelves had been pilfered, hadn't they? I played the light over them again and saw the answer to the conundrum. No one had taken any books. The empty spaces here and there on the shelves made a symmetrical pattern. There had been knickknacks placed among them, some of them probably old and valuable. Take the knick-knacks, leave the books.

I flicked off the light and closed my eyes softly, barely letting the lids meet. Squeezing them shut sets off retinal fireworks that you don't want to have to cope with in a dark environment. It's sort of like looking for a firefly through a barrage of Fourth of July skyrockets. When, at the count of twenty, I let my lids open, my pupils felt as dilated as an owl's. I found I could see a slight variation in the darkness around me. The portion of the living room framed by the archway was just perceptibly paler than the entrance hall, which was as dark as the hole at the bottom of the world, where the souls leak out. And then, when I looked up the stairs, it was, somehow, darker *still*, as though it had been reduced and thickened, like a sauce. And the baby powder smell was stronger in that direction.

The house chose that moment to let out a remarkably low, grinding groan, the kind of sound a yawl might make capsizing in a high sea. Almost simultaneously, the solidity of the carpeted stair beneath my feet went a little gelati-nous for a couple or eight long-feeling seconds, and then held still again as the house subsided into a displeased aftermath of yips, barks, and creaks.

Okay, just a wee seismic jolt, commonplace in Califor-nia, the kind that always startles TV news anchors who are working live. All the painstakingly acquired smoothness goes out the window to be replaced by a few seconds of borderline yammering in suddenly high-pitched voices with regional accents, and some apprehensive glances up at the thousands of pounds of lights hanging overhead. When it's over, if one of them is a male, he'll use his palm to smooth his tie. The woman will usually touch her hair. Those will probably be the last human gestures at the end of the world: smooth the tie, touch the hair.

I saw again in my mind's eye that outrageous orange Dynel hair. She *had the key*. Why didn't she just come in and get whatever it was herself?

I was *stewing*, unusual for me, so I blamed it on the house. In my life I've spent uninvited time in probably four hundred houses and I'd never liked one less than I liked Horton House.

The carpeting on the stairs killed the sound of my footsteps as I climbed, and by staying right next to the banister, I managed to ascend relatively quietly. The penlight was off since, for all I knew, there were people upstairs— unlikely but not impossible—and after about fifteen steps I started very softly kicking the riser of the step in front of me, just to make certain that one was there. Nothing feels more like slapstick than lifting your leg in expectation of a step that's not there and then putting it down seven or eight inches lower than you'd anticipated. It's like stepping into a hole. Fred Astaire couldn't have made it look anything but klutzy.

And, of course, it's noisy.

When my little forward kick didn't hit anything and I knew I was at the top of the stairs, I stood there and waited for something to say *boo*.

Nothing did, but if something had I probably would have preferred it to the smell of powder, which was much heavier up here, as cloying as a face full of lilies. It was almost enough to tint the darkness pink. It amazed me that any high-priced designer of fragrance molecules would have offered it up for sale rather than chucking it into the bin labeled *Stenches*. I turned my head, inhaling slowly through my mouth. The floor plans had put the master bedroom at the back of the house, farthest away from the racket and stink of horse-drawn buggies that once rattled down the street. That put it to my left, and that was the direction where the powder's smell was strongest. Miss Daisy, as the sole remaining Horton in Horton House, would have claimed that room. That she had remained there, rather than being shifted against her will into, say the cook's bedroom, raised my hopes that the rooms upstairs, the rooms in which she lived, hadn't been scavenged into the humiliation I'd seen on the ground floor.

When you've done this as often as I have, you learn to listen around corners. The first step in doing that is to go as still as a pond and then close your eyes, which was unnecessary in the pitch-blackness of the second floor. Breathe with the tip of your tongue touching the roof of your mouth, which, as people who work around microphones know, is the quietest way to do it. Then stay there until you get a sense of the house's regular noises, and listen *through* them. Up until now, Horton House had been making too much random noise for me to do that, but the little seismic hiccup seemed to have calmed things down for a moment, settling months' worth of resentful, grudge-filled stresses and strains in a single, cranky jolt. For the first time since I'd gone in, the house was silent. Above me

I suddenly heard the faint, rapid tapping of rain, finger-nails on the soundboard of a stringed instrument.

All my experience told me I was alone up here. And the unvarying velvet of the darkness told me that the windows on this floor were covered, too, which meant I could use the penlight without attracting any attention outdoors. I punched the button.

The stairs ended in a landing with a magisterially high ceiling. Directly across from me was a wall, bare now, but with an enormous dark patch indicating a missing picture. The patch was perhaps six feet long and four wide, hung vertically, a standard portrait format for someone worth wasting twenty-four square feet of wall space on. In this case, it was almost certainly the man whose name—well, whose alias—the house bore, the nineteenth-century claim jumper who, as a young thug in his twenties, had begun to accumulate what would become the Horton fortunes by stealing silver and gold from mine sites in Nevada until around 1890. At that point, things got too hot, and he ran; he ran, in fact, all the way to England, via New York, with his victims in highly motivated pursuit. According to *A Miscellany of American Rogues*—a decorous, almost courteous exposé of some of the nation's dodgiest rich, written in the 1940s—the Atlantic stopped the law in its tracks while the claim jumper seems to have crossed in style. If the book is accurate, he spent a couple of quiet years in London, where he changed his real name, Edgar Francis Codwallader, to the less Welsh and less memorable Henry Wallace Horton, Jr. I thought the *Junior* was a nice touch, and not because it's my given name, but rather because people who invent names for themselves so rarely think of it.

By 1894 he had obviously re-crossed the Atlantic to the

land of his birth because he was arrested, under the name
of Horton, in Brooklyn, New York, for aggravated jewel
theft, the aggravation being assault and battery via fists.
It wasn't much of a crime, since the jewels had belonged
to a widely disliked *arriviste* rather than a member of one
of the establishment clans who owned the judicial system,
and fist fights were accepted at the time as a diverting form
of masculine conflict resolution. Still, the arrest made the
papers during a slow news week when a search of Horton's rooms turned up two complete sets of documents in
two names, Horton and Codwallader. There was no way
to sort out which, if either, was real and which was bogus;
it was still seven or eight or nine years before the first
criminal was convicted on the basis of a fingerprint and
more than a decade before the military and police depart-
ments began storing them as a means of identification. The
Man with Two Names, as the papers styled him—it was
a *very* slow news week—disappeared after being released
on bail, and both of his sets of identity papers, which had
been in the custody of a small police precinct station, disappeared with him. As was often the case in those days,
the questioning of the cops charged with safekeeping the
documents seems to have been, well, mild.

He then worked his way back west, where he was
spotted by vengeful victims in Virginia City, Nevada. They
tracked him to the vicinity of San Diego, where he left
misleading signs suggesting he'd fled into Mexico. He then
ambled north, and as Henry Wallace Horton, Jr., he bur-
rowed into Los Angeles, grew a beard, talked with a mild
British accent, distributed his money in attention-getting
quantities among several local banks, learned some manners, married above him, built the house I was currently

disliking so much, and bought his way into the social register. In his stout, prosperous sixties, he capped his saga by siring the girl-child who, ninety-seven years later, would wither away at the center of a cloud of baby powder in the master bedroom just to my left. *A Miscellany of American Rogues* hinted that there might have been another kid or two, by a mistress or several mistresses—it really was a man's world back then—but no names were given, either because they were unknown or because the publisher's lawyers got nervous.

And at some unknown point, before, after, or during Horton's sojourn in England, something extremely valuable had found its way into his hands, something that the woman with the rented children and the orange Dynel hair wanted very badly. Something small enough to be concealed in a nineteenth-century doll.

Okay, the evidence said I was alone. I turned right and made a quick pass down the hallway, walking on the balls of my feet. The floor responded with resentful protest, so I sidestepped to the right-hand wall and hugged it until I came to the first door. There were two on this side and two on the left side, and all were wide open.

The first room was a bedroom that no one had used in a long time. There was a leak in the roof and water had probed its way down to the ceiling above the bed, where someone, perhaps in the '30s or '40s, had installed a ceiling light, a nice, circular piece of thick etched glass in a heavy brass fixture, now tarnished to a dull, ashen gray-green. The water had found the hole that had been drilled for the electrical wire and followed it down around the fixture and onto the bed. As I stood there, I heard a *plop* that sounded like someone dropping a quarter into a bowl of pudding. The bed had, at some time in the past, grown so heavily soaked that one side of the frame had snapped, creating a v-shaped break in the middle and putting a valley in the center of the mattress, where the old ruffled fabric covering the box spring had become a black ripple of mold. The place stank of rotting cloth with an undertone that might have been wet feathers if the mattress was old enough, which I doubted. Whatever it was, it reeked, but I preferred it to the baby powder.

An old book, its covers warped and its pages puckered, sat on a small table at the head of the bed. Beside it were a pair of dainty wire-rimmed spectacles. The whole room said *maiden aunt*, a term not currently much in use, consigned to the linguistic trash heap reserved for so many thoughtless and casual insults. Whoever she was, she was undoubtedly long dead by now. But, unlike the portion of the house I'd seen so far, in this room the furniture and fittings seemed intact.

I'd intended to check the bathroom, but when I stepped onto the bedroom's carpet it made a disorienting squelching sound, and I figured, what the hell. Above me, the tapping of the rain increased in volume and another *splorp* landed percussively on the bed.

The next room, which was on the street side of the house, was probably the sitting room, although there wasn't much left to sit on; like the first floor, it had been picked over. Faded dark spots on the carpet, places unbleached by the sun that had poured through the big rippled windows in pre-paper bag days, made it clear that someone had carried off the furniture. In this case, judging from the disembodied shadows left behind, the furniture had been a couple of short couches and what might have been an armchair. A nice cherrywood table, as yet unlooted, stood at the juncture of the *L* that had been formed by the couches. On the room's long wall, opposite the door, were more bookshelves, but these had fewer open spaces. The *expensive* knickknacks had probably been downstairs where they could impress visitors.

I almost missed the single long shelf on the wall to my immediate left because it was down at about hip height. Stretched along it I saw, with a sudden increase of interest, a line of dolls.

The carpet was dry in here. I stepped through the door and beamed the little yellow light at the small figures grouped there in an unlikely assembly, a mixed lot that ranged from cheap old toys to some that had gradually become collectible. Five of the fourteen dolls on the shelf were rag dolls, and two of those had black faces—"calico and button dolls" from the end of the nineteenth century. While some black-faced dolls from that period are racist caricatures, these were nicely, if inexpensively, clothed, not wearing the patched rags and head scarves that distinguish the more judgmental dolls. Cheap when new, each of these was worth almost a thousand to the right buyer, probably more than some of the knickknacks that had been swiped from the bookshelves on the first floor. But the people who had been emptying this place had been looking for substance and shine, and these folk art dolls, beautiful in their way, didn't make the cut.

I scanned the rest of the shelf quickly; the rain was coming down harder, and my car was more than a block away. A few of the dolls were very nice indeed, including a fancy one from Paris, but nothing of Maison Jumeau quality. Not even close.

The room across the hall was completely empty. Even the carpet had been pulled up, leaving strips of wood at the juncture of floors and walls, into which the carpet tacks had been driven. There was a leak in here, too, slowly expanding a small dark puddle in the far right corner. Hurrying a little now as I headed back toward the master bedroom, I peered into the third room and saw a child's bed, a glorified cradle of sorts, set into a small gondola that had been carved, it appeared, from a single piece of heavily lacquered wood, a cream color that probably emphasized the pink flesh tones of the child—presumably Miss Daisy—who slept there. I went over and touched it. The wood felt cool and smooth, and the gondola rocked gently side to side, with a surprised creak. Mice had nested pungently in the snarl of sheets. I figured this was probably the mistress of the house's first bed, and it seemed to be time to stop postponing my look at her last.

4

Intimate Agonies

When I pushed on the door to the master bedroom, which was ajar, it bumped against something, making a little *thunk*, but it kept going. Whatever it hit hadn't been alive, so I just stood in the doorway and played the light around the room.

It was a big room with a higher ceiling than the others, as befitted the master or mistress of the house, and more window space; both the opposite wall and the one to my right were covered in brown shopping bags. In the far right corner was a fireplace, its tiles black with use, and in the fireplace were two scorched and blackened twists that I could identify, even from where I was standing, as cloth. The charred, knotted forms nestled among the charred hearts of some thick logs.

Up close, they were just clothes: some kind of patterned dress, it looked like, and a few lighter-colored things that could have been either shirts or blouses. They'd apparently been wadded up and tossed in on top of the tag end of a fire so that they'd sparked and blackened and stiffened without actually bursting into flame except the outer layer or two. The sheer volume of smoke it put off, I thought, must have been formidable for anyone who remained in

the room. I bent at the waist and sniffed the acrid aftermath of the fire. Sharp as it was, it smelled better than
the floral excess of the baby powder, the scent of which
was almost overwhelming in here. The clothes, whoever
owned them, had probably been burned after Miss Daisy's
final departure. Surely no one would have intentionally
created such a choking stench in a room containing a
woman who couldn't walk.

Or maybe they would have. I straightened and turned
to face the bed, which I was surprisingly reluctant to look
at. My instinct had been correct. For all her money and
her hard-bought social standing, Miss Daisy had passed her
final years in a cheap, flimsy hospital bed, barely as big as
the miserly single mattress in the room behind the kitchen.
At some point the bed had been kicked or had banged into
something so forcefully that the wheel at one corner of
the mattress's foot had been bent, tilting the whole thing
down a little, like a derelict pool table. It looked incredibly
uncomfortable.

But the sheets eclipsed everything else that was wrong.
They were splotched and filthy, a map of various intimate
agonies: incontinence and bleeding and hair loss and the
sharp wrinkles caused by fear- and pain-sweat, and above
all of that, the sheer, monstrous indifference of those
who'd been tasked with caring for her. I closed my eyes,
inhaled that fucking powder, and forced myself to go to
work.

A little gathering of blankets at the foot of the bed
released a puff of scented powder when I lifted it, looked
beneath it, and let it fall again. Nothing there. Nothing
under the bed. Nothing on the two shelves along the
windowless wall to the left of the door except some old,

worthless books, mostly Reader's Digest condensations of best-sellers from the '40s and '50s: stately names like Thomas B. Costain, Daphne du Maurier, Kathleen Winsor, Samuel Shellabarger. Each sounded whiter than the last. I had read du Maurier's *Rebecca* and Shellabarger's *Prince of Foxes,* both found on my mother's shelves, but what I remembered most clearly was that Shellabarger had married a woman with the indelible name Vivan Georgia Lovegrove Borg. In these volumes these writers' imaginary worlds had been shrunk and repackaged, boiled down to size for people who would rather talk about books than read them. There was no doll behind the books.

No doll in the closet, not hidden in or between any of the clothes, musty and moth-eaten, that hung disconsolately there, abandoned decades ago; nothing on the shoe racks other than Miss Daisy's old but almost unworn twenty or so pairs of shoes. Nothing in the shoes. In the bathroom, nothing. Four moving boxes stacked in a corner contained nothing but more books, some baby clothes that practically disintegrated when I picked them up, a couple of tarnished necklaces—costume jewelry from another time—and, at the bottom of the last box, a stack of folded newspapers all with the same front page, brittle enough to break between my fingers. They were dated 1931, and in the lower right-hand corner was a story about the death of financier and philanthropist Henry Wallace Horton, Jr.

In other words, nothing *anywhere.* I got on hands and knees, pushed the grate with its burned clothes aside, and pointed the penlight up the chimney. Nothing but soot and bricks.

Harried Mom had said it would be in the bedroom.

I turned back to the door and stopped. Sticking out from behind it was a piece of smooth wood.

When I moved the door, I saw several pieces of what had once been a chair made out of some light wood: just a seat, four dowelled legs, and a curved back. One side of the back had been forced down, wrenching it hard enough to pop the pegs that had held the legs in place, splintering the wood.

Because of where the chair was, it was impossible not to see how the damage had occurred. It had been propped beneath the door knob in an attempt to close it against someone who fully intended to get in. The door could only have been barred from inside. Miss Daisy, I knew, had been unable to walk. Had she *crawled* out of bed and across the room to force that chair into place? And had she made it back to bed before the chair shattered and the door flew open?

Fifty thousand bucks wasn't enough for this.

But here I was, and I figured that the house, vile in so many ways, had shown me its worst. I clenched the light between my teeth so I could use both hands and ransacked the entire second floor, just barging room to room, moving everything, tossing things aside as an outlet for the anger. Looking everywhere and finding nothing. Coming back toward the master bedroom I saw the pull-down in the hallway ceiling that would give me access to the attic, and I climbed up the steps that unfolded when I yanked it down. The attic was dark, dusty, wet, and empty. I could see where things had been stored by the trails through the dirt that they'd created when they were shoved toward the pull-down, but other than that, my beam bounced off nothing between me and the walls. The water was dripping pretty good up here.

I stood there on the rickety fold-down stairs and thought until I began to sneeze like a machine gun, probably from the dust. When I had it under control, I went down the ladder, shoved the pull-down back into place, and drifted into the nursery, avoiding even looking into Miss Daisy's room. There was a folding chair beside the gondola-shaped baby's bed, and I sat there and rocked the gondola, listening to the creak, and thought some more. After I ran out of things to think about and got my anger under control, I got up and went down the stairs, figuring I might as well backtrack all the way to the front door, search the elephant's foot umbrella stand, and then go over the house inch by inch, including, this time, the basement.

At the foot of the stairs, the scent of baby powder suddenly blossomed. It increased as I passed the archway to the living room, but by the time I registered the conundrum and slowed, a light had snapped on behind me, and someone said, "Stop." I must not have stopped quickly enough because an instant later I heard a soft *thup,* and the hardwood floor beside my right foot erupted into splinters.

5
The Way Some People Have Dobermans

After Harried Mom left McDonald's, $27,500 poorer, I'd done exactly what she'd made me promise to do.

I sat right where I was, without getting up, without going to the bathroom, without picking up my phone, without looking at or speaking to anyone, keeping both hands in plain sight, for ten minutes. For the first sixty seconds or so I was counting my heartbeats, which were coming hard and fast; I *knew* I'd made a mistake. The phone rang twice, but I ignored it and sat there, breathing in enough airborne fat to clog an artery, and wishing I'd gotten up and left when I first wanted to.

But Ronnie and I needed the money. And we needed it *now*.

When my phone said the ten minutes were done, I got up and went to my car without looking around, started it, and headed north on Western with the phone on my lap. When it rang this time I punched the speaker button without picking it up, and Louie the Lost said, "Nobody touched your car. Guy with a head of hair like a porcupine looked at it from eight, ten feet away and wrote down your license plate, but nobody planted nothing on it."

"Thanks," I said. "Did you get a picture?"

"*Lotta* hair," he said. "Looked like an exploding arm-chair. I got him sort of sideways, but it's mostly hair and the tip of a real honker of a nose. Hair's gotta be a wig."

"Okay," I said. "Where are you?"

"Five, six cars back. Nobody suspicious between you and me, by which I mean nobody who pulled out from Micky D's. Why don't you haul over to the curb for a minute and let me make sure nobody slows down. Hang on. I'm pulling over in about five seconds. You see a space?"

"I do," I said, heading for it. The curb was red, but I wasn't getting out. "In," I said.

"Okay, I'm just watching here."

A couple of cars went by. I said, "God, this is an ugly street."

"Rents are going up anyway," Louie said. "You know what I like about crooks?"

"No. I haven't even wondered—"

"The whole fucking world economy has turned into a giant sponge that the only reason it exists is to squeeze all the money there is up to the One Percent. That's why these rents are going up. It's like, whatever river you're on, the water flows into Lake Fatso and stays there. But us, we don't do that, crooks don't. We steal it and keep it all for ourselves. The thick-fingered assholes on top never even smell it."

"Makes me all patriotic. Can I move yet?"

"Think she's in position?"

"If I didn't think she was in position," I said, "I wouldn't move. She's had plenty of time."

"Little cranky, huh?"

"Yeah," I said, pulling back into traffic. "I *hate* not having choices."

It was one of K-Town's biggest malls, four immaculate floors that would have stood out even in Seoul. I'd chosen it because of the layout.

I punched the speed-dial for Ronnie's number as I crossed the second level of the garage, heading for the double door I wanted. "Coming in," I said. I put the phone, still on and connected, into the pocket of my yellow T-shirt so I could be heard while I was out of sight and pushed the doors open with my free hand. The other was holding the thick manila envelope, which now had the smaller envelope inside it.

Polished floors, *very* bright lighting, shops everywhere, with some of the clothes pushed toward the cute end of the spectrum: Korean cartoon heroines, animated super-heroes, and some sort of Asianized Yogi Bear, offset by clinically clean cookware with a high gleaming-knife ratio, and, everywhere, makeup, with all the operatic fragrance that makeup brings. Not many people visible, but a lot of audible, if echoing, conversation.

"Got you," Ronnie said on the phone. "Browse around a little."

I looked at things I didn't want for a couple of minutes, feeling as though time were standing still, until Ronnie said, "Nobody. Not the door you used, not the other door, either. Come on up."

Even though it was clear no one was watching me I gave the place one last look out of force of habit, a customer trying to figure out where some shop had moved to, and got onto the escalator, very conscious of not looking back over my shoulder. Two stories above me, in the food court on the top floor, the attractive young woman from McDonald's looked down at me.

"Pictures of the kids," Ronnie said when we sat at the

table she'd chosen. In front of her sat a little flying-saucer-looking disk with some colored lights on it. It would blink when the order she'd placed at one of the food stalls was ready. She pushed her phone over to me.

"Pretty good," I said, flicking through them. "Couldn't get the guy outside, huh?"

"I had no idea he was with them until it was too late. I got the kids coming out, before they passed me, but I couldn't turn and shoot as they clustered around that guy. By then your friend in the clown makeup was looking at me, anyway."

"She was pretty alert."

"Good thing she's so irritable. She gave you a look I thought was going to freeze you to your seat, so while she was distracted I put the lens right on her in burst mode. Maybe ten shots in a couple of seconds. By the time she looked up, I was eating fries. So what's the story?"

I pushed the envelope at her. "More than twenty-five K," I said, "with the same to come. Take it home and put it in the box up the chimney."

She was looking at the envelope as though it might contain a pit viper. "What do you have to do?"

"Same old."

"Don't give me that," Ronnie said. "You were about to blow her off. Your spine was as stiff as—"

"It was," I said, "but that was before I saw the money."

The flying saucer began to blink and vibrate. It did everything except play "Melancholy Baby." I picked it up and said, "Which stand?"

"Bulgogi House," she said. "Second from the left, but you know what?" She put her hand on my wrist, international language for *stop*. "It'll wait. Who cares if it gets cold? Why so much money?"

"I'm not a cheap date," I said. "Stinky told her—"

"It's too much. I mean, what could that be a percentage of, the Hope Diamond?"

"Don't worry." It sounded hollow, even to me. "I'm good at this."

She looked at me for a long moment, successfully suppressing whatever fondness she might have felt, and then said, "I'll get the food." She took the flying saucer, and I watched her go, her shoulders high and tight with anger. This was going to be a difficult discussion for her, which meant it would be rough for me, too.

But still. We were confronting something that had to be confronted, something impossible to ignore.

When I'd met her, a year and a half or so earlier, I was being forced—by the crooked cop I'd told Orange Hair about—to investigate the murder of a blackmailer. The blackmailer happened also to be Ronnie's husband, so naturally she was the prime suspect, although that didn't keep us, on the erotic level anyway, from eating each other alive at the earliest possible opportunity. As the relationship expanded upward to the higher chakras and turned gradually into love, Ronnie unspooled lie after lie about the most commonplace things: where she came from, how she got to California, what she'd done before we met, not even bothering to avoid contradicting herself. At the same time, my work put her into situations that most people would find stressful, and her responses made it obvious that she possessed the finely honed set of the skills and instincts necessary to live outside the law.

Despite her inventive dishonesty about facts, emotionally I would have trusted her with my life. I'd even shared with her a secret even my daughter and my former wife didn't know: my apartment in a Koreatown building, a slum on the outside and polished perfection within. For years it had been my ultimate hidey-hole for the day when a lifetime of transgressions would finally catch up with me, and now Ronnie and I played house in its big rooms with their polished wooden and marble floors. We'd been sitting on one of those floors late on a wine-sodden Christmas Eve two months earlier when she'd finally presented me with her secret: the two-year-old son, Eric, who had been taken from her by his father, a New Jersey mob doctor. He had made it clear that she'd never see the boy again, so naturally I promised that we'd get him back. *Men*. When will we learn?

Some crowd somewhere in the world erupted into tinny cheers at a kick or a goal or something in a soccer game on one of the big flat screens that hung over the food court tables. I avoid watching soccer because to me, all the games are the same game: kick the ball and run around and then kick the ball and run around again. As a result, I was looking down at the tabletop, still damp from its last wipe-down, and wondering how to navigate the upcoming conversation with Ronnie when Louie the Lost said, "You were clear all the way." He pulled out a chair and his nose wrinkled. "Jeez, so this is where all the garlic goes."

"Right," I said. "Like the Italians have never heard of it."

He was looking past me, at Ronnie. "What's she getting?"

"Whatever she ordered, I guess."

"Jeez," Louie said, "don't go out on a limb or nothing."

"It will be pork or beef, it will be spicy, it will be accompanied by pickled cabbage."

"Shoulda eaten at McDonald's." He looked around the place. "Lotta Koreans."

"That's why they call it—"

"So what did she want? How much did she give you?"

"Ten thousand," I said. Louie was a friend, maybe my best friend, but the twenty-first-century code of thievery, unlike Robin Hood's, says that you steal from whoever and keep it to yourself. "I need to know whatever you can find out about a house. It was built back at the beginning of the twentieth century and it's called Horton—"

"You don't want me," he said. "You want *Architectural Digest*."

"Get someone. You had some smart UCLA kids a couple of years back—"

"Still got 'em," he said. "'Course, they're different kids now."

"How much an hour?"

"Same as before. Seventy-five."

"How much of it do they keep?" I asked.

Louie smiled. He had a cherub's smile. "How much in the envelope?"

"I want all there is about the house, including descriptions, pictures, floor plans, applications for architectural changes, and absolutely *everything* about the guy who built it, named Horton, I suppose. And I'm especially looking for anything hinky in the family, any crimes, murders, misdemeanors, divorces, in-law problems, addictions, black-sheep kids, property fights, sudden windfalls, challenged wills, whatever. Anything that seems even vaguely interesting. Anything that says conflict or—"

"You're gonna need a lot of kids," Louie said.

"Get me the best ones you can, the ones who work fast," I said. "Envelope or no envelope, money's tight."

"Right," Louie said. "I forgot." He knew what Ronnie and I were going through. As a telegraph, someone whose job was to acquire and sell information about who and what and when in the criminal world, Louie had already put us in touch with Francie DuBois, the disappearance specialist who was working out the very expensive kidnapping and subsequent total and untraceable disappearance of Ronnie's child. Now he looked up, apparently surprised, and then stood, a crook with manners.

"You forgot what?" Ronnie said. She was carrying a huge tray, stacked with plates, which Louie gallantly took from her, glancing uncertainly at the food they contained. "Hey," he said, his eyebrows going up. "Spare ribs."

"What did Louie forget?" Ronnie said. Louie had left after eating most of the ribs and apologizing for it a couple of times while he swiped the tip of a finger through the remaining sauce.

"Forget?" I said. "How would I know? *He's* the one who forgot—"

"What you were talking about, Junior. You *do* remember what you were talking about."

I said, "Ronnie." I took a long breath, a delaying tactic while I tried to find a different response, but none came. "We need the money. There's no point in discussing it."

She said, "There's nothing that can't be discussed."

"I keep hearing that."

She leaned forward with her elbows on the table and cupped her face in her hands. It was such an abject pose that I reached across and circled one of her wrists with my fingers, and we sat there like that for a minute. I could feel the glances of people at other tables.

Into her hands, she said, "I'm so sorry."

"Why? Because you want your son back? Is it your fault his asshole father keeps the kid behind stone walls? Is it your fault he's got gunmen the way some people have Dobermans? What are we supposed to do? Walk away? We knew when we started to talk to Francie that it was going to run into some bucks. None of this is news."

"I didn't like that woman with the plastic hair," she said. "I don't like how much money she's offering."

"Neither do I," I said. "But I'm going to learn everything I can about her and those kids between now and the time I go into that house, and Louie's got his honor students pulling as much history as they can find."

"I don't know." She rubbed her eyes with the heels of her hands. "How are you even going to figure out who she is? I mean, she was Miss Halloween."

"Through the three kids she had with her," I said.

"And how are you going to learn anything about the kids?"

"I think I've got exactly the person," I said.

She withdrew her wrist and sat back, eyeing me with an attitude it was hard to mistake as admiration. "You *always* do that," she said. "Men do, in general. The harder something is likely to be, the more confident you act. If you were a woman, you'd be laying the whole thing out, asking for ideas, looking for something you might not think of by yourself. But no, not men. You assume you're carrying around everything you'll ever need. No wonder we go to war all the time."

"It doesn't *help* me to say things out loud," I said,

knowing how irritated I sounded. "It helps me to think about it and then go do whatever it is."

"And look at you," she said. "You haven't gotten killed yet. I suppose that's a kind of success."

"Relax. It's an old house. No one lives there, no one has lived there for months. I've even got a key. I mean, what could go wrong?"

6

Positional Good

"*Whoops*," said the person behind me.

It felt like my back was ten feet wide and had a target painted on it. I said, "That is *so* unreassuring."

"It's this gun. Goes off if you *breathe* on it."

"Then why don't you take your finger off—"

The person behind me said, "*Hic*," and a bullet whirred past my ear.

"Listen," I said, "*Take your goddamn finger* off—"

The person behind me hiccupped again, but this time without a potentially lethal aftermath.

"I'm going to hold my breath," the person behind me said. "That doesn't mean I'm not here. Don't move, don't turn around."

I said, "The best thing is to stand on your head and drink a glass of water. I'll hold the gun if you—"

"*Hic*," said the person behind me. "Don't think I'm not dangerous just because I've got hiccups."

"No," I said. "The scariest part of the movie is always when the killer gets hiccups. Makes my hair stand on end every time."

"You're making that up."

"And you call yourself a crook," I said.

"I'm the one with the gun. You're the one with his hands in the air. Hey, put your hands in the air."

"Death and hiccups," I said, putting my hands in the air. "They've gone together for centuries. That's why the deadliest man in the old West was called Wild Bill Hiccup."

"Was not. It was *Hic*-Hickock."

I said, "A common mistake, but one that I, as a working criminal, would be ashamed to make."

"Wait a minute, wait a minute. How am I supposed to drink water while I'm standing on my head? You're making fun of—"

"Not at all. Just do it, you'll see. Look, I'll even go get the water. Hell, I'll hold the gun."

"You stay right there. No, don't turn around." She, because it certainly *was* a she, hiccupped again.

"At least you haven't got your finger on the trigger."

"I can put it back a lot faster than you can turn and jump me. Don't talk. I'm holding my breath and counting to ten."

"Signal if you get stuck."

"Be quiet."

I was quiet. After what must have been a very slow count, she said, "How'd—*hic*—you know I was here?"

"I smelled that fucking baby powder in the hall. Had to be something that came down from Miss Daisy's room. I figured, the doll."

"Not bad," she said.

"Not good enough to know you were here the whole time I was."

"This is true."

"In the *basement*."

"Sure, why not? Oh, right *you* didn't go down there. Afraid of the big spidies? The ratsy-watsies?"

I said, "Can I turn around?"

"I'm still—*hic*—thinking about that."

"Look, we're obviously in the same situation. My neck itches."

"Well, don't scratch it. What situation?"

"Neither of us has it. Both of us have, essentially, failed."

There was a pause. "What do you mean, failed? I have the doll, that's what you smelled, right?"

I said nothing, and a few seconds later, I heard, "Okay, neither of us has *what*?"

"I don't know, and neither do you. Or if you *think* you know, maybe you could share it with me."

"So you don't know what it is and you think I don't know, but you're certain I don't have it? *Hic*."

"The only reason for you to stay here when I came in was to see if I got it. You could have left a hundred times while I was banging around upstairs and the house was creaking—"

"Boy, *doesn't* it?" she said.

"So by a process of really low-grade reasoning, that means you don't have it, either. Even though you've got the doll, since I could smell the damn thing. You'd have been out of here. So what about—"

"I'm *thinking*. How do I know *you* don't have it?"

"Because I was looking for the damn doll, same as you. Let's make a deal. If I can teach you to stop your hiccups, we'll go sit on those awful chairs in the dining room and talk. You can keep your gun on me."

"Wow," she said. "What a generous offer. I can keep my—*hic*."

"Up to you," I said.

"*Nobody* can cure my hiccups. I get them whenever I'm nervous, not that I'm nervous now. My whole life. My last year of high school, all I did was dream about the prom. I was going to dance with the guy I liked if I had to ask him myself. Oh, *forget* this, you don't want to hear it."

"You're the one holding the gun. You can talk about whatever you want."

"So he *finally* came over and asked me, after I'd like stared at him like an owl for like an hour, and I hiccuped through the whole song. Everything I'd wanted to say to him all year, it had a hiccup in the middle of it. When the song ended, he *patted me on the shoulder.* Like a puppy. He never spoke to me again."

"He was probably a jerk. Most of us were."

"He's a mortgage broker now, so, yeah. Anyway, sure, you've got a deal. You cure my hiccups and we'll go sit and talk. And you promise me that I can pat your pockets and wherever else I want to pat without you trying to get my gun."

"I wouldn't touch that gun if I was wearing full-body armor."

"So what's the big secret?"

"Okay. First, just breathe normally."

"Don't get funny or anything. I can breathe and shoot you at the same time."

"Breathe evenly and slowly, a little more deeply than usual. And pay attention to the place where your hiccups start, down like in the middle of your chest. And then, just before you hiccup, say, '*Now.*'"

"You're kidding."

"Try it."

She let a couple of more hiccups sneak by, and each time I said, "Missed it. You've got to concentrate." And then, after a silence so long my back began to itch, she said, "Well, hell, let's go sit down."

"It was obviously not the doll," she said. "It took me two minutes to find out that none of them, even in top shape, is worth that much."

I said, "*How* much?"

She shook her head, which is what I'd have done if she asked me the question. She was still holding the gun, although at this point it was just a cautionary totem. We were sitting on opposite sides of the crappy Formica table with the doll, which she hadn't yet let me touch, lying on its back between us, its wide, dusty eyes fixed on the ceiling as though it was hoping that a boy doll might rappel its way down, paying out line like a spider, to rescue her.

My new acquaintance barely came up to my shoulder and probably weighed less than eighty-five pounds. She was shrouded from head to toe in flowing black robes topped off with a *niqab*, the black headdress with eye slits favored by some Muslim women, a disguise no cop dares to question these days. Just visible at one corner of the eye slit was a long straight tress of silver hair that confirmed my guess about who she was, although I hadn't let on. Female burglars are relatively unusual, and female burglars with prematurely white hair are rarely seen even at burglar conventions, which are, as you might imagine, held infrequently. Lumia White Antelope was a one-time protégé of my mentor, Herbie Mott, although her name then had been Luz Ginzberg. Sometime after I knew her, she'd gone to the desert and dropped psilocybin with a

Polish post-hippie who told potential squeezes he was Native American. In the blaze of a chemically enhanced sun she'd had what Herbie had described as "an epiphany. Or something." I hadn't thought about her in years, although at one point I had thought of her practically all the time.

She'd patted me down so thoroughly I wasn't sure I'd tell Ronnie about it.

I wrenched myself back into the present. "Ballpark figure," I said. "Just in the neighborhood. How much did they offer?"

"Way too much," she said. "It almost stopped me from taking the job."

"Me, too."

"But not quite," she said.

Since I wasn't going to explain my need for the money, I said, with the sincerity of someone totally baffled by a disguise, "It's not fair that I can't see your face."

"What's not fair," she said, "is that I have to look at yours. Wow," she said, sitting back and fanning her face with the gun, "I made a joke and I didn't hiccup."

"If it was too much money, why did you take it?"

She fiddled with the gun some more, and I got ready to duck under the table. "Do you read economics?" she asked.

"Not if there's anything else on hand."

"If you did, you'd know that price has nothing to do with intrinsic value. Back in the 1970s an economist named Fred Hirsch invented the term *positional good* to describe something that's valuable only because other people want it. You know, like the way the rope line outside a nightclub and a couple of bodybuilders saying *no* makes stupid people think whoever's playing inside must be good, even though they'd probably run for their lives if the same band was playing for free in their grocery store."

"I was thinking something like that a little while ago. About books."

"So it sort of reassured me. I mean, the idea that the doll isn't worth anything even close to—to what they offered me. Not worth enough to kill for. But at the same time it kind of put me on the thorns of a dilemma."

I said, "Horns."

She shook her head. "Horns? What kind of sense does that make? Dilemmas are *thorny*."

"The early Greek word *dilemma* means 'double proposition.' In other words, an either-or choice is necessary. Animals with sharp horns have two of them, at least ever since the last unicorn took the long hike."

"Okay, okay. I'd write it all down but I'd have to put down the gun."

"So what *are* the horns, if we can get specific for a minute?"

"Well, which is more dangerous, having something that's worth so much that everybody wants it, or having something that might not be worth much at all and only a *few* people want but they want it really, really bad, and they're the kind of people who hire burglars?"

I said, "That qualifies as a dilemma. Are you looking for an answer?"

"No. Anyway, I think I've eliminated one of those groups. I think it's worth a lot. I wasn't sure I was going to show you this, but you cured my hiccups."

I said, "The doll has been cut open."

"How did—oh, that's right. I remem—I mean, someone

said—that you were pretty smart. Take a look, under the back of the cloak."

I picked up the doll, which was heavier than I'd expected, and ran my fingers over the smooth, cold face. The whole thing was so over-finished, so precious, so finicky, it was impossible to imagine its being given to a little girl to play with.

Apparently reading my mind, she said, "I don't think it was really a toy. I think it was an aspirational role model. Middle-class family, brainwashing their eight-year-old, *This is who you can be if you marry up*. Makes me—*hic*—really pissed off. I hiccup when I get mad, too."

"This is still economics?"

"Well, left-wing economics. Have a look at it while I breathe."

I turned it over and lifted the cloak, which was heavily beaded. The fabric was beginning to split and fall away from the beads, and beneath it was a polished, flesh-colored composition material that I knew was a blend of very fine sawdust, water, and glue that had been mixed, molded, dyed, sanded, and lacquered. A slit had been cut in a straight line that would have run from one shoulder blade to the other if the doll had a skeleton. The two diagonals cut below created a triangle that could be pried out. I worked it free and saw that a little wadded linen or muslin stuffing, old enough to be brittle, had been tamped down to make room for something rectangular and sharp-cornered, maybe two-thirds the size of a box of playing cards, but not as thick. It would have to have been slipped in vertically and eased out the same way. A snug fit. I said, "And you found it empty."

"As you said yourself, if I hadn't, why would I have waited around for you?"

"Why *did* you? You obviously knew I didn't have it. I came in after you did."

"I was going to force you to tell me who sent you. The person who hired me is not going to be happy about this, and I thought some information about the competition might make the encounter a little less unpleasant."

I said, "Are you worried about that?"

"The person? No." She looked at the table top for a moment. "I've got a winning personality," she said. "I *do*, don't I?"

"Absolutely. Okay, here's what I know about the one who hired me, but it's not going to help. It was a woman, Anglo, probably early forties, and kind of heavyset. Real cold eyes, not very tall. Nothing remarkable about her voice."

She said, "Well, I suppose that eliminates a few people, but I was hired by a go-between."

"Who?"

"Skip it. Hey, was tonight when you were supposed to come?"

"Last night. If it can be avoided, I make it a point not to show up on any night when someone knows I'm supposed to be doing something illegal. You?"

"Yeah." she said. "Tonight. They're going to be waiting to pick me up. Two of them, I think. What they're *not* going to be is happy."

"Who are they?"

"Don't know. The people who hired me, I guess."

"When are they supposed to—"

"Any old time now. In fact, you've held me up. So to speak. So there's nothing more you can tell me? As like a consolation prize for them?"

"No. I mean, she had three kids with her, but she'd rented them."

"Right."

"No, really. They were actors."

"Okay," she said. She got up, almost no taller than she'd been when she was sitting, and took the doll. The gun dangled from her free hand. "I don't think there's any chance that they're going to come in here," she said, "but there's a good space just under the steps down into the basement. You can get in there and even if they shine a light all over the place they won't see you."

I said, "That's really nice of you. Do you actually think—"

"No, no, no," she said. Then she shook her head for emphasis. "No. Worst comes to worst, I'll just give them their money back." She hiccupped. "Some of their money, anyway."

"You could give me your gun, and I could cover—"

"It's not mine," she said. "I borrowed it. I think I should—"

"No problem. Well, I could watch through the hedge or something."

"I'll be fine," she said. She looked down at her hands, the gun in one and the doll in the other. "Although you might get the front door for me."

"Sure," I said. I got up.

"You know who I am, don't you?"

"I do," I said, feeling apologetic. "The hair."

"Well, Junior," she said, "it was nice to see you again." She turned away, hesitated, and turned to face me again. "Would you let me phone you once in a while?"

"Sure," I said. "It'd be great to hear from you."

She put her stuff on the table, pulled out some kind of Android phone and entered the number I recited.

When she'd thumbed it in, she looked up at me and said, "We can catch up or something. Maybe just talk about nothing. I don't have a lot of friends now." And she picked up the doll and the gun. I followed her to the door and opened it for her. Then I sprinted into the living room, peeled away a corner of thick brown paper, and put my eye to the window.

Seen through the old glass, she rippled like a mermaid as she walked to the gate. Tucking the doll under one arm, she used the free hand to open the gate and step through it. The gate swung shut. I couldn't hear it latch behind her.

But I did hear a car door close. Through the little spaces in the hedge I saw headlights come on. And then I heard a remote little *pop* that, I was dead certain, was a gun being fired inside a closed automobile. By the time I got out to the sidewalk, the car—something wide and white—was making a leisurely right turn onto Pico Boulevard.

7
Itsy Winkle

I just kept kicking the front door, yelling, and jamming my thumb against the bell. It was after 2 A.M. and I was making a lot of noise for a sedate, upper-middle-money neighborhood full of TV series supporting actors, second-tier studio executives, and record producers who hadn't had a hit since Big Hair, but that was the point. Stinky had a couple million bucks' worth of reasons not to want any of his neighbors to get alarmed and call the cops. At any given time the house had three or four rooms full of extremely expensive objects from all over the world, improbably jumbled together as though Sotheby's had held a garage sale.

"Minute, minute," someone said from the other side of the door. It was the kind of voice the South Wind might have, long on breath, somewhat moist, and well above body temperature. It belonged to the latest in Stinky's infinite conga line of Filipino folk dancers, lured from their touring troupes to overstay their visas and serve as his houseboy. This one, an almost unreasonably slender wisp of good cheer, seemed to be named Crisanto, which, he'd informed me, means "golden flower." Crisanto's two most recent predecessors—there was a *lot* of turnover—had been named Jejomar and Ting Ting, both of whom, like Crisanto, came from impoverished small towns where English was, at best, a third language. Jejomar, regrettably, was no longer among the mobile, but I was friends with Ting Ting, who now lived in improbable bliss with a short-tempered hit woman, a hippie throwback who hadn't signed on to the *peace and love* part of the lifestyle. Her parents, bless them, had named her Eaglet.

I was thinking I might have a use for Eaglet when the door opened.

"It's *you*," Crisanto said with apparent delight. He put three straight fingers to his mouth, the picture of a man who has forgotten something unpleasant, and his eyes crinkled in infinite regret. "Mr. Stinky will be so *sad* he miss you."

"Where is he?"

"He is—" Crisanto put his hands palm to palm as though in prayer, brought them up to one cheek, closed his eyes, and rocked slightly. "Him sleep," he said, opening his eyes.

"Well, get him up. And excuse me," I said, brushing past him, "I don't mean to be rude but I'm going to have to be." He took up so little of the doorway I could get by without even side-stepping. "I'll be in the living room."

"Mr. Stinky will not be happy," he said, following me. He was plucking at my shirt as though that would bring me to a screeching halt.

"Tell him I'm going to wait for exactly two minutes, and after that I'll break something valuable every thirty seconds. And I'll start with the best stuff." I headed down the hallway, not looking at the excellent seventeenth-century silverpoint portrait of a young woman, a work I had coveted for years, and made a left into the enormous and compulsively redecorated living room. The huge picture window in one wall looked down at the lights of the San Fernando Valley, burning extravagantly away in defiance of the energy crisis even at this hour. I'd always figured that view added about $350,000 to whatever Stinky paid for the place.

"Mister Junior." I turned to see Crisanto standing in the doorway, being visibly, almost tidally, tugged toward Stinky and his primary responsibility, but stranded here by manners. "You wan' a Coc'Cola?"

Looking at him, seeing the grace he maintained in what had to be a difficult life, I felt a little of my fury ease off. "Okay," I said. "I'll wait *four* minutes. And no thanks, no Coke."

I used the time to survey the latest treasures, including a fine nineteenth-century spinning wheel, which looked fragile enough to qualify as the first thing to put my foot through. I'd have to walk a line with the destruction, though; I'd known Stinky—probably the San Fernando Valley's best high-end fence—long enough to respect the blinding speed and total commitment with which he could turn from harmless, finely tuned aesthete, the kind of man who can draw a delicate butterfly's wing from memory, into a homicidal maniac.

I'd been here only a few days ago to pick up my $2,500, but there were already some new acquisitions. I knew where the best small objects would be, and was staring at the exquisite eighteenth-century French cylinder desk, like a roll-top but with a single thin, curved piece of wood where the roll-top's slats would be, when I heard Stinky grumbling to Crisanto about making some tea. I stepped away from the desk and closer to the spinning wheel than he would want me to be.

"You're not going to need the tea," I said as he came in, wearing a long Victorian nightshirt big enough that four Ebenezer Scrooges could wear it while stealing a car, with yardage left over. I'd never awakened him before, so I was surprised by the man-bun on top of his head. It was exactly as flattering as all the ones you've seen, and it was hard to imagine him doing it in a mirror without averting his eyes.

I said, "I need one thing from you, and then I'm gone."

"It's *chamomile* tea," Stinky said icily. "It's for me. It's for going *back* to sleep."

"One thing, two words," I said. "The name of the person who called you."

He crossed his arms. "Not on your life."

"It's not *my* life I'm talking about."

Stinky's eyebrows went up, one a little higher than the other, something I was pretty sure he practiced. "Is that a threat?"

"Well, of course, it is, you dope. And it's not limited to your copious body, either. For example." I kicked the delicate wooden spokes of the spinning wheel hard enough to send splinters flying in all directions. Crisanto appeared behind Stinky, eyes wide. He had a teacup dangling from one finger.

"That. Will. Cost. You." Stinky's face had gone Arctic white. He didn't care about people but he was crazy about things. "And so will anything else you destroy. Good night." He turned his back with a dramatic whirl and came face to face with Crisanto. They stepped to Stinky's right once and then to his left, trying to get past each other, and while they were dancing I went to the cylinder desk and opened it hard enough to bang the curved piece of wood home.

"Wonder what's in *here*," I said.

Stinky grabbed the teacup, turned, and heaved it at me. He had a terrible arm. It missed me by five or six feet and pretty much disintegrated against the wall.

I said, "Must have been pretty thin. Limoges?"

"Get away from that desk." He was quivering. "If you're not out of here in sixty seconds I'll shoot you."

"I'm fucking terrified," I said. "Do you know Lumia White Antelope?"

"Mediocre," he said. He drew several deep breaths. "Even for a woman."

"My guess right now is that she's dead, and that she's doing it as well as any man could, and I *need the name of the person who called you.*"

"I can't go all Sarah Bernhardt tragic on you," Stinky said. "I didn't know her well enough, and what I did know didn't inspire confidence."

"Stinky," I said, "I *will* attack you physically."

"Can't do it." He uncrossed his arms and then crossed them again, a nice, defensive tell.

"Okay, then, what's your favorite thing in this room?"

"Why didn't you call me today?" he demanded. "You were supposed to have gone last—"

"Well, I didn't," I said. "I went tonight instead."

He held up a hand, palm facing me, international sign language for *stop*. "And you're telling me that—that *girl* was . . . was there?" He looked like someone who'd glanced into a mirror and seen someone else's reflection.

"Yes."

Stinky said, "Where's that *tea*?"

"I am making," Crisanto said. Over Stinky's shoulder he gave me a beatific smile that said, *See? Everything is fine.* He disappeared into the kitchen.

Stinky blotted his upper lip with his index finger, brought down the corners of his mouth and pushed his lower lip out, making what I think of as *Mussolini mouth*. His eyes were all over the room, as though he were counting to make sure I hadn't pocketed anything. It was unusual to see him lose his composure to such an extent, so I just relaxed and enjoyed it.

"Let me get this straight," he said at last. "You went tonight and there was another—"

"*And* I think she's dead," I said. "And remember, I know what a compassionate person you are, so if I keep harping on her probable death, it's because I think it suggests a risk to you. *You*, Stinky Tetweil—"

"Shut up," he said, but he didn't put much into it.

"Because, you see, that suggests either that you sent *both* of us and the customer is displeased, *or* the customer went to *another* talent agent in case your nominee screwed up and couldn't find it. In that case, not only will the customer be displeased, but so will the other talent agent, who's going to assume that I found whatever it was and that we—that's you and I, in case you're not following along—have whatever it is and are out looking for a better price. Which is, of course, what the customer will think, too. So they're probably *both* displeased, or about to be."

"Don't be—" he said, and broke off. "That means you didn't—" he said, and then the phone rang. It was almost 2:20 A.M. He stood immobile for a moment with his mouth open and then Crisanto sang out, "I get it," and Stinky gathered vast reserves of breath and bellowed "NOOOO," loudly and deeply enough to compete with a marine buoy warning ships away from foggy rocks. "Do not—*do not*—"

"Okay," Crisanto said. "I do tea."

"*No*, no. Turn off the lights in back, all of them. Leave them on in here."

I said, "You don't even know where your *light switches* are?"

"Hurryhurryhurry," Stinky called out. "You," he said to me although we were the only two people in the room, "Where did you park?"

"Two blocks—"

"Good, good. Come with me, *now*."

As Crisanto scurried to the back of the house, Stinky led me through a kitchen that could have fed a battalion. At the far end was a door. "If anything is ever missing from here," he said, one hand on the knob, "I will have you killed. Is that clear?" He opened the door to reveal a large pantry, packaged food of every kind lined up obediently on shelves from floor to ceiling.

"You're safe," I said. "I don't eat canned goods."

The phone stopped ringing.

Stinky said, "Shut up," but I didn't think he even knew he'd said it. He pushed aside a huge can of baked beans, and the back wall slid about two feet to the right, just enough to let me in. "I'm serious," he said, "now or ever. If *anything* goes missing—"

"Why didn't you turn off the living room lights?" I asked, but Stinky was using his not-inconsiderable body weight to shove me through the door.

"He would have seen them go off. The light in there comes on when the door closes," he said, and then I heard someone pounding on the front door.

The last time I'd been with Stinky when he was in danger he had begun to recite the Lord's Prayer in Tagalog, something he'd learned from Jejomar, but this time he just went so pale that his white nightshirt looked beige by contrast and he said, "Jesus Christ our lord and savior." He started to slide the door closed, slowed, and said, "There's a little speaker in there. If it sounds like we're all getting killed, step on the pedal next to the door and go straight out through the back. If he's inside, you should be able—"

More banging on the door, real hinge-benders. I was hearing it in stereo, both through the door to the pantry and from the speaker inside the hidden room.

"—to get down the hill without being seen," Stinky finished. "Now get the rest of the way in there." A moment later, the door slid closed and a little 20- or 40-watt bulb came on.

I was in Aladdin's cave if Aladdin had been a twenty-first-century fence specializing in high-end swag who was tight on storage space. The room was only about eight feet long and four wide, but the stuff it contained, piled floor to ceiling, made the living room look like a Salvation Army store, and some of it was small enough to pocket. I was expanding my image of Stinky's operation when the front door got pounded on again.

"Moment," Crisanto said. "Coming, coming."

Whoever it was responded with a kick.

"Hello, *hello*," Crisanto said, all delight, and then there was a kind of soft-edged sound that might have been a body hitting a wall, and Crisanto stopped talking.

"Get him," a man said. It was said quietly but it was the quiet of someone who's known for a long time that he doesn't have to speak up to be listened to.

"Going now," Crisanto said, and then he said, "Eeeeek." Another soft-edged sound, followed by a sharp one that might have been something falling off the wall.

"Why are the lights on?" the soft voice said. I ended that line with a question mark, but it wasn't an interrogative, it was a demand.

"I cleaning?" Crisanto said, and I noticed he was allowing his English skills to regress. "Every night, I—look, look, vacuum cleaner. See?"

"Get him," said Soft Voice, "and then get the hell out of here."

"Get and get," Crisanto said. "Moment."

My cell phone purred. Ronnie. I accepted the call and said, very softly, "I'm okay but I can't talk."

She said, "Do you need help?"

My heart ran an extra lap. Not many people ask you that question when you're obviously in danger. "No. Call you later." She hung up.

I listened to nothing for a couple of minutes, long enough to wonder whether Stinky was getting dressed, had gotten his throat cut, or had slipped out the back. Then I heard him, but it was a Stinky I didn't know, a querulous supplicant with a tone of voice that seemed to be wringing its hands. Grandeur was an indispensable and, I was willing to bet, hard-earned part of Stinky's personality, and hearing him now was oddly uncomfortable, like coming on someone who prizes himself on his looks but hasn't had time to put in his teeth.

Stinky said, "Yes, but" a couple of times and then, "I don't know." At that point they must have moved away from the microphone in the entry hall because I didn't hear anything until Stinky said, more distantly, "No, he didn't, not when he was supposed—" and I was pretty sure I had just become the topic of discussion. I could no longer hear Soft Voice. "Because that's how he *is*," Stinky said. "He's a pain in the ass." Soft Voice must have responded because Stinky said, "No, it's not only that. He's careful. He doesn't think it's smart to tell people when and where he'll—" And then, "Right, right, of course. I'll get hold of him."

This time Soft Voice must have had a lot to say because it was a full minute, a unit of time that goes remarkably slowly when, on the one hand, you have nothing to read and, on the other, when you're wondering whether you're about to die. The silence was long enough to tell me that Soft Voice meant business.

When Stinky spoke this time, he surprised me. He said, "No. Out of the question. Not even for you." Then he said, "Because that's how it works. I won't give him your name and I won't give you his. It's *okay*, Crisanto, go somewhere else, we're just talking."

Stinky inspired loyalty although I'd long wondered why. Maybe I was hearing it now.

"Whatever you want to do, you'll do," Stinky said. "I won't pretend it won't hurt my business. On the other hand, who's better than I am? Who keeps you more secure? This is—"

The other man must have interrupted, because I didn't hear anything except some sibilants for thirty or forty seconds, and then Stinky, sounding a little shaky, said, "You know what? Fuck it. And fuck you, too." And a moment later I heard the front door slam, hard enough to shake the wall of my little room.

I became aware that I had put something in my pocket while I wasn't looking, so to speak, so I fished out a beautiful necklace, maybe eighteenth-century Chinese, a fluid alternation of pearls and perfect spheres of imperial jade—that breathless, first-day-of-spring green that

Thai jewel dyers have been trying to forge for decades—in a long strand that met in a heavy, hand-fashioned gold clasp: museum stuff. I slapped the back of my hand, tried to figure out where I'd taken it from, and then I put it into an open mahogany box that I was willing to bet played music. At that moment, the door slid open.

Stinky's eyes went at once to the box, and then he shook his head and said, "Good decision, bad memory. It was over there."

I said, "I haven't had much practice putting things back. Feels awkward and clunky. Like writing left-handed."

He backed up a couple of steps. Sweat was beaded at his hairline. "Do I have to ask Crisanto to search you?"

"I was just coveting it. Up close. Why didn't you give me to him?"

"He didn't ask nicely. Come on out of there, I don't want to have to keep watching your hands. I want you to sleep here tonight."

"Can't."

"Surely," he said with a crimped little smile, obviously fighting to keep his tone neutral, "*surely* you can call her."

"Sure, I could, but that's not the issue."

"I don't know how long he'll be out there."

"I'll take my chances."

"It's not you I'm worried about, you idiot," Stinky said, "it's *me*. You never, *ever* let a client think they own your business, not even for a moment, because if you do, he will. Sooner or later, he will. The man who was just here would drive a tank through a kindergarten to get to a quarter if he thought he could get away free and clear. But I lied to him anyway because my business rules say my clients don't meet my specialists, not any more than a specialist, like you, is allowed to meet *him*. He's furious that I wouldn't give you to him, but we've done enough business that he's going to be okay with it until something says otherwise. You strolling down my driveway would be rubbing his nose in it, and he will not let that pass."

"He won't see me."

He had backed all the way to the kitchen by then. "Come *out* of there."

"Have Crisanto turn off all the lights, and I mean *all* of them."

"You don't give me orders in my own—"

"Fine," I said, coming into the kitchen and blinking against the light. "Let him spot me through the windows."

Stinky blinked and called out, "*Crisanto.*"

"Itsy Winkle," he said after a long and wearying argument. "Lumia was represented by Itsy Winkle." We were sitting in the dark living room, me surrounded by pillows on the plump, fussy couch and him in the nineteenth-century partner's chair positioned directly between me and the French cylinder desk. Guarding the goods, which I found insulting. He had a leg crossed, revealing that he wore socks beneath thongs. "But you didn't hear it from me."

"I thought Itsy went away for keeps, for that thing with the giant black pearls seven, eight years ago. She beat the shit out of the woman who owned—"

"What a pleasure to know something you don't. There was a second confession years later. It absolved her."

"Must have cost her a fortune."

"It did. Do you remember the Armor-Rite job? Spring before last?"

"The nine million, right? The driver and the guard

were attacked outside a business where they were doing a pickup, a dry cleaner or something, by pit bulls—"

"Staffordshire terriers," Stinky said. "Pedigrees and everything. They lifted their little doggy pinkies when they drank tea." Reminded, he reached over to an exquisite, almost translucent, teapot, and filled his cup, ignoring mine. Stinky had being Stinky down cold. "Several witnesses saw the dogs drag their owner, a young woman, down the sidewalk on her stomach, screaming, and rip into the Armor-Rite guys. In the meantime, someone helped himself to most of a Friday bank pick-up, climbed into a car idling in traffic beside the truck, and drove off. No one even glanced at him, with all that reality TV action on the sidewalk. Woman got bitten, too, when she tried to pull the dogs off."

"And she wasn't arrested, right?"

"Questioned, of course, but no. She had no record, clean as the driven snow is commonly and incorrectly supposed to be. She'd been raising the dogs for five years, she was even certified by the dog racial purity people, whoever they might be—"

"American Kennel Club."

"If you say so." He sighed at the sheer banality of the idea and picked at some lint on his gown. "Itsy had been sent up for stealing the pearls, and clubbing half to death the nice lady who owned them, a full year before the young woman began to raise the dogs. Entered them in shows and everything. Patience is a virtue, perseverance furthers, all that rot. Unbeknownst, et cetera, she'd been Itsy's girlfriend, the dog lady had, for a few years, when she was seventeen or eighteen, but that was definitely off the record. Then, about a month after the Armor-Rite robbery, someone from Pacoima stepped forward and turned

himself in for the job with the pearls that Itsy had done. At
his wife's insistence. The little woman said he'd been gone
that night and that he—" he squinted up toward the ceiling—"*Pedro*, I suppose, had shown her the pearls when he
got home. Described them perfectly."

I said, "Pedro."

"One of those names." Despite his fondness for Filipino
folk dancers, Stinky occasionally displayed the snow-white
trust fund child's not-uncommon lack of interest in the lives
of people in traditionally lower-economic minority groups.
"Maybe Juan? An immigrant, I believe. He even produced
one of the pearls, a perfect match for the set, which brought
together some of the biggest black pearls ever on the market. The pearl was persuasive, since the necklace had never
been recovered. It was probably the least valuable stone in
the haul. Said he'd given the others to a representative of *el
Eme*, the Mexican mafia—"

"I know who *el Eme i*s."

"—who had set up the job. The man who came for the
pearls, he said, had black hands tattooed all over his chest.
Apparently, removing his shirt was equivalent to showing
his ID. As it turned out, a notorious *el Eme* what-would-
you-call-it, a *functionary*, with identical tattoos had been
killed in prison about six months before Pedro's wife's conscience began to bother her. So, you see, they'd thought of
everything. He had the story, he had his wife saying he'd
been gone the night of the robbery, he had the tattoos all
over the thug's chest, he had the pearl. Left over, of course,
from Itsy's haul. By comparison, the prosecutors who put
Itsy away had a *weak case*, which they won only by con-
tinually pushing witnesses to say things about her criminal
past that the judge told the jury to disregard."

"And Pedro's wife?"

"Waiting for him in their new house in Hidden Hills, bought with the money stolen from Armor-Rite."

"So when Itsy got out, she set herself up as a contractor."

"She'd done a little of it before, dabbled in it, but yes, she started to specialize. In girls, and not just burglars, either. Plausibles," he said, meaning con artists, "even hit-girls. It's like a little franchise."

"Hitwomen," I said reflexively.

"Oh, who *cares*?" Stinky said. "She is, was, whatever, the fence and the contractor for that young lady with the absurd name."

"Lumia," I said. "So somebody, and you don't think it was the guy who was just here, went to Itsy and hired Lumia—"

"So it would seem."

"Do you know how to reach her?"

"Itsy? My recommendation would do you no good, my boy. She loathes me."

"Still."

"I'm disinclined," he said. "If you didn't please her, and you wouldn't, she'd be on my doormat, kicking and shouting as you just did. She can be impressively unpleasant. So, no."

"Final answer?"

Stinky yawned and looked at a gold watch thin enough to be transparent, probably a tuxedo watch from the 1930s.

"What time is it?"

"A little before four." He looked up at me, and he said, "If you don't find that thing, whatever it is, he *is* going to come after you. And me. Maybe you should just return the money."

"Not an option," I said, getting up. "Sleep tight."

8
Infinite Black Nothing

The car that had taken Lumia away after I heard the shot had turned right onto Pico. My car had been parked a long block away from Horton House, pointing south, which meant that I'd dropped south to Venice Boulevard instead of up to Pico and taken it west for a bit before angling up to the freeway to get to Encino and Stinky. It had been gnawing at me the whole two hours-plus I'd been at Stinky's that I hadn't at least cruised Pico for a mile or two, just out of concern. They'd been long gone by the time I finally left Horton House, but who knew? There might have been some signs somewhere. There might even *still* be, I thought as I drove back down into the Koreatown area.

Were there ever.

I got off the freeway at Alexandria and went up to Pico. Horton House was about a mile to my left, but I turned right, figuring if they were going to do anything they'd get a little farther from the scene of the crime first. I'd barely gone another half-mile when I saw the red lights ahead and then the cops in the street and the sawhorse barriers they'd put up to give them both of Pico's eastbound lanes. A blinking arrow sign on the pavement transformed the suggestion to merge left into an imperative, and about twenty or thirty yards from the obvious center of the action up ahead, a cop directed me into the oncoming lane, which had been blocked off in the other direction a couple hundred yards down. Normally it would have been a terrible snarl, but at four-thirty on a weeknight, I would barely have had to slow if it weren't for the rubberneckers. LA is a city obsessed with automobiles, a place where live car chases, covered by multiple helicopter cameramen, bump international affairs off the TV news. Los Angeles drivers reserve their right to gawk at traffic accidents with all the energy that some people in Texas put into defending their right to wear a gun in church. So I had lots of time to see what I didn't want to see, and it didn't even look suspicious when I slowed.

A big white car parked at the curb with the rear doors open. Cops crawling all over the place. A gurney standing behind the car, covered by a white cloth with a strap around its center. The body beneath the cloth was no more than five feet long. It could have been a child.

So the hit had been on the cards whether she got the doohickey or not. They shot her, it had seemed to me, the moment she'd closed the car door, before they even pulled away from the house, knowing that another car was waiting for them a couple of miles up Pico. Pull over, park legally, leave the stolen car with the dead female burglar in the backseat, and drive off into the night. She'd probably sat there, alone in the backseat, until someone on the sidewalk slowed to look at her.

Pretty fucking cold.

Swearing furiously at the gawking rubberneckers and also at myself, I worked my way up to the first right and headed back to Horton House, pulled back by Stinky's warning that his client would come after me if I didn't find whatever the hell it was.

As far as I could tell, the house hadn't been ransacked, discreetly tossed, or burned down. None of the three would have surprised me. It loomed like a right-angled glimpse of infinite dark matter sliced into the night sky, paled by the city's neon glow bouncing off the low clouds. More than ever, Horton House seemed like a place where the dead slept badly. This time I'd brought a real flashlight and this time I knew for *certain* that I was looking for something tiny. I also knew I only had about an hour before the night's cover of darkness was diluted by the daily warmup to sunrise. The first paling in the sky would be deferred for fifteen minutes or so by the clouds, but the sun itself was scheduled to shoulder its way into the new day around 6:40 and it would already be too light for comfort by then. Burglars usually can tell you what time sunrise is, give or take ten minutes.

So I hauled ass.

First, I ripped to pieces the sagging, stinking bed where Miss Daisy had breathed her last. The blankets, when I tore them off, released an eye-stinging cloud of baby powder. Nothing there, nothing under the mattress, nothing in the toilet tank, nothing in any of the jars and bottles of makeup, most of them decades old: brands like Zell, Max Factor, Tangee, Coty. I even poured into the sink two full shakers of the loathsome baby powder and forced myself to plunge my fingers into it. Zero. In a moment of stupidity I tried to get even with the powder by running water into it, but all that did was turn it into a vile-smelling cement in the basin. The water refused to drain.

Nothing in the light fixtures, nothing behind the wall outlets (which popped right off, the screws embedded in clots of rotting plaster), nothing in the pockets of the clothes or the cushions of the room's only easy chair. Nothing inside the books on the shelves. Nothing in similar places in any of the other upstairs rooms. Nothing in the cradle. Nothing in any of the dolls on the shelf in the sitting room, which slowed me down for about fifteen minutes as I checked them individually. I hurried downstairs to the basement door, crossed myself with a certain amount of embarrassment, and followed the stairs down into the damp, which was almost as hard on my sense of smell as the baby powder. In one damp, filthy, cobwebbed corner I found a bunch of tools that included a wrench, and I took that back up to the second floor and removed the old U-shaped trap beneath the sink in the master bathroom, cursing myself for doing things in the wrong order as the powder poured through and gave me a sneezing fit. Nothing in the trap. Nothing in *any* of the traps on the second floor.

This was not looking good, and I only had about thirty minutes of real darkness left.

I was certain that whatever it was would have been on the second floor, if only because that's where Miss Daisy had been confined, but I went into the kitchen anyway and ransacked the cupboards and drawers. In one drawer I found a yellowing booklet that said *Names and Numbers* in that faux-handwritten Betty Crocker font so popular in the 1950s. Around and between the grease spots and food smears on its pages, I saw entries in both pen and pencil and in several people's handwriting, and I tucked it in between my belt and my stomach to keep my hands free. Out of sheer desperation I ransacked the servant's bedroom for three or four depressing and unproductive minutes and then went into the living room.

It was a broad room, much wider than it was deep. The floor was bare and gritty underfoot with all the dirt that sifts through carpets like the one that had been in this room for decades until it was peeled back for sale. From the state of the floor it was apparent that the carpet had stretched almost from wall to wall, leaving a margin of six inches or so on all sides. It had obviously been custom-cut by its installers to make space for the marble hearth, once white, that claimed the space in front of the fireplace in the center of the long wall. It seemed to me the room had an awkward shape for a place in which so much family life is supposed to be transacted and, ideally, shared. The room's shape would have dictated two or three separate groupings of furniture, one in front of the fireplace and one at some distance on either side. Maybe they had exhausted their family-gathering spirit around the dining room table. Maybe this family wasn't all that eager for face-to-face time. When I tried to imagine them gathered here, in this forbidding room, what I came up with was something like cocktails at the House of Atreus.

Before checking out the bookshelves, I put the light on the wispy-looking photos on either side of the fireplace, and they were so appropriate to this awful place that I popped a full set of goose bumps.

Years ago, I had a short dalliance, a bit hair-raising and thin on laughs, with a young female plausible who called herself Angela Havilland and specialized in delivering messages from the Beyond, at a hefty mark-up. She had enormous, melting eyes that looked like they could see

through walls, a voice softer than a spring breeze, a soothing, empathetic manner, and a heart like a carbon-steel
fist. At first I'd thought, or perhaps hoped, that she did no
harm, just applied a kind of warm towel to the wounds
of severance. While I was kidding myself, she dazzled the
fact-collector in me with her encyclopedic knowledge of
centuries of attempts, both heartfelt and fraudulent, to
bridge the void between life and death. And here were two
prime examples of her favorite curiosity, hanging on the
walls of Horton House.

They were "spirit photographs," a particularly nasty
phenomenon from the latter half of the nineteenth century
and the first two or three decades of the twentieth. Essentially, they were double exposures made for an audience
who had no understanding of how photography worked
and who ached for evidence that their dead were still at
hand. The most common hoax was a photo of a living
person and, in the background, hovering weightlessly, a
transparent image of some dearly departed. In none of the
spirit photographs did the spirits look alarmed or even
vaguely surprised at being dead, which was, of course,
because they'd been alive when they'd had a camera
pointed at them. The scam started in America, where the
most notorious spirit image was a picture of Mary Todd
Lincoln, careworn and baffled in her widow's weeds.
Behind her floated a spectral, barely recognizable Abe,
his hand resting protectively, if immaterially, on her left
shoulder. It would be kitsch if it weren't so callous, if it
weren't for the hopelessly lost expression on the widow's
face.

Spirit photography was practically *made* for England,
where every third stately home boasts at least one resident

spook and where photos of the recently deceased, often children—hard to look at today without profound uneasiness—were hung on walls as framed memento mori. It seems ghoulish until we remember how high the child mortality figures were at the time.

So imagine, in a society that made space in their family gathering rooms for photos of the physical remains of the departed, the hunger there must have been for images of their enduring *spirit*. Perhaps the most famous of the British spirit photos was hanging to the left of the Horton fireplace: the "Brown Lady" of Raynham Hall, caught descending an empty staircase, taken at the height of the Spiritualist movement, in 1936. People who were on hand when the picture was taken saw nothing out of the ordinary, although the photographer's assistant supposedly *sensed* something and told the photographer to make an exposure, which revealed a woman no more solid than a cloud taking the stairs in the conventional manner, although she certainly seemed insubstantial enough to float. The photo, published in a popular magazine, *Country Life*, caused a sensation. The image on Horton's wall seemed to be a direct copy from the original negative, which would make it a genuine rarity; as closely as I looked I couldn't find the dot pattern that betrays the magazine printing of the day.

The other photograph, equally famous, had been taken almost forty years earlier, in 1895. The sister of the second Viscount Lord Combermere, an enthusiastic amateur photographer, created a panoramic image of his extensive library by setting her camera for a one-hour exposure while Lord Combermere was fully occupied several miles away, being buried. When she developed the film, she found that the Viscount's customary chair was occupied by an extremely transparent individual who could conceivably have been her brother, although to my eyes, it might have been anyone, including a large terrier.

And here it was, hanging to the right of the fireplace, so Horton had the one-two punch of British spirit photography displayed in his living room. Obviously, I thought, he'd brought them back from England otherwise he'd have had American photographs, of which there are thousands—but why have them at all? From what I'd learned about Horton, he didn't seem to be someone who was afflicted with the spiritual vapors.

The house did its creaking act again. I thought I'd become immune to it, but at that moment, it was enough to make me turn and look behind me. Just for a second, I wondered whether he could have built this wretched house just to house those eminently spooky pictures.

I didn't really want to handle them, but to be thorough I took them both down: nothing glued to their backs, no hidey-holes in the wall behind them. With a certain easing of tension, I re-hung them and turned my attention to the books. Maybe some carved-out . . .

My, *my*.

Tired as I was, for a few minutes there, I actually lost track of time.

An absolute mob of first editions: George Eliot, Anthony Trollope, Arthur Conan Doyle, Wilkie Collins, George Gissing, and other cream-of-the-crop late Victorian and Edwardian writers, although no Dickens. Eliot's *Middlemarch* was definitely the real deal, four octavo volumes instead of the standard three-decker, a concession to the book's length. It was originally serialized in eight smaller volumes while Eliot was still struggling to finish it—talk about *pressure*—but the first complete and corrected edition was the one staring at me from the shelf. A couple of other Eliots were probably firsts, but *Middlemarch* was the most valuable.

While I couldn't see anyone who would own these things having the insensitivity to deface them, I opened ten or twelve volumes at random; no secret hiding places carved through the hearts of the pages.

I exhaled in relief and stood back to get a broader perspective. This was a serious collection. Some of these old pieces of paper were more valuable, probably, than most of the things that had been taken, but as I said, nobody steals books.

Except me. I went into the kitchen and opened the cupboard with the paper shopping bags packed into it and pawed through them until I found one that seemed less brittle than the others. I grabbed a second to be on the safe side and hustled back into the living room.

All the Eliots went into one bag, accompanied by a couple of beautiful Trollope firsts, not the rarest and most expensive of his books, but two I loved, *The Way We Live Now* and *The Eustace Diamonds*. Gissing's *Grub Street* went into the second bag, and then I hesitated over the Sherlock Holmes books. Conan Doyle, like many nineteenth-century British writers, was published first in magazines. If demand for an author's stories justified the expense, the tales were collected and re-released as books. Holmes caused a sensation, and the first two collections, *The Adventures of Sherlock Holmes* and *The Memoirs of Sherlock Holmes*, each contained twelve stories. First editions of those collections have pretty good value, and here they were. I considered them for a moment—I've never been a big Holmes fan—but then, I thought, the first guy ever to equip a detective with a magnifying glass deserved the tribute of being stolen.

I happened to know one of the telltales of the first book, *The Adventures*, not because I'm an expert but because it's famous among book collectors, if only because it's so memorable. On page 317, the character named "Miss Violet" is referred to as "Miss Violent." So I pulled that volume down, approving in passing the very Victorian peacock blue cover, and flipped it open, and there, waiting for me, was Miss Violent.

I was putting it into the second shopping bag when I registered what I'd seen somewhere in the book's first few pages. I reopened it to the title page, and there I found, in surprisingly dark blue ink, "To Henry Wallace Horton with thanks for the divine spark, Arthur." Beneath "Arthur," as though added in some embarrassment at how personal it was to sign a first name only, was the rest of it: "Conan Doyle." *Really*. My claim-jumping, jewel-stealing, assault-and-battering American millionaire was on a first-name basis with Sir Arthur Conan Doyle? Henry Wallace Horton's sojourn in merry old England had been more interesting than I'd imagined.

The second Holmes books also went into the second bag.

I also snapped up good editions of a couple of Galsworthy novels, a beautiful first of Collins's *The Moonstone*, and four or five others. I stepped back, regarded the shelves for one more covetous moment, and then, lugging the bags, I went out, wincing, into the first tenuous light of the brand new day.

PART TWO

DAY FOR NIGHT

What hath night
to do with sleep?
– John Milton, *Paradise Lost*

9

Apartment 302

People had their headlights on, which made it relatively easy for me to play loop-the-loop on the narrow neighborhood streets as I kept one eye on the mirror. I didn't seem to be dragging anyone behind me, but just to be on the safe side I took a long way around—east toward downtown, then north all the way up to Sunset before heading west again and, finally, south on Western to get home. The sun barged its way into the sky behind me and poked its big nose through the clouds as I turned west, and I squinted like a cave fish caught outdoors at high noon.

I was wearier than I'd thought. I'd been up for twenty-four hours, and a lot of them had been high-adrenaline hours, but that was no excuse not to keep an eye out for anything interesting going on a few cars back.

The woman with the orange hair had said she'd "researched" me, but that could have been an empty threat. I wasn't that easy to research. The only spot on the map I'd visited that I was certain she knew about, other than Mickey D's, was Horton House, so if she were going to pick up my trail, that's where she would do it. Of course, if she'd tried, she would have done it the night before last, when I was supposed to be there. And after she and her bushy-haired friend had picked up and shot Lumia (if I was right about who had been in the car), she'd have had no reason to return. That gun had gone off only moments after the car door closed; Lumia couldn't have had time to say I was in there. Nor, I thought—and the thought struck like a punch in the gut—would she have. Lumia never would have told them about me. She'd even shared her hiding place with me.

I was going to need to process how I felt about what had been done to Lumia, how I had felt about Lumia, what I could *do* about Lumia.

Back to worrying about myself. I supposed that Orange Hair *could* have come back, although I hadn't spotted her either time when I left the house on foot. It was probably within the realm of possibility that there was a whole platoon behind me, expertly changing places to blend in. But if you believe that, then, first, you're usually overestimating your interest value, and second, if they're any good, there's really no way to detect it. I turned left into the maze of streets east of Western Avenue—once, as the name suggests, the westernmost edge of built-up downtown LA and even now a border between urban cramping and the big, sprawling lots that surround some of the town's most beautiful houses. And then a thought, one I'd been pushing away, shouldered its way in. Perhaps the reason she wasn't following me was that she already knew where I lived. The prudent thing to do would be to get Ronnie out of there.

Not that the place would catch the eye of Orange Hair as she drove by. My address was inside one of three energetically run-down apartment houses that sit at the corner of two streets I'm not about to name, the kind of urban ruins whose good bones hint at an interesting, perhaps even glamorous, past but that look today like all it would take is one good shove to push the whole thing over, dominoes-style. It's hard even to read their names from the fractional neon tubing that remains in their signs; a recently broken *W* has transformed The Wedgwood, where I live, into *The edgwood*. Similar damage had turned The Lenox into the toxic-sounding *The nox* and The Royal Doulton into *The Royal Doult*. All three apartment houses had been named after the premier manufacturers of formal china in the 1920s, which is why, in their rather considerable heyday, they were collectively, if informally, referred to as the China apartments.

And there'd been a lot of *hey* in their heyday. The area just a mile or three south of Griffith Park had been the first great neighborhood for movie money, the earliest Beverly Hills, so to speak. The houses and apartments in the area were home to well-paid but name-beneath-the-title talent: screenwriters, art directors, actors and actresses on the way up and down, mistresses, multiple mistresses, tag teams of mistresses, the occasional mister, and so forth. So, for example, studio royalty—the Cecil B. DeMilles of the world—lived in castles in Griffith Park, while Cedric Gibbons, who designed both the Oscar statuette and MGM's lushest movies, bunked luxuriously in the Lenox before building one of Los Angeles's most extraordinary houses in the wilds of Santa Monica.

Inevitably, over the next few decades, the film industry moved west, pushed by a landslide of money that demanded hills with views, and houses on lots large enough to qualify as city-states; and the Western Avenue neighborhood started a long economic skid that continued through the 1970s. The big houses were cut up into apartments, the apartments went unimproved and became undervalued and overpopulated, sometimes with two and three families to a unit. When land values reached their nadir, a secretive, cash-only Korean syndicate bought the China apartments and brought them back to their original state of glory on the inside while distressing even further the buildings' exteriors until they looked like convalescent homes for rats. They even pulled up the lawns and planted weeds. The absolute poster of urban decay.

But inside, if you could get past the inconspicuous Korean guards, they were perfect palaces: big rooms, high ceilings, Art Deco windows, endlessly polished mahogany and marble floors, such long-forgotten amenities as cold pantries, nurseries, and libraries. The units were marketed to those who had a *lot* to hide, many of them "small businessmen" with huge profits, men with second and third secret families, and a staggering variety of criminals— representatives of virtually all the major tribes of Crook Nation. Almost all of them were Korean.

I had been given possession of unit 302, a six-room beauty with a view of the downtown lights, five or six years earlier by a Korean plausible named Winnie Park whose life I had saved in an uncharacteristic moment of physical bravery. Several of her schemes had simultaneously gone rancid and she'd fled the country, handing me the lease as a thank-you before taking off for Singapore. But she blew it in Singapore, too, and now she occasionally writes me wistful letters from prison, where she's serving a really solid chunk of time.

With one last, cautious look in the mirror I pulled into the basement garage beneath the edgwood. By bribing every building inspector in sight, the syndicate had knocked the previously separate underground garages into one vast subterranean space. Since the buildings stood on a corner, it was possible to dip down into the edgwood's parking basement and emerge a moment later from beneath The Royal Doult, on a different street altogether. If, like me, you kept an extra ride down there, you could come out not only from a different building, facing a different street, but also driving a different car. I thought this arrangement testified to the management's deep and thorough understanding of their customers' needs.

For years after my wife, Kathy, and I split, I had lived in off-brand motels, moving frequently from one dump to another, trying to stay ahead of the rapidly growing list of crooks whose bad side I had managed to locate. After Winnie's departure I had tossed her stuff and filled Apartment 302 with the simple but expensive period furnishings it deserved. I'd signed up for the syndicate's cleaning service to keep its surfaces gleaming, and I'd filled the shelves in the library, but I visited it only rarely, and even then with one eye on the mirror. It had been my sole real secret, my one-person bomb shelter for the day the world turned on me, as it had on Winnie Park. Even Kathy and my daughter, Rina, didn't know about it. But, at a turning point in my relationship with Ronnie, when I had been modestly unfaithful in spirit if not in body, I'd gone full metal jacket on commitment: I took her to the place and asked her to live there with me. Together we had created my first real home since Kathy and I broke up.

The pretense of squalor extended from the dim garage to the battered elevator with its preprogrammed lurches and jiggles, its recorded soundtrack of alarming noises no one wants to hear in an elevator, and its hidden camera so the guards could stop you on the ground floor if they didn't recognize you. It extended even to the corridors on each floor, whose ceilings dropped flakes of plaster, like architectural dandruff, on the slightly squishy carpets. It took me three keys to open my door, both bags of books held tentatively in my free hand as I fiddled with the locks.

Once inside, I released a long breath I seemed to have been storing up forever, since the moment Lumia's wretched little gun went off. The place was blessedly dim and silent and cool; Ronnie didn't like the heating system, which produced warm but faintly dusty-smelling air. A vase of out-of-season carnations radiated its pungent scent all the way from the living room. I went into the library, floor-to-ceiling shelves on three walls, and put the supermarket bags on my favorite place to sit in the world, an old armchair made of a leather so supple it seemed to have been buttered for decades. Then I tiptoed to the door of the bedroom, moving burglar-quietly, and peeked in at Ronnie, who had one foot poking out from the blanket. Its Technicolor rainbow of toenail polish (she never did them all the same shade) served as a sort of cheerful flag of greeting. I gave her a Laurel and Hardy fingertip wave, eased the door closed, went to the kitchen, wrapped the grinder in a couple of dish towels to shut it up, and made some coffee.

The fragrance of the coffee, steaming on the little library table beside my chair, combined with the carnations to create a scent almost pungent enough to scrub the stink of Miss Daisy's baby powder from my memory. I unpacked the first editions and flipped through them, putting them to my nose to catch another favorite scent, the perfume of old books. These volumes were in good shape; no Philistine had dog-eared them or underlined in them (a sin I commit compulsively), no children had enlivened the color scheme with their crayons, and the pervasive damp of Horton House seemed to have given them a solicitous miss. It was relatively late in life that I'd begun reading— reading seriously, anyway. I'd read as a kid primarily as a way of hiding in a world my father wasn't in. My mother was fond of really thick books, the originals of the "condensed" versions I'd seen on Miss Daisy's shelf, thoughtfully de-boned and reduced to gruel by Readers Digest, but I'd learned early that fatness in a book wasn't a warning sign but rather a promise that you would be allowed to remain in its world for a longer time.

English girls in the seventeenth century, I had read somewhere, were often criticized for reading novels rather than sermons. The printing press, like every other technological advance, had been demonized as the death of civilization even as it opened life up and even made it bearable for so many, as it did for me when I was a kid. After I escaped my father's house I entered into the slightly schizophrenic existence of someone who was a college student when it was light out and a burglar after dark, and I pretty much quit reading anything that wasn't assigned and likely to be on a final. And then an English professor, an avuncular, brilliant, big-hearted, basso profundo Faulkner scholar named Marvin Klotz, with whom I had taken two classes, said to me, "You know what the curse of being a teacher is, Mr. Bender? It's constantly looking at some kid and thinking he or she is brighter than the external evidence would indicate, and being wrong over and over again." I had said something like, "Yeah?" because I wasn't used to having faculty members address me as a person rather than a paying customer, and he said, "Yeah." He reached into his briefcase and took out a book that was fat even by my mother's standards—more than nine hundred pages, as I would learn almost immediately—and he handed it to me and said, "Let's see what you get out of this."

What I got out of it was that I didn't know shit.

The book, William Gaddis's *The Recognitions*, was about an art forger who is tormented by the questions of what he owes to God and which God he might owe it to. It opened to me the worlds of religious history, the names and idiosyncrasies of some now-obscure gods and their avatars, the painters of the Flemish Renaissance, the lives of some of the quirkier saints, and the world of Greenwich Village in the 1950s, to name just a few. It also put me on a long-term course of reading that, in the short haul, completely replaced my college curriculum and, in the long run, was responsible for the books on the shelves of the room I was sitting in. It was very satisfying to know that I already owned a first edition of *The Recognitions* to share the shelves with Trollope, Eliot, Conan Doyle, and the others I had just brought home.

A yawn ambushed me. I blinked away the tears and asked myself where I would put Mr. Horton's masterpieces. Rearranging bookshelves, especially *full* bookshelves that will require some deletions to make way for the newcomers, is sort of like adopting a clutch of kids when your bedrooms are all filled to capacity: Which children will you push prematurely into the world? I thought about the three little actors whom Harried Mom had used as props and made a mental note to visit, later in the day, the person who might be able to help me identify them. Without warning, time imploded completely, just folded up and disappeared, and the next thing I knew, someone was tapping lightly on my knee.

10
Swifty

"You came in quietly," Ronnie said. She was standing a couple of feet away, silhouetted against the flow of morning light in the doorway behind her, and she had a fresh, steaming cup of coffee, complete with saucer, in her hand. She waved it around as I sat up and blinked at her, my eyes feeling so crusted they could have belonged to a century-old tortoise.

"I was singing opera when I came in," I said. I yawned. "You could sleep through Armageddon."

"Better than being awake for it." She was wearing the yellow T-shirt, which she had claimed and laundered in water hot enough to take it down two sizes. Ronnie liked yellow. She even looked good in it.

I squinted at the yellow and said, "What time is it?"

"Just past ten-thirty." She stepped forward, looking down at me. "You were all collapsed in here like a crumpled newspaper. I didn't have the heart to wake you up."

"It was a long night," I said. "Is that coffee for me?"

"Sure. The stuff you made had turned into asphalt." She backed up a step instead of handing the cup to me and said, "Want to drink it in the living room? That way, I can sit down, too."

I said, "Why don't you sit on my lap?"

"It's just one grim condition after another. Angle around so I can get my pretty little feet on the footstool." She set the coffee on the table, put both arms around my neck—she was still minty with toothpaste—and slid onto my lap. It always amazed me how someone I loved so much could weigh so little; you would have thought the sheer volume of affection I'd poured into her would weigh her down, if only a tiny bit. Maybe love is lighter than air. She said, "Rough night?"

"A stinker." I picked up the cup, leaned to one side so I wouldn't spill any on her, and drank about half of it. It was *much* better than mine. When I went to put it back, I hit the edge of the table with my forearm, and only her reflexes kept the saucer from sliding off and hitting the floor.

"It *must* have been a bad night," she said, putting the saucer back. "Usually you're as precise as a cat."

"Cats knock all kinds of stuff over."

"Yeah, but they do it on purpose," she said. "What went wrong?"

I gave her the two-minute summary. When I'd finished, she snuggled up against me and said, "I don't like this chair half as much without you in it. Did you know her very well?"

"She was one of Herbie's pets for a while. A nice person who kind of undervalued herself. Always looking for a version of her she could like better. She, um, she got the hiccups when she was nervous." To my surprise, I'd had to take a deep breath to finish the sentence.

"I never met her," she said, but it was partly a question.

"No, you didn't. We hadn't seen each other in years."

"And you didn't get the McGuffin. Does this mean that we're in danger?"

"I think it does," I said. "How would you feel about going back to motels for a while?"

"No problem," she said, "as long as you're there, being as uncomfortable as I am."

"Wouldn't miss it for the world."

"So you think two people are competing for this thing you didn't get."

"That's what I think."

"And they're both dangerous."

"From what I've seen so far, that's an understatement."

She sighed. Then she said, "One suitcase, right?"

I said, "I haven't actually been to bed yet. You look like you might benefit from a little sleep, too."

"*Sleep*, he says. Fat chance." She got up and offered me a hand. "Come on, gramps. Morning's slipping by."

"You can call me gramps all you want," I said, letting her pull me up, "but I'm still spry."

Stinky yawned into the phone, and I involuntarily yawned back at him. He said, "You just *left*."

"Who fences furniture, carpets, paintings, house stuff?" I was in the living room, looking at the skyline and working on my third cup of coffee, reinvigorated by the caffeine, a little friendly exercise, and a shared shower. Ronnie was in the preparatory stages of packing, a process with several phases.

"Well, paintings are a category unto themselves. The rest of it: contemporary or antique?" Then he said, "Thank you, Crisanto."

I said, "Fences have specialties? What did he bring you?"

"If you must know, it's a hot infusion of chamomile, blessed thistle, and black tea, *Tanyang Gongfu* from Fujian."

"Easy for you to say. Does it wake you up?"

"I don't require the same amount of *waking up* that you do."

"Really. Are you aware that black tea was an accident, just some old crap tea that was left in the sun too long—"

"You are *not* going to spoil—"

"—and that the Chinese sold it to the British and made up this big story about it because they figured the Brits wouldn't know any—"

"Three," Stinky said, counting down. "Two."

"Why can't you drink coffee, like real people?"

"If you *insist* on an answer," Stinky said, "coffee is blunt-force trauma for the nervous system. Fine, I suppose, for the insensitive and the low-strung—"

"Those of us who have to shave the backs of our hands."

"Figuratively, of course. Most of the time. *Yes*, there are specialists. But if you've somehow bagged, or, rather, come across, something that would interest one of them, I'd be very happy to take it to the best—"

"I'm sure you would," I said. "But what I need is information. I'd like you to give me their names and then call ahead and tell them they can talk to me."

"Let me see," Stinky said, "which favor am I returning?"

"The one I'm going to do you when I don't tell the guy who banged on the door there last night that you're the one who sent me to him."

"You don't know who—"

"I will," I said. "And you *know* that's true."

"You'll be walking into the lion's den."

"I have dealt," I said, "with television and movie producers."

"And, of course," Stinky said in one of those dazzling reversals that are possible only to people whose innermost convictions are shallowly held, "you'll tell me *immediately* after you've talked to him. Let me know how it went. If you're still walking, I mean."

"I will."

"And if there's money to be made from whatever you're doing with this old furniture or whatever it is, you'll remember who opened the door for you."

"You're so *dependable*," I said. "It's a comfort to have at least one friend, or maybe acquaintance, who always jumps the way you think he will."

"So you want the name of a fence?"

"And a number, please."

"And you promise you won't start taking things to this fence, things that I should get."

"And a number, please."

"I'm waiting for your word of—"

"Do you remember when you said that if I didn't find the gizmo, your visitor last night would come after me? And do you remember who else you said he'd come after?"

Stinky gave me a long pause that was difficult to interpret as *thoughtful* and said, "Do you have a pencil?"

Ninety minutes later, Louie the Lost said, "That was a nice girl." He chewed for a moment, but without his usual gusto, although, to be fair, *gusto* wasn't the likeliest reaction to the food we were eating. "Little bit of a thing."

Louie and I were in yet another of his favorite San Fernando Valley restaurants, each of which was distinguished by one thing it did better than any other San Fernando Valley restaurant Louie knew of. In this one the highlight was pie which, unfortunately, we hadn't yet gotten to. The courses preceding the pie were memorably forgettable.

"She was," I said, and then I said again, "She was," and realized that I wasn't really ready to talk about her yet. Then I said, without knowing I was going to say it, "She was lonely."

Louie gave me a quick glance with a lot of questions in it, so I changed the subject. "Are *any* of your restaurants good at more than one thing?"

"Nah," he said. We were sitting in front of a big window in the full cold glare of the afternoon, and I was startled to see strands of gray in Louie's ponytail. How long had I known him, anyway? Did I have gray in *my* hair? "Somebody tells you he can do two things great," Louie said, "stand back because his nose is gonna grow. Most people work their whole lives to get to the point where they do one thing okay, not great, just okay. People who get great, they *only* do one thing. Most great singers can't swim for shit."

I said, "I'd love a look at the data that supports that."

He blew on his coffee. It was almost gone, so I knew he was stalling before saying something he wasn't sure of. "You wanna talk about her or not?"

"Yeah." I was looking out the window. "I, uh, when I knew her she was a kid. Maybe seventeen. Maybe eighteen. She was so little she looked thirteen, fourteen. I saw her last night for the first time in eight or nine years. I mean, she took a shot at me, but that was the gun's fault."

"You have a forgiving nature."

"She said she was sorry. She had the hiccups."

"That can be murder, no joke intended, when you got a gun in your hand. Not as bad as sneezing but a lot worse than a yawn. Yawn can be kind of cool, you're pointing a rig at someone and you yawn. They gotta figure they're fooling with the iceman. You want me to keep talking or you want to give me the details?"

I gave him the details.

"I wish I hadn't heard that," he said. He lifted the edge of his plate, dropped it, and pushed it to the center of the table. "Now I've eaten all this crap and I don't even want the pie."

"She wanted to stay in touch with me," I said. Louie just waited. "And now she's dead. So I've got to talk to Itsy."

Louie picked up a fork and used it to squash flat a little Matterhorn of mashed potatoes. When he was finished, he said, "Well, I can tell you where she is but I can't make her talk to you."

"How did she feel about Lumia?"

"Probably felt the same about her as she would about your prostate gland. Itsy saves the battery acid for guys but she's a bear, even with chicks."

"I'll have to risk it."

"Okay." He elbowed the plate farther away and reached into his pocket, coming out with his wallet, which had both a little pad and a miniature pen sort of built into it. For all I knew, if you unfolded it a certain way you'd find an oxygen mask and a map of Atlantis. He'd bought it from some efficiency guru during one of his occasional attempts at getting organized, a campaign that always ended with him jamming into his car everything that didn't have what the guru called "a natural home" in the house he and Alice shared. The junk sat there for weeks, until he either put it all back in the house or sold the car. "Oh-two-oh-three," he said aloud as he wrote the numbers.

I said, "You didn't have to look that up?"

"Why would I?" He tore off the page but I put up a hand.

"From what you say about her, I need her address, too. I have a feeling a phone call won't open the door."

"Okay." He started writing again. "It's the one with the drawbridge."

"The drawbridge? Wait, you know her *address*?"

"*Sort* of a drawbridge," Louie said, tearing off the page and handing it to me. "I know lots of things."

And he did. When he was a kid, Louie's ambition was to be a getaway driver. He'd seen all the movies: three cranked-up crooks toting bags of cash jamming themselves into the waiting car, sweating buckets and yelling *Go-go-go*, while the cool-headed guy at the wheel checks his mirror, gives a full, if ironic, signal, raises an eyebrow, blows a smoke ring, and pulls into traffic, postponing the screeching tires and the daredevil maneuvers for a block or two, until they're out of sight. Maybe flicking cigarette ash out of the wind wing (these were *old* movies) and saying, "Calm down, boys, enjoy the ride," before delivering the loot and the gang safely to the hideout. When they get out of the car, they all say, "Thanks, Swifty."

But there was a problem. Louie had the speed and the wheel skills and the right kind of snap-brim hat, and he was aces with up and down, but he couldn't tell north

from south even with a compass in his lap. A getaway
driver with no sense of direction is going to earn nick-
names a lot more pungent than "Swifty." After a jewelry
job that was supposed to terminate seamlessly with a
quick dip across the border into Tijuana instead ended
up stuck motionless in traffic in pre-rap Compton, the
word went out. It went out so often that it generated its
own acronym, ABL, as in the phrase, "I need a driver,
ABL," meaning not only "able," as in *competent*, but
also as in *Anyone But Louie.*

His dream shattered, Louie retired his collection of
miniature getaway cars and expensive racing tires, and
considered his future. He'd always been affable and easy
to talk to. He had a trusting and trustworthy face. People
liked him, even people he'd driven.

People *told him things.*

Information, as we are ceaselessly informed, is money,
and nowhere is information more *directly* linked to
money (and survival and, occasionally, revenge) than
in what I'm tempted to refer to as the shadowy world
of outlaw life, although, of course, I won't. So Louie set
himself up as a telegraph, an informational intersection.
Like Fagin with his network of street kids, Louie developed hundreds of low-paid sources who were experts on
the various facets of what I'm not even remotely tempted
to call the vast, malign jewel of crime. With lines set up
and info in hand, he opened his shop and made it available
both for cash and on a quid pro quo basis. The enterprise
was so successful that Louie, an enthusiastic Italian cook,
named one of his most Mediterranean dishes "squid pro
quo." He bought a house. He began accumulating automobiles with multiple license plates that he made available

at a price for one-time use, a profitable sideline that let him get rid of some of those old racing tires.

Much better than getting sworn at from the backseat.

He also enriched graduate students by hiring them out, at a hefty markup, for custom research, a service I took advantage of on a regular basis. I'd already asked for information about the family and the house, but now I said, "I think I need more on the old guy. Can you put your gnomes on him? Anything they can find."

"He's been dead a long time," Louie said. "Pie?"

"Sure, whatever kind you want."

"Rhubarb."

"Except rhubarb. I took a bunch of good first editions out of the place last night. They were the right vintage for him to have bought them when he was in London, but it just doesn't fit in with who I thought he was. And one of them was signed by Arthur Conan Doyle. Personally, I mean."

Louie said, "Signed to the *guy*?"

"That's it. *Thanks for the inspiration* or something. So I obviously don't know enough about him. Maybe there's something somewhere about where some of the money came from. Maybe there's something I don't know about his wife."

Louie flagged a waitress, who gave him the universal *two minutes* signal. He said, "There's gotta be a million things you don't know, but why you going back so *far*?"

"I'll take peach, if they've got it," I said. "You know, everything about this says *old*. The money that built that awful house is nineteenth century, the books I took last night are nineteenth century, the doll that contained whatever I was supposed to take was nineteenth century. The family was born, so to speak, in the nineteenth century, when he changed his name. The whole thing feels to me like the kind of tangle—I mean two of us were sent, presumably by different people, to steal the same thing. So as I said, it feels like a tangle that's had lots of time to turn into a snarl, to tie multiple people into a complicated knot."

"Why now?" Louie said. "If this goes all the way back, like, to the middle ages, what suddenly kicked it into action?"

"It's because Miss Daisy is finally gone. Because they're going to knock down that house," I said. "It has to be that. Whatever these people want, Miss Daisy had to be out of the way. Whatever they want, they think it's in the house."

"Okay," he said with a shrug. "It'll run you maybe another twenty-five hundred and expenses, whatever they might be. Parking or something."

I said, "Do you think of the past as being darker or lighter than now?"

He did me the courtesy of thinking about it for a moment. "Darker. Not just 'cause of gaslight and no TV or Internet. A lot of people, they see old times as all silver forks and curtsies and *yes, my lady,* but, you know, it was Jack the Ripper and kids walking the street, too. What about you?"

"I don't know. I'm not sure people aren't darker now."

"Aahh, listen to you. You know what it is? Back then people could keep all their bad shit in a bag. Today it's all over our living rooms every night. You got some guy keeping a fourteen-year-old chained in a storage container for a bunch of years and we all know about it. Thing is, back then they all *didn't* know about it."

The waitress, who was standing over us, pad in hand, said, "In a *storage container?*"

"Don't worry about it," Louie said. "It was in Omaha, one of those places." To me he said, "You said peach, right?"

11
Unresolved Hostility

"Are you about ready?" I said into the phone.

"Packed up. Packed for you, too."

"What did you pack for me?" I was standing in front of the restaurant, pretending I wasn't cold. Louie went by in one of his cars and waved at me. Louie is the kind of guy who waves from cars to people he knows, even when he's just said goodbye to them.

Ronnie said, "Why? Don't you think I'm qualified? Two pairs of jeans, the obligatory thirty T-shirts, two nice shirts—"

"Which nice shirts?"

"*The shadow knows,*" she said with an old radio-mystery delivery. Ronnie loved radio shows from the 1930s and '40s. She had complete MP3 collections of *My Favorite Husband*—Lucille Ball's show before she moved to TV—*The Shadow, Yours Truly, Johnny Dollar, Mr. Moto,* and a bunch of others. She liked the acting, completely on the surface and devoid of subtext, as though it all took place before the invention of the subconscious, and the way people started their sentences with "Say . . .", a once-ubiquitous linguistic tic that seems to have been exclusively American and is now a verbal fossil. "And, let's see," she said, "a couple of sweaters and your awful Dodgers jacket."

At the mention of the jacket, I did a little involuntary shiver. The sunlight was gone, stopped in its tracks by the sliding clouds that can close the sky like a giant window shade in February and March. "Do me a favor," I said. "Get me a jacket that doesn't have a great big word written on it. If someone's going to describe me, they should at least have to work at it. And then, if you're finished, do me *another* favor and get out of there."

"Where to?"

I said, "Where would you like to go?" There had been no prediction of rain, but after last night's showers while I was in Horton House, the meteorologists may have been the only people who didn't know it was coming. A trillion dollars to predict the weather, and they give us percentages. No wonder nobody trusts the government.

"The Ritz-Carlton." she said. "But since that's kind of a stretch, maybe a Travelodge?"

"How about Minnie's Mouse House?"

"Oh, my God," she said. "Who says you can't revisit the past?"

"The best way to hide," I said, "is to be somewhere no one in his right mind would expect—"

"I'd hoped we'd gotten past that. Anyway, I thought you'd used up all those places."

"I've got dozens of them. And it's right over in Burbank, close to Disney in spite of a bunch of lawsuits over the name, so it's sort of on the edge between the Valley and LA proper, which is where all this stuff seems to be happening."

"Should I call and make a reservation?"

"No need to confuse them," I said. "I doubt they've ever had one."

"What about room service?"

I said, "What *about* room service?"

"Silly me. Well, gee. It'll be like being young and stupid again. Or maybe just stupid."

A wind kicked up, a rain wind, and I turned up my collar. Unlike Ronnie, I hadn't remembered a jacket. I was not liking the day very much.

"I *am* sorry about this," she said. "I know how much you love your place—"

"Our place."

"Our place. And I, well, I—"

"It's not your fault," I said. "I knew I shouldn't have taken this job."

"But I'm the *reason* you took—"

"I'm sorry to interrupt, but blame that asshole in New Jersey, blame the clowns who guard him and the baby, blame the hoods who pay him. All you did was have a son with someone who turned out to be a double-scoop of shit."

"Fine," she said, and then she cleared her throat and changed the subject. It had taken her more than a year to confide in me, and even now that we were taking first steps to do something about it, she could only talk about it for so long. "Okay, Minnie's Mouse House it is."

"Get something to eat somewhere, first. She doesn't change the cheese in the traps very often."

"You *have* stayed there, though, right?"

"No," I said, "but it's been on my list for a long time. Listen, leave soon, okay?"

My phone had rung twice since I'd left the apartment. Both times the screen read UNKNOWN, and the caller left no message, but it wasn't hard to guess who it was, although I hadn't given her my number. It upped the urgency quotient.

Louie's pie place wasn't far from one of my storage units, one I liked because there was no need to check in—you just slipped a card into a slot beside the gate, waited until it groaned its way open, and drove straight to your unit. I had come to get one of my guns, but the layout of the place reminded me of something else, and that gave me an idea. I took the automatic out of the lightly oiled cloth in which I wrap it, slipped in a clip and grabbed another, replaced the books that covered the weapons in the cardboard box, relocked the unit, went to the car, and called someone who essentially *lived* in a storage unit.

"*What?*" Anime Wong said on the other end of the phone, in the aggrieved tone of one trapped in a world gone wildly and irrevocably wrong in a manner that points directly and solely at her, an attitude only teenagers can muster. Fortunately, most of them outgrow it, although it's always amazed me that more of them aren't murdered before they do. Still, Anime was usually sunnier than that.

"Gee," I said, "What a greeting. Was it something I did?"

"It's *you*, isn't it?" she said. "You only call when you want something."

"That's not fair," I said. "I'm just checking in, you know, seeing how you are and stuff."

"That's pathetic," she said. "I've gotten Trader Joe's *valentines* more sincere than that."

"Why so sour? Oh, never mind. How come you picked

up? I usually get kicked to voicemail and I have to wait until you've got a break between classes."

I'd known Anime and Lilli, her life partner, if you can have one of those when you're in your mid-teens, for a while now. They worked with an adult hacker named Monty Carlo at a high-profit, low-risk cyber dodge that skimmed loose money off the funds states set up to hold the proceeds from abandoned safe deposit boxes and bank accounts. Their office was an intensely wired double-garage size storage space in a facility much like this one, which I think the three of them owned. Monty was a career criminal, but Anime and Lilli were funding minutely planned and *very* expensive higher educations up to, and including, doctoral degrees in computer science. They planned to change their last names when they turned eighteen so they would be called one after the other to receive their diplomas and could go up holding hands.

"We're not going to school these days," she said. "We're *protesting*." She wrung the word out as though it were saturated with vinegar.

"What?"

"Food," she said. "And it's really Lilli, and I don't want to talk about it. Why did you call?"

"Well, you know, I was thinking about both of—"

"You already tried that."

"Okay," I said, and I told her why I'd called.

"Give me an hour," she said. "I'll get the stuff. In fact, we've already got it. Bring cash to pay me back. Do you think you can put it together yourself?"

I said, "Um."

"Right. I'll do it."

"I'm not sure it's safe for you."

"Make it safe," she said. "Isn't that one of the things you do, protect people? So protect me."

"Got it," I said. "You sure *you* know how to put it together?"

"I was the one who set it up here. We've even got backup equipment. I just need to pick out the right ones from the backup stuff and test it all. And later I'll need to buy new ones, which is why I need your money."

"Okay. At the, uh, office, right?"

"Sure. My parents still think I'm at school."

I said, "I keep forgetting you've got parents."

I needed the hour anyway, because I had to contact someone else, see whether she had an opening in her schedule, and then, if she did, swing by to pick her up.

When I called, Ting Ting answered the phone, eager as always to learn which friend was on the other end of the line. For someone who had once beaten me up so decisively it made a doctor inhale sharply when he saw me—not a reassuring reaction—Ting Ting was as blithe as a daffodil. He regarded the entire world with goodwill and trust; he was the kind of guy who once, in my company, chased down a kid who had dropped a quarter on the sidewalk. He'd only beaten me up because I'd pissed Stinky off, and Stinky called Ting Ting—then the houseboy of the month—to usher me out. I had resisted being ushered. It's especially demoralizing to be beaten to a pulp by someone who keeps apologizing in between kicks to your head.

"Hey, Ting Ting," I said. "How are you?"

"I play marimba," he said. "Drive Eaglet *crazy*."

"Good. It'll help her keep her edge. I worry about her, getting all soft and happy. Why marimba?"

"We make a band," he said. "Three *pinoy* and me. Playing at Pilipino nightclub."

"How much money?"

"We pay them fifty dollar one night."

I said, "Wow."

"We getting better," he said. "Before, we pay one hundred."

"At that rate," I said, "you'll be playing for free in no time. Is Eaglet around?"

"Oh," he said, sounding excited. "You have something for her? Somebody she can shoot? She so—so *boring*."

"*Bored*, dammit," I heard Eaglet say, "not boring. Who is that?"

"Is Mister Junior."

"Well, do I get to talk to him anytime soon, or are you waiting for Imelda Marcos to die? And can you *not* play the marimba while I talk?"

"I play quiet," Ting Ting said. He was the first person in her adult life who acted like she was a harmless *hausfrau* from a 1955 sitcom, and she loved it. Everyone else was terrified of her.

"Jesus," she said to me. "It's like being held captive by a ray of sunshine."

"He is sweet, isn't he? If I played on the other team, I'd be on him like hot fudge."

"For all the good it would do you," Eaglet said. "Every fragrant bit of him belongs to me." Behind her, I heard an interval being struck on the marimba.

"So?" I said, "Other than that, how are you?"

"Like he said, bored. You know how it is. Kill somebody, sit around for a long time, kill somebody, sit around for a long time. It's like being a pitcher."

"No uniform, though."

"Wouldn't the cops love that? *Hey, we got number 17.* Are you planning to get to the point any time soon?"

"I need protection for a few hours. Me and a teenage girl."

"I don't entirely like you," Eaglet said, "but I admire the fact that you didn't tell me only about the girl and pretend that you were bulletproof. Even put yourself first. When?"

"I can be there in maybe thirty minutes. Might take a couple of hours, total."

"A thousand," she said.

I said, "Yikes."

"Okay," she said. "Since you're an old whatever—acquaintance, I guess—five hundred, plus an extra five if I have to shoot anyone."

"Do I have to pay for the bullet, too?"

"I'll throw it in for old times' sake."

"Thanks. And you can go soon?"

"You already *said* thirty minutes. I'll be sitting on the curb. Anything to get away from this fucking marimba."

The first thing Anime said when she saw the big black SUV was, "Where's your terrible car?"

"In the parking lot of a terrible restaurant," I said. "We're using Uber. For security."

"I didn't know they had SUVs."

"It's Uber Whopper or something. There are some people who know what my car looks like, and I don't want to make things any easier for them than they already seem to be."

Anime was wearing a baseball cap that said "Lemon

Meringue *pi*" on the front with her ponytail drawn through the loop at the back, a plaid shirt that looked like it had made its way down from Oregon on its own power, and a pair of skinny jeans that accentuated the fact that she probably didn't weigh eighty-five pounds. As always, she was makeup-free, but she'd once told me that Lilli wore so much it averaged out. Under one arm she had a box designed to hold a pair of men's sneakers for somebody with big feet.

We were most of the way to the car when something shifted behind one of the darkened windows, and Anime stopped and said, "Who's in there?"

"That's our protection for the day," I said. "She's a hitter. Her name is Eaglet."

"God, her parents must have hated her."

"They changed their last name to Sunshine."

"Literally?" The word *hitter* must have dropped because Anime's eyebrows did a high jump. "And she *shoots* people?"

"Not indiscriminately."

"I'm sitting in front."

"No, really, she's fine. She just shoots the people you point her at."

"Don't be silly," she said. "I don't care about that. I get sick in the backseat."

"Fine," I said. "We've probably been standing here talking about her long enough for it to be rude, so let's go."

Eaglet and Anime exchanged purely social smiles as they sized each other up. When I got into the backseat, Eaglet said to me, in the tone of one who doesn't believe teenagers understand English, "You didn't mention kids."

"Why would I?" I said.

"You said a *teenager*."

Without turning around, Anime said, "It's not *his* fault you're a bad judge of age."

Eaglet said, "You barely look—"

Anime said, "I'm in my teens. I live in that storage unit. Do you know a *lot* of pre-teens who live in a storage unit?"

Eaglet's eyes widened. "Do you really?"

"Off and on. Things are a little rough at home."

"You poor thing." I'd never heard that tone from Eaglet. The driver glanced at Anime, pulled through the storage facility's gate, and turned right.

"My mom is trying to figure out how to break up with her hair stylist," Anime deadpanned. "It's dominated family conversations for a week. There's not much room for personal growth."

"Not easy to do," Eaglet said, accepting that she'd been outmaneuvered. "My stylist knows everything."

As the driver pulled through the storage facility's gate and turned right, I said, "I hope to shit not."

"Within *reason*," Eaglet said. "It's like the confessional. As I understand it, I mean. You know you're supposed to talk about everything, but there's always that little bit everybody holds back. How they really hate their little brother or something."

"Anyway, Junior needs me," Anime said. "Probably as much as he needs you. He's technologically illiterate."

I said, "Hey."

"So, your job, I mean, what you do," Anime said. "What are the requirements?"

"A steady hand and a profound indifference," Eaglet said. To me, she said, "Big mouth. Don't you have to tell this nice man where to go? Or is he driving at random?"

"He knows," I said. "I worked it all out before you got in the car."

"Big secret," said the driver. He was a jovial Jamaican and I could tell he'd been dying to get into the conversation.

"Into town?" Eaglet said as we signaled for a freeway on-ramp.

"Good guess. In fact, when we get off the freeway I'm going to need you to cover your eyes for nine or ten minutes."

"People who have my job do not cover our eyes," Eaglet said. "Professional code. It's a deal-breaker."

Anime said, "I'll get car sick."

"It's okay," the driver said. "I can see."

"Oh, come on," I said to Eaglet. "You know I wouldn't do anything—I mean, Jesus, how long have you known me?"

"I've known Corney Swinster a hell of a lot longer than I've known you," Eaglet said, "and he took a whack at me last month."

I said, "Corney? But I heard he got—" A perfumed hand was clamped over my mouth.

"Finish the thought *silently*," Eaglet said, removing her hand, "and yes, he did."

"Poor Corney," I said when I could talk again.

"That's not a very friendly sentiment," she said. "Considering."

"Well, I wasn't suggesting I wished the outcome of your meeting had been different. It's just that he was one of the guys who played poker with Herbie, back when I was just getting going. He was a terrible player, so everybody liked him."

"Aces and eights," Eaglet said. "Wasn't that what Wild Bill was holding?"

"It's amazing," I said. "You can go a decade without thinking about Wild Bill Hickock and suddenly he's everywhere."

Anime sniffled.

"The little girl, she crying," said the driver.

"It's okay, sweetie," Eaglet said. "She'll find a new stylist in no time."

"It's not that," Anime said. "It's Lilli."

"Who's Lilli?" Eaglet and the driver asked in unison.

"My—my friend." She craned around to look at me. Her face was gleaming, so she'd been crying silently for a little while. "I lied when I said we were boycotting, protesting, whatever I said. About food. Lilli, she, she stopped eating things, first it was sugar and then it was gluten and then it was soy or nuts or meat or rice or fish or salt or—"

"I know where this is going," Eaglet said, and the driver nodded and said, "Yes, yes, yes," and Anime said, "And I said something really stupid, like, *It doesn't matter what you don't eat, you'll never be transparent*, and she went all quiet for a couple of weeks and then I noticed she was wearing different clothes, a shirt I hadn't seen before, and I asked her something innocuous, like where she got it, and she leaned over to me like there were a hundred people listening, and she whispered, 'I'm too fat.'"

"Yes, yes," said the driver. "My wife's sister's child, too."

"And I was trying to talk to her and it turned out it was something *I* said, something about her butt, and now she's lost, *she* says, twelve pounds, but it looks like more to me, and you know, Junior, you know she wasn't very big to start with, even when—"

The driver said, "Stop, child," as he merged right, and Eaglet said, "You didn't do it. Listen to me—"

"And now she won't go to school and she's throwing up all the time and her breath smells *terrible* and I'm scared that—"

"You listen to the lady," the driver said. "I can tell the lady knows."

"I *went* through this," Eaglet said. To my profound surprise she leaned forward and put a hand on Anime's shoulder. "How old are you, honey? I mean, really?"

"Fourteen. Honest."

"And your, your—"

"My girlfriend." Anime swiped at her cheeks with the back of her hand. "She's fourteen, too, we're both—"

"And her parents?"

"They're old."

"No, I mean, what are they—"

"Doing about it? Nothing, they haven't even *said* anything," Anime said, and her voice scaled up a little, "but her mother is skinnier than that horrible old woman who wanted to be the Queen of England—"

"The Duchess of Windsor," I said.

"My mother saw her," the driver said conversationally. "When she was living in Bermuda. Not fat."

"That's her," Anime said. "And Lilli's mother, she talks about how she can wear *child sizes*. The way she says it, it's like she cured cancer or something."

"It's not your fault," Eaglet said. Her hand was still on Anime's shoulder. She was sitting behind the driver, so it was a diagonal stretch. She hit me with her left knee to move me over. "It's her mother, it's what we see on TV all the time, it's pressure on girls, it's a *lot* of things. For me, it was—I mean, I did it too. I weighed seventy-five pounds, and I'm taller than you are."

Anime turned and looked at her. "What did you do? To get better?"

"Oh, well," Eaglet said, shaking her head. "I'm not exactly typical."

"But you must have—"

"My parents were Christian Scientists," Eaglet said with some resignation, "until they found what my father called *the vegetarian route to God.* Which was peyote, mostly, with some mescaline thrown in for variety. So when I'm eight or nine our whole middle-class life—school, the house in the suburbs, and regular names and so forth— turns into a crowded Quonset hut in San Bernardino with me starving myself in the corner while my parents, who are now the Sunshines, loop out over a book of paintings by Hieronymus Bosch as they peak on the day's dose. And then they added weed to the mix and my mother began baking day and night, anything that was sweet, and they knocked all of that back with bottled spring water because their systems were so *pure*, right?"

"The hungry herb," the driver said. "Makes everybody eat."

"Except me," Eaglet said, "and after a few months my mother realized I wasn't eating any of the donuts she'd baked, and she said, 'Don't you like it, honey?' or something, and I just lost it, I squeezed them into crumbs and threw them all over the place. She hadn't even noticed I was starving myself to death."

"So," Anime said, "what? A doctor?"

"No, 'cause they'd been Christian Scientists, remember? No doctors. And then they turned to the sacrament of the cactus, which is *natural*, they kept saying, so no technology, no chemicals, no medicines, no anything. Listen,

I'm not your basic case history. They handed me to this shaman, an old Mexican guy who made me sign a piece of paper saying I was a member of the Native American Church to make everything legal and then he took me up into a big rock formation about twenty miles away and gave me some peyote, first time I'd ever had any. And after I finished throwing up—"

"Lilli is cool with throwing up," Anime said. "She does it a lot."

"I'm not *recommending* this, honey I'm just telling you what I—" She patted Anime's shoulder as though she were soothing herself, and Anime allowed it. "Anyway, we spent about ten hours up there talking about my life, and around five-thirty, when I thought I was getting a pretty good handle on my life and the sun was about to set, he made me stand up and he introduced me to my shadow, which was really *long* by then. He made me bow to it and see how it bowed back, and he said I had to *remember* my shadow when I was losing weight because when I got smaller I was making my shadow smaller and weaker, too, and I needed my shadow to be powerful. See, he said, just before you're born there are *two* spirits that are both you, as close as the two sides of a window, but at the last moment, just before you slide into the world, a decision is made somewhere, and one of those spirits becomes you and the other one is your shadow, and you're responsible for your shadow's well-being. Because your shadow is like your visible spirit and it's there to *remind* you that you're part spirit, and that spirit can be blown out like a candle. Just *poof* because of something you do. He also said your shadow is there to keep you from darkness, 'cause when you're someplace dark, your shadow disappears, right? And that's how it reminds you that you're always just one doorway away from *real* darkness, the bad kind. Your shadow is there to nag you not to go through the door into that kind of darkness because if you do, it will disappear forever. Both you and your spirit, both of you, lost forever."

"Huh," the driver said. "My sister's child—"

"So," Eaglet said, "it got my attention. I'm not saying it *worked* exactly, but it gave me someone else to think about, even if it was my shadow. I don't think I believed anyone knew I was alive. My parents were lost in the dope, my life had been taken away from me. What I wanted didn't count for anything. My eating was something I could control. So that thing with the old man was like a push, and over the long run I sort of found my way back."

"You're saying I could be her shadow, sort of?" Anime said.

"You're together a lot?" Eaglet said.

"Only like all the time."

"Well, I've read a lot about this for the obvious reason, and one thing that seems to work, unless there's clinical depression in there somewhere, is actually *feeding* them. A lot of parents have coped with this by feeding their kids, by hand, if necessary, just showing how much they care."

Anime's nose wrinkled, and she said, "Really?"

"Look," Eaglet said. "There's *three things* here. There's what's happening to your friend, there's how you're reacting to it, and there's what you can do."

"What I can—"

"You need to stop blaming yourself. You didn't cause this, any more than my parents caused it in me. People are complicated, it's almost never just one thing. So that's first, stop feeling responsible. Next, assume some *real* responsibility. Hold her fucking hand, make her talk. Feed her. *Try*, at least, to feed her."

"But if she won't eat—"

"You'll be *doing* something," Eaglet said. "You'll be loving her. You'll be sitting right next to her, showing her how much you care. The best doctor, the best nurse in the world, they can't love her the way you can. That old man who took me up to the rocks, for weeks he came by and looked at my shadow and then at me, and he'd say, 'Make us happy, girl. You can make us happy because we *care* about you.' You care about your girlfriend, right?"

"She's the only person I ever loved," Anime said.

"Then you know what? You're the person who can help her. I'm not saying it'll be easy, but eventually she'll let you in. Maybe not at first, but this is one of the things love can fix."

The driver said, "She's right, child. You the only one can help her."

"I don't know," Anime said, blinking fast.

"Well, excuse me," Eaglet said, "but who the hell is going to do it if you don't?"

Anime said, "Oh."

"Tell you one other thing," Eaglet said. "There's something fighting with itself inside her, and she *needs* to eat, she needs energy for the fight, to work it out. You can't solve it for her, but you can help her get to the point where she can solve it herself. For me, once I got back to my fighting weight, so to speak, I realized I had a lot of hostility inside myself, a lot of unresolved hostility."

"What did you do about it?" Anime said.

"I *resolved* it," Eaglet said flatly. She turned to look out the window. "I'm still resolving it. I resolve it a little more every time I do a job."

12

Time to Talk

When we hit the bump before dropping down into the underground garage, Eaglet made a little *eeep* sound that I knew she hoped I hadn't heard. Anime, who had been peeking between her fingers for blocks, was quick enough on the uptake to say, "Whoops" so that she'd sound surprised, too.

Eaglet, to my amazement, was playing fair, her jacket pulled up above over her eyes. She said to me as we sloped downward, "If you ever tell anybody I let you talk me into this, you're going to be looking behind you for months."

"I won't. And you can look around now."

I was used to the place, but seeing it through their eyes, it was creepy in the extreme. It was so big and so deep and so badly lighted that the farthest wall disappeared into apparent infinity, like a hallway leading into a black hole. Eaglet looked around and said, "Where are the seven dwarfs?"

"This is fine," I said to the driver as we approached the elevator to the edgwood. Like the other elevators, it lacked both a name and an address. You either knew which elevator you wanted or you had a sixty-six percent chance of winding up in the wrong building. I gave him a twenty as a tip as I climbed out, and he nodded thanks and said, "Take care of the little one," and I promised I would, then went and pushed the button for the elevator,

Anime squeaked a bit at the first jolt-and-slip-back effect, and neither of them looked reassured by the creaking cables and structural groans on the sound track. "Don't worry," I said. "Even if we went into free fall it'd probably just be broken hips, something like that." They both moved to the walls of the compartment, seeking reassurance in contact with something solid, so I said, "That part falls just as fast as the middle." Anime responded with a barely audible puff of irritation.

When the doors opened and they saw the corridor, Eaglet said, "Do the people who live here name the rats?"

I said, "Shhh," pulled the automatic out of my pocket and said to Eaglet, "You go check the fire stairs at the end of the corridor. If anyone is there, make them *stay* there."

"Until," she said. She took a gun from her purse. It was pink.

"Until I see who they are or they're dead. Do you have a silencer?"

"I do." As though it were a nail file, she took from her purse a black tube that I recognized as a Gemtech, although I didn't know the model number. "They don't make it in pink," she said, fitting it to the barrel and giving it a twist. Anime's eyes widened. "Although God knows I've complained. What's the signal to shoot?"

"The moment it seems appropriate."

Eaglet said, "Fine," and moved quietly down the hall.

Looking around, Anime said, "How can you *live* here?"

"Whisper, please," I said. "It's not as bad as it seems. Stay here for now."

"I want to go with you."

"Okay, make a deal. You go with me to the door and then keep going, all the way to Eaglet. But for now we'll both wait here until she's had a look, okay? Then you can go wait with her while I peek inside."

"Okay," she said. She had the sneakers box with the stuff in it pressed to her chest with her arms folded over it like a shield. She took a step forward and I put a hand on her shoulder to stop her as, at the other end of the hallway, Eaglet pressed an ear to the door. She stood there, immobile, for a long moment and then she stepped back, very slowly turned the knob, and opened the door a few inches at a time, staying out of sight behind it. When it was halfway open she went onto her knees, holding the door steady, and then very quickly looked around its edge, her head well below the area anyone on the other side would probably have been aiming a gun at. Then she stood up, stepped through the doorway, and stood there, her back to us, obviously listening.

Anime was holding her breath.

"It's okay," I said. "She shoots extremely well."

Eaglet came back in and shook her head. "Nobody," she mouthed.

"Here we go," I said. I led Anime down the hall, and she kept going when I stopped and keyed the locks. When I'd finished with the third I turned and whispered to Eaglet, "If anything happens, you get her down those stairs." Then I pushed the door open and waited.

The place was cool and silent, and the sun was low enough that dust motes air-waltzed in a rectangle of light falling across the end of the entrance hall. The place looked, sounded, and felt empty, but I went in quietly anyway, leaving the door ajar and waiting at the end of the hall to listen for another minute before I stepped into the sight lines of anyone who might be in the living room.

No one was. Ronnie had left half a cup of coffee on the table in front of the couch. The surface was filmed with non-dairy powdered limestone or whatever the hell it is, which she generally skipped when I was around. Beside the coffee was one of the books I'd taken the previous evening, which felt like six weeks ago. She'd used a nail file as a bookmark, and it slipped out and hit the table with a tinny protest as I picked up the book, which was Trollope's *The Eustace Diamonds*, the story of the ambitious and only marginally honest Lizzie Eustace and the stolen necklace that gave her so much trouble. Great book, even if he did bag some of it from Thackeray.

I put the nail file back—page 34—and toted the book one-handed through the rooms with the gun in the other. It took me about three minutes to know that I was alone. Then I went to the front door, said, "It's okay" to Eaglet and went into the library.

I had just decided to keep Mr. Horton's first editions together, giving them their own two feet of shelf space, and was pulling out some things I figured I'd never open again when Anime came in, still carrying the sneaker box.

"This place is like a *movie*," she said. "Who would have known, from how ratty it looks in the hall—"

"That's the point," I said. "And you should see the outside." From the living room I heard a low whistle of appreciation.

Anime said, "Most women don't whistle."

"Is that a fact?"

"Wow," she said, her eyes going to the shelves, "have you read *all* of those?"

"And others."

She nodded. "You're smarter than you act."'

"Reading doesn't make you smart," I said. "Reading makes you human."

"Yeah, but you don't have to kill all these *trees*. Ebooks, you know?"

"We all have our paradigms," I said. "Every generation has different ones. For my generation, it's books with covers. For yours, it's selfies and what you ate for lunch and dwarfs doing calisthenics on YouTube."

"Thanks, Grampy," Anime said.

"You would think," Eaglet said, coming through the door as she put the pink gun back in her purse, "that you two didn't like each other, the way you talk. Jesus, look at all these books."

"You say that as though it were a beetle collection."

"Well, I mean, who's got the time?"

"Getting back to business," Anime said, "I guess you want it pointing right at the front door, right? That's the only way in."

"Sounds good to me."

She shifted the shoebox to one hip and held out her free hand. "Give me your phone." When I'd handed it to her and recited the code she jammed it into a pocket and went out, carrying her sneaker box.

"Where did you find her?" Eaglet asked.

"She, or rather she and her girlfriend, found me."

"Can you just go straight to any book on these shelves? Without having to walk around with your neck at that uncomfortable angle, reading the titles?"

"With my eyes shut," I said. From the other room I heard Anime pushing something across the floor.

"Oh, bullshit," Eaglet said. "Turn around and close your eyes."

"Well," I said, "within two or three books."

"Hedging already."

I closed my eyes, and a minute later I heard her back away from the shelf. She said, "*The Snow Leopard.*"

"Okay. Here goes." I knew which set of shelves and which actual shelf it was on, so it was easy to find the right set of shelves by touch and count my way down to the right shelf. Then, taking an educated guess, I ticked off six books to the right with my index finger. I pulled the book out about an inch and turned so my back was to the shelves, opened my eyes, and said, "Check it out."

"Ha," she said. "*At Play in the Fields of the Lord.*"

"Yeah, I missed. Two books to the right," I said. "That's *The Snow Leopard*. The one in between them is *Shadow Country.*"

Eaglet said, "Wow."

"Useless, but a good trick," I said. "You can probably do that with your handguns."

"Hey," she said, sounding insulted. "I read. Once in a while."

Anime called out from the hall. "You've got a text."

"Ignore it," I said. "On second thought, read it to me."

"It says, 'Time to talk.'"

"Well," I said, "you can't always get what you want." I looked over at Eaglet. "Maybe you should be in the hall outside."

"Put it into the purse, take it out of the purse," she said, opening her purse. "I should charge extra." Gun in hand, she went into the hall while I went back to clearing a space on the shelves. I didn't really care about the chore, but this kind of busywork allowed my mind to wander, and by the time Anime came back in, maybe four or five minutes later, I had the rest of the day planned.

"Here," she said, handing me the phone. "Why don't you have any apps?"

"I have a little speaker that talks in my ear," I said, "I have a teensy microphone that's sort of near my mouth. I have this little thing that makes bad guesses at the weather. I have the gizmo for the Apple Store if I ever want an apple."

"This phone is wasted on you," she said. "It's like giving a piano to someone who's only got elbows." She tapped the phone's screen. "This one, the one with the eye, is called Eyes24," she said. "Tap on it."

I did, and I was looking at my front door from inside.

"Whoa," I said. "Where'd you put it?"

"The ceiling is really high," she said. "Nobody's going to look all the way up there, so I put it at the corner of the wall and the ceiling, pointing at the door."

"So I just sit around looking at this all day? Are there commercials?"

She said, "Do you know what push technology is?"

I said, "Give me a minute."

"I don't know how you've lived so long—"

"Hey," I said.

"—and learned so little. Okay, wait here."

She left the room. A moment later, my phone emitted a little sound, a new one, like a cello being played in mud, and a little rectangle surfaced on top of the few apps I hadn't been able to delete, and inside it was Anime, waving at me. I watched her on the screen as she called from the hallway, "Tell me you figured it out."

I said, "You've changed your hair?"

"It's a motion detector. The camera is always on, and when something moves in front of it, it beeps at you like that, like a text. Do you know what a text is?"

"Judging from the root," I said, "I know it's got something to do with words."

She rubbed her eyes. She really did look weary. "Well, is there anything else I can do? Want me to set your alarm clock? Get your TV off ESPN?"

"No, Ronnie knows how to do all that. Let's get out of here." She had disappeared from the screen, and a moment later she came through the doorway. "Wow," I said putting the phone next to my ear and shaking it, "how'd you get out of the phone?"

"If I lived here," she said, looking around the room, "I'd never leave."

"That was my plan, too. But in the darkness fate moved its heavy hand."

"So who do you think this setup, the camera and all, is going to show you?"

"Someone," I said. "I don't know who she is, but I need to know when she's here."

13

Bride of Plastic Man

"Here's my number." Eaglet pushed me sideways to reach across the back of the seat and hand a rectangle of paper to Anime, who had claimed the front again. "Any time you need to talk."

Anime said, "Thanks," and looked at it.

Peeking over Anime's shoulder, I said, "Is that a *business card*?"

"It is." Eaglet reached into her purse and pulled out the pink gun, the barrel pointing toward me. I resisted an impulse to cross my legs.

"What's it say? 'Have Trigger, Will Pull?'"

"One-Shot Solutions." She was keeping the gun down, out of sight of the window and the driver's mirror, as she removed the silencer. She saw me looking at it and said, "It snags on the lining. This is an expensive purse."

"And One-Shot Solutions is?"

"My sole-proprietor corporation. C-corp, if you know what that is."

Anime said, "Can I have Lilli call you?"

"I think it might be better if we met each other," Eaglet said. "This kind of stuff is best when people can look into each other's eyes. It's harder to dismiss them."

I said, "What's the business description? You know, you need to give the state a—"

"Public relations," she said. "That's what I do, isn't it? I adjust relationships among members of the public. Ease strain, and so forth."

Anime said, "Okay, I'll get something lined up. Is any day better than any other?"

"Mostly, I sit around," Eaglet said. "Listening to the marimba."

"I'm going to bail in a minute," I said as we approached the off-ramp nearest to Louie's terrible restaurant. "This gentleman will take you home. Off at Lankershim," I said to the driver. "Then right." I reached up and handed him a twenty. "For the extra stops."

The driver said, "Sure thing."

"Thanks, Eaglet. And thanks, Anime, for setting me up with the camera system."

As the driver swerved onto the off-ramp, Anime said, "You guys helped me, too."

To the driver, I said, "Up there, behind that parked car, is fine. Get them back safely, okay?" I got out, knocked twice on the window, and watched them pull off.

The afternoon was dimming, dragging us all toward night, some of us possibly faster than others, and I needed to talk to the person who might be able to help me identify those three rented kids.

I hadn't been to the chateau for a while, not since I'd barely survived the high-voltage tango with the Hollywood studio head everyone called King Maybe. I'd been double-crossed into that confrontation by the lord of the chateau, Jake Whelan, and that betrayal had brought to an end the intermittent, almost nostalgic fondness I'd once felt for him, in spite of his extravagant collection of character flaws.

Once the most powerful man in motion pictures, Jake was dwindling irreversibly, going from bold-face headline to footnote. For years I'd thought that time flowed around him, like water around a stone, leaving him untouched, and that hundreds of pounds of cocaine could vanish up that Roman emperor's nose year after year without tarnishing his psyche or denting his bank accounts. Last time I'd seen him, though, he'd looked a little scraped and ragged at the edges, like someone who'd spent a long time facing down a high-velocity sandstorm, and the chateau, which he'd had shipped stone by stone from France and reassembled above Coldwater Canyon during his glory days, had already acquired some of the melancholy of a deserted building.

But I wasn't prepared to see the high gate at the bottom of the driveway sagging open and hanging on one hinge and the call box that had always stood beside it decapitated and lying upside down in the weeds. I was *especially* unprepared for the weeds; the condition of the gate and the call box could be recent developments, but the weeds had taken months.

I had to get out and push the gate a few feet aside to get past it—making me, I figured, the first guest in some time—and then I drove up the curving pavement to the house.

Never one to miss an opportunity to flaunt, Jake had designed the approach so that visitors caught details of the house like quick cuts in a film, a montage of overindulgence: a gray stone corner here, a mullioned window there, a turret floating above the trees, until, at the top of the drive, the structure finally revealed itself in its full, widescreen, quasi-royal, anachronistic splendor. But now the approach was a caricature of decline: a glimpse of missing roof tiles, a black diamond where a pane of glass had been punched out, military-green patches of lichen colonizing the walls. The expensive foliage, exotic bushes and flowers imported from God only knew where, was slowly losing its battle against those tireless peasants of the plant world, hillside scrub.

I pulled into the circle in front, where there had always been several vehicles parked: a couple of Jake's, some for the housekeepers, and a few more for the hard cases who had been providing security since the late 1970s, when rumors began to circulate about exchanges of really serious amounts of cash for glistening white buckets of Peru's top export. (One urban legend among burglars was that the spaces between the walls were insulated with stacked cash.) The security doubled down later, when Jake started to build his private museum in the basement, extending long sticky fingers into the secret market for stolen paintings. In those days it was routine for a visitor's car to be surrounded by guys whose suits bulged with heat before the driver had time even to get the door open. Cocaine has been known to contribute generously to its users' paranoia.

Today, my car was the only one there.

A mockingbird let loose as I walked up to the front door. I put my finger on the bell, but before I could push it, the door opened and Jake squinted at me or, more likely, at the light of day.

"You," he rasped. He hadn't shaved in days and he

was wearing a maroon silk robe that had probably cost a couple thousand bucks when it was new but looked now like something I might use to dry my car. The sash was knotted over a little pot belly that I'd never seen before.

I said, "Me."

"Drab as ever," he said. He cleared his throat against the rasp; at his apogee, Jake's voice had been silken, and never more so than when it was gelding some subordinate. "In movies, criminals are *interesting*."

"Well," I said in a flare of spite, "I see that you've put on a few."

For a moment I thought he was going to shut the door, but instead he took a couple of steps back. "And *thank* you for pointing that out," he said. "You've gotten shorter, haven't you? You're almost as short as an agent these days."

"It's just, you know, you've always been so . . . *trim*." It was true: Jake had been one of the handsomest young men in Hollywood for an unreasonable length of time before he became one of the handsomest old men in Hollywood. He'd started out as an actor, long on face and short on talent, but he'd quickly developed a reputation for taking control of the pictures he was in—even when he had a supporting role, as he usually did once it became apparent that his talent had to be stretched very little before it became transparent. Directors complained bitterly about his behavior, but producers' ears went up: here, improbably handsome, like someone wearing reverse camouflage, they recognized one of their own, an expert in wielding power he didn't deserve. In no time Jake *owned* Hollywood. It was said that he paid for tables for four to be held for him seven days a week at his nine favorite restaurants, just in case the spirit moved him or he got hungry when he was being driven through the neighborhood. And I mean held *all the time*, all through lunch and all through dinner.

"*Trim*," Jake said in the tone of someone who had just remembered an ancient Arab curse. "You haven't reached this stage of life, yet." He turned around and went back down the stone-floored hall, leaving me to close the door and follow. He'd apparently started dyeing his hair by himself, because he'd missed a tuft in the back, and it gleamed like a silver weed. As we passed the enormous living room that no one ever used, he said over his shoulder, "And the way you're going, you might *not* reach it, so allow me to share some of the highlights with you. Things begin to hurt, especially things that bend, like knees and elbows, and even though you used to play two, three sets of tennis without even wrinkling your whites, you gradually find yourself avoiding stairs, waking up eight or ten times a night and wishing you could sleep next to the toilet, and feeling in the morning like it might take, I don't know, a piece of earth-moving equipment to get you out of bed. So you're slowing down, you can't work off the calories so easily. Next in the parade of blessings, your secondary appetites fade and, well, *narrow*. I used to put in a half hour or so every afternoon flipping through my daybook, just trying to decide which famous or semi-famous stranger, acquaintance, contractee, friend, lesser princess, or ex-wife I wanted to tuck in with that night. Now, all that's left of what was once a really sybaritic range of pleasures is a mild enthusiasm for sugar. If you were to ask me right now what I want most in the world, it would be to die while I'm eating crème brûlée."

"Sorry to hear it."

Ahead of us was the kitchen, and to our right was the den Jake pretty much lived in, so he stopped and looked back at me. "No, you're not. You're still pissed at me because of King Maybe."

"I am," I said. I watched Jake hobble quite slowly, one hand on the rail, down the three stairs to the sunken room with its eternal blaze crackling and snapping in a fireplace the size the stable Jesus was born in. "And you invited me in," I said, "because you feel guilty about it."

"I've got calluses on my guilt impulse," Jake said, easing himself into the room's best chair, a butter-colored leather masterpiece that always faced the fire. His knees cracked. "I sleep okay, once I finally *fall* asleep, and in between hikes to the john."

"I'm sure you do." I sat, too, sinking into a perfectly nice armchair that probably cost a third of what Jake's did. "What happened to the movie?"

"What movie?" He put out an arm and made a flicking gesture with the back of his hand in the direction of the fireplace. "Could you poke the fire a little? It's cold in here."

It wasn't, but I got up. "The movie you were so *worried* about, the one you supposedly sent me to King Maybe's office to find out about. Something long about a women nothing ever happens to."

"Not much of a *TV Guide* slug."

I moved a couple of logs at random, feeling as though my eyebrows were about to burst into flame. "It was going to be your—I don't remember the word you used—your apology or something for all the crap—"

"I don't *owe* anybody an apology." His tone had a lot of teeth in it. "I made five of the nine highest-grossing pictures ever, up until the Chinese started buying tickets. Fucking Chinese," he said. "Do you know what they've—"

"Yes, you've told me. Sequels, franchises, tentpoles, all that."

"Don't do that," Jake snapped. "Don't tell me I've told you something when I haven't."

I managed to roll the log over in an eruption of sparks. "But you did tell me. We were sitting right—"

He slapped both hands, fingers spread, on the arms of his chair. "Well, don't fucking *tell* me about it. I may not be enjoying this stage of my life, but I don't want to be told I don't even *remember* it. My mother," he said, bouncing a little against the cushion behind him, "toward the end of her life, she watched the same four *I Love Lucy* shows over and over again. I got them for her on film from Lucy herself. My mom laughed at them like all the jokes were brand new. Before she died, like a parting gift or something, I brought Lucy over, in person, and my mom looked at her like she'd never seen her before. Like she was the new nurse or something."

"I'm sorry," I said.

"We come out of the room, Lucy says, 'It's hard to get a laugh these days.'" Jake barked out a laugh of his own, as brief and unamused as the sound of a trap snapping shut. "So guess what. Dying isn't the only thing you got to worry about, you gotta worry about forgetting you're alive. Leave that fucking fire alone and sit down. Why are you here?"

"Right," I said. I put the fire tools back and wiped my hands on my jeans. "I'm giving you a chance to work off a little bad karma."

"Don't worry about my karma. I've been who I am since before you ate anything you had to chew."

"Well what I need is easy, I think. Are kid actors still in those books, those directories, with the head shots for casting directors?"

"If their agents pay for it." He shook his head. "It's mostly a scam now, not like it was years ago. Now it's all online. Directories are for bottom-level. Con artists."

"Con artists sounds exactly right. Here." I reached into the pocket of my T-shirt and handed him Ronnie's two best shots of the kids. She'd cropped to the faces and blown them up. One of the pictures of the little girl was good enough for her to use professionally. "I want you to get one of your people—do you still have people?"

He didn't even look up at me.

"One of your people to comb though those directories and find these kids and get the names of their agents."

"Tell me again why I'm doing this."

"You know exactly why. King Maybe. So, yes, you're going to do this for me, and if you don't, I know a fence, a fine art specialist, with half a dozen guys working for him who'd love to get a few minutes in the museum downstairs. Just looking around this place, it doesn't seem like the fortress it was, back when you had all the live-in muscle."

"You're not only as short as an agent," Jake said. "You *act* like an agent, pulling out the heavy artillery when a simple *please* would do the job."

"Please."

"Yeah, sure. But tell me something. You got a payday in here someplace?"

"I do."

"I'll set it up, you foot the bill. Run you twenty, thirty an hour."

The old Jake would never have asked for money. I said, "Sure. And here's another one." I fished out the picture of Harried Mom.

"Jesus," he said, holding it at arm's length. Jake never wore his glasses. "What is this? 'Bride of Plastic Man?' She's so ugly you could use her as bat repellent."

"I'll ignore the sexism—"

"Look at me not yawning."

"—but the way she looks is obviously a matter of personal choice."

"Gee, you think?" Jake said. "She's made up to the teeth, and they're not even her real teeth. This goop around her jawline, her neck? Prosthetic. Makes her look heavier than she is. She's got stuff wadded up under her upper lip to change the shape of her mouth. That hair. What color were her eyes, green?"

"Yes."

"Well, then. The defense rests. Green eyes occur ninety-five percent of the time in genre fiction. How many times you actually seen green eyes? Listen, I made all three of the *Face Shifter* movies, seventy-million buck opening weekend for the second one, and she'd have fit right into the eighth reel, when Julia Roberts has turned halfway into John Goodman. I probably would've used her on the poster."

"So you're saying the picture is useless."

"That's what I'm saying. No way to tell what she really looks like."

"Well, the kids then. I want their agents' names and whatever other contact information your guy can get."

"Yeah, yeah," Jake said. "So that's why you came."

"That's pretty much it."

He slipped the pictures into the pocket of his robe and looked over at the fire, chewing on his lower lip. "You, uh, you want to stay for lunch?"

"I ate lunch about four hours ago, Jake, but thanks."

Jake stretched out his legs and crossed his ankles, then uncrossed them and crossed them the other way. Gazing down at his feet as though he wasn't quite sure what they were, he drew a breath to say something, shook his head, exhaled heavily, and then said, "Dinner?"

14

Not Replaced with Junk

If I were given to being melancholy over the lives of people I don't particularly like, I might have been feeling melancholy for Jake as I coasted down his driveway, popping the clutch to bring the engine to life when I was halfway down and mentally thanking Louie for installing the manual transmission after I bought the car. *I really hate automatic transmissions,* I thought, practically out loud, and then I realized I was trying to divert myself from the fact that I actually *was* feeling melancholy. For Jake.

"Fuck him," I said, not very convincingly. That was, after all, what he would have said about me. Probably was what he was saying at that moment.

Still, despite the massive ego and the tiny moral code, he'd had a *vitality* I'd admired and envied, even if the energy was fueled largely by malice; malice seems to slow time for men of a certain type, keeping them young, or at least a malign imitation of young. Whatever the source of Jake's energy—and adding to the anger, you had to remember, were the products of global drug smuggling operations and a lot of sub-rosa chemistry—he'd once seemed to be walking proof that there actually were people upon whom Time couldn't lay a glove. In my uneasy late thirties I'd taken a small amount of comfort from that, and I could almost hear the hiss as another illusion slowly deflated.

I stopped at the bottom of the driveway. The cars streaming by had their headlights on; it was that awful time of day when it's neither as light nor as dark as you think it is, or would like it to be. I hit speed dial, and Ronnie said, "I can't believe you're leaving me here alone."

"I know a few people who survived a night there," I said. "Is it too awful?"

"Too awful for what? Too awful for *Architectural Digest*? Yes. Too awful for people who shoot up elementary schools? No. Close, but no."

"Well, sorry if this sounds tactless, but is it too awful for you?"

"Oh, no. *Certainly* not. I mean, it's got walls and everything."

"I've got one more stop to make. Could be an hour, could be more. Do you want to check out and go someplace nicer? There's a Sheraton on the Universal lot, about two miles away."

"Wouldn't dream of it," she said. "I'll be able to use this against you for years. But here's what I *am* going to do. I'm going to go to the best restaurant within a fifteen-mile radius, order two complete dinners, pick at both of them, and bring nothing back for you."

"Have a steak," I said.

"I don't want a steak."

"No, but I do. What kind of revenge would it be to have a kale mash or something like that? I wouldn't be upset that you didn't bring me any. I'd probably thank you."

"Right," she said. "One rare, prime rib-eye, bone in, at

Taylor's, left intact and untasted on the table while I chow down on the kale mash. No, I'll bring you one small piece of cold fat."

"Everything okay on the security front?"

"You mean, do I think anyone might be looking for me at Minnie's Mouse House? No. And I did absolute figure eights getting here. I'm alone."

"Okay," I said. "Love you."

"Oh, well," she said, "if you put it *that* way." And she hung up.

I sat there at the bottom of Jake's steep, unswept drive, projecting a sequence of events in roughly chronological order onto the inside of the car's windshield: the first call from Stinky; the Bride of Plastic Man with her hired kids; the creaking, ransacked darkness of Horton House; the broken chair that a frantic Miss Daisy used to keep someone out, probably having crawled across the floor to wedge it there; Luz Ginzberg, aka Lumia White Antelope, hiccups and all, hired by the competition, afraid of them, but nevertheless going out into the night and that waiting white car; the heavyweight who barged into Stinky's in the middle of the night at the center of a whirlwind of threats; and then, in the more distant past, Henry Wallace Horton, Jr., aka Edgar Francis Codwallader, dragging his fake name, his stolen gold, and his English first editions across raw, scratchy stretches of the West in the nineteenth century; his surprisingly bookish journey to England; an antique French doll with a triangle cut into its back; the building of the worst house I'd ever been in.

Sort it out, boil it down. One object, small and worth killing for. One helpless old woman, dead. One nice female burglar, someone for whom I'd once had a secret, unexpressed affection, murdered. Two people—presumably, anyway—who wanted the small object badly enough to hire competing burglars to go into a house they either wouldn't, couldn't, or were afraid to enter. Behind it all, more than a century ago, one old claim jumper who liked to read.

Why did they kill Lumia? Was it anger, or would they have killed her even if she'd brought them what they wanted, just to dead-end the connection? Was I on someone's shoot list, too, whether I delivered or not?

It had gone full dark while I'd sat there. It was also evening rush hour, so Coldwater was a serpentine necklace of lights as it wound its way up toward Jake's eyrie.

Okay, I thought, don't worry about getting killed, worry about working it out so they don't get a chance at me. There are balls in the air. Be methodical. Check things off. I had Jake putting someone to work to find the kids. I had Louie digging up everything he could on old man Horton. I was about to barge in on Itsy Winkle and try to pry her competing client's name out of her. I had the name of a fence for the kind of stuff that had been stolen out of Horton House, I had the old notebook that probably contained the names of the faithful servants who had presumably stolen it . . .

Just on reflex, I mentally challenged my assumption that the best stuff had been *stolen* from Horton House, as opposed to having been removed in an orderly and lawful fashion. The place was, after all, about to be torn down. It's standard procedure, I thought, when a house is waiting for the bulldozers: Haul off everything worth selling, and sell it. It was virtually guaranteed to happen.

But in that case it wouldn't have been *replaced with*

junk. There would have been no point in that crap furniture if the house was just being cleared. No, Miss Daisy had been nailed to that bed for a long time, the rest of the family apparently unwilling or forbidden to visit her, and during her long illness the best stuff was toted off for sale, one or two pieces at a time, by people, at least two of them, who remained in the house, who still needed a table to eat dinner at, a place to sprawl in the enormous living room.

So, the servants. What, if anything, did they know about the forces that were in play? Maybe the notebook from the kitchen would lead me to them. If not, maybe the fence whose name Stinky had given me could direct me to the shops where the stuff had been sold. The shop owners would have the names of the people they bought it from, just in case it turned out to be hot.

I was sitting there, thinking, *I'm missing something*, when a car pulled into the driveway at considerable speed, jammed on its brakes so hard that it bounced when it stopped, and then hit its high beams a couple of times, in case I had somehow failed to notice its arrival.

I flicked mine back, just indicating that my car was occupied, and then opened the dash compartment to get the automatic. Who knew? I decided to let whoever it was come to me. After a short *my-dick-is-bigger-than-your-dick* pause, the driver's door on the other car opened and I discarded the modifying phrase because it was obvious, even with her headlights half-blinding me, that the other driver hadn't framed the delay in those terms. She was unquestionably, conspicuously, even notably female.

Lush was the word that came to mind, lush as a Rachmaninoff chord. I tucked the automatic out of sight but still within reach and put my window down as she approached, and then, as my headlights hit her face, I recognized her as the leading actress in a sitcom from ten or fifteen years ago, a strikingly beautiful comic talent. If she'd been born a little earlier, she would probably have been a movie star, able to explore all the dimensions of her gift instead of debasing it in the same fucking limiting way every week for six years until she went up in a tabloid-celebrated mushroom cloud of cocaine.

Laney Profitt. I hadn't heard her name in more than a decade. The car was a well-worn BMW sedan, maybe from 2004 or 2005, that had lost its share of arguments. Not a star's ride.

"You just gonna sit here?" Laney Profitt said, putting a steadying hand on the car's roof and leaning in. If I'd been a Breathalyzer, she would have blown *go to jail.*

"Sorry," I said. "I was grabbing a little time to think."

"Yeah. Jake doesn't allow that in the house. You wanna back up or what?"

Up close, I could see that time had worn away at her as surely as it had at Jake. The quicksilver fluidity that had made her look different in every shot had thickened and calloused into a weary mask framing jumpy, anxious eyes. I said, "I'm a big fan."

"Yeah?" she said. "You don't look that old. Listen, Jake's gonna be wondering where I am. Can you . . . ?" and she made little hand gestures to scoot me back up the driveway.

"Sure," I said. I looked past her car and saw the traffic still streaming up Coldwater; no way she could back into it to let me out. "It's going to take a minute or two, though. Lot of curves. How long have you known Jake?"

"I don't know," she said, turning to go back to her car. "How long have I known you?" She stumbled a little when she got to her door.

I backed all the way up the drive, which wasn't any easier than I'd thought it would be. Whatever Jake had offered her to get her here, she wanted it pretty badly; the front bumper of her car was never more than a couple of feet from mine, and she was leaning over the steering wheel as though she could get at least part of her there a few seconds earlier.

The instant we got to the circle she pulled past me and jumped out of the car, leaving the door open. I really *really* didn't want to see her run to the front porch, so I headed back down the driveway, trying to replay the thoughts I'd been working through when her headlights interrupted me. Obviously it was a defensive reaction, taking refuge in the Horton House situation so quickly, ransacking my brain to avoid thinking about Jake and his guest and the lower-depths world it seemed likely they shared, but sometimes the way my brain works surprises me, and halfway down I suddenly knew what I'd overlooked. The end of a once-prominent family. An almost-historic house, being torn down. What an *idiot*. I stopped right where I was and called Louie.

"I don't got anything yet," he said.

I said, "How long does it take a will to get through probate?"

"Depends on whether anyone wants anything," he said. Then he said, "Oh, yeah, shoulda thought of that myself. I need her whole given name and the county where the will was filed."

"Daisy Laurel Horton," I said. "Los Angeles."

I sat there, letting the car idle for a moment after he hung up. If he could get the information—and it shouldn't be a major problem because wills in California are public documents the moment they go into probate—and if Itsy would talk to me, I figured that within twenty-four hours I'd have my cast of characters: family members, servants, lawyers, the crooks who hired Lumia and me, the kids the Bride of Plastic Man had dragged into that restaurant, and the names of the agents with whom she'd negotiated their services. With any kind of luck at all, they would have *her* name. It almost felt too easy.

No kidding.

I'd never met, or even seen, Itsy Winkle, but years ago a burglar on her string had told me a little about her one evening over coffee in a Ventura Boulevard restaurant, mediocre enough to be on Louie's list of one-item favorites. The burglar lived downtown but had accepted a job in the Valley and, for some reason I've forgotten, couldn't get into the house until eleven. Sally Everest was a gregarious, energetic young woman who honored her old-fashioned name by wearing her hair 1940s-style, just below shoulder length and curled under at the ends like a big band singer, and who bored easily. She didn't want to just sit around watching her knee jiggle up and down, she said, waiting to commit to a burglary that had given her a case of the anticipatory willies.

So she'd called me. I was living at the time in a motel called The Viking's Pyre, big on color illustrations from the 1920s by artists of the Howard Pyle school, in this case meticulously painted panoramas of extravagantly bearded, very dead Norwegian men, probably named

Harald, being pushed out to sea in flaming and obviously expendable boats. The place's owner was Danish and *serious* about it. I'd slept in cheerier environments, so when Sally called, I said sure, just no Scandinavian food.

She didn't want to talk about the job—bad luck, she said—and we didn't really know each other all that well, so when the topic of Itsy sort of wandered into the conversation she grabbed it like a life preserver.

"Everybody says she's awful," Sally said, "and they're right. She is."

I said, "Really." Itsy at that time was still primarily a do-it-herself crook. She'd only just begun to branch out as an entrepreneur, assigning to other burglars the jobs that didn't interest her personally but had good money attached. Thinking back on it, it must have been in the year just before she went to jail for braining the nice lady with the pearls. "What makes her so awful?"

"Well," Sally said, "there are two ways to answer that because it's really two questions, isn't it? First question is what's inside *Itsy* that makes her so awful, and the second is what is it in *me* that makes me dislike her so much? In other words, in my own personal *experience*—"

I said, "Pick one." Our waitress was standing behind the counter like someone frozen in time, unable to tear her eyes from Sally's hair.

"Well, on *Itsy's* side, so to speak, there's the way she looks. I mean, that's enough to embitter anyone, right there."

"I guess it would be," I said, not wanting to admit my ignorance. It's a character flaw that I'm trying to deal with. Still. "Yeah, sure, I can see that."

We were sharing a booth, and Sally narrowed her eyes

and leaned across the table toward me, practically a silent movie parody of someone who is speaking confidentially. She did everything except half-cover her mouth and talk past the back of her hand. "Is that woman *looking* at me?"

"Which woman?"

"The one who's dressed like a waitress."

I said, "She's not just *dressed* like a—"

"All right. Our waitress, then."

"Yes, she's been staring at you since you walked in."

She settled back in her seat. "Just wanted to make sure. It would be kind of deranged to think people were looking at you when you're actually the furthest thing from their—"

"Itsy," I said. "What's so terrible about her?"

"You really *are* task oriented, aren't you? Well, let's see. She's dishonest, she's unpleasant, she's manipulative, she just *grabs* an opportunity to be violent, she's unfair to the people who depend on her, she's a right-winger—"

I said, "Most crooks are."

"She thinks people who don't work for a living are parasites."

"What about *her*?"

"I didn't say it was a flawless world view. She also foams at the mouth about how her tax dollars are spent when she doesn't hardly pay any. But that doesn't keep her from stumping up and down that living room cussing a blue—"

"Stumping."

"You know," Sally said. "*Stumping*. The way she does."

"Right," I said. "My mind wandered. That waitress really has her eye on you."

"Maybe she thinks I want the silverware." She picked up a spoon, blew on it, and rubbed it on her blouse. She raised both eyebrows and lowered her lids, going for mysterious. "She should just *know*."

"I think it's your hair," I said. "She should just know what?"

"I'm the silverware *queen*. You know the Mildenhall Treasure?"

"Sure," I said. "That treasure from Mildenhall." I *am* working on it.

"Biggest find of Roman silver tableware in history. Literally priceless, although I always think that's nonsense, don't you? I mean, priceless to who?"

"Whom," I said.

"Yeah, whom. The farmer who dug it up used the utensils every day like he bought them on eBay or something, and the great dish—there's a huge dish that's so great they call it *the great dish* even in the museum catalogue—he used *that* to plunk down whatever kinds of birds they eat over there, partridges or something. I mean, can you imagine?"

"The mind boggles."

"So, yeah." She drummed on the tabletop with the handle of the spoon. The coffee was terrible. Each of us had choked down one cup and had chosen to let the second round get cold. She lifted the spoon and showed it to me, framed between her index fingers as though it were something I had just won on TV. "I specialize in silverware," she said. "Especially eighteenth-century English, the work of Thomas Wallis One and Two, when I can get it, which is almost never. But even the prospect makes me go all creamy. Do you know anything about silverware?"

"Not much." It sounded more authoritative than *zero*.

"Well." She sat back, looking disappointed. "There's silverware and then there's silverware. A good tray from, say, Thomas Wallis, who died around 1790, will run you seven to ten thousand bucks. A serving spoon could bring five to eight hundred."

Eight hundred seemed like a lot for a spoon. "This is pure silver?"

"There's no such thing," she said. "Well, there is, obviously, but it's too soft to use for anything. Sterling, which is the purest kind that's *useful*, is a little more than seven percent something else, usually copper. See, they call it sterling because—just yawn or something if I'm putting you to sleep."

"So far, both eyes open."

"So, okay, there wasn't much silver in Europe until the Spanish started hauling hundreds of tons every year out of South and Central America." She took a quick survey of the place, possibly to make sure no one was making notes. "Before that, it was pretty much for the church and castle crowd, and it was also used for money. Problem was countries would mix tin and other cheap metals in so they got more for their money than the money was actually worth. Except for the kraut straight-shooters in the Hanseatic League, which started someplace that's now in Germany. *They* kept their silver money close to pure because their trade depended on it. The Hanseatic League began on the Baltic, which was then called the East Sea, so people outside the league referred to them as Easterlings and began to ask for payment in Easterling silver, which got shortened to Sterling."

"Damn," I said. "Who knew? So what's the problem?

"Well, there are forgeries, some pretty good." She glanced at the waitress and intercepted a full-bore, double-barreled stare, but then the woman looked away, blushing as red as a brake light. "Forgeries can be hard to spot."

"So that's it? That's the problem? *Forgeries*? Seems to me that everything you swipe has a different problem, a *tactical* problem, I mean. In addition to forgeries, I'd figured the problem with silver would be weight."

"Because I'm a woman?" she said, accompanying the words with a meaningful squint.

"No. Because it's *heavy*."

"I *wish*," Sally said. "I'd love to score enough good stuff to have trouble carrying it out. Uh-uh, the big problem is *noise*. You ever empty your silverware drawer? Wake up the whole cemetery. See, there's too *much* silver, in some ways. The Victorians, who had rules for everything, decided, around 1840, *Thou shalt not eat anything with thine fingers*, and all of a sudden, the whole kingdom went all dainty. The people who made silverware saw a boom market. Within a few years there was one knife for bread, one for butter, one for meat, a dozen kinds of forks, and God only knows how many spoons. That old thing about not knowing which fork to use? That's a leftover from the Victorians. Thanks to the Industrial Revolution, there was a whole new class of really rich Brits who weren't nobles, and they were a little *touchy* about that, so they invented all these new table manners tests so they could look down at anyone who might have grown up with a single fork. But in this day and age, for somebody like me, what the great age of British silver means is that we've got weight and noise and *awkwardness*, all at the same time, and the issue becomes how you carry a bunch of loose, noisy pieces when you've only got two hands. So you want to know how I do it?"

"Always. This is my favorite *Jeopardy* category"

"*Burglar Jeopardy*," she said, and she clapped her hands. "I always take three of those long cloth shoe organizer things you hang inside a closet door, so that's twenty-four slots per, and you can roll them up when they're full. For the odd-shaped pieces, I've got knitted golf club covers. They're perfect, narrow at the mouth and wide farther down. I used to use men's running socks, but the merchandise slipped out once in a while, and you *really* don't want it hitting the floor. So the stuff is all packed and muffled. Oh, and a Santa sack to throw everything into."

"Have you ever done a job where you used all of it?"

"Three or four, and may there be more. What do you specialize in?"

"Getting away," I said.

"Do it backward," she said. She stirred her coffee with the spoon.

I said, "Absolutely. That was the first thing I learned: Imagine getting out before you go in. When you open a drawer, imagine putting everything back in the same place before you take anything out. Who told you that?"

"Henry Timmerman. He always said—"

"*Sure*. Henry. He was one of Herbie Mott's guys."

She looked at me until she was certain I'd finished talking. "You interrupt a lot," she said. "Henry always said that when you interrupt someone you might have cut off the only thing you really needed to hear in the whole conversation. Do you have sisters?"

"No."

"Didn't think so. Guys with sisters, especially older sisters, usually learn not to interrupt women."

I said, "Do you know a burglar named Lumia? Since your teacher learned from my teacher."

"No. Pretty name, though." She looked at her watch and said, "Getting near time."

The waitress spotted the gesture and started toward us, but Sally held a hand up, just a request for a minute or two more. The waitress stopped as though she'd walked into a force field, and then she reached up and did a little air-primp to an invisible fall of hair at her shoulders, held up two thumbs, and smiled.

"I love women," Sally said. "We're so much nicer than men. Except for Itsy, of course."

I said, "Of course."

"If you're ever over at her house," Sally said, putting a twenty on the table, which was a tip of about 400 percent, "look out for a gun. Little, no more than five inches, but big enough to do it to you."

"Where does she carry it?" I asked.

"Them," Sally said. "They're all over her. She *bristles* with them."

15
No Swimming

"It's the one with the drawbridge," Louie had said, with the implication, *You can't miss it*.

But I almost did. It was dark, for one thing, and for another, well, okay, it wasn't *literally* a drawbridge, but it was a modern equivalent. And when I finally spotted it, it told me two things right off the bat. Itsy did not like drop-ins and she was doing *extremely* well.

The house was in a relatively undeveloped area of the northwest San Fernando Valley, above Chatsworth and near Box Canyon, well up on a narrow, hilly, scraggy sagebrush street that was being built as it rose, beginning at the Valley's floor. *Chez* Itsy was five or six vacant lots above its nearest neighbor, with no one yet building above it. It looked to me as though she'd bought two lots and slapped the house down in the middle, so even when the street filled in, as it inevitably would, she'd still have space on either side.

The clouds were hogging the entire sky, declaring victory over what the King James Bible, with characteristic condescension, terms *the lesser lights* of the stars and moon, and since the neighborhood still lacked street-lights, I once again found myself in a darkness that felt thick enough to bite off and chew. I spared a moment to ask why—after decades of wondering why people sought *enlightenment* but not *endarkenment*—I suddenly found myself unnerved in the absence of light.

Itsy's house might have had something to do with it. It was a two-story postmodern cube that looked black, although up here pretty much everything looked black. It might have been dark blue or even gray. Not a gleam of light came from it. Surrounding it, and dimly illuminated by a thin neon strip set into the ground at its base, was a fence made of sharply pointed steel spikes about eight feet high, four inches in diameter, and six inches apart. There were no horizontal stabilizing bars, meaning nothing to pull yourself up by or wedge a foot into: a burglar's defense against burglars. I figured each of the bars had to be anchored in at least a foot of concrete, and they looked like they'd been made personally for Vlad the Impaler.

The purpose of the light strip was to direct attention to the fence. The purpose of the fence was to direct attention to the gate. The purpose of the gate was to direct you to turn around and go home.

On the other side of the spikes I saw a stream or moat or water hazard about eight feet wide. It didn't look deep, but it didn't have to. Posted every eight or ten feet on the far side of the moat was a colorful placard on a stick, each with its own little light, the kind of signs that, in a critical phase of the election cycle, might have said VOTE FOR FENSTERMACHER, except that what was on them was a picture of a middle-size fish with really significant teeth, a dentist's daydream. I'm not an ichthyologist, but to me those teeth said *piranha*. There was also a sign that, I supposed, suggested something about the sense of humor of the house's owner. It said NO SWIMMING.

The final source of illumination, since the house emitted none, was a yellowish squint of a lamp placed above the transparent gate, which looked like Plexiglas. I estimated it as at least four inches thick and roughly eight feet high, slick as ice. On the other side of the gate was the water. Anyone smart enough to figure out how to go over, or through, the spikes or scale the gate would also have to be dumb enough to get into the water. Seemed to me like that eliminated pretty much everyone.

So I pushed the button beside the gate.

Almost a full minute passed, and I pushed the button again. This time, I got a mechanical-sounding voice that said, "Go. A. Way."

I said, "No."

Another pause. Then the mechanical voice said, "No. One. Is. Home."

I said, "I was with Lumia last night, just before she got killed. You remember Lumia?"

After what might have been a reflective moment, the voice said, "Where."

"You know where. You sent her there. Don't you want to know whether she found it?"

An even longer pause, and then the mechanical voice said, "Shit."

I heard a sound somewhere between a rumble and a rasp, and a rectangle of what might have been concrete, about four feet wide, began to slide toward the gate from the far side of the water. As it came, I saw the narrow steel I-beams over which it traveled. It kept moving until it snicked into place just on the other side of the gate and

then, noiselessly, the gate swung inward. It was, I supposed, an invitation.

The front of the house had no windows, which explained its
nonexistent light profile. The extra-big door—maybe nine
or ten feet high—at the end of the walkway was ajar, and
I went through it into a hall that disconcerted me in the
same way Jack, of beanstalk fame, must have felt when
he invaded the home of the giants in the sky. Everything
was at least a foot taller than it should have been. Without
being aware of it, we get used to the notion that the things
that surround us will conform to standard sizes. Tables,
for instance; the average dining table is twenty-eight to
thirty inches tall. A drafting table, which is conspicuously
taller, runs a maximum of forty-four inches. Hall tables
are usually a little higher than dining tables because the
people who put things on them are standing up. The tops
of the two tables in this high, dim hallway were even with
my elbows.

The mechanical voice said, with no emphasis whatso-
ever, "Hold. Arms. Away. From. Body. Spread. Fingers.
Turn." The door behind me, which I had left ajar, clicked
shut. Then it clicked again.

I turned halfway and paused; the machine said, "Turn.
Slowly."

I did as I was told. The floor was a deep gray slate,
beautifully polished, and the walls were the same gray. The
house felt colder inside than it was outside. As I completed
my revolution, I saw that a painting hung on the wall at
the far end of the hall. I had to do a squinting double-take
before I recognized it as a museum quality print of El Greco's *El Coloso*, the terrifying vision of a naked giant, left

arm raised threateningly, with a bent elbow and a clenched fist, glaring over his shoulder at the tiny, frantic horde of people who are fleeing like disorganized ants in the lower-left foreground of the painting. The print was something like actual size, almost four feet high. I'd never seen it that big before, but it had curdled my blood in much smaller representations. Some people doubt it's really an El Greco, but the quality of the nightmare says to me that it is.

I said, "What now?"

The mechanical voice said, "Your. Name."

I said, "I don't know about that."

A break in the conversation, if you could call it a conversation.

I said, "So far, you haven't even said hello. I'm about thirty seconds from saying fuck you and going home."

Through an archway to my left I could see a large dark windowless room, almost certainly the living room, which looked lightly, if at all, lived in. Much longer than it was wide, it seemed to be all gray: furniture, carpet, walls, everything the same gray as the exit hall. Without my having requested it, my mind emailed me an image of how conspicuous a spill of blood would be in that room. On the top of several tables were frozen silhouettes of a form that made me vaguely uneasy.

There had been no reply, so I said, "And I'm getting tired of talking to Robby the Robot, too. Either come out here—"

"Or what?" It was a female voice, but not much warmer than the machine had been.

"Or, as I said, fuck you."

"Tell me why you came."

"Well," I said, "in the best of all possible worlds I

would personally like to kill the people who murdered Lumia. Either you can help me do that or you can't."

Another pause, but then at the far end of the living room, a light went on. It was just a table lamp, one paltry cellophane-yellow bulb, but in here it felt like the sun announcing the end of the Long Dark Night of the Soul. Sitting motionless on the table, one paw in the air, was a cat. The woman's voice, still conspicuously not seeking approval said, "Come in."

I went in.

The room had a vaulted ceiling like the entrance hall at Horton House. All the furniture seemed to be leather and a little too big, and with the light on I could see it was a shade or two darker then the plumage on a dove. The carpet was thick enough to trip over. There were four or five tables, and each one had an immobile cat on it. A *very* immobile cat. I eyed them warily as I walked through the room. When I was most of the way to the lamp, I said, "Cat got your tongue?"

"Sit," the voice said. It came from behind me.

I said, "I wouldn't dream of it. After you."

"I would prefer you to be seated."

"And I would prefer to have both my feet under me, right where they belong, in case I decide it's time for them to do their thing. Nothing personal."

"I *personally* would prefer that you sit down."

The tone wasn't much different, but the words were. I said, "Oh, what the hell," and sat on an armchair across the room from the table with the light on it, allowing me to turn toward the front door without the bulb's glare, comparatively speaking, in my field of vision. I was also slightly put off by the reflected points of light in the cat's eyes, motionless as buttons. To fill in the royal flush of unreassuring details, I'd had to boost myself up to get my butt into the chair, making my feet dangle a few inches above the floor like a four-year-old's, and there was *another* cat, this one with its head turned and its tongue out to groom itself, on the table beside my chair. It wasn't purring. It wasn't grooming, either.

I heard a sort of squeak from the right, probably the dining room if the house was built on a conventional floor plan. The squeak sounded like the legs of a pair of leather pants rubbing together, and it turned out to *be* leather pants. They were black, they were tight, they had many pockets, they matched a black leather, form-fitting top. All that black leather clothed the almost emaciated form of the tallest woman—perhaps the tallest person of either gender—I'd ever seen off a basketball court. She had to be seven feet and an inch or two, thin as the blade of a knife, with enormously long, spidery fingers that probably could have curved around a bowling ball with the fingertips almost touching. As she drew nearer, I realized that, slanting and skeletal and angular as she was, the least reassuring thing about her was her eyes. They were wide, *wide* open, far enough that the entire circle of the iris was visible. When I was a kid and made an unpleasant face, my mother always told me that it would stick. Itsy Winkle looked like someone who had suddenly come face to face with something absolutely terrifying and instead of running had decided to stare a hole through it. And it had stuck. To make her face even more unsettling, her upper lip was considerably shorter in the center than it was in the corners, baring the four upper incisors. They looked like they got dry a lot.

She kept coming toward me until she was disconcertingly close, only a few feet away, and then she bent stiffly at the waist as though to see me better, bringing those unsettling eyes to bear on me, slowly tilting her head to the right. I sat there, trying to keep my eyes on her hands, thinking about the little gun I'd been warned about, and half expecting a five-foot tongue to flash out, fast as a frog's, and do me some obscure but memorable damage. She saw it in my face and smiled. Sort of.

"Excuse the rudeness," she said, without a hint of apology in her tone. She spoke quite slowly, giving each word the time and effort it required to make it mildly threatening. "I'm very nearsighted. It's part of the condition. Marfan, you can look it up later. The height is partly Marfan, too, although both of my parents were well over six feet tall, so the syndrome just added to it." She straightened and turned, the pants squeaking again, and went to the couch opposite, where she collapsed, folding up one joint at a time, like a giant praying mantis, and stared at me. "So," she said. "How did you come to see Luz last night?"

"We bumped into each other at Horton House."

"Who sent you?"

I said, "Uh-uh. You should know better than—"

With a creak of leather, she leaned forward. For half a second I thought she'd spread wings and fly across the room at me, but what she did was say, "Don't you *dare* take that tone with me." The lamp to her right made her eyes shine like giant marbles, bigger and even more disconcerting than the cat's eyes. The shine seemed to take up half of her face. Below them, the exposed teeth glinted. She licked them with the tip of her tongue.

"Sorry about the tone," I said. "To answer your question, as far as I'm willing to, the person who sent me was someone like you." Mentally, I was trying to put words to the air she gave off. What Itsy projected was an insect-like *indifference,* a completely neutral, even mechanical reaction pattern that suggested she could kill you in one moment and, in the next, be standing there wondering why she had your detached head in her hands. I said, "Who paid you to send Lumia?"

She clasped those immense, spidery hands over her left knee and rocked back and forth for a moment, creaking like Horton House, looking at me and through me, and said, "Who was Luz—all right, Lumia—to you?"

Well, good question.

"A long time ago, when I first met her, I sort of fell in love with her."

"Sort of. Only a man can *sort of* fall in love."

"You want to know, or not?"

She nodded, which I interpreted as a prompt to go ahead. I said, "I was on the rebound. My wife had kicked me out because I wouldn't take a straight job. She was tired of worrying which way I'd wind up, dead or in jail."

She said, "Did she have a preference?"

"People told me you were a pain in the ass," I said, "but they understated it."

"So," she said. "Lumia. Continue."

"I met her when I was working with another burglar, who was kind of mentoring her."

"That Mott man, the one with the dandruff," she said. "So the two of you, you and Lumia, were an *item*? She wasn't exactly stingy with her affections."

"You know," I said, "I can probably figure out who

killed her without spending another fucking second with you."

"Just trying to get a rope around your desire to avenge her."

"I *liked* her," I said. "We never got together, but back then I liked her. And I liked her again last night. As a general rule of life I don't let people who kill my friends just skate away."

"Last night," she said. "Did she find it?"

I smiled at her. "Hasn't your client told you?"

For the first time, I saw her actual feelings: a ripple of irritation that, I was sure, was the watery tip of a huge, submerged mountain of rage.

I said, "They haven't called you, have they?"

She pursed her lips as though to spit but then she swallowed, loudly enough to be heard across the room.

I said, just twisting the knife, "Were you supposed to get a *bonus* if she found it?"

"If you have it," she said, "I'll pay you much more than you were promised by whoever hired you."

"So you *were* supposed to get a bonus. So they *haven't* called you. So let me make a little leap here. I don't have it, either, but I will."

"When?"

"When I do. And I'm also going to kill the people who killed Lumia."

"The people who killed her are invertebrates. They didn't make the decision."

"Maybe not," I said. "But one of them pulled the trigger, and that's good enough for me."

She tapped the long fingers against her knee and looked at me. "I'm waiting for the *leap* you promised."

"First, I need an answer. Whoever sent her into Horton House did it through you because he or she didn't want to hire her directly. So why did they pick her up there?"

I got a lift of the chin.

"So they could kill her," I said. "That's what I figure, anyway. But if they were going to kill her, why not just hire her directly?"

She continued to tap her fingers, as though she could hear music I couldn't. Then she said, "If what you're asking is whether I knew they were going to kill her, the answer is no. They hired her through me, obviously, because they didn't know where to find a burglar." She leaned back, her head only inches from the upraised paw of the stuffed cat on the table. Its coat gleamed.

"But you *did* know they were going to pick her up. You had to be the one who told her they were coming. She'd never talked to them."

Tap, tap, tap. Then she said, "They didn't trust me. They were afraid I'd take whatever it was. Tell them she didn't find it, and then go sell it to someone. They said they had to pick her up and search her, and then they'd bring her straight here."

I said, "And, of course, it wasn't your neck." She actually blinked. "So when she didn't arrive, what did you think had happened?"

A pause, but at least she wasn't tapping. "I thought they'd killed her."

I said, "And that was all right with you." I looked at her for a few seconds. She didn't wriggle or look away or clasp her hand to her heart. I said, "Why did you let me in?"

"You wouldn't go away."

"And?"

"And you might have represented them. The clients."

I said again, "And?"

"And when you said you'd seen Lumia last night I thought *you* might be the one who killed her." She shifted her weight to her left and reached into one of the many pockets in her leather pants. When her hand came back up, it had a very streamlined little automatic in it. In my experience, a gun that's pointed at me always seems bigger than it is, but this one was almost swallowed up in her huge hand. That may have been part of why I didn't feel any special menace. I'd been warned about it, and in contrast to everything else in the room, it felt like a prop.

"So you thought I'd killed her," I said. "And now?"

"No, now I don't. You haven't got that."

"Got what?"

"What it takes to kill someone when it's not personal. You're not in that league."

I said, "Here's the deal. You tell me who hired you. I'll kill the people who murdered Lumia and the person who hired you. When I find what we're all after, I'll give you a cut."

"Why would you do that?"

"Because you're going to make it all easier by telling me the name of the person who hired you."

"Not a cut," she said. "I'll sell it for you."

"I don't think so."

She started to shake her head, but instead stopped with her face turned partly away, regarding me from the corners of those awful eyes. "Do you know what it is?"

"I know it was supposed to be hidden in a doll—"

"A Jumeau."

"And I saw the doll and I saw where a piece had been cut from its back and the stuffing pulled out to make a hiding place."

"How big a piece?"

"A rectangle, smaller than a deck of cards."

She said, "Did you find the doll, or did Lumia?"

I said, "I did." I didn't want to raise the prospect that Lumia had removed the McGuffin before showing me the doll and that her clients might already have it. I didn't believe it; as I'd realized at the time, if she'd found it, there was no reason for her to stay in the house when I went upstairs. Also, I didn't want to bring the conversation to an end. I needed her to think I might still find it.

She was leaning toward me again, making the room seem a lot narrower than it was. "Where is the doll?"

I said, "I gave it to her. She seemed—umm, *worried* about getting into the car with nothing to show." I had to swallow, and even though I wasn't looking directly at Itsy I could see the interest kindle in her eyes and knew that, to her, that would seem like a weakness. I cleared my throat and said, "So I gave it to her, so she'd have something in hand."

"You're soft," she said.

I said, "And proud of it." I looked at my watch, although I didn't bother to read the time. She said nothing. I counted to five, and when it was clear that she thought it was my move, I said, "Lot of cats. Were they yours? Wee fluffos you couldn't bear to be parted from?"

The upper lip that bared the front teeth rose enough to show me the gums, too. "Don't be silly. I hate the little fuckers."

"So you what? Set traps for them?"

"Please," she said. "You can get in more trouble for killing a cat than a person."

"Then where did they come from?"

"I bought them on the dark web. There's nothing you can't find there."

"Enlighten me," I said. "If you hate cats, why would you buy these?"

"To remind me that at least some of the world's pussy-cats are dead. Anything else?"

"Your client," I said. "Yes or no?"

She said, "His name is Allan Frame. I'll get you his address. It's a good address. I checked it before I hired Lumia."

16
The Hard Hello

It was only a little after eleven, but I still had to ring Stinky's doorbell half a dozen times before Crisanto opened it and placed every one of his hundred and twenty pounds in my way.

"I need Stinky," I said.

"Mr. Stinky in toilet."

"He'll come out eventually," I said. "He always has in the past." I put both hands out and tilted them to my right, an invitation for Crisanto to get out of my way. "Please?" I said.

Crisanto licked his lips and spread his feet slightly, the image of someone who's decided to tell a bully to suck it up and swallow it.

"Is he putting someone in that cute little room behind the pantry?" I said. "Shall I go and see who it is?"

"Let him in," Stinky said from the living room. "No manners at *all*."

The confrontation averted, Crisanto gave me a welcoming smile and stepped aside. I went down the hall, running my fingertips over the silverpoint drawing—just because I was angry enough to put my fingerprints on it—and into the living room. Stinky, wearing a kind of luau caftan with prints of tropical birds all over it, was sitting in front of his cylinder desk. It was closed. On the table in front of the couch was a cognac snifter half-full of something that was exactly the right color. I went over and sat in front of it as Stinky followed me with his eyes.

I picked up the glass and sniffed it. Well, well. "Company?" I said. "Brought out the good stuff and everything, didn't you? Even the nice crystal. Doesn't seem to me I've ever tasted—"

"Would you like some?" The words were polite but the tone was pure poison.

"That's okay," I said. "It'd be wasted on me. Just do me a favor for a second, and look at me."

Stinky said, "With both eyes?"

"Please," I said. "This will take less than a minute, and then you can get back to the person you actually invited."

With an aggrieved sigh, Stinky swiveled his chair to me and waited, his eye on mine, expressing no curiosity at all.

I said, "Allan Frame."

For all that happened on Stinky's face I might have recited the first five letters of the alphabet. But then he reached out and scratched the side of his tiny nose.

"Okay," I said, getting up, "now you can play with your *real* friends." To Crisanto, I said, "I'll let myself out," but he still followed me all the way to the door, and after it closed behind me, I heard him throw the deadbolt.

"I should have known that the person who hired me through Stinky was also the one who went to Itsy to hire Lumia," I said. "Here I was, fantasizing competing camps when, in fact, the Bride of Plastic Man is actually behind everything."

"The Bride of—" Ronnie said from the bed. There was only one chair, and I was in it. "Oh. *Right*. Who called her that?"

"Colorful old Jake." I was in the motel room at Minnie's Mouse House, working on a cold but perfectly cooked ribeye from Taylor's. Ronnie, who loved crisp fat, had thoughtfully trimmed every bit of it off and eaten it for me. "Jake seems to be getting the old age he's earned."

Ronnie said, "You sound like you feel sorry for him."

"You know?" I said. "You see a lion that's lost its teeth and claws, and its coat is all mangy and falling out, and you don't think about all the lives it chewed up and swallowed. You kind of mourn the loss of power and beauty."

"Bet an antelope doesn't feel that way."

"Antelopes are peaceful and beautiful and boring. Whatever else they are, lions aren't boring."

"Returning to the real world for a moment," she said, "why should you have known you were both hired by the same person?"

"Because he showed up, furious, at Stinky's after Lumia got killed. What that suggests to me is that he figured I'd gotten the McGuffin out of the doll but left the doll behind the previous night, when I was supposed to be there, and he figured Stinky hadn't told him about it."

"But then, why shoot her? She didn't know what she was looking for, she didn't—"

"I don't think it was the fixer, it was the clients. Fixers don't get their hands dirty. So it was one of his two clients, either the Bride or that fuzzball with the big nose who was with her at McDonald's. Maybe they were furious, maybe panicked, maybe doing her in cold blood was part of the plan. *Invertebrates*, Itsy called them. Maybe he or she always meant to shoot Lumia and would have shot me if I'd been there when I was supposed to be. Maybe, maybe, maybe. Lumia told me where to hide if they came in, and for a moment I thought they might, but they took off. There they were with a dead woman in their car, and they obviously decided the best thing to do was get the hell out of there.

"Anyway, the guy in charge, whose name is Allan Frame, figured he could get to me through Stinky. But when he showed up to do a little strong-arm, Stinky surprised him—and me, I have to say—by hiding me in a sort of treasure cave and blowing him off. I should have known right then, the moment the guy started pushing Stinky around, that he had hired me through Stinky and then got Lumia through her own manager or whatever you want to call them. So it was his clients who were waiting for Lumia. I need him to tell me who they are." I put down the fork and rubbed at my face, fighting a fast-moving tide of feelings at the thought of her, friendless and terrified, in that car with the gun pointed at her while I sat safely in the house, a clueless asshole.

"Poor baby," Ronnie said, watching me. "You must be exhausted."

"It's just, you know."

"I know," she said. "She meant something to you."

"Just someone I liked," I said. "If you, um, if you saved this whole steak for me, what did you eat? Except for the fat, I mean. You ate almost *all* of the—"

"I ordered the kale mash," Ronnie said, "which I set in the center of the table because the room needed some green, and then I had a couple of almost raw lamb chops. I asked the chef just to put them in a plastic bag and then

slip them into his pants until they were body temperature."

"Hope they weren't frozen."

"I think I would have heard him scream." She smiled
at me, essentially an interrogative smile to see whether I'd
smile back.

I forced one but couldn't hold it, so I looked around the
room, something I'd been avoiding. I said, "Sorry about
this place."

"Wouldn't miss it for the world," Ronnie said. "It's *got*
to be a personal growth opportunity. The carpet alone hits
a new lifetime high on the creep scale."

It did indeed. It had once, in a distant millennium, been
white, but now it was the gray they point at in TV commercials to convince you to change your detergent. The
gray was enlivened by hundreds of thin, twisty black figures that might have been little snakes or individual sperm
cells swimming valiantly for glory, but that, on closer
inspection, turned out to be mouse tails in various degrees
of curliness. Worst of all, they were heaviest where the
carpet met the wall, where they formed a sort of black
fringe that suggested enormous platoons of mice sitting
cheek by jowl with their butts to us, just on the other side
of the thin plaster. To make the experience even more vivid,
the bottom of the wall had mouse-holes *painted* on it at
irregular intervals. I had been told that one hole in each
room was real, not painted, and inside it was a coupon for
a free two-night stay. I didn't have to fight an inclination
to search for it.

"I have to admit," Ronnie said, "that I made it from
the door to the bed in a single leap. That was before I
looked at the bedspread." The bedspread, on which she

was reclining—one of Ronnie's guides to the good life is never to miss an opportunity to get horizontal—was patterned in little mouse footprints. "If this place had a chandelier you would have found me hanging from it."

I said, "Did you sample the cheese?" Sharing the room's one table with my steak was a dusty Plexiglas dome that covered a plate with three desiccated, melancholy looking pieces of cheese on it. The plate said NIBBLE NIBBLE NIBBLE all the way around its edge. The table was in front of the room's sole window, and the window was covered with a red, white, and blue drape that featured about sixty images of Mickey Mouse giving the onlooker a cheery four-fingered salute. About twenty yards away from the window the motel's magenta sign glared away, with just enough of its light bleeding through the drape to turn Mickey's friendly world a wee bit demonic.

"You have to arm wrestle a rat before you're allowed to open it, so I passed," she said, rearranging herself among the lumps in the mattress.

I picked up the bone to gnaw on it. It's my favorite part of a steak, except maybe the crisp fat.

"That's so *carnivorous*," she said, watching me. "'Thousands of years of civilization, erased like chalk.'"

"A new stage in our relationship," I said. "You haven't criticized my eating before."

"Wouldn't dream of it," she said. She rolled over on her stomach and propped her chin on her hand to watch me work on the steak. "My mother always said you can learn a lot about a man from the way he eats a bone."

"She *always* said it? Not the easiest phrase to work into a conversation."

"I've been staring at that curtain," she said with a nod

at the window, "and given that you're a font of useless information—"

"Useless?" I said. "Forsooth. Obscure, perhaps, but never useless."

"—I just know that you can explain to me why Mickey Mouse only has four fingers."

"Actually," I said with my mouth full, "he has four *digits*. Three fingers and a thumb."

"Mice don't have thumbs."

"Yeah, well, they don't wear gloves, either." I put down the bone, swiped at the cold fat on the plate with the pad of my right index finger, and then put the finger into my mouth. Around my finger, I said, "Mmmm."

"So, no answer. Life is just one disappointment after another."

"I didn't say I had no answer. I was just busy eating. In fact—and this is the solemn truth—Walt, as the whole world called him, was asked that very question."

Ronnie said, "I'll just bet he was."

"And this is what he said, word for word: 'Artistically five digits are too many for a mouse.'"

She looked at me long enough that, in a film, there probably would have been a dissolve. "That's it?"

"I don't make this stuff up," I said. "I'm stuck with the truth."

"So," she said, "why would that person have hired *two* burglars, you and Lumia?"

"Being double-careful is my guess. The only reason I even learned Lumia was there was that I went the night *after* I was actually supposed to go. Way it looks to me, if I came out empty-handed on my scheduled night, she was supposed to give the place another shaking."

Ronnie said, "Do you think they were waiting for you outside on the night you were supposed to be there?"

"That's exactly what I think."

"Brrrr," she said. "So that woman with the orange hair, she wanted—"

"Looks like it. Dessert?"

"I ate it. Are you doing anything to *sidestep* all this? I'd hate to have to move out of the edgwood. Not that *this* isn't nice, of course."

"I think Jake's going to find her for me, through the kids."

Ronnie rolled over on her back, staring up at a bit of the ceiling that looked to me just like all the other bits of the ceiling. She let the silence stretch out and said, "It's tomorrow at ten, isn't it? The meeting with Francie."

Francie DuBois was the disappearance specialist—she called herself a travel agent—who was going to help me get Ronnie's two-year-old son, Eric, out of New Jersey without a trace, once I figured out how to get my hands on the kid. Francie had opened the exit door for a great many people who had been just one wrong turn away from the hard hello, and now they were all living in some off-brand country, eating sheep' testicles or something else prized by the locals, but free of mortal terror. I wasn't personally certain it was a trade I'd make.

"Ten it is," I said. "We can just lounge around here and soak up the atmosphere until it's time to go. Memorize *Hickory Dickory Dock* and *Three Blind Mice*. Not much character development, but they're classics of their kind."

She said nothing. I figured I knew what she was thinking about, and I was right.

"Are you *sure* you want to take on that woman with the orange hair?"

"I don't think I've got any choice. I think I can either take her on or sit around until she comes after me."

"So if you just returned the money, she wouldn't—" She broke off, rolled onto her back and put her arm over her eyes to shut out the room. She said, "I don't know."

"About what."

"Any of it. I don't know whether you shouldn't just try to find a way not to come up against that woman, and I don't know whether Francie, even if she seems pretty smart, can really erase your tracks out of New Jersey. I don't even know whether you can get in and out of that house in one piece."

I pushed back from the table and got up, just to move a little. "To take the points one at a time, I think if I try to give the Bride of Plastic Man her money back she's going to figure I have the doohickey and come after me with guns. As far as Francie is concerned, all we're doing is looking at potential plans. And getting in and out of houses is what I do."

She put the heels of her hands to her eyes and kept them there for a moment. Then she rolled back onto her left side and said, "In case I'm not making myself completely clear, I'm *worried* about you. I'm worried about how I would handle it if anything—anything bad—were to happen to you. I'm not sure I could survive losing you."

I said, "Oh."

"You think you're immortal."

"Not to start an argument, and not to downplay the way I feel about what you just said, but if I thought I were immortal I would have been dead a long time ago."

"Well," she said, "I'm glad you're not."

"Me, too," I said. "I would have missed this room."

She said, "Oh, fuck you."

"But you mean that in a good way."

"Of course I do, you idiot. Well, if you're going to take her on, we might as well talk it over. I do have some survival experience, stuff you don't even know yet. What's your plan?"

"It hasn't actually evolved to *plan* status yet."

"That's not exactly what I wanted to—"

She broke off because I'd gotten up, and she must have read my expression because she said, "Don't touch me until you've washed the grease off your hands."

"I was going to give you a chance to lick it off. I mean, considering the way you went after all that fat."

She pushed herself to a sitting position. "If I do lick it off, will you *bother* me?"

"Absolutely."

"Well, trot that grease over here. Something about this place just gets the old hormones pumping. But there's a condition."

Almost close enough to touch her, I wagged my index finger at her and said, "A mere stumble on the path to paradise, a faded stop sign I can blow through, a ripple on the surface of—"

"As much as I usually love to hear you talk, shut up. There's a time and a place for everything."

She put the greasy finger in her mouth, and I shut up.

17
Gateway to Stardom

Despite my recent lack of sleep, I snapped bolt upright at the sound of the mouse's xylophone, which was what my dream had turned it into, a sort of all-rodent version of the Modern Jazz Quartet with a xylophone made of tiny bones played by a mouse wearing white gloves and sunglasses. But the sound continued after I opened my eyes, and once I had pushed through a moment of yawning incomprehension the mice turned into John Prine and I saw my phone blinking on the table where the remains of the steak still sat, silhouetted against what, given the fuchsia tint of the light outside, looked like a hundred Mickey Mouses waving for rescue from the ninth circle of Hell, the Mouse Inferno.

Ronnie said something to someone in whatever dimension she was in. It sounded like *cantaloupe* or, I suppose, *can't elope*. I cast a mental vote in favor of melon and got out of bed.

Unknown number and a text: LOSING MY PATIENCE.

I said out loud, "We *do* have something in common." I read the text again, for no reason except that I still had one foot in the Land of Nod. Nope, I hadn't missed anything; she was losing her patience. Just for the hell of it, I brought up Anime's app and found myself looking down the entry hall toward the door of our apartment. The light all came from the left side of the screen, which was as it should have been; I'd left two table lamps burning in the living room.

I pulled the chair to the table, pushed the cold meat a little farther away, and watched my own front door on the bright little screen. The experience was unusual without being interesting, and after a minute or two I went to Facebook and read the latest creative slagging of the president, and a bunch of people making irate complaints about spoilers in some TV show with dragons in it, and then, with a yawn that was loud enough to make Ronnie say, "What?" in her sleep, I went to my email.

There he was: Jake. I looked at the time on the message: 4:20 A.M. About twelve minutes ago. Whatever he and Laney Profitt had been doing, it hadn't made him sleepy. The message read, *Have info. $1500 cash.*

Like an idiot, I emailed him back, *How could it possibly be $1500?*

My phone sang. It said *Jake*, and I thought there should be a nightmare font a phone's user can assign to people he doesn't want to talk to.

"Because you're my friend," he said when I picked it up.

I said, "Do you know what time it is?"

"I've got it," he said, "the name you wanted. I thought this was important to you."

"At this hour? And fifteen hundred dollars' worth of important?"

"Sliding scales," he said. "Every value has its place on a sliding scale. And night is the same as day, except it's darker and I look better."

Ronnie sat up and surveyed the room. "Damn," she said. "I hoped this place was a nightmare."

Jake said, "You got a girl there?"

"How much would it be if you weren't my friend?"

"A price far above rubies." He inhaled sharply, with the kind of decisive vigor that usually means it's not for the purpose of respiration.

"The Book of Proverbs?" I said.

"Practically the only book in the Bible no one's tried to make a movie out of. You know why?"

"Too episodic."

"Smartass," he said. "So come over. You're awake. As awake as you get, anyway."

"Who *is* it?" Ronnie said.

"It's Mister Movie."

"What?" Jake said.

"Tell him to go to bed," Ronnie said.

"Mortals go to bed," Jake said. "So look, I want fifteen hundred now. It's not that I'm broke, it's that I no longer keep cash around. *Now*, as in within thirty minutes. Otherwise, you can go whistle for your name because I'll be asleep most of tomorrow. And it will cost more tomorrow, too."

I said, "Okay."

Jake said, "Make it two thousand."

I hung up. Ronnie was looking at me questioningly, and I raised a finger. The phone rang.

I said into it, "You were saying?"

"You can't get a *yes* if you don't ask the question," Jake said. "Fifteen. But thirty minutes. I'm not kidding."

"Fine." I disconnected. To Ronnie, I said, "I'm contributing to the delinquency of a senior citizen. Good thing I've got the stash from the Bride of Plastic Man."

Outside, it was definitely nighttown. The world felt abandoned and thick with sleep, and the gleam of my headlights
shifted the colors in front of me toward the yellowish area
of the spectrum, the colors I associate with bruising and
decay. The clouds had cleared but the moon was mostly
a memory, an icy curl as thin as an eyelash, far, far to
the West as it lowered itself toward the Pacific. The stars
are never much in Los Angeles, but with the moon on its
way out they stippled the sky in an orderly, domesticated
fashion as though they weren't all lethal, perpetual atomic
meltdowns burning their way toward us across billions
of miles. They disappeared deferentially near the horizon,
where the city lights absorbed their glow.

Traffic was as light as one would expect, so it was just a
couple of long straight hops and an uphill climb from the
cheap kitsch of Minnie's Mouse House to the expensive
kitsch of Jake's transplanted chateau. The valley's lights
in the rearview mirror signaled me to turn around and go
back as I took the curves up Coldwater Canyon.

In my headlights, Jake's fancy foreign foliage looked
even rattier than it had that afternoon. When I got up
to the top, I found Profitt's old Beamer angled carelessly
across the circle with the driver's door still open. The inside
light was out, so I figured Laney might have some trouble
starting it in the morning. The thought was accompanied
by a twinge of sympathy at the idea of anybody wanting
to leave Jake's place and not being able to.

I went to the door and lifted the five-pound iron
knocker, but it was pulled out of my hand as the door was
yanked open.

Laney Profitt looked like she had spent the evening in
a clothes dryer. Her hair was in her eyes, she was missing

one shoe, and her clothes were disheveled in a way that suggested they had been repeatedly ripped off and rebuttoned wrong. The thick mascara on her left eye had been smudged into a diagonal line that took off at a jaunty angle in the direction of her hairline. She looked ten years older than she had nine hours ago. I could have stood behind her in a supermarket line for half an hour without recognizing the woman I'd enjoyed so much on TV.

"Shit," she said, obviously expecting someone else. "He's waiting." She turned her back and went down the hallway, walking like someone who hurt.

"Waiting is good for him," I said, following her down the hall. "It builds character." Somewhere inside me there's a tiny alter ego that goes messianic in a snap when I encounter certain kinds of self-induced tragedy. He's rarely greeted warmly when I let him out to play, so I've learned to keep him under control.

"That's my boy," Jake bellowed from the sunken room with a ghastly attempt at heartiness. "He comes on the wings of the wind."

"Sounds messy," Laney said, drifting to her right to take the steps down.

I stopped on the top step. The place looked like giant babies had been wrestling each other. The lights were off, so the only illumination came from the hallways that opened into the room on either side. The armchair I usually sat in was on its side and Jake's buttery throne was askew, two or three yards from its usual place. Pieces of wood, some of them substantial, littered the floor in the approximate area of the fireplace as though they'd had a contest to see who could miss it by the widest margin. Wads of what looked like toilet paper were crumpled here and there. On an almost never-used couch against the wall on the side of the room opposite the fireplace were two small, white-streaked mirrors and a glass pipe, caked inside with residue that had achieved the shade of brown I used to see in the filter of a cigarette that I'd smoked to the point where I burned my fingers. The place smelled too sweet, like overripe melon, and the heat was pumping. The fire, though, was just a few sullen coals.

Jake was sprawled on the stairs across the room. He looked like he might have fallen anywhere from a minute to an hour ago and hadn't yet made his mind about getting up.

I asked Laney Profitt, "Is he okay?"

"Talk to him directly," she said. "He can hear." She went to the couch in the center of the wall to my right, moved a mirror aside, and sat, bending forward so sharply her head was almost between her knees.

I said to her, "Well, then, how about *you*? Are you okay?"

She didn't straighten up. "Ask him," she said. "It's his stuff."

"See?" Jake said. "One way or another, you gotta talk to me."

My messianic alter ego shoved me aside long enough to say, "Jake. You've got to get hold of yourself."

"Don't start," he said. "You got it?"

I said, "Do you?"

"Sure, sure." He fished in the pocket of his safari shirt and then fished in a different pocket. "Fucking shirt," he said. "More pockets than a pool table. Ah-*ha*." He brought out a little piece of paper, obviously torn from a larger one. "Let's trade."

"Name?" I said. "Address? Company name? Phone number?"

"Come on, come on, come on." He waved the paper in the air. "The old swapperoo. I'm sure you've got someplace you want to go."

"Almost anyplace," I said. I didn't want to go into that room.

"Well, it's not going to come to you," Jake said. "Come on, have pity on an old man and bring it over here. Move it."

I fished the money out of the pocket of my jeans and counted it in front of him. "Fifteen hundred-dollar bills, okay? Want me to do it again?"

He said, "Don't be an asshole. Just get over here." He tugged up at the piece of paper like someone testing resistance on a fishing line, and I went.

I tilted the paper to the light coming in through the hall and read, in a fine, slanting Spencerian hand,

Althea Beckwell-Stoddard

The Beckwell-Stoddard Agency

Your Gateway to Stardom

Then an address in a not-very fashionable area of North Hollywood and a phone number.

I said, "Whose handwriting is this?"

"Mine," Profitt said without looking up. "Centuries of nuns." She sneezed. "You know why nuns wear black and white? Because they're the whole keyboard of misery."

"She's a shuck," Jake said. "Not Laney, but that broad. That's what my guy says. On the side, runs a school for young thespians, charges their parents a fortune, teaches kids how to walk using one foot after another instead of hopping like kangaroos, takes a markup on head shots, takes a markup on everything, does a little 'screen test' at a markup of about a thousand percent. Then, when the kids get to be fourteen, fifteen, she cuts them loose."

"Well," I said, "thanks."

"Other side of the page," Jake said. "Names of two of the kids, the girl and one of the boys."

I turned it over. "My, my. A bonus."

Laney Profitt straightened and fell back against the couch with the heavy sigh of someone whose stimulant of choice has ceased to amuse. "So you can go now."

"Gee," I said. "I guess I can. Hope you guys don't overdo it."

Profitt snorted. I guessed it was a laugh.

"See you, Jake," I said. I turned around and went back down the hall and out the heavy front door. The world was just perceptibly brighter than it had been when I came in, daylight slipping the thin edge of the wedge beneath the darkness.

Silhouetted on the other side of Laney's dead BMW was a car that hadn't been there when I arrived, a low, mean-looking Maserati that might have been red. I could see the silhouette of someone behind the wheel, but he or she didn't bother to track me as I crossed the circle, just sat staring dead ahead. I started my car, did a three-point to turn it around, and as I began to drop down the driveway the light came on in the Maserati and the door opened. I couldn't see much of whoever got out, but I figured it was probably someone who knew a lot of movie stars.

18
Why, Miss Peabody, You're Beautiful

One night a million years ago, or so it seemed—I was seventeen—Herbie Mott caught me idly casing a house he planned to burglarize. Although I was a rank amateur who had never broken into anything riskier than a box of cookies, Herbie didn't chase me off, even if he did briefly threaten me with a squirt gun. Instead of giving me the boot, he deputized me to stand lookout. This was before cell phones were omnipresent, so I was told simply to park, facing out, at the mouth of the circle on which the house sat and, if someone entered it, honk twice and then get the hell out of there. He had confounded my stereotypes about crooks by paying me $500 in advance, trusting that I wouldn't just peel off into the night the minute he was inside the house.

About forty minutes later, he came out with a satisfied expression and a bag of swag, gesturing me to follow as he climbed into his car. He led me down the hill to an all-night Du-par's coffee shop a few blocks away. There, in a booth he claimed as though he'd owned it for years, he gave me the first of what was to be a series of seminars on The Art of the Steal. It was, so to speak, my baptism, and the seminars evolved over almost eight years into a transfer of a lifetime of both knowledge and philosophy, including a set of ethics designed to allow the sensitive burglar to go to sleep at night. Foremost among those was *never take the best thing they own.* It might not sound like much to you, but I'd seized the line as a lifetime maxim and it had spared me a good many guilty sleepless nights. Even crooks, at least the ones who aren't sociopaths, have a conscience.

Actually, some of the sociopaths I know are all right, too; Eaglet, who would probably shoot a troupe of Girl Scouts in full uniform if the price were right, seemed to love Ting Ting and had been surprisingly sympathetic to Anime. I'd gotten along with a couple of other hitters, too, although it would have been nice to have been certain, each time I saw them, that they hadn't just accepted a contract to turn me into fertilizer.

Du-par's, which has been pouring bad coffee and serving so-so food since the 1930s, used to be all over the place, but tastes, thank heaven, change. One doesn't want to go to one's parents' favorite restaurant, and the management had fiercely guarded against anything that could be called hip, so the customer base had aged and died, and the chain had dwindled to four or five outlets that weren't visually interesting enough even to qualify as retro. What they had, mainly, was that the surviving restaurants had been in the same locations for genera-tions and they were open twenty-four hours a day. My personal Du-par's, the one in which Herbie initiated me into the art of burglary, was right on Ventura Boulevard, only a couple of blocks from where Coldwater emptied itself into the valley, and I headed for it so automatically that I was slightly surprised to find myself in the parking lot. Since I was there, I went in, perhaps thinking I might commune with Herbie's spirit.

I was so tired that the restaurant floor seemed to pitch beneath my feet, and the place was bright enough to feel like a personal insult after the slowly warming gray of the early morning. What I always thought of as *Herbie's booth* was full up with a party of—as the gods of cheap irony would have it—cops. Three beefy males and a relatively wispy female, the female practically driven into the wall by an epidemic of manspreading. On the other hand, she was the one who was talking, and the three beefers seemed to be listening.

I could almost hear Herbie saying dismissively, "Female cops." Herbie wasn't much bigger on change than DuPar's was.

A couple of protect-and-serve antennae went up as I passed, prompting glances from the woman and the porkiest of the men, but it might have been simple curiosity. This was definitely the cigarette-butt end of the night, and cops on the late shift are always interested in the people who share the dark hours with them. I nodded as I went past, and the porkiest one nodded back. I skipped the booth behind theirs and slid into the next, and then I closed my eyes and rested my face in the palms of my hands and felt the restaurant rock on the swells of my exhaustion.

I don't know how long I held the pose, but I suddenly became aware that someone had spoken to me and that she was clearing her throat to give it another try. I opened my eyes, and there was my waitress, a night bird if I ever saw one: a 1960s beatnik, or perhaps an homage to Nico in the Velvet Underground, with enough eyeliner to stripe a zebra, hair so straight that it might have been ironed falling to mid-back, the fashionably starved look that amphetamines once made so easy to attain, and, in a nod to the twenty-first century, what seemed to be an entire graphic novel tattooed on her forearms and neck.

She said it again. "Help you?"

"Is it that obvious?" I rubbed my eyes. "Yeah, thanks. Coffee, two cups, black, and what are the pies?"

"You expecting somebody?"

"No. I drink coffee with both hands."

"See, here's the thing," she said. She leaned forward, put a hand on the appropriate hip, lowered her voice, and glanced at the cops. The two male ones facing us were already looking at her. "I don't know, maybe you're made of money or something, but you order two cups, I gotta charge you for two cups. You order one cup and I promise to keep it filled, it costs you half as much, and you can switch hands whenever you want. Apple and lemon meringue."

I glanced at her name tag. It said *Glinda*. I said, "Witch of the north part of Oz?"

"*Everybody* gets it wrong," she said. "The south. I'm the leader of the Quadlings, I am attended by fifty beautiful maidens—in the traditional sense of the word—and protected by a large army of female warriors. It's *heaven*." She rolled up her already-short left sleeve and I saw a line of women wearing armor and holding spears at various martial angles.

I said, "Do you need a recruit?"

"Pffff," she said. "You wish. Go for the lemon meringue. The apple has been here since the fruit was picked."

"Thanks. You don't hear much about the Quadlings these days."

"We keep a low profile," she said, turning away. There was a period, during my long development into a responsible adult male, when I was known to glance appropriately at the female *derriere* from time to time, so glancing at hers was sheer force of habit. I won't objectify her by describing it.

"Hey, Glin," the porkiest cop said, waving her over.

I thought *Glin*, and pulled out my $1500 piece of paper. There, in Laney's throwback parochial-schoolgirl script, was the information on the hyphenated Ms. Beckwell-Stoddard. Hadn't seen the name Althea in a while, but the whole thing, hyphen and all, felt like a Gatsbyesque invention masking something much less glamorous, something along the lines of Ethel Frimp.

Your gateway to stardom. A particularly unpleasant racket, pitching people who, like most parents, thought their children were exceptional, milking them for everything she could get, and then, as Jake had said, cutting them loose, poorer and disillusioned, with the kids probably doubting, possibly for the first time, their talent and their beauty or *whatever* it was that they hoped made them special, different from everybody else.

What kind of person could do that to family after family, child after child?

I suddenly found myself thinking about three dark women—dark, at least, in the way the word is commonly used to describe a personality: Althea Beckwell-Stoddard, Itsy Winkle, and the Bride of Plastic Man. The landscape was littered with dark females. Perhaps the least remembered of the major Greek deities was the amazingly named Nyx, one of only two beings to be born directly from the very first form of creation, Chaos. (The other was her

brother, Erebus, who was darkness itself.) At first Nyx
played the ingénue: she created light, for one thing. But
either she soured over time or she let all that primal power
go to her head, turning out one downer after another—
pain, death, doom, jealousy, retribution, strife, a whole
bouquet of miseries, everything except adolescent acne
and singing out of tune. (In fairness, she also came up with
friendship.) By 700 BC, she had also become the mother
of the goddess Hemera, who personified day, and that
relationship locked her into a sort of permanent rotation,
fighting Hemera to a standstill at the close of every day
until she could take over as night and, in turn, losing a
struggle each morning to her niece, Ushas, the dawn. Sort
of musical chairs, but with light.

The Greeks knew that there was no act so foul that
only a male could perform it. Beginning with Nyx, they
gave the female principle full honors in the world's vile
curriculum. Still, personally, I thought, three at the same
time was a bit much.

I turned the scrap of paper over and read *Hannah Sanders* and *Danny Wynn,* so I had names for two of the three
kids who'd been dragged into McDonald's. I brought
Ronnie's pictures up on my phone. Hannah Sanders,
whom the Bride of Plastic Man had called Dorothy, was
a gamine with a smile that might suggest trouble in the
future, and the name *Danny Wynn* seemed to fit one of
the boys better than the other, a kind of puggish, thick-
featured kid, probably, I thought, a juvenile character
actor who, if he worked at all, probably specialized in
"hero's funny-looking friend" roles, with a character
name like "Butch" or "Slugger."

I went to the Web and entered Danny's name. There

were a dozen guys named Danny Wynn, but there he was, the kid I'd pegged as a Danny. If the photos were representative of the quality of Ms. Beckwell-Stoddard's work, the photographer was lucky to be paid at all. In one, Danny had his baseball cap on sideways, implying, I suppose, comic skills; and in another he had a black eye that had obviously been drawn on by an unskilled and shaky thumb. There were others, but I couldn't force myself to look at them.

"Just wave for more," someone said, and I looked up to see Glinda sliding a cup of coffee across the table. Her forearm was decorated with a furious man with a pair of ram's horns emerging from an aggressive snarl of hair. He looked like no one had consulted him. "Black, no sugar, right?"

I said, "Right."

"We witches can tell," she said. "Pie on the way."

I thanked her, but she was already in retreat, and I was surprised to see that several of the tables had filled up and that the windows had gone the charmless gray of an aircraft carrier. The coffee wasn't very good, but it was strong.

Hannah Sanders had her own website, and she photographed much better than poor Danny had, even posing for someone with no talent at all. She was more conventional as child actors go, a modestly pretty and obviously energetic little girl with a really exceptional smile. Even in Ms. Beckwell-Stoddard's miserable photographs you could sense a forceful character, and I suddenly remembered her bargaining unshakably for Fashion Barbie. *A kid who gets her way*, I thought. On the scanty evidence available, she seemed to have a brighter future than Danny.

Okay, time to take a look at the dragon.

The Beckwell-Stoddard Agency proclaimed itself "Hollywood's Finest Nursery of Young Talent," the words surrounded by pictures of kids from, say, five to fourteen. The sample skewed moderately female and heavily Caucasian, with a few Hispanics and Asians mixed in, perhaps to slow the eye as it hurried across the wretched photography. Only one African American child, a handsome pre-teen of eleven or so who seemed to be daring the camera to do him justice. I spent some time going through the talent but couldn't find the other boy I'd seen in McDonald's.

Althea Beckwell-Stoddard had been photographed—by someone who knew what he was doing—sitting on the corner of a big white desk, an apparent pillar of rectitude if you skipped the almost accidentally displayed legs. She wore expensive, up-tilted wireless glasses, her hair was under martial law, and her mouth was pursed like someone who's trying to master French vowels. Late thirties, I guessed. In a movie of a certain vintage she would have been called "Miss Peabody" or something similarly stultifying until the lead actor pulled off her glasses, messed up her hair, and said, "Why, Miss Peabody—you're beautiful."

"That's a mean-looking woman," Glinda said, coffee pot in hand. "Whoops. Hope you're not engaged to her."

"No," I said as she poured. "I've never met her. But I think you're right, I think she's probably a wretched piece of work."

"Most guys," she said, "you could know them for years and they'd never use the word *wretched*. What do you do?"

"I'm in property reallocation."

The hand went to the hip again. "Yeah? You're work-ing at this hour?"

"You never know when a really prime opportunity for reallocation will arise. What about you?"

"Well, *this*, obviously." She used the hand with the cof-feepot in it to create a semicircle that took in most of the restaurant, and then she put the pot on the table. "But when I'm off, I work on my sorcery."

"How's it coming?"

"The transubstantiation of matter," she said, "is a bitch. Whoops, forgot your pie."

"I thought transubstantiation was a religious ritual."

"Where do you think magic came from?" One of the cops pounded the table and held up a fan of money, and Glinda said, "Striking it rich here," and went to the table.

I figured I had some time before she'd be back with the pie, and I used it to research child labor laws in California. When I had what I needed, I called Louie. It wasn't quite seven and Louie often said he didn't even turn over in bed before eight, but I knew his voicemail would pick up around the clock. When it did, I said, "It's me. I need a few business cards that have to look right, so get Benny, okay? I'm Dwight Sykes again, and this time I work for the State Department of Industrial Relations, the Division of Labor Standards Enforcement. The seal is online, and you can use the picture of me from the Sykes driver's license. In fact have Benny make another copy of the license, too. Mine is in a storage unit halfway to Pasadena. By noon today, will that be a problem? Say hi to Alice."

I put the phone down and tapped it to bring Ms. Beck-well-Stoddard's bright, hard, equivocal face back on the screen. I spent a minute trying out opening lines, looking for the right tone, and mapping out the likely flow of the meeting. Then I spent a couple of minutes trying to figure out which string I should pull when I was through with this one. There were a lot of them, but some would lead nowhere and some others would probably snap. Maybe Louie would have something new by this afternoon.

Glinda had apparently forgotten my pie but she'd compensated by leaving the coffeepot on the table. I poured myself another cup and asked myself whether it was worthwhile to try to get to sleep for an hour, hour and a half before going with Ronnie to the meeting with Francie DuBois. It was probably the lack of sleep, but suddenly the whole errand sounded improbable, even impossible. I felt once again like the boasting boy I used to be before I finally stopped trying to impress my father. I was, it seemed at that moment, just wasting everyone's time and possibly putting myself into a situation that could break Ronnie's heart and kill me, all in a very condensed minute or two.

Maybe an hour's sleep, I thought, and then remembered where I'd be doing it, all those mouse tails on the carpet. A wave of something close to despair swept over me and I had one of those moments when my entire life felt like a turned-out pocket, empty at last, once and for all.

I skipped the pie, put a ten on the table for Glinda, and went out into the chilly-looking dawn.

19

Are There Dogs?

Since the room key had a laminated Mickey Mouse hanging from it, it wasn't hard to locate it in my pocket. I slipped it into the lock as quietly as possible and eased the door slowly open.

The bed was empty.

For a moment, I was gripped, even shaken, by one of the most complex reactions of my life, a potpourri of the kinds of things you might throw into a mental blender to whip up a schizophrenia smoothie: abandonment, fear that someone had taken her, a sudden sensation that I was being watched, and, least credible of all, a dawning relief about not having to go into that walled mansion in New Jersey.

Then I heard the toilet flush.

I imagined her opening the bathroom door, wrapped in the almost meditative sense of privacy that usually accompanies our interactions with the toilet, and suddenly seeing a man silhouetted in the doorway. I stepped back and pulled the door closed again. Then I counted to five and knocked, saying "Ronnie?"

"Hark," she said inside the room, sounding very awake. "'Tis the nightingale."

"*No*, Juliet," I said. "It's the lark. You keep getting it wrong." I reached for the door, but she pulled it open and gave me a smile that wiped away most of the grime and residue of the night.

She was all dressed up in a pair of briefs with bluebirds on them and a sleeveless T-shirt. "You're lucky," she said in a blast of Pepsodent. "I'm *so* minty." She put her arms around me and kissed me, and quite a lot of the emotional sewage I'd been fighting my way through since the coffee shop got swept aside, under furniture and into dark corners, where it would patiently await its next opportunity. "Are you hungry?"

"I can imagine a point at which I might be. A shower would help."

She mimed hitting her forehead with the palm of her hand, "Oh, that's right, you've been up all night. Tell you what. You clean up and I'll go get us something with no nutritional value. Croissants, maybe. There's a nice French bakery a couple of streets away. I ate there on the way to Taylor's last night and on the way back, too. Sound good?"

I said, "Boy, you really are minty."

"I smell good without this stuff, too," she said. "Some do, some don't." She went to the room's tiny closet, the hinge of which squeaked like a mouse, and opened the door. "You want me to pull anything in particular out of the suitcase?"

"I don't even know what's in it."

"You go get wet. It'll be a surprise."

I went into the bathroom and started the ritual of rebirth with soap and hot water. My razor was still in the suitcase and I didn't want to look like I was spying on

Ronnie as she assembled my outfit for the day, so I figured I'd go for the one-time cutting-edge *bristly* look. If she'd packed a pair of slip-ons, I'd wear them without socks. Maybe stop somewhere and buy a pipe. Raise an eyebrow from time to time. Mr. Hip Anachronism.

In the shower I found myself thinking about Anime and Lilli. My daughter, Rina, who was the same age as they, had a friend who had come through an eating disorder, and a couple more who were still struggling. Maybe she'd have something to suggest. I also asked myself whether I should set up some protection for Rina and my ex-wife, Kathy, by having their house baby-sat by either Eaglet or Debbie Halstead, a tee-tiny, button-nosed hitter whose specialty was getting friendly enough with guys to shoot them through the ear. Debbie once saved my life with a single long-range shot and, I'd been told, had briefly gone kind of sweet on me, so maybe Eaglet was a better idea, although either of them could be trusted to spot and repel unfriendly incoming. A woman sitting alone in a car attracts less attention than a man, which just shows you how dangerous an assumption can be. Maybe I'd hire both of them, switching off in twelve-hour slots around the clock. I had no idea how good the Bride of Plastic Man's research actually was.

I turned off the water, found a towel that was thin enough get a sunburn through, and tried to dry my hair. Then I wrung the towel out over the tub and used it to move around the water on my skin. As I wrung it out a second time, I made a decision: move to the Sheraton at Universal City. As someone who had endured some of the worst motels since Norman Bates closed up shop, I felt an obscure little pang of regret. A growing inability to endure discomfort, I'd always thought, was one of the sure signs of advancing age. Bumming around Europe, carrying your stuff on your back, thumbing rides, and sleeping in cheap fleabags is *romantic* when you're young. Doing it when you're old is just sad.

Making lists in my head, I heard the door close behind Ronnie on her way out, so I dripped my way into the room she had just vacated and looked at the phone. Still early enough to get Rina at home. I dried my hands on the bedspread's little mice feet and punched up the number.

Kathy answered. "Where in the world have you been? We've been so *worried* about you." It wasn't anywhere near as affectionate as it sounded.

"I'm sorry, I'm sorry. I really am. It's been a difficult time." I picked up the greasy steak plate and toted it across the room. Staying out of sight behind the door, I put it just outside. Either the staff would get it or the mice would.

Kathy said, "You've chosen a difficult life. There, I've said that, and I can let up on you. Are you okay?"

"Yeah, so far. There are clouds on the horizon, though." I wiped the grease on my thighs, figuring I could rub it in later, like lotion.

"Into every life," she said, "a little rain—"

"I thought you were letting up."

"Sorry," she said. "How's Ronnie?"

Kathy and Ronnie actually liked each other, which was more than I can say about me and any of the men Kathy had seen since we split up. Another thing I didn't like, to return to the present for a moment, was the shirt Ronnie had picked out, a Christmas gift from Kathy, who had been trying for years to nudge me toward the Junior Executive school of dress. Faced with the possibility of rejecting, on some obscure level, both of the women I loved, I put the shirt on. Ah, romance.

"Ronnie is great," I said. Kathy didn't know anything about New Jersey and probably wouldn't until the issue was resolved. One way or the other. "She'd like to get together sometime soon."

"When you're out of mortal danger. It's not that I don't worry about you, I'd just like to keep Rina out of the line of fire. I suppose you want to talk to her."

"I do. I need to ask her something about some kids her age." Looking down, I saw that I had put a greasy thumbprint on the shirt, which gave me an excuse to wear something else.

"You mean those two? Are they all right? Anime and, and—"

"Lilli. It's Lilli who's the problem." I opened the closet door. "She's getting kind of weird about eating."

"Poor baby. We know all about that. Hang on."

While I hung on, I abandoned the closet and used the wet towel to get the rest of the grease off of my hand. Then I went back to find a different shirt.

"Hey," Rina said. "The vanishing American."

"How are you, sweetie? How's Tyrone?"

"I'm okay," she said, "and Tyrone is better than I deserve."

"Not in my opinion. *Nobody* is better than you—"

"My self-esteem is fine, Dad, and I've got to get moving. School plows right ahead without me if I'm not there. And I've learned to accept that. I guess you'd call it a kind of maturity. Are you proud of—"

I said, "Thought you were in a hurry."

"Only when *you're* talking. So?"

I gave her the short version, skipping the counseling session with a hit-woman. There was a pause.

"Well," she began, "Tiffany—"

"Tell me you don't *actually* know someone named—"

"Three, actually. You snob. There are whole bouquets of girls named Tiffany now. Anyway, Tiffany—*one* of my Tiffanys—went through it and she can talk about it. Are you thinking that I should go see them? We, I mean, me and Tiffany?"

I said, "Me and Tiffany? *Me and Tiffany* should go—"

"I have an English teacher already. Yes or no?"

"Yes. But I think I'd better bounce it off Anime first. Will you see, uhh, Tiffany today?"

"Yes, you elitist. In two classes." There was a pause, and then she said, not to me but to someone in another room, "Just a minute."

"Gotta go, huh?"

"Yeah. I'll talk to Tiff. What then?"

"Tell you after I check in with Anime. Love you."

"Yeah," she said. "Me, too."

She hung up and I stood there, still wet and tired but feeling much better. My daughter always did that to me. Even the shirt looked nicer. I took it into the bathroom, got one of the microscopic slivers of soap, small enough to have been meant for the mice, and began to scrub at the grease spot.

"Not easy," Francie DuBois said. It was about quarter after ten. We were in an ugly little ten-by-fourteen room with the blinds drawn over the only window, looking at a big, clunky something-pad containing an image of a compound that couldn't decide whether it was a house or a fort. About the size of Xanadu in *Citizen Kane*, but not as warm and welcoming, and surrounded by a stone wall perhaps nine feet tall. The picture was one of a dozen taken from a helicopter that had been hired for just that purpose.

I was beginning to understand why Francie's services cost as much as they did.

"They've cut down all the trees near the wall," I said.

"I thought you'd notice that," Francie said. "Aren't you going to ask if there are dogs?"

"Are there—"

"One of the ways to tell if someone is a burglar," Francie said to Ronnie, "is to show them, or tell them about, a house. If the first or second question is *Are there dogs,* odds are pretty good."

Ronnie nodded. She hadn't said much.

"Well?" I said.

"Yes," Francie said. "But they're lap dogs, little yappers."

"The age-old question," I said. "Which is better, a big dog that will try to kill you silently or a little pincushion that won't shut up?"

Ronnie said to me, "And?"

"It's moot," I said. "Best is cats. Dogs take it personally but cats don't give a shit." The word brought to mind Itsy Winkle's dark living room with its menagerie of stuffed cats. I shook my head to clear it.

Francie's ugly room was a rented office in a building full of rented offices, in the middle of Van Nuys. The building was essentially a chest of drawers, each drawer containing a bunch of offices that were more or less the same as all the other offices. Francie had told us that all twelve of the place's floors were absolutely the same, exactly like hers, and I immediately recognized raw material for a burglar's nightmare in which everything would depend on my going through the right door, and *only* the right door, on my first try.

As Louie had explained it to me, Francie used an office for two, or at most three, clients and then put her stuff in her purse, wiped the place for prints, and moved on to a similar setup miles away. The people from whom she was helping her clients escape were usually heavily armed and short-tempered. This particular office contained a good-size steel desk, three folding chairs, and a lot of linoleum. The only thing on the walls was a big photographic blowup of a piece of wood with the word *Home* stenciled into it in bullet holes. It was, I assumed, Francie's reminder to her clients of why they were sitting here.

From her side of the desk, Francie brushed the screen with her coral-tipped fingers. Suddenly we were looking at a dark world where solid objects were a queasy, semi-fluorescent green, the color range you see in military footage of rocket attacks at night. We were about six feet up and heading smoothly for a wall, but then we turned right and paralleled the wall for twenty or thirty seconds before rising up and over it and dipping down again, into a backyard the size of Pasadena. The camera stopped and hung, motionless as a hummingbird, looking at the yard below.

"Drone," Francie said. "I had to bring in a guy from North Carolina to work the damn thing. Nobody within fifty miles would even think about it."

"That's Eric's charm," Ronnie said. She was barely audible. I looked over at her, and she cleared her throat as though to say something more, but just swallowed and looked down. Francie glanced at her and then at me.

The backyard was formally gardened within an inch of its life, green, glowing flower beds everywhere, foaming up along paving-stone paths that branched and curled like streams on a flood plain. The paths were the brightest things in the image because the stone had retained the largest amount of the day's heat.

"He hates anything random," Ronnie said. She blinked a couple of times, a dead giveaway of tension. "He'd pave the whole place but a realtor told him it would lower the value of the property. He would have paved me if I'd held still long enough."

Probably hearing the strain in Ronnie's voice, Francie pulled the tablet back to her side of the desk and said, "Do you want to take a break, maybe pick it up a little later?"

Ronnie used both index fingers to massage the bridge of her nose. Then she closed her eyes and rubbed them. "No," she said, eyes still closed. "I'll try to keep the drama private."

Francie glanced at me again, and I shrugged. She pushed the tablet back toward us.

"Dog houses," she said as the drone slid over the landscaping. "I'm pretty sure that insubstantial-looking stuff surrounding it is chicken wire, so even if the dogs wanted to rend you with their tiny jaws they probably wouldn't be able to."

"That's just going to make them bark louder," I said.

"He doesn't want them pooping on his nice concrete." Ronnie shook her head and said, "Sorry." Then she said, "Wait. *Stop*. Go back a little."

Francie backed it up, and we were looking at a cluster

of kid stuff: two swings, what might have been a sandbox, a play house. Ronnie's index finger followed the path of something straight and diagonal, "A teeter-totter," Ronnie said. "What does that suggest?"

Shaking her head, Francie said, "I don't know, what?"

I sat forward. "That there are two kids," I said. "What's a solo kid going to do with a teeter-totter? Sit on one end for a while and then go sit on the other?"

"Maybe it was part of a playground set," Ronnie said between her teeth. "Maybe that was cheaper than buying them one piece at a time. If there's any fault Eric missed out on, it's not being cheap."

"But on the other hand," I said.

We all sat there. The room was made even smaller by the nose-clogging scent of imitation pine, pseudo-fresh air from a can. The only thing in its favor was that it smelled so little like the real thing that, clearly, no actual pines had been injured in its production. I breathed through my mouth while Francie moved the drone back and forth, not looking for anything, just dancing in place. Then I said to Francie, "We need more information. If there's another kid, if he's married someone who has one, or he rents one by the week, whatever it is, we need to know. This opens up whole avenues of complication, maybe even tragedy."

Francie nodded. "I'll see what I can—"

"Is there someone *you* can talk to?" I asked Ronnie. "Someone who might know something about him?"

"Maybe. I don't know. I'm not sure I can trust . . . I might get traced."

"That's easy," Francie said. "Hop a plane to Iowa City or someplace else you'll never go again, buy a burner phone there, make the call, drown the phone in a public toilet, and fly back home."

I said to Ronnie, "You don't think you can trust her? Him?"

"Her." She tilted her head back and turned it from side to side, probably trying to loosen muscle tension. "I have no idea. Things change all the time back there. It's like a Medici court."

Francie got up. She was wearing a coral blouse that picked up the blush undertones of her dark skin and she'd done something loose and spiraling to her hair. Wherever she was, she was an automatic finalist in the contest for the title of best-looking person in her zip code. When I'd first met her, two or three months earlier—when she'd taken a timely shot at a guy who was following me in a car—I'd been slightly overwhelmed by her intelligence and the physical package it was wrapped in. I'd taken her to dinner and kept that part of the evening secret from Ronnie, the only time I'd ever done that. I could sense Ronnie looking at me now, as I looked at Francie. I felt my face heat up.

Francie said, "I'll put things on hold until we know something. No point in spending money on false assumptions." She went to the wall and took down the HOME picture. "When you're ready to start again, give me a call."

Ronnie said, "Your hair is so beautiful. Does it have a name, the way you do it?"

"It's a Senegalese twist," Francie said. "Not as tight or as much work as a box weave, which look great but you gotta stay after it all the time and it's murder to sleep on. This is, I don't know, softer. A little less upkeep."

"It's gorgeous," Ronnie said.

"Thanks," Francie said, "It's lower maintenance than some of the alternatives." She opened the desk's top drawer and took out a big leather purse and a couple of manila folders. She slipped the whatever-pad into the purse and put the folders on top of the picture. Then, from the purse, she pulled a package of alcohol wipes and went to work on the surface of the desk. The pine scent was so bad that the alcohol was a relief. "We're done here," she said to me. "Next time it'll be a place in Hollywood. Probably. Got a view and everything."

Passing me to open the door for us, using the hand with the wipe in it, she slowed, looking at my chest. She said, "Do you know you've got a spot on your shirt?"

20

Yousies-Mesies

Loose ends.

It wasn't even eleven yet, so I couldn't swing past Louie's to get the business card and driver's license, which would be ready at noon. Or, more realistically, a little past one, crooks being not much more obedient to the clock than they are to life's other little strictures. It seemed to me there were a million things I could be doing, but I couldn't think of any of them. Somewhere in my mind was a recurring image of Lumia, walking away under a series of overhead spotlights that grew dimmer as she receded. She was a little smaller at each pool of light, looking back from time to time as though all I had to do was call her, and she'd turn around and come back, with her prematurely gray hair and her silly name and her hiccups.

I could have called her back before she got into that car.

I must have looked a little lost because Ronnie said, "Knock, knock."

"Sorry," I said. We were on the sidewalk, only a few yards from the office building Francie had just vacated. The car was a couple of blocks away, in front of a meter I had packed with quarters, thinking we'd be an hour or more. I started walking. "I haven't had much sleep."

"She's an attractive woman," Ronnie said. "Francie, I mean."

"You've met her before," I said, feeling the side-step in the reply.

"But this was the first time I really looked at her. She likes you, you know."

"She likes you, too."

"Don't be silly. I'm not accusing you of anything. I suppose I could even congratulate myself, the guy who loves me is attractive to other women, even knockouts."

"Sounds like a two-edged sword to me."

"Yes," she said. "Doesn't it."

I stopped walking, so she had to stop, too. When we were looking at each other, I said, "You don't have to worry about me."

She blinked as though I'd made a sudden move toward her face. "I do, though. I worry about you all the time."

"Well, it's a waste of energy."

"This may not sound like much of a compliment," she said, "but I feel like I've missed every lifeline anyone ever threw me. Or maybe they threw them too far away for me to get to them. Maybe they did it on purpose, I don't know. So I guess what I'm saying is that I worry about you because I love you and also because I need you so much right now." She took the fabric of my shirt in her fists and pressed her forehead against me. Without raising her face to mine, she said, "It's a really, really shitty feeling because it confuses two things, how much I love you and how much I need you until Eric is here. And how afraid I am that it might go wrong and I'd lose both of you. So, yeah, I go on red alert when I sense that some woman is interested in you."

"All right."

"All right," she said, stepping back. "You've nailed it. It's *all right*."

"What can I say? No, wait. Here's where it is, here's where I am. If I look at that house from every angle and can't find a way in the world to get out once I'm in, I'm not *going* in. I'm going to pass and look for a new way, a better way."

"Fine," she said. "Better than fine. Let's go back to Ratville."

"Let's not. Let's go to the Sheraton. We can get all our stuff packed—"

My phone rang. I didn't recognize the number, but at least it wasn't blocked. I held up one finger and answered it.

"Where are you?" It was a woman's voice.

"Depends on who's asking"

"It's me, you idiot. Itsy. Where are you?"

I pointed to the phone and shrugged, and Ronnie took the front of my shirt between thumb and forefinger and led me, like a two-year-old, down the sidewalk.

"The Valley," I said. "I'm in Van—"

"Do you know where Lumia lived?"

"No.

"Are you *sure* of that?"

"No, actually I'm not. I have a rare neurological disorder called Advanced Address Amnesia. I can never find the same place twice."

"Then you *have* been here."

"No, I have not, and if you have a point, get to it."

"I want you to come over here. Now."

"We all want something," I said. "Don't we?"

"You say you felt something for her. If that's true, get over here."

I put a hand on Ronnie's wrist, and we stopped walking. I took a deep breath and said, "What's the address?"

The address was a two-story apartment house in a charm-free block of Reseda, a flatland area that was once apparently covered from horizon to horizon with the spiky flowers called mignonettes in English and French, and *resedas* in Spanish. Since those flowery halcyon days, the San Fernando Valley has been paved remorselessly, and few places are *more* paved than Reseda, so the *resedas* are, at this point, a meaningless verbal indicator, about as accurate a description of the current reality as "pacific" is of the world's biggest and stormiest ocean.

The Valley had a million apartment houses just like Lumia's. I'd even lived in a couple of them: two stories of Confederate-gray stucco, flat roof, aluminum-frame windows, and an external stairway dead center in the building, leading to the upper floor. Not a moment's thought had been given to charm or grace or even whimsy. Cost-effectiveness, 100; aesthetics, zero. From the spot where I parked the car, I could see that the door of the third apartment to the left of the stairway on the second story was wide open. The day was dull and gloomy, as though it had only partially won the battle with the night and was half-considering throwing the match and turning in early. Making way for Nyx.

Dark as the day was, the open doorway was a rectangle of black. I went quietly up the stairs, stopped at the top, and, from sheer force of habit, listened for a moment. What I heard was a low, unvarying, almost mechanical string of repetitive profanities, the sort of semi-conscious, anti-prayer monologue that comes to someone who expects to be disappointed and furious about everything in life and has been proved right over and over again.

Not much question about who it was. I made a point of scuffing my shoes as I walked. Itsy Winkle didn't seem like someone it would be safe to surprise. Even so, when I got to the door I found myself looking straight into the barrel of the little gun I'd seen the previous night.

And there she towered, peering down at me over the gun, all knees, eyes, elbows, and predatory intent, seeming even bigger in a place that hadn't been built to fit her. When she recognized me, the gun stayed right where it was, aimed at the bridge of my nose.

I said, "Hello to you, too."

She said, and her voice was stretched thin with what sounded like rage, "Did *you* do this?"

Since I'd seen essentially nothing but the gun and those awful eyes, it took me a minute to figure out what *this* was, but then I took in the state of the apartment, which looked like a giant had picked it up and shaken it like a doll's house. The floor was strewn with books, clothes, silverware, and all sorts of other stuff. "You think—" I said. "Why would I—" I stopped. "Right," I said. "If I'd gotten here first, I would have suspected you."

"*Me*," she said. It was more a threat than a question. She even brought the gun up a few inches so she could site down it. Head shots require more precision than gut shots. It was remarkable how steady her hand was.

"Sure," I said. "For the same reason you thought of me. The money she was given to do the job. It had to be *here*."

"You think I'd steal that—"

"Of course I do. Why not? It's not like she's going to get a chance to spend it. Tell you the truth, if I'd known where she lived, I probably *would* have come after it. I'm running up expenses all over the place, researchers, fake documents, will probates, hotel rooms, hired protection, you name it." The gun came down a few inches. I said, "But if I'd been the one who searched this place, *Itsy*, you wouldn't even have known that I was here. None of this mess. And not just professional pride, either. I'd never handle *her* things that way. I'd handle them the way she would have wanted me to."

She let the gun hand drop to her side. "Probably true," she said. "People do say you have skills."

"If I come in there, are you going to shoot me?"

"Am I—no," she said, slipping the gun into one of her leather pockets. "The moment has passed." Her eyebrows contracted to a point where they almost met. "But why do you want to come in?"

"For the *other* reason you called me, if you decided to let me live. They tossed the place, but that doesn't mean they *found* anything. Burglars are better than most people at hiding stuff, and you, if you'll excuse me, are out of practice, so you thought of me. If you mentally reverse engineer a few hundred successful boosts, like I have, you come to realize that the average old bear has no idea how to hide anything."

"And if you find it?"

"Fifty-fifty. Sound okay? I really *am* running up a tab on this, and you know she'd want me to find these assholes."

I needed to get Itsy out of my way. It made me uneasy to have to keep walking around her, where I was within strangling reach of those fingers, while she teetered and creaked above me. So I cleared a space on the couch and searched every cubic inch of it before I asked her to sit down. The first objective was to restore some sort of order, see if I could look at the place as Lumia had. There wasn't much I could do about the pile of hair, dirt, and mystery waste that had been shaken onto the carpet from the bag in the canister vacuum cleaner, but everything else could be sorted and categorized. Step one was to pick up each item that had been tossed and/or ransacked, pat it down, and then find an appropriate place for it, and I did all of it under the gaze of those startled and startling eyes. The process seemed to interest her, but I realized she was probably making sure I didn't locate and pocket anything she might want. When I had a few piles of stuff, I said, "Pitch in a little, would you? No, no, stay on the couch. You're a woman. As I hold these things up, you tell me where you think Lumia might have kept them."

We did that for a while, operating in an absolute vacuum of small talk, and when I had things sorted into six likely locations—living room, kitchen, bedroom, closet, bookshelf, bathroom—I put each pile in the appropriate place, neatly segregating them both from the stuff that had been trashed and the smaller number of items that hadn't been yanked out of place. When that was finished, we went back into the living room and she resumed her spot on the couch.

"So, money," I said. "What shape is it?"

"Rectangular," she said as though to a small child, with a carefully modulated undertone of pity. "Flat."

"And that was their operating thesis, too," I said. "That's why all the attention to the books and the couch and the stacks of dishes and the layers of the bed. That's why they pulled all the towels out of the linen cupboard. How did you get into matchmaking?"

She gave me the owl's eyes for a moment longer than was polite, and then she said, "Safer than doing the jobs myself. I'm conspicuous. My last job, which everyone in the world seems to know about, the one with the pearls? The reason I hit that old woman so hard is that I was trying to kill her. And I thought I had, but unfortunately I misjudged the spot I hit her in. She'd seen me and even in the dark she could give the cops a very general description of me, and that was that. I was good at what I did as long as I was in a completely empty space or in absolute darkness, but let any light hit me, and I'm done for if someone is looking. Burglars should really be inconspicuous," she said. "Like you."

"I work at it."

"What do you drive?"

"A white Camry."

"My, my," she said. "A cloak of invisibility. Are you happy with Stinky?"

"No one could be happy with Stinky." I was passing my hands across the bottoms of the bookshelves that were below eye level to see if anything was taped there. Nothing was. "But if you're asking do I want a change in representation, the answer is no."

"You're loyal to him, then."

"I know when he's lying," I said. "He's got a tell, and I always know when he's lying. *You*, on the other hand, you could tell me San Francisco is moving toward us at fifty miles an hour on the 101, and I wouldn't know whether to believe you."

She rearranged all those sharp joints into a position that probably would have looked comfortable on anyone else and said, "What's his tell?"

"Ah-ah," I said. "Why women only?"

"Are we *chatting*?"

"Humor me. This isn't very interesting work. Why women?"

She licked those perpetually drying front teeth. "I like women better than I like men. I don't like either sex very much, but women have a thin edge over you people. Then, too, women are less direct than men, more Machiavellian, which is probably a product of thousands of years of getting beat up. Get three smart women in a room and give them a challenge and let them talk, and you'll get some very underhanded answers."

I said, "Hmmm" and took my shoes and socks off.

"And they're easier to frighten than men because they're not so given to bluster. When you've frightened a woman, you usually know it. Why are you doing that?"

"I'm going to walk the carpet, all of it within a few feet of the walls. That was one reason I needed the stuff picked up."

"You'll be able to feel it?"

"If it's in any kind of wad at all. If she spread it out, a bill at a time, I'm out of luck, but I'd be surprised if she did that. She'd have had to move a lot of furniture, and I doubt she peeled back the carpet that far. It's likelier to be in four to five stacks, close to a wall."

She made a sound I couldn't spell in a million years, seemingly devoid of both vowels and consonants. Then she said, "Do you have people in your life?"

I moved a sad little dinner table and its single chair away from the apartment's longest wall. "Several."

"Don't you think they're weak spots? Pressure points that people can use against you?"

The small four-shelf bookshelf, one of two in the room,

was light because the books had all been pulled out, pre-sumably fanned, and then splayed facedown on the floor, although they were now neatly stacked in its center. "Actu-ally, I think they make me stronger."

"What an odd idea. Where do they live?"

I said, "You must be kidding."

"See?" she said. "Pressure points."

"Have it your way." I did six trips up and back, then turned and did the wall with the front door in it. The book-case on that wall, which had also been emptied, couldn't be moved, so it shrunk the potential hiding area. They had dumped the stuff from the vacuum just to the right of the bookcase, so I shoved aside as much of it as I could with the edge of my foot before stepping on the carpet. That kicked up some dust, and Itsy sneezed.

"Bless you," I said, turning around to take the next pass.

"Yeah, yeah, yeah," she said. "This could take days."

"Good thing they went through all the books, then. You don't *have* to stay."

"I didn't know she read."

"Why would you?" I said, and she didn't reply. When I was finished with that wall, I said, "Please get up. Time to move the couch." I picked up the vacuum cleaner and laid it on the coffee table, then pulled the whole thing away from the couch. Itsy reassembled herself into a standing position and took one end of the couch. Between us, we got it about four feet from the wall, and I did the back-and-forth until I'd run out of room. I went back to my end of the couch and waited, and eventually she made that unspellable sound again and picked up her end.

Then we repeated the furniture moving routine wher-ever it was necessary to clear the carpet in the short hall and the bedroom. In the bedroom, Itsy collapsed, looking like a collision between isosceles triangles, on the mattress that had been pulled off the bed. When I'd finished with the carpets I went through the piles of clothing on the floor. There was no reason to search the drawers because they'd all been yanked out of the dresser and turned upside down. I did reach into the empty space where the top one had been and feel the bottom of the wood above the opening.

"People forget about that," Itsy said. She sounded almost approving. "They look at the bottoms of the drawers but forget what's above the top one."

"You don't need to pass an I.Q. test to qualify as a burglar." Hanging crookedly above the dresser was a picture of Lumia and a guy, just a guy, kind of a schlub, but a cheerful-looking schlub. They were someplace with trees, and they both seemed happy enough. I took it down, ran my fingers over the back, and said, "Who's this guy?"

Without even looking over, Itsy said, "How would I know?"

"Right." I stepped back from the dresser and went to the closet. About ten minutes later, I said. "Kitchen."

After half an hour of hard and sometimes greasy work, I could almost see the black cloud of frustration and anger above her head. "Okay," I said, "between them and us, I think we've exhausted most of the places where I'd hide something flat and rectangular. That leaves the other shape."

"Which is?"

"Tubular," I said. "A roll." I went back into the living room, pulled the hose off the canister vacuum, and looked into the hose. Then I pulled the changeable power head off the hose's other end, stuck two fingers into the tube and said, "Voila." Then I said, "My fingers are too fat."

Her eyes had shimmered when I spoke, in a way that made me uneasy. She said, "What does that mean?"

"It means Lumia put a couple of strips of tape across the inside of the roll, with a few adhesive inches sticking out on either side to hold it in place. Her fingers were slender enough that she could slide the roll in and then reach in through it and press the tape against the walls of the tube. I haven't got enough room to scrape the tape off."

"Long, thin fingers," she said. "Hmmm, I wonder who has—"

"Right," I said. I handed her the end that had slipped into the power head. She held it up in the not-very-bright light from the open door, peered into it, then inserted two of those prehensile-looking fingers and began to work on the tape. She must have seen me moving out of the corner of her eye, but by the time she looked up, I already had my gun in my hand. I said, "Just in case."

After a moment of staring at the gun, she said, "So you're *not* stupid." A minute later, she had a thick roll of hundred-dollar bills in her hand. "There's another one farther up," she said. After a little muted swearing she held it up, too.

"Okay," I said, "time for yousies-mesies. One for you, one for me, until they're all gone."

She spun the second roll around her index finger. "You don't trust me?"

I didn't say anything. A couple of seconds later, we both started to laugh.

We were facing each other over our stacks of money. Lumia had gotten fifteen thousand and no signing bonus, so in all, that was about half what I'd been paid. Income inequality extended easily to the criminal world, where Congressional committees were unlikely to try to regulate it and unions hadn't gotten much of a foothold except as a profitable and seldom-audited business enterprise. I didn't see any good reason to share the disparity with Itsy. I had doled out the bills, and she felt the need to count them twice. I'd double-dealt her once, giving her one extra bill as a character test, which she failed, then folded the money and slipped it into two of her leather pockets. She looked at me suspiciously, checking, no doubt, to see whether I knew I'd overpaid her.

"So," I said, "The piranhas."

"What about them?" She was lying on her right side on the couch in a posture of sharp-angled collapse. I was sitting on the little chair that had been pulled up to the dining table. Itsy used those otherworldly fingers to flip through the edges of the stack in one of her pockets, not the one with the gun in it. I watched closely.

"Well," I said when she was through playing with the money, "guess. What *would* I be asking about piranhas?"

"They're hard to train, if that's what you want to know." There was no sign of humor in her face.

"Okay, since you're having so much fun, are they really there?"

"They were for a couple of months. They're not easy to buy, by the way."

"Glad to hear it."

"But you can't *believe* how much you have to feed them. Piranhas will eat you out of house and home. I spent hours just standing there throwing raw hamburger into the water, not a particularly interesting activity. And the hamburger they don't eat rots and floats to the surface, and then the water stinks. I can see why they're in so few pet stores."

I looked at her, but she seemed as serious as a straight razor. "Did they come with a handbook or something?"

"No." She lifted her head and rolled her eyes over to me. I could almost hear them click into place. "Why would they?"

"I had a roommate in college once who bought an alligator, a baby, I guess, maybe ten inches long. And with it came a little booklet entitled *Enjoy Your Alligator*. Just like that, in the imperative, like if you didn't enjoy having your fingers bitten off, you hadn't held up your side."

She put her head back down on the cushion and rested the back of her hand on her forehead, very Sarah Bernhardt. "Where did he keep it?"

"In the bathtub."

"How thoughtless."

"I learned not to drop the soap and how to do aerobics and shower at the same time."

"What happened to it?"

"I accidentally flushed it down the toilet. So what's in the moat now?"

"Electric eels."

"You're shitting me."

She moved the melodramatic hand and gave me the stare again. "Do I look like a woman who shits people?"

"Yeah."

"Well," she said, "occasionally. But don't let it get out. Suppose I said it was a rare bacteria that kills on touch."

"I'd believe you, of course, although I'd love to see how you handled it. How did you disarm the piranhas?"

"Six or eight gallons of bleach. Piranhas don't like bleach."

"So," I said. "Allan Frame. The guy who came to you to recruit Lumia. How dangerous?"

"Very. And not as tolerant and easygoing as I am." She studied the ceiling as though there were a mural painted on it.

"Where can I find him?"

"You don't want to. He's connected."

"So am I."

She said something that sounded like air escaping from a tire.

"I need to know where to find him."

"And I'm sure *someone* will help you."

"Okay. What did he tell you about his client?"

A long blink, and then she tore her eyes away from the ceiling and turned them on me. "He said that the person I gave him had better play it straight, or we'd all be dead."

"Did you tell Lumia that?"

She blinked, and then she told me a lie. "I did."

I just sat there, looking at her but seeing Lumia walk to the hedge and through the gate to get into that car.

Itsy said, "Do you know you've got a spot on your shirt?"

"Yes, that's been brought home to me rather forcefully by a cross-section of the population."

"Do *not* fuck with Allan Frame."

"Did you *see* his client? Do you know her name?"

"Of course not. That's what he's for, one more layer between his client and the person who ultimately goes into the house."

"And yet she talked to *me*, face to face."

"Yes," Itsy Winkle said with a conspicuous attempt at patience, "but she thought she was going to *kill* you, didn't she?"

21
Thinning the Herd for Laughs

In the end, I told her that I could get to Allan Frame without her, but that if I did I'd tell him that she had sent me. I got a kind of a mad-cat hiss and then an address and a request that she be invited to my funeral. I told her I'd do the best I could from Beyond, and she said she'd try to derive contentment from the fact that I *was* Beyond.

Then she tried again to steal me from Stinky.

Halfway down the stairs of Lumia's building, leaving Itsy behind to burn sage or plant curses in the corners, or perhaps even to mourn in some entomological way, I realized that it was almost one, time to swing by Louie's and get the stuff I would need for my chat with Ms. Beckwell-Stoddard in Hollywood's Greatest Weedpatch of Young Talent or whatever it was. Looking at my two potential approaches to my primary objective, I realized that Althea Beckwell-Stoddard, dragon though she seemed to be, was an easier and probably less dangerous route to the Bride of Plastic Man than the route that had Allan Frame in the middle of it. I called Louie.

"*Hey*," Louie said, even before I'd said hello. "Your guy wrote a book."

"My guy."

"The rich guy, whatever his name is. Was."

I stopped at the foot of the gray stairway and looked up at a gray sky, a sky the color of industrial sludge. "What do you mean, a book, you mean—"

"Not like a real book, not a *book* book like you'd get in a store, with fancy covers and *Better than James Patterson,* but it's as *long* as a book. As long as a short book, anyways."

I started the hike to my car. "Where is it?" A little wind kicked up, smelling sort of wet.

"UCLA. He left them his papers and stuff and some money to look after it all. You know, they'd take John Wayne Gacy's papers if there was enough money in there. For someone who's writing a thesis—"

"Got it." The day had darkened an f-stop or two.

"—about really serious twists. Title would have those two dots top and bottom, you know those two—"

"A colon."

"Yeah, they all gotta have those two dots to separate something that's actually interesting from the rest of it, something like *Thinning the Herd for Laughs, colon, Inside the Mind of John—*"

"I get it. How did—" I stopped talking as my remote, rather than unlocking my car, locked it instead. I'd forgotten, therefore, to lock it, something I *always* do, a sign that I was even more wary of Itsy Winkle than I'd thought. I got in, feeling the stiff wad of cash in my front pocket.

"How did what?" Louie said when he got tired of waiting.

"How did you find out about the book?"

"My girl found it."

"Your *girl*?"

"At UCLA. Where she's a student. Barely out of her teens, okay? But worth every penny you're paying her."

"Can she bring it to me?"

"No. There's only one copy. It's in, like, a reading room, you know a room where—"

"You read something," I said, "but can't take it out. Then what good does it do me?"

"You need like a special card even to look at it. You're really jumpy today, you know? Hey, you coming over here?"

A raindrop ended its long leap on my front window, making a circle the size of a quarter. "Yes," I said. "I've got to—"

"You got to get your papers. You know what? You should slow down, take a calm pill. She's copying it. She's not supposed to, so it's taking her a little time."

"What kind of a book? How is she copying it?"

"Like his life story, like *I did this, I did that*. Lot of God in it, she says. What do you mean, how is she copying it? On a *copier*."

"Tell her to stop. Tell her to go someplace where no one will be looking at her and take a picture of every two-page spread with her phone. Give her my phone number and tell her to send the pictures to me. If there are no page numbers, she needs to put a little piece of paper with the page number on it in the upper left-hand corner of each left-facing page. That way she doesn't have to stand around at a big machine with this thing in her hand and maybe get caught, and also I'll get it faster. Tell her every ten, twelve pages, send me two-page spreads of what she's done."

"Wow," Louie said. "You just think of that?"

The rain had built to a sparse spatter, not a lot of drops but they were all whoppers. "No. It's been done *ad infinitum*. Can you phone her?"

"They don't like those things going off in the library. Might make somebody forget his colon, which sounds kind of messy. She's on airport mode or something. Anyway—"

"Airplane. Does she check it regularly?"

"Regular as anybody that age does, which is like all the time, but the problem—"

"Call her or text her, leave a message to change the approach and text the first batch to me as fast as she can."

"Problem is her camera's busted. Did you really think I didn't think of that? The camera?"

"Then why did you—"

"You seemed to be having a good time. I sent her a text, asked her to get hold of somebody with—"

"Good. How we doing on the will?"

"I got somebody downtown. He's a law student, so he's supposed to know how things work, but you know, you got *civil servants* down there. Can't get fired, can't get demoted. Worse than crooks, almost as bad as the DMV."

"Well, let me know."

"Where you going now?"

I started the car and turned on the wipers. "Toward you, to pick up the papers, and then to see a talent agent."

"Well, I mean, jeez, you're a nice-looking guy, but—"

"Bye, Louie,"

"Wait a minute. Where you at?"

"Reseda."

"And your agent is where?"

"North Hollywood."

"I'm like a zigzag out of your way. Tell you what. I'll meet you at Du-par's, save you a little—"

"I was just there."

"It's not a *date*, it's a hand-off, okay? Save you a little time."

"Great, thanks. Ummm . . . it's going to take me longer than it'll take you, so please call the person who's waiting for the will and tell him to get there, too. Tell him we're going to bribe the civil servant. He can go up to five hundred. I'll give him cash at Du-par's, but he needs to get out of there right now. That way, he can get back to the clerk's office today. He's got to haul ass because it's starting to rain."

"Moving fast, huh?"

I turned on the lights and checked the mirrors, then swung into sparse traffic. That would end soon: people in Los Angeles pay the same kind of attention to a little rain as Noah did to the Deluge, and a sprinkle can bring the town to a dead stop. "I *have* to move fast," I said. "I hate this thing. I want it over."

"He's my next call."

"Have the lemon meringue," I said. "And don't tell me I've got a spot on my shirt."

"Are you all moved in?" I asked Ronnie.

"Yes, and we've got a bed big enough to lose a state capital on. Mouse count, zero. It's heaven. Although I miss our place."

"Me, too. Not for long, I hope."

"And there's this huge theme park down below."

"It's raining."

"Not here, it isn't. Not yet, anyway. And I've been wet

before, and it didn't do anything permanent to me. How's your day coming?"

"I'm going very, very fast, and it's going very, very slowly." I turned south on Reseda Boulevard, heading for the 101.

Ronnie said, "You ever think about a tree's perspective?"

"No," I said. "In all honesty, I can't say I have."

"It's doing its thing at what must seem like the only correct pace in the world, and we're probably going so fast it can't even see us. Or maybe we're blurs or streaks. They must pity us, all that herky-jerky movement for nothing. We live, all frantic, we want something, we die, and the tree adds a couple of rings."

"Well, let's hope none of them writes a book, it'd be longer than *Ulysses*. Although it'd have to be an ebook, wouldn't it? Be kind of awful to print a tree's book on paper. Makes the tree an accessory."

"You're pretty quippy for someone who's barely slept." The rain turned up its volume.

"It's talking to you," I said, and it was true. I felt almost completely awake.

"You shouldn't talk while you're driving. Some cop—"

"You're right. I'll check in with you during the occasional pause in my day."

"Nothing dangerous, right?"

"I laugh at danger."

"As I said, nothing dangerous?"

"Not so far as I can tell."

She said, "I've been thinking about that teeter-totter."

"Me, too," I said. A guy in a black matte muscle car swerved in front of me, throwing a tsunami of muddy water with a little gravel in it across my windshield. I got even with him in a manly fashion by blinking my brights for a nanosecond. "But you go first."

"If there's another kid there," she said. "If he's got, you know, a *friend*, it kind of changes things. He might be . . . *attached* to someone."

I wanted to hug her hard enough to make her squeak. "We don't know enough yet to come to a conclusion. Let's park it and think about it."

"Maybe we could get some images from the daytime."

The freeway onramp was coming up, two lanes wide. I pulled my little Camry next to the muscle car and got an almost audible snort of disdain from the hormone at the wheel, who had a cleft in his chin so deep I wouldn't have been surprised to learn it went all the way through to the back of his head. When the light changed I goosed the enormous old Detroit engine that one of Louie's guys had shoehorned under the Toyota's hood and left him with the ever-welcome fumes of exhaust and burnt rubber, plus, out of the window, a popular traditional gesture that goes all the way back to rude old Ancient Rome, where it was called the *digitus impudicus, or* "unchaste finger." He received my gesture in the appropriate spirit, with a loud bray on his horn, and I waved goodbye with the *impudicus* and slalomed across three lanes to the center, which was moving right along.

"Where'd you go?" Ronnie said.

"Participating in an age-old ritual," I said. "Guy stuff. Honor and all that. We can ask Francie about what you just said, but I'm not sure she'll be able to find someone who'll be willing to put a drone in that backyard in full daylight. I think maybe first you need to take all the precautions you can, go to Iowa City or someplace like that, see what you can find out from whoever it is. I'll fly with you once I'm finished with the current situation. Think of it. Just you and me and Iowa City."

"I didn't know there even *was* an Iowa City."

"It was the capital before they moved it to Des Moines."

"Why did they do that?"

"Because they wanted something harder to pronounce. I mean, I'm kind of honored that you assume I'd know the answer, but I don't."

"I thought that was your specialty."

"What was?"

"Useless and unrelated bits of information," she said. "You unwrap one all the time. Mickey's fingers, for example."

"Here's something I've never told anyone. When I was fourteen, which is the same as saying sex-obsessed, I once looked up *esoteric* in the dictionary because I had confused it with *erotic*. I read the definition of esoteric, and it was like a bolt of lightning. I thought, Oh, my God, there's a *name* for it. Whoops."

"Whoops what?"

"Truck won't share the road."

"A truck? Where are you?"

"On the 101, heading for North Hollywood."

"The freeway? And you're talking to me? Goodbye. I mean, I love you, but goodbye." And she was gone.

I scanned the rearview for the muscle car but didn't see it. With the cheer Ronnie had given me evaporating, I settled simultaneously into driving mode and a deep funk.

The lack of new threats from the Bride of Plastic Man was unnerving me. Why wasn't she coming after me? I could only think of two reasons, neither of them comforting: first, she had something else on her mind; and second, she didn't *need* to come after me. For some reason she felt she could reach out and touch me whenever she wanted. In some ways I might have felt more secure if the threat were more evident. I knew what she had done to Lumia, and I'd seen what she'd done to Lumia's apartment. Not a lot of apparent remorse.

That was enough of a prod to get me to an off-ramp and down to a surface street where I could park for a moment. I checked out the app Anime had installed and looked at my entrance hall. Nothing. No one in camera range, no broken door. Same lights on. Why was she leaving me alone?

A new thought: somehow she'd gotten her hands on whatever she'd sent me and Lumia to find. I had been rendered superfluous. I sat there, listening to the engine tick as it cooled, and trying to find a perspective. After murdering Lumia, she'd gone and tossed Lumia's place to get her fifteen K back. She'd paid me almost double that and hadn't tried to recoup it. Yet. So, one theory: she had what she wanted, she no longer cared about the advance, and she didn't actually know where I lived.

Another theory: she had whatever she had wanted, and she knew *exactly* where I lived and had it under surveillance so she could pick up her money and kill me at the same time. At her convenience, so to speak.

Either way, my priority still had to be to figure out who she was so I could say hi to her before she could say hi to me. I worked the cash out of my pocket, pulled thirty hundreds off, and popped open the glove compartment. And almost kicked myself.

There it was, the little notebook I'd taken from the kitchen drawer at Horton House. I'd tucked it into my pants in the kitchen and then forgotten about it as I ransacked the library in the living room. After I put the bags of books into the trunk and went to sit behind the wheel, the notebook had announced itself by cutting into the tops of my legs. Without thinking, I'd tugged it free and tossed it precisely where it now lay and closed the door on it. I pulled it out, doing a vigorous mental self-critique in language that would have tightened my mother's mouth, put the money into the compartment, and snapped it shut again. Then I sat, turning the little book over in my hands.

It was at least fifty, maybe even sixty, years old. The paper was brittle enough to have broken, so cleanly it might have been cut, along several diagonals where a corner had been dog-eared. I flipped through it as the rain drummed down and the world went wavy with the water flowing over my windshield. It made me think, for a moment, of the old glass in the windows of Horton House that had looked out at a rippling world as it changed over more than a century, or at least until Miss Daisy had turned her back on it forever and insisted on her ficus hedge and the paper-covered windows.

What had she hated so much that she refused to let any impression of the world outside the house leak into her vision? Was it really just a neighborhood that, from her perspective, was going downhill? It felt as though there had to have been something more. Maybe it was a symbolic gesture; maybe she had turned her back, once and for all, on something or someone in her life, something she couldn't control. So she'd banished it or him or her forever from her sight.

The notebook had been used in the conventional way, front to back, although clumps of empty pages had been skipped over as though rejected for flaws I couldn't see. Here and there, a slender cluster had been torn out, reasonably neatly, probably someone putting a ruler near the margin and pressing down on it as she ripped the pages upward. The entries, in faded ink or pencil, comprised a sort of chronological flip chart of the various approaches to teaching handwriting in the public schools, which meant that the earlier entries were much better spelled and easier to read than the later ones. The earliest handwriting, in fountain-pen ink now faded almost to a pastel, was nearly as tidy and obedient as Laney Profitt's had been. The most recent were in prosaic ball point and the occasional Sharpie, in a haphazard chicken-track printing.

A car splashed by me, bringing me back to myself. How long had I been sitting here? I called Louie, who accused me of misleading him on the pie, which tasted like it was made from a sugar-free lemonade mix, and said that Walter—the guy who'd been waiting for the will at the registrar's bureau—wasn't there yet, and where the hell was I, anyways?

"I don't know," I said. "But I can't be more than ten, fifteen minutes away. What about the book-copying thing?"

"She's got somebody coming."

"It's taking long enough."

"I knew you'd be happy that we'd solved it."

I noticed something in the book and looked at it more closely. Louie said, "What, you've stopped speaking to me?"

"Be there in a bit." I hung up.

The majority of the book's individual pages had been

written in only one hand, with only one kind of writing implement; it was rare to see two hands on any single page. But here, right under my nose, was one entry in at least *four* hands and possibly five: a name and a list of phone numbers. And it was relatively early in the book.

Eduardo, the first line said, and then there was a string of five phone numbers, all but one of them with a line through it, each number different. The name and two of the numbers—the first two—were in an early hand, written in fountain pen. The other three were clearly written by three different people. The last, and certainly the most recent, was the chicken-scratch hand, written with a black Sharpie.

In all, there were nine people, first-name only, listed on that page, Some of them had only one number, some of them had two or three, and two were followed by a chain of numbers—written, if my assumptions were right, over a period of many years. But only Eduardo spanned so *many* hands, only Eduardo had five phone numbers.

Who has only a first name? The help. Why the chain of numbers? Obviously because the people to whom they belong had moved over a period of years, or the phone company changed prefixes or, who knows, they got too many junk calls.

I felt like I was looking at a wall in Pompeii that someone had scribbled a grocery list on. It was the most vivid glimpse I'd caught of the actual life of that frozen, stillborn house. All these people, coming and going, all these phone numbers that rang somewhere else, maybe someplace where people laughed every now and then.

Eduardo, I figured, would be in his eighties or nineties by now if he still ate, drank, and slept. There was no way on earth I could prevent myself from dialing that number.

A man said, "Hello?" in a gruff voice that didn't sound like it got a lot of use. After a moment, he cleared his throat and said, "*Dígame?*"

"Eduardo?" I said

He said, "Yes. Who is—"

I hung up. I could feel my heart pounding. I had a living link with Miss Daisy's past.

22
Dead for a Century

The wanna-be lawyer who'd been downtown at the registrar's office was skinny and severe, with a pursed, disapproving little mouth like a puckered buttonhole, pale, red-rimmed eyes, and bloodless-looking papery skin that flaked freely wherever it was exposed. If you'd put him into a snow globe and shaken it, you'd have had a blizzard. At first sight, he was a Dickensian drudge who seemed to regard everything apprehensively, as though he doubted his eyes and was waiting for the real, and much worse, form of whatever it was to present itself. Louie had two sticky-looking pie plates in front of him, and the flaking man had a cup of herbal tea, his third, judging from the little foil envelopes in which the teabags had been brought to him. They had been lined up in tight formation on the place mat to his right, their edges precisely parallel with the edge of the mat.

"This is Walter," Louie said, sounding apologetic.

I said, "Hey, Walter," sliding in next to Louie and looking for Glinda. She wasn't there, and I realized it would have been a pretty long shift if she were. Still, with her in it, the place had felt a little less like an artifact of history, an amusement-park curiosity frozen in time.

Louie said, "Walter doesn't eat pie," speaking the

sentence with the kind of precision one might use for the code phrase that will prompt an identifying and equally meaningless response from a fellow spy, "It's sunny in Oslo" or some other non sequitur.

"Pie is full of sugar," Walter said, with the weight of someone who had studied the issue long and hard and felt it needed wide dissemination. "And you are?"

Ignoring him, Louie handed me the driver's license and business card, saying, "By the edges. It's still a little sticky."

I took them as directed, gave them a critical glance, fanned them in the air a little to hurry the drying process, and said to the flaking man, "I'm your employer. You may call me Dwight Sykes."

Louie said to me, "Did *you* know there was sugar in pie, Dwight?"

"My mother warned me about it," I said. "Or maybe it was something else. Swimming right after eating, maybe. Or while eating."

"You're joking," Walter said, sounding like a lifelong member of the Brotherhood of Far-Off Laughter.

"You're right," I said. I put down the cards so I could reach into my shirt pocket. "It's a bad habit. Here. Five hundred. Just tell the clerk you're in a hurry."

Walter started to reach for it but drew his hand back. "I don't know," he said, as though struck by doubt for the first time. "Bribery . . ." He allowed the thought to sputter off into nothingness, something too dire to face without at least a warm-up. He even chewed his lower lip like someone auditioning to play Doubt in a medieval mystery play.

I put a couple of fingers back into the pocket and came out with two more bills, neatly folded in half and waiting for him. "And for you," I said.

He took both, opened the folded ones, raised the pale eyes to me, and said, "Why does she get more than I do?"

Slipping immediately into Bad Cop, Louie snarled "Because we can't replace *her*. You, on the other hand, I got a thousand—"

"Okay," Walter said. The tight little mouth got almost small enough to disappear.

I peeled off three more and gave them to Louie, putting them one at a time into the palm of his open hand as Walter watched. "Get it before closing time," I said, "and put it in Louie's hands tonight, and you'll be all even-steven." His forehead furrowed, and I pointed to the bills and said, "These will be yours, in other words. Okay?"

"Okay," Walter said, getting up. "Thanks for the tea." With a little spurt of venom, he said, "It had too much tannin."

We both watched him scuttle to the door. Louie said, "Sorry."

I said, "I always think it's kind of touching to see someone cling to a life he's obviously not enjoying."

Louie raised his hand for the waitress. "Pie?"

"Coffee," I said. "Walter has drained me of my life essence. Where are we with the pictures of Horton's book?"

"Someone is bringing her a phone with a camera that works. Might even be there by now. What do you think it's going to tell you?"

"If I knew that," I said, "I wouldn't have to read it." A waitress appeared at my side, and I said, "Where's what's her name?"

She said, with big-league waitress attitude, "You're gonna have to do better than that, Jack."

"Where's Glinda?"

"Ah," she said, "a night owl. My guess is that she's either asleep, trying to levitate the *Titanic*, or getting another tattoo."

I said, "That's Glinda. Black coffee, please, and— Louie, which pie did you like best?"

"I liked the mince, but you want peach. You always want peach."

"You guys didn't have that last night," I said to the waitress. "Peach, please."

"And you?" the waitress said to Louie.

"French fries, more coffee."

"It's your heart," she said, and left.

Louie said, "You suppose there's a school somewhere, Waitress Improv? Pay it off with a cut of your tips?"

I got up and went to the other side of the booth, used a paper napkin to wipe away the skin flakes, and sat down. "Call old Walter when you figure he's not driving, make nice for a minute to get him off-guard, and then tell him I need the old man's will, too. Henry Wallace Horton."

"Died when?"

I had to think for a minute. "1931."

"Jeez," Louie said. "That's a long way back."

"It's there," I said. "That's what bureaucracies do, they enshrine worthless documents and defend them with their lives. If the clerk gets difficult, tell him to offer her the extra two hundred. In fact, erase that, tell him to *start* with two hundred for Miss Daisy's will, just to entice the clerk across the bribery line and when she's said yes, offer her the other five hundred for the old man's. Tell him we'll give him five hundred when he brings them both to you."

"I guess that's psychology," Louie said. "I could just tell him I'll shoot him."

"But he knows you wouldn't."

"He doesn't know shit. Under that *I died eight months ago* attitude, he's thrilled about hanging with a crook. He probly thinks I got a whole room full of Lone Ranger masks somewheres."

I was looking for my pie. "How do I get the address that goes with a phone number?"

"Reverse directory," Louie said. "Used to be only the cops had them, but they're online now."

I rubbed my eyes and said, "I'm really tired. I actually knew that."

"Some of them want you to sign up, though, which always makes me think *cops* even though it's probly not. And it's no good if your number is unlisted."

"Can you handle it, even if it's unlisted?"

"Yeah, sure. Give me the number. You know, you're running up a tab here."

I gave him Eduardo's number, and then, pulling more money out of the pocket as he wrote the number on the pad in his magic wallet, I said, "Here. A thousand, wait, fifteen hundred. I can give you a couple thousand more if you want to go to the car with me."

He folded his wallet and put it away. "Ahhh. You're good for it. Hey, I got the names of some used-junk shops within ten, fifteen miles of that old house. Some of them are like retail outlets for fences, selling boosted stuff. You want them?"

"Not now," I said. "That phone number might be a short-cut, a direct line to one of the people who took the stuff out of the house in the first place. Hang on to the names, though."

"They're filed away," he said, and he wasn't kidding. News that a court order had been issued for Louie's files would probably drive a thousand crooks straight to Mexico.

I said, "I'm really tired."

"You already said that."

"See?" I said.

"You survived Itsy. No bite marks anywhere I can see."

"I wore a repellent. Her house is full of stuffed cats."

Louie's mouth fell open. "That's sick," he said. "Don't tell Alice." Alice was his wife. She practically spoke cat. An appalled silence descended on the table. My phone buzzed, and I looked down at it as my pie arrived and said, "Jackpot."

The waitress said, "It ain't *that* good, honey."

The pictures the student had taken of the book were serviceable, but just, photographed closely enough to get a two-page spread into the frame. The pages rose sharply up from the center crease to form little parallel mountain ranges on either side of it, and then tapered down again left and right to create a sort of gentle downhill ski slope all the way across the margins to the edges. This gave the lines of type a ribbon-like curl, and the words closest to the camera and farthest away were slightly out of focus but readable. The book was simply standard-size paper that had been typed on both sides on an old manual typewriter operated by someone who felt emphatic enough about the material to turn the periods into tiny holes that went straight through the paper. The pages had then been crimped and bound crudely at the center margin. Here and there an occasional line had been deleted by energetic repetition of the letter x, and less frequently a word or a passage had been crossed out in ink and a correction hand-written above it in a precise, printed hand as legible as the text on a blueprint.

With a certain amount of squinting and occasional enlarging, the old man's story was largely legible.

It began:

It has been said by wiser men than I that Fate is a jokester. In my life I have seen little that would persuade me otherwise. In point of fact, as I now pick up my pen to tell my story before I slip into dotage, it seems to me that I can take the wiser men one step further. The central fact of a man's life is not whether it has been a joke, but whether he is the butt of the joke or the one who survives to tell it.

If you are reading this, and if my wishes have been honored, I have now been dead for at least seventy-five years. You will, in fact, be inhabiting one of the first years that does not begin with a one in the more than 2000 that have passed, taking both fools and saints with them, since the death of Our Lord. I have now joined the departed. For much of my life I feared death, terrified by the question of which extreme of Eternity, the lower or the higher, I would occupy. As you peruse these pages, should they continue to deserve your attention, you will see that there was good cause for my early uncertainty (later dispelled) about my final destination, and also for my wish that my story should remain a secret until my children are likely to have departed this surprising and endlessly treacherous world.

I said to Louie, "The dead *will* find a way to speak."

23

Not Fluffy and Foo-Foo

Rain drummed impatient fingers on the roof of the car as I waited for it to lift enough to give me some driving visibility. As heavy as the downpour was, the thin clouds allowed some of the sun's light, now the chilly, luster-free color of pewter, to seep through. Most of the people who were driving, I saw when I looked up, had their headlights on. I went back to my phone.

After a youth and a young adulthood imprisoned in the cold dungeon of disbelief, I received a gift I had done little to deserve. If this gift, a vision of the unseen world that has brought me comfort over the past four decades, is accurate, as I firmly believe it to be, I may well be standing beside you as you read these words, perhaps even peering over your shoulder. If my spiritual superiors are correct in their understanding of the soul, Heaven and Hell may be empty ideas; and the departed fools and saints of all those immemorial years may yet lurk transparently among us, waiting only for the summons of someone they loved. Even my abandoned child, I believe, will be residing there, close to me, beyond all earthly injury, even, perhaps, in friendship with my implacable daughter.

However, I anticipate myself. For many years my life was spent willingly, nay, eagerly, in darkness. Indeed, as these pages will show, some of it was dark as night itself.

Another one knocking the dark, I thought, resisting an impulse to look over my shoulder. Then I did a mental double-take: I said aloud, "Abandoned child?"

The spattering rain hit the roof like a handful of tacks. The windows had steamed up, so I checked the downpour's slant—left to right, from my perspective—and half-lowered the passenger-side window. The air was cold, wet, and welcome.

But the tale of my misdeeds, many and varied as they were, will have to wait its turn in this narrative.

I came into this squalid world, without my wishes in the matter having been sought, in the shattering year of 1860. As I lay in my rough-hewn Kansas cradle, great things broke to pieces around me, creating the blood-soaked world through which I would have to find my way, and which would misshape my character. Mr. Lincoln was elected and the great peeling-off of the South was begun. I would come of age in a world where mankind, as Mr. Tennyson says of Nature, was red in tooth and claw.

My phone vibrated and John Prine began to sing "Fish and Whistle," the ringtone that had awakened me to Jake's call the previous night. I saw a number that I didn't recognize for a moment, and then I did: Eduardo, from the notebook I'd taken out of the kitchen drawer in Horton House. Curiosity getting the better of him, I thought. He probably didn't get many calls. Maybe a little guilty conscience picking at him. I rejected the call to let him stew a little.

The next few pages of Horton's memoir outlined a childhood Dickens might have created: the death of a beloved mother, the brutality of a drunken and apparently stupid father, a grinding daily routine of trying to coax crops from baked earth, and then this:

> During my seven years of intermittent atten-
> dance at school, the only light in my world
> was shed by my teacher, Miss Greening, who
> encouraged me to read. But we should be as
> selective in our reading, she said, as we were
> in our choice of friends. A bad book, like a
> bad friend, has the power to lead us astray.
> Several times she told us that we must always
> ask ourselves why a man has written a book.
> What does he wish to make you believe? How
> will he gain from your belief? Will it enrich
> him? Will it give him the fame so many men
> seek? Will it enthrone him in some earthly
> fashion? Will it rescue his name from infamy?
> Will it injure an enemy? Or does he merely
> possess something he wishes to share with you,
> a moral approach to life or a story in which
> he hopes you will find delight? There are more

bad reasons for a man to pen a book than good ones, or so Miss Greening believed, and while she encouraged us to read widely she also said that only when we knew how the writer regarded his reader should we consider ourselves free to honor him with our belief.

It is because of Miss Greening's words of caution regarding books and my desire to be a narrator who is worthy of your trust that I announce here and now, at the beginning of my own book, that the child whom she educated and befriended in the tiny Kansas schoolhouse where we broiled and froze in alternation was not named Henry Wallace Horton, Jr. Rather, he bore the name with which my parents baptized me. Miss Greening knew me as Edgar Francis Codwallader, a name I was later to disgrace and then abandon out of a combination of prudence and craven fear. My mother had died by then, young but beaten down by circumstance, and although my father still lived it was not to protect him that I discarded the name I inherited. I had no thought of how he might think of me; indeed, I had no thought of him at all. It was because I wanted to become the man Miss Greening had envisioned when she taught me, and I could not do that without adopting a new name and leaving behind the one I had sullied. If I have achieved any good in my life, and people have assured me on occasion that I have, it is due to Miss Greening and, later, to the wise friends to whom fate delivered me in, of all places, London, when I had the most

need of them, and who opened to me the world of
the spirit.

Like a lot of crooks, I've witnessed more than my share
of impromptu deathbed confessions—some from people
who, under any other circumstance, wouldn't have trusted
me with a handful of small change although, when the time
came, they were eager enough to spill their last to me. I have
to admit that I've heard some whoppers from the mouths
of those who knew that their flight had been called and was
already boarding, and that it would be strictly one-way.
Some people just can't help lying; some people have sani-
tized their past so often they've come to believe the G-rated
version; and some people apparently figure they can pull
the wool over the eyes of the Welcoming Committee.

Horton's pious claim that what mattered most to
him was becoming a person Miss Greening could admire
was undercut by the fact that he'd continued to commit crimes after adopting his new name. I had no way
of knowing whether he had been on good behavior in
England, when the world of the spirit, whatever that
was, seemed to have been opened to him, but he was
passing himself off as Henry Wallace Horton, Jr. when
he stole that jewelry from the New York social climber
and topped it off with a little assault and battery. It just
goes to show you, I thought as I pocketed the phone and
started the car, that a writer will go out of his way to
present himself on a good hair day even in a book no one
will read until after he's dead.

Horton's tribute to Miss Greening ended the installment of the book that Louie's "girl" had sent in her first
burst. I took a couple of deep breaths, started thinking

about the script I was going to spring on Althea Beckwell-Stoddard, and started the car.

To employ a child in the entertainment industry, the production company needs a special permit. To represent children for work in the entertainment industry, an *agent* needs a special permit. To work on a set, the *child* has to have a special permit, signed off on by the kid's parent. Any time a child is on a film set, even if it's only to walk by in the background for a second or two, there has to be either a teacher or a social worker, and sometimes both, in attendance. Every one of those laws is enforced by the California State Department of Labor Relations, in the person—for this afternoon, anyway—of the upright and incorruptible Dwight Sykes.

I quick-checked myself in the rearview mirror. I didn't look like a Dwight. But then, I've never felt that I looked like a Junior, either, and I've gone through life without people chasing me, crying out "Impostor." I supposed I could be Dwight again for an hour or so.

My guess was that Ms. Beckwell-Stoddard had her agency's permit all in order and one or two of the children might, too. What I was almost certain of was sloppiness on the part of the phony production company the Bride of Plastic Man had used to get hold of the kids for the day. She wouldn't have been able to show the bona fides necessary to get a permit. And Beckwell-Stoddard, focused on conning her kids and their parents left and right, would be so happy about an actual job that she wouldn't go all obsessive over a detail like that. I was also betting that the guy with the bushy wig and the honker nose who had shepherded the kids was neither an accredited teacher nor a social worker, as opposed to someone who alternated between moving large pieces of furniture from place to place and punching people on the nose for small change. I could make a very persuasive case, if Ms. Beckwell-Stoddard was reluctant to show me her client's identification, that the Garden of Children, or whatever she called it, was in danger of being closed for neglecting the protection of its defenseless clients. And *think* of the lawsuits that would follow.

How did someone wind up ripping off kids and their parents? I know I'm kind of compromised when it comes to moral condemnation of how people make a living, but these are *kids* with a precarious sense of self. These are loving *parents*, emotionally invested to the hilt in their children's happiness. These are *families* in a time when so many family incomes are stretched to the point of breaking just to keep food on a table that has a roof over it. And to exploit the love among them—the most precious thing they all share—as an entry point to rob them blind—well, it didn't predispose me in Althea Beckwell-Stoddard's favor. I realized, with no guilt at all, that I was going to have a good time sweating her.

It was a little before four, with the daylight prematurely on the wane as the clouds continued to bulk up, by the time I found the Gateway to Stardom, Hollywood's Finest Nursery of Young Talent, and so forth. All that hype and promise had been packed into a small but somewhat graceful older building, perhaps from the 1940s or even the '30s, set well back from the street in an area that mixed residential properties with commercial ones and backed right up against some scrubby hills that were too steep to develop. A dead lawn at the rear of the lot marked an abrupt end to the untidy, undomesticated tangle of the chaparral. Curving across the lawn was a sinuous concrete path, bordered on either side by the skeletons of last summer's perennials, now brown and spiky. They looked cold to the point of shivering. The building was white stucco with—surprise—a domed roof, like a miniature observatory, a lucky find for a con woman who pretended to deal in stars. I was so ready to unload on its inhabitant that it was almost a disappointment to realize that I wasn't going to get a chance to do it. Although the reaction quickly grew much more complicated.

I smelled it before I saw it. The door was a few inches ajar and she'd had some time in there alone. I stood absolutely still, five or six feet from the small one-step porch with its silly little classical pillars, my heart playing bass drum in my ears, and tried to scan the street without being obvious about it. I brought up my wrist as though to check my watch, looked around in a disoriented fashion, scratched my head like a bad silent-movie actor, and then squinted at the building, just someone searching for an address. I saw no surveillance cameras. I deeply desired not to go in, but I had to.

I took a good, lung-filling breath, held it, stepped up onto the porch, and used my elbow to push the door open and then, as something exploded toward me and past me, I used every bit of that breath in a scream like the one you hear from the heroine in a bad horror movie, the one who keeps turning her ankle as she runs, with the Beast so close behind you can hear it panting.

I'd been ambushed by cats, five or six of them, maybe more, bolting from the room, some of them even darting between my feet, as the door opened. I turned away, unwilling to look at what the cats had been doing. These weren't someone's beloved Fluffy and Foo-Foo, these were half-starved feral cats lured down from the hills by Ms. Beckwell-Stoddard's inadvertent self-advertisement. At two or more days dead, she was a buffet as far as they were concerned. There's even a nicely unemotional scientific term for it: *postmortem predation*. If Itsy Winkle were here, she'd have given me a triumphant smile.

And if she'd been here, I could have sent *her* in, but she wasn't, so it was down to me. I had to try to find something that would help me identify the Bride of Plastic Man, some agreement, contract, *something* with a name and some identification on it. I took that lung-busting breath one more time, seeing poisonous little flowers blossom in my field of vision, and elbowed the door open again, keeping my gaze elevated, well away from the thing on the floor. But this tactic did not give me any kind of a break. There was a desk in the middle of the room, the very desk she had dangled those long legs from in that photo, and behind the desk was a corkboard with a lot of long pins pushed partway into it. I didn't have to look down to know that the woman at my feet had been shot through the back of her head: dangling by one wing at a lopsided angle from one of the pins were her expensive, stylish rimless glasses. The lenses were no longer transparent, and much of the cork was covered in a black spatter pattern that had attracted more flies than I hope ever to see again.

I had the time to register a filing cabinet, open and rifled, papers scattered on the floor around it, many of them dappled by reddish-brown smudges, before I turned and fled, somehow doing it at a stately, unhurried walk across that dead lawn, four accelerated heartbeats per step, until I got to my car. Then I drove away at a languid pace, turned the corner, pulled to the curb, opened the door, and lost all of my peach pie.

Ten minutes later, I had Eaglet on her way to watch Kathy and Rina's house.

PART THREE

BEFORE THE SUN CAME UP

How did it get so late so soon?
– Dr. Seuss

24

If I Wanted to Talk to a *Pisher*, I Would Have Called a *Pisher*.

Although I hadn't been able to force myself to look directly at what was left of her, the peripheral image of Althea Beckwell-Stoddard chased me all the way out of North Hollywood, through a stop-and-go stretch of Ventura Boulevard, and then up Coldwater Canyon, which was clogged with the pre-rush-hour rush hour. I hadn't realized I'd seen it at the time—or maybe I'd suppressed it—but my memory, idling with nothing to occupy it as I inched uphill at three miles an hour, mercilessly supplied the final bit of the design, an intricately interwoven lacework of dainty cat tracks, a kind of frilly border surrounding the body, each symmetrical print the dark brown of dried blood.

I also saw those spattered glasses hanging drunkenly on the corkboard, and then the eyes that had looked out through them in her official photograph. The pose had been a little Hollywood-cheesy, probably knowingly so, and the eyes had seemed to comment on that. There had been just a bit too much going on in Althea's eyes, not only intelligence but also assessment and a certain wary distance. If I'd met her in person she might have seemed warmer and more trustworthy, but on the basis of those eyes alone, I wouldn't have let her near my daughter.

Still, she hadn't deserved *that*. I'd known some bad, bad people in my life but I could think of only one or two whose actions might have led me to regard their being eaten by cats, even postmortem, as justifiable punishment. It was horrific enough to make me wish I had some sort of religious perspective, or the access to the spirit world that Henry Wallace Horton seemed to have found. *Something*, anyway, that would give me a ten thousand-foot view from which I could have put what I'd seen into some kind of comprehensible panorama, preferably one that would re-frame it as a rite of passage—although a particularly ugly one—to a better existence.

But I didn't have anything of the kind. So I just heaved a sigh that clouded the windshield as I crept past Jake Whelan's broken gate, wondering whether Laney Profitt was still there or whether, in the second-rate light of this particular day, she and Jake couldn't bear the sight of each other for a moment longer. I was wondering how she'd gotten her car started when I reached the top of Coldwater and made a right on Mulholland Drive, the road that stretches along the spine of the large hills or small mountains that separate the San Fernando Valley from the southern expanse of the Los Angeles basin. I was able to express my anxiety by speeding up a bit on Mulholland, if only because sheer economics thinned the traffic. A mile and a half later I made a left and dipped down into the El Dorado of Los Angeles property values, where the annual state taxes on a single house can cost more than it would take to buy some of the newer homes in lesser areas down on the flats. When people say "Hollywood" what they really mean is Brentwood and Bel Air.

The hedge and wall that completely blocked the house from view had gone up in 1947, the year the founding thug of Las Vegas, Benjamin "Bugsy" Siegel, was shot many times in the head at his girlfriend's Beverly Hills home, the 30-caliber bullets having passed through a brightly lighted window on their way to his skull. Walls instantly became a high-demand item, even (this being Los Angeles) a status symbol among the city's more prominent crooks. The wall I pulled up to, like Miss Daisy's ficus hedge, would probably have required special official dispensation for height, although in this case the name of the house's owner was undoubtedly all the dispensation that was needed.

I was here because I couldn't think of anything else. Althea Beckwell-Stoddard's murder had deprived me of my relatively safe route to Allan Frame. The person who lived here, I hoped, might yank Mr. Frame's fangs, or at least make him think twice before burying them in my throat.

A light went on above the no-nonsense wrought-iron gate as I pulled into the driveway. The moment my finger touched the intercom button, a man said, "He's not seeing anyone right now." The last time I had heard that voice it had been singing Barry Manilow's "Copacabana" from the kitchen and putting a lot into it. Given the size of the house, he *had* to have been putting a lot into it for me to be able to hear him at all, much less identify the song.

"Is he all right, Tuffy?" I asked.

"He's as all right as you can expect."

"What do you mean, *all right as he can expect*?" said the master of the house, from a distance. "What am I, the Wandering Jew? On the hoof since the Year One?"

I said, "What's he doing that's so important he can't see me?"

"Anything you can think of," Tuffy said. "Trying a new part in his hair. Looking at a tooth implant catalogue. Watching PBS. He's not entirely happy with you."

I said, "Ouch."

The master of the house said, "He doesn't call, he doesn't write . . ."

"Awwwww," I said, "did I hurt its little feelings?"

"Careful," Tuffy said.

"You're right," I said instantly, feeling like I'd just had cold water poured down the back of my neck. "I didn't mean to say that. So, uhh, what are you doing that I'm not invited to?"

"You *know*, Junior," the master of the house said, obviously having waved aside Tuffy, who outweighed him three to one, "if favors were a teeter-totter, my end would be on the ground without me sitting on it, and you'd be way up in the air talking to the birds."

"I know," I said.

"You do?"

"I do."

"Well, I'll give you that you got chutzpah," he said, "but so what? Tuffy, do I like chutzpah?"

"You hate it," Tuffy said.

"So tell me what you're doing." I was getting a little desperate. "Maybe it's something I can help with."

"You?" said the master of the house, and Tuffy said, "You?"

"I can do—"

"Now you're interrupting me?" the master of the house said. "Long time ago, I learned, *first they interrupt you. Then they shoot you over dinner.*"

I said, "I didn't."

"Don't argue. Never argue. What we're *doing*? We're going to taste a *wine*, a wine I wouldn't share with the Pope, not even with Lenny Bruce, rest his soul. And I'm going to share it with a sponger like you?"

"Make a deal," I said. "I know *all* about wine. I grew up in a vineyard. I named all the grapes. They came when I called. I taught their children. Give me one little sip—I won't even swallow it, if that's what you want—and I'll tell you more about it than any of those clowns in the restaurants with the ladles around their necks."

"This is wine with an actual *cork*," said the master of the house.

"Okay. Fine. Up to you. That sound you hear is me abandoning all hope. But listen, if you don't like my critique, you can have Tuffy throw me over the wall."

"Over the wall?" said the master of the house.

"Or *through* it. God knows he's got the muscles for it."

"Deal." And the gates slowly ground open.

Tuffy came out to meet me. In defiance of all I thought I knew about human limitations, he had bulked up a little more. He'd had to cut slashes into the ends of the short sleeves of his Hawaiian shirt to let his biceps breathe. The shirt was a primary-color phantasmagoria of South Sea themes, an island so dense with clichés even Moana would have given it a miss. He said, "You're the first person he's seen in a week."

"Why? Is he okay?"

"You decide. You know why he said he'd see you? After the intercom went off?"

"No idea."

"He said the way you stick it up his nose reminds him of

himself, sixty-five, seventy years ago. Said *he* never knew when to shut up, either. When he was young, he meant." He turned to lead me in, stopped, and said, "How much do you really know about wine?"

"Nothing at all," I said. "But I watch old James Bond movies. I know how to swish it through my teeth and raise one eyebrow. I can say, '*Hmmmmm.*'"

"You can raise one eyebrow?"

"Not exactly. I mean, I can, but the other one goes up, too."

Tuffy blew out a little air. "Well, he's waiting. Don't say anything about his weight."

I said, "His *weight*? What is it, what's the problem?"

He shook his head. "Nothing. He said a couple of days ago that eating is too much trouble because he just has to do it again in a few hours."

"Is he depressed?"

"Who can tell? You think he talks about *feelings*? He's not eating, he's too thin, he's grumpy, he watches old *Dancing with the Stars* shows two and three times when he already knows who won, he doesn't sleep for shit. Does that sound depressed to you? Maybe you can cheer him up, although I don't know why you would cheer anybody up." For Tuffy, that was a long speech. He turned away again, and I followed him through the door.

The shrunken little old man in the eye-searing plaid golf pants was sitting exactly where he'd been when I saw him last, dead center on the endless white leather couch, staring at the enormous flat screen on the room's opposite wall. The screen was dark. The man's name was Irwin Dressler. For almost fifty years he had been the most powerful man on either side of the law in Southern California:

a mob boss who had never been arrested; a financier who had started several of California's major banks for money laundering purposes and then taken them straight; a civic force who had looked at Chavez Ravine and seen a good place for his favorite baseball team to play, despite the fact that there was no stadium there and his favorite team was in Brooklyn; a lawyer who had represented, at one point, both the movie studios *and* their unions, leading some wit to say, "When the studios got a strike on their hands, Irwin goes into a room alone for half an hour and comes out shaking hands with himself." He had testified before Congress several times and had been thanked heartily at the end of every session.

And, sure, he'd had some people killed, but in some cases it was a public service. He was, for example, widely believed to have been responsible for the bullets that put the aptly named Bugsy Siegel under the sod at long last. It was rumored at the time that work had started on Dressler's wall several weeks *before* Bugsy sat on the wrong couch.

Dressler had summoned me a few years back, sending Tuffy and his secondary muscle, Babe, to bring me in when I was reluctant to come under my own power. Well, okay, not so much reluctant as *terrified*. Irwin Dressler was known as someone who could make people disappear quite literally with the shake of a head. In one famous incident in the 1970s, he had dispatched three panicked subordinates to catch up to and intercept a hitter who had left the room five or six minutes earlier because a fly had landed on Irwin's nose during a discussion and he'd shaken it off. They all thought the hitter had gotten up to go to the bathroom.

I'd never heard how that story ended, and I wasn't sure I wanted to. I had done him one service by helping him dish out retribution to another old mobster, but he was right: favor-wise, I was deep in the hole.

"Boychik," he said without turning to look at us. The skin beneath his chin had a couple of deflated-looking new folds, and the tongue of the belt that held up his awful golf pants passed through the buckle and continued all the way out of sight behind his back, with several amateur holes punched through it. His thinning white hair was slightly yellowed and longer than I remembered, slicked down in a way I hadn't seen before, a way that accentuated the shape of his skull. "You were the only thing I didn't have today," he said, still with his eyes on the dark screen. "Cramps, I had. A headache, I had. People falling down on *Dancing with the Stars*, I had. Boredom like there's no tomorrow, and that's okay by me, I had. But you, you I didn't have. So look, a royal flush."

"Are you eating?" I said.

"At the moment, no. Why, are you hungry?"

"No, thanks."

"I could get you something," Tuffy said.

Dressler waved the words away. "Enough about that. He's hungry, he can eat on his own time." There was an edge in his voice that froze Tuffy in mid-turn. To me, he said, "So tell me, Mr. Wine Smart Guy, what kinda grapes go into a Merlot?"

"Only the best," I said. "Grapes like they wish they had in heaven. Picked by left-handed virgins, singing in Latin, beneath a full moon."

He held up a hand, all knobbed knuckles and blue veins. "Back it up. Red or white?"

I said, "Red or white."

"That's what I said."

"I know," I said. "I was admiring the way you said it."

"You don't know shit, do you?"

"*Red*." I made a kind of scornful French laugh, a little *pfff* that I didn't even know I could do. "Merlot. Red or white, it is to laugh. What a question. *Pfff pfff*."

Tuffy said to him, "I told you."

"Told me what?"

"That he couldn't find his ass in a blizzard."

"Red, indeed," I said. "A peasant's notion, a blunt-force instrument, no refinement at all. In the trade we refer to the color of Merlot as *arterial raspberry*."

Dressler gave me a look that might have been the last thing some people ever saw, back in the old days. Then he slowly shook his head.

I said, "Can I sit down?"

"Sure, sit." he said. "You want to do your trick with the wine?"

"It's not a *trick*," I said. "It's the result of a lifetime of—"

"Tuffy. Bring *Schmendrik* here a little wine. You, sit down, sit down. My neck doesn't bend as good as it used to. Just a couple spoonfuls, Tuffy, in one of the good glasses. Give him every chance. Used to be one of my rules," he said as Tuffy headed for the kitchen. "Before you pop somebody once and for all, you give them whatever they need for you to see whether they're worth anything. *Then* you pop them. What's your favor?"

I did not have control of this conversation. I said, "Allan Frame."

"Allan Frame," Dressler said. "The favor is Allan Frame, huh? Okay. You know, when you talk about dangerous people, there's mainly two kinds. You got your hot dangerous people and you got your cold dangerous people. Like Allan Frame. Give me the hot ones any time."

"Which one are you?"

He looked at me as though I'd asked which way was up. "I'm *me*," he said. "When you bring it to *me*, what you get is what you bring, hot *or* cold, it doesn't matter."

I said, "You've lost weight."

He surveyed the room. "It's around here someplace."

"You're not looking like—"

"Don't tell me how I look. I don't tell you how you look, you should return the favor. You're not exactly this year's model, you know."

"I worry about you."

"Tell you something," he said, "for years I wished people weren't so afraid of me. I walked into a room, people stopped talking. They *vibrated*. You could smell the sweat. Now, *nobody's* afraid of me. I got you *worrying* about me, I got TV shows want to talk to me with their cameras, I got fruitcake actors, pluck their eyebrows, want to play me in the movies, I got guys knocking on the door, want to write my life story. Like I went seventy-five years without saying *how are you*, and suddenly they think I want to tell the whole world everything I ever did, right out loud."

"It's just this year's stupidity," I said. "Everybody's supposed to want to be famous."

"There's only one kind of stupid," Dressler said. "They just wrap it different."

"I'm still worried about you."

"Who the hell wants you to be worried about him?"

I didn't answer.

It took him a little time, but he reached over and patted my hand. "Don't tell Tuffy," he said. "I got a little something. Here." He indicated the general area of his right kidney.

I felt the whole room drop fifty or sixty feet straight down. Dressler said, "Hey, look at you. What's it gonna do to me, kill me? You think maybe I haven't been alive long enough? You think maybe I never want to stop getting up in the morning? How many times can you get up in the morning before you say, every fucking *day* I do this, and what do I get for it? I'm a day older and that's my future, I gotta do it again. Maybe I'd just like to sleep."

"You and Jake Whelan," I said.

"Jake Whelan," he said. "Jake Whelan is a teenager compared to me. What happened to him, he got a wrinkle?"

I said, "I'd miss you."

"It's a small club, the people who would miss me. Would you yell to Tuffy, ask what the hell he's doing in there? The bottle's open, breathing or sneezing or something, and the glasses are right next to it."

"I'll get him," I said. I got up, trudged through the deep carpet to a dining room the size of the one in Versailles, crossed it, and then angled down a short hall to the kitchen. Tuffy's eyes were almost as wide open as Itsy Winkle's. He looked like someone had just fired a gun about an inch from his ear.

He said, "No."

I said, "Don't show it. We have to get him to a doctor."

"He won't even talk about it."

"Well, we can't solve that now. Give me the wine. You bring the glasses, okay?"

Tuffy took two steps toward me and threw his arms

around me, squeezing me so hard I almost squeaked. "He can't," he said. "He just . . . *can't*."

"Maybe he won't, it's not over yet. We'll get him to a doctor. Come on, he's going to figure we're talking about him."

Tuffy stepped back and scrubbed his forearm across his face. "You first."

I took the bottle and my glass, which already contained an infinitesimal amount of wine, and carried them back through the hallway and the dining room. Dressler had been sitting with his chin lowered to his chest, an attitude of exhaustion, but the moment he heard me he sat up. "About time," he said. "You and Tuffy been having a gossip?"

I said, "Not everything is about you. I was checking the color and the aroma, memorizing the label."

Dressler said, "And?"

"And bottoms up." I knocked it back, nodded, and said, "Pretty damn good."

He said, "That's it? That's all you got, Mr. Expert?"

"What do you want me to tell you? That it was aged for ninety years in oak from the True Cross and then strained through the Shroud of Turin?"

From the dining room, Tuffy said, "It's French."

"So the water is from the grotto at Lourdes. But who cares? Here's what it is. It's the kind of wine where people decide between buying a case of this or a new car, an *expensive* car, one that runs on bird song or something else with no emissions except maybe music. And since I'll never have anything like this again, I'd like some more."

Dressler said to Tuffy, "Go bring those glasses. If it's as good as our expert here says, you should have some, too." Then he turned to me and said, "Allan Frame."

"Yeah," I said as Tuffy trudged toward the kitchen.

"I'm not going to set up a meeting."

I said, "Well, shit. All that wine expertise—"

"I'd miss you," he said, and then he released a creaky little laugh. "Allan Frame, you don't want to mess with, believe me. I'll take care of it." He raised his voice. "Tuffy, can I get the phone over here?"

"Sure thing." Tuffy came in with the glasses and put them on the table. He poured some for me, a little for himself, and considerably more for Dressler. He put Dressler's glass close enough so Dressler wouldn't have to reach for it, and then went to a little niche I'd never noticed, in the wall that had been on our right as we came into the living room. He pulled out an old Princess phone in a queasy shade of graying avocado. It was the ugly clamshell version that had buttons instead of the old-fashioned dial. It looked like a dollhouse toy in Tuffy's huge hand as he brought it over, trailing yards of twisted and knotted cord behind him.

I said, "You're kidding."

"It was my great-granddaughter's," Dressler said. "Sentimental." To Tuffy he said, "When was the line swept last?"

Tuffy looked at his watch. "They all get swept on the hour and it's ten to six, so maybe fifty minutes ago."

"Good enough for Allan Frame," Dressler said. He punched a couple of numbers, paused, and hung it up. "Maybe I should know what this is about before I bother the man."

"*Bother* him? You're *Irwin*—"

"Thank you for reminding me who I am. That, I still remember. But Allan Frame is putting together a *lot* of weight, more weight than anyone has had in the Valley since that thug Annunziato, who gave all of us a bad name, got shot. So tell me what this is about."

"Someone needed a house burglarized and she didn't know how to find a burglar—" I stopped because Dressler had his hand up, palm facing me, a gesture that has probably meant *enough* for thousands of years.

"Not Allan Frame," he said. "Nobody who just needs a *burglar*, you should forgive my tone of voice, would go to Allan. They wouldn't dare. Someone eight, nine levels down from Allan, maybe. But even then they'd have to be stupid, because if what they were after was worth more than a buck-fifty, Allan would have it before it even got warm in the burglar's pocket."

I said, "He hired *two* burglars to hit the same house. On successive nights. Used two fences to do it, so he was one remove from both burglars."

"And the fences told you who he was?"

"With some persuasion."

"I'm glad I'm not their life insurance company. But I'm telling you, Allan Frame doesn't operate at that level. There's gotta be something you don't know."

"There are a million things I don't know. But the main thing I don't know is who his client is. She, or someone working for her, killed a friend of mine. And she's just killed someone else, someone who's no loss to the world, but she's dead in a way that's bad enough to make me personally nervous. Whoever his client is, she's knocking them down left and right."

"It's a she," Dressler said, shaking his head. "Always a complication."

"So, can you still call him?"

"You shouldn't expect much. Whatever is going on, it's

outside the usual rules." He looked off into the middle distance for a moment, picked up his wine glass and drained it, put it down—Tuffy got up and refilled it instantly—said, "Ehhh. Not bad," and began to punch the buttons on the silly little phone.

I hit my own wine again as he waited for an answer. It hadn't deteriorated. Tuffy didn't leap to pour me more, but Dressler made a *tsk-tsk* noise and pointed at my glass, and then he leaned back, turned away from me and said, "Is he there? This is Irwin Dressler." He listened. "For a minute," he said, "I can wait for a minute, but no more."

We all sat there. Tuffy's eyes were wide and he was fidgeting a little, but Dressler did the *tsk-tsk* thing again, looking at Tuffy, and Tuffy subsided instantly.

"Allan," Dressler said in a new voice, a younger, deeper, and stronger voice. "It's me. Yeah, yeah, good, what about you? Okay, we're both good, it's good to be good. Listen I need to ask you a question. See, there's—"

He broke off, both sparse eyebrows raised in surprise. Then he said, "*No*, it's not something I can discuss with Harvey. If I wanted to talk to a *pisher*, I would have called a *pisher*. You're the one I want to talk to, so just hang on for a—" He broke off and looked up at me. If it had been anyone but Dressler, I would have described his expression as *puzzled*. He said, "Son of a bitch put me on hold."

Tuffy, who was sitting on the floor, shifted nervously and cleared his throat.

"*Yeah*, I'm here," Dressler said. "Where would I go? I called you, remember? Listen, somebody's telling me you got some kinda client, you're hiring burglars for them or something, and I know you don't do that but I—" He blinked heavily and then he said, "Hold it, hold it, *hold* it.

I want to know who your client is, and, *no*, I'm not going to tell you who told me about—" He pulled the phone away from his ear, blinking so hard I could almost hear it, and then put it back and said, obviously over whatever Frame was saying, "*Hey*, hey, you gotta watch that. That kind of thing is bad for the heart, you remember being *polite*, how people are supposed to be—" He looked at me and did the spiraling finger at his left temple that means *crazy*, and said, "Not to talk over you or anything, but no, I don't know who that is, what kind of a name is *Junior* anyway and I've got to tell you, I don't much like your—"

His mouth dropped open, and he sat back on the couch, holding the phone out in front of him and looking at it. He tapped it a couple of times against his palm as though to fix it or get its attention, listened again, and said, "He *hung up* on me. Sonofabitch hung up on me." Slowly, carefully, deliberately, he replaced the handset, the way he might handle a Faberge egg, drew two or three deep, soothing breaths, and then threw the phone across the room. The cord, whipping out behind it, knocked over and broke the crystal wine glasses and flipped the bottle end over end, creating a Jackson Pollack spatter in arterial raspberry across the white carpet.

"Tuffy," Dressler said. "More wine. I need Allan Frame's home address and office address and the license plate number of whichever car he drives most, they'll all be in the yellow notebook, third drawer, so bring it here, get me the number for Phil Romero, he used to work for Allan, give me a hitter's list, and get that Annunziato girl—"

"Trey," I said.

"Who the fuck cares?" Dressler said. "She'll come to

whatever I call her, she's got acres of skin in this game, that
vonce took away her business and most of her employees.
She'll be happy to pitch in. What are you *doing*, Tuffy,
am I a TV show that you're just sitting there looking at
me with your mouth open? Wine, yellow notebook, Phil
Romero, hitters, Miss Annunziato."

"Got it," Tuffy said, getting up.

"And call Dr. Fleiss, tell him I want him to come to his
office at seven. Time is it?"

"Six straight up," Tuffy said, and my phone rang.

"In his office at seven, okay? I need a once-over, this
thing in my side. I can't go after somebody like Allan
Frame if I'm dying, can I?"

"No," Tuffy said with a fierce grin, "you can't."

"So go get the stuff. Don't forget the bottle. You," he
said to me, "answer that fucking phone."

"I'm here," Eaglet said. "How long do you need me to stay?"

I was standing in the hallway between Dressler's front door and the living room. I could hear Tuffy opening and closing drawers somewhere. "Can you make it to midnight? Do you have anything that you can, uhh, that you can use—"

"A bucket, but I won't need it. I've been invited in. I assume they've got toilets."

"How did you get—"

"What do you think? I knocked on the door? *Hello, I'm your friendly gunperson for the evening.*"

"Then how—"

"You know," she said, "your daughter is really something. She came home just when I got there—"

"At that hour? Why was she so late? School gets out at—"

"I'm *telling* you. She took two friends of hers, both named Tiffany—"

In the background, I heard Rina burst into laughter.

"—to go see that little Chinese girl, the one with the girlfriend who—"

"Anime," I said.

"Yeah, Annie. And they talked for a couple hours or more, at some Mexican restaurant, and she says Annie—"

"Anime"

"—is feeling a lot better from the talk, and they're all going to get together with Annie's little girlfriend, whatever her name was, because both of the Tiffanys have been through this and come out okay, and you know, I like to think I might have helped, but, I've got to admit it, my experience was a little on the *special* side, what with the mushrooms and the shaman all, but you know what? They invited me to come, too. *Me*, with, you know, just regular girls—"

"You're regular," Rina said in the background. "Well, mostly regular. You've got the coolest business card."

"This never happened to me in high school," Eaglet said.

"That's very interesting," I said, "but—"

"I'm not talking to you. So anyway, I can stay all night because I can sleep on the couch and be right up front to blow the shit—sorry, Rina—out of whoever comes in. If anyone does."

"Have you talked to Rina's mom? To Kathy?"

"Sure, she's right here," she said, and I squeezed my eyes shut like someone expecting a punch. "Say hi, Kathy."

Kathy said, "Hi," but her tone wasn't quite as effusive as Eaglet's and Rina's. It was a tone that promised additional discussion in the future.

"Hang on a second," I said as Irwin Dressler rounded the corner, walking slowly but with considerable purpose.

"Go away," he said. "If you should ever be asked to

testify about what happens here tonight I want you to be able to say you left, and not make the lie detector even hiccup a little. Shoo, shoo."

"I'm shooing," I said, and my phone buzzed to indicate a text.

Opening the front door, I said to Kathy, "Gotta go. I just got a text I have to—"

"We're fine without you," Kathy said. "Aren't we fine, girls?" There was female chorus of *yes*, and she said, "And you and I will talk about this later." She hung up, and I went to the car.

The rain was coming down with serious intent, so I cracked the windows just a little for air and retrieved the new text, which told me to check my email, which in turn had an attachment for me to download. Louie's researcher had apparently accelerated her photo-taking so as to hurry things along and then amalgamated them somehow into a big document. I looked at the time and understood why: the library would be closing soon, and she wanted to get me all she could. Whatever Louie was paying her, she was earning it.

```
When, at the age of seventeen, I fled Kansas to
seek my place in the wider world, I possessed
the unstoppable brute force of an ox and a com-
mon variety of low cunning. Like many young men
who are still under the spell of their as-yet
untested self-delusion, I mistook my force for
strength and my cunning for intelligence. It took
several years and many mistakes, some of them
inexcusable, before I could identify the errors
```

in that appraisal and see myself as I truly was.
It was a frightening awakening.

Those qualities, however, had been required
of me if I were to survive my life with my
father. He was a man who passed judgment first and
sought clarification later. Indeed, he delighted
in passing judgment, both because it gave him
an opportunity to feel superior to me and also
because he enjoyed inflicting the punishment that
would follow. My mother's death was a kind of
furnace that burned away any softness or affection
my father might once have possessed. He became
as hard and unyielding as stones in the field he
plowed so doggedly every year. When I think of
my father now, I see a narrow, rigid man guid-
ing a plow that is being pulled by a mule and
scratching a dry, shallow line in the earth. My
father knew that the earth would fail him and
that the crops, in the main, would die before
they were ready for harvest, but he could see no
farther than the end of the furrow he was cutting. I hope my father's spirit is at rest now.
I am sure it is.

I know it is unfilial of me to confess, even
in a book that will not be read for decades (if,
indeed, it is ever read), that I could not love
my father. It was not until I was much older that
I could understand somewhat how he became the man
I knew, and it took me even longer to recognize
him in myself, like looking in a mirror and seeing suddenly an unexpected likeness in the mouth
or around the eyes. Indeed, as I sit here, pen

in hand, devoting some of what will surely be my last days to this book that may never be read, I see again that straight, useless furrow, being cut this time into paper. So it may be that I am indeed my father's son. I am afraid also that he taught me how to be a father, perhaps the worst thing he ever did to me. When people claim that we revisit the sins of our fathers, I am sorry to say, from my own experience, that we often revisit them upon our children. I know I did upon my daughter.

But this is not the time to talk about my bungled relationship with my family. That will come in its turn. Suffice it to say that when I left Kansas I was running not only toward an unknown world but also away from my father. Later, when I did the things of which I have grown to be most ashamed, it seemed to me that I was somehow evening the score with my father, doing deeds that, had he known of them, would horrify him, trapped as he was in his useless, profitless rectitude.

Well. As someone who'd had his own issues with his father, I found myself finding common ground with the founder of the short-lived Horton dynasty. I'd demonstrated my contempt for *my* father by replacing him with Herbie Mott and embarking, as soon as was humanly possible, on my own relatively modest life of crime. I had more in common with the old claim jumper than I'd thought. One problem with looking at people we dislike more closely, I've found, is that we usually see ourselves in them.

The young woman in the library was hauling ass,

because a little buzz and shimmy broke my concentration on the book to announce a third installment. That made me wonder how late the library was open, which in turn made me look at my watch, and *that* led me to wonder what was happening with the wills, and at that moment my phone rang.

"It's that sparkler, Walter," Louie announced. "He's got them both, although he says it cost him an extra couple hundred of his own. I asked him did he get a receipt, and he didn't even chuckle."

"Nobody actually chuckles," I said. "The chuckle is a fictitious form of laughter."

"Whatever you say."

"Come on," I said. "Let me hear you chuckle. Three to one you'll give me some kind of snort."

"Are you even *interested* in these wills?"

"I'm interested in anything and everything that'll help me get past what I saw this afternoon."

"Yeah? What's that?"

I told him.

"Why didn't you lie to me?" he said. "Tell me you bought Girl Scout cookies and one of them went bad or something, anything except that. I would have lied to *you*."

"I had to give part of it to somebody," I said. "You're my best friend."

"Yeah? Do me a favor, make another friend."

"So is old Walter with you?"

"Nah. He's on his way, but it's raining and it's rush hour."

I looked out the window. It was, in fact, still raining and it was the raggedy end of rush hour. I was parked in Dressler's driveway, just outside the gate. No one had come out yet to tell me to beat it. "What's your guess at an ETA?"

"What're you, NASA?" Louie said. "His ETA?"

"All right. Where and when do you think we should meet Walter? Is that better?"

"Du-par's," Louie said. "We can put sugar on everything. How about we give him forty-five minutes?"

"I'll be there."

"Come a little early," Louie said. "We can get some quality time."

I have to admit that I found the rhythm of Codwallader's prose, stiff though it was, sort of hypnotic. It was so much more *languid* than most of the contemporary language I'd read. He had a story to tell and he assumed that his reader, if there ever was one, would have a lot of time to devote to it. The issue of free time without much of anything competing for it helped to explain the sheer length of novels like *Middlemarch* and the other triple-decker doorstops laid at the feet of the public by people like Dickens and Trollope and Eliot. None of those writers could have guessed that a time would come in which the standard attention span could be measured in seconds.

It would take me a good twenty or twenty-five minutes to get to Du-par's, so I began to skip a little. He had gone bad in the conventional way, one misdeed at a time, with the intervals between them growing shorter as his confidence grew and his conscience shrank. He stole, he betrayed, he stole some more. He terrorized the helpless. When he finally killed someone, at the age of twenty-four, it shook him, and he did a pious page or three about remorse and the blown-out candle of the spirit and death being a one-way street and all that, but the eventual upshot was that he accepted who he was; as he said, what was the alternative? At the same time, he became more violent; where before, he had used violence as a threat, in his mid-twenties it became his tool of first choice, a way of dispensing with the warm-up. Draw the gun, grab the stuff, clobber the sucker silly, and take off for the horizon. And also, for the first time—or at least the first time he admits it on the page—he began to look over his shoulder. As the malfeasance added up and the list of victims and double-crossed confederates grew, and the occasional *wanted* poster appeared, he spent less of his time and energy on crime, and more on making sure the trail behind him was clear. He was operating mainly in Nevada during this period, and while the unsettled West was enormous and empty and easy to get lost in, the towns were claustrophobically small; sooner or later *everyone* rode through. Codwallader was spending a lot of his time with one eye on the street.

The narrative, for all its *I'm being frank because I'm dead* claim of honesty, was pretty vague on how much money he was pulling in. He was stealing mostly silver and a little gold, but he didn't get very specific about how much of it he swiped or what he got for it. The most detailed description of his takings comes almost incidentally in a story about the time one of his saddlebags burst open beneath the weight of the silver it contained, silver that had been purified and melted into bars. At the time, he was being chased by people who were no more than a few miles behind him, and his horse was tiring. But the bag broke and he didn't have the luxury of slowing down to pick up his haul, and the spill of silver across his trail distracted and delayed his pursuers. He was able to hole up in some convenient rocks until he could venture out without risk of being hung on the spot. After that, he kept a handful of silver bars within easy reach in case he ever again needed to put distance between him and the people who were after him. What that said to me was that he'd bagged considerable quantities of gold and silver.

This was just a few months before the time when, after a hair's breadth escape from the mining boomtown of Virginia City, that he began to think about going to New York, and perhaps beyond.

26

It's All in the Wrist, Like Everything Else

Traffic was heavier than I'd thought it would be, courtesy of the rain. I'd only just made the turn from Mulholland onto Coldwater when my phone rang. Louie again.

No cops behind me. I put the phone on speaker and said, "Fifteen minutes."

"You're not going to *believe* what's in this will," Louie said.

"Which one?"

"The daughter. Daisy. Jeez, she hated *everybody*."

"Is Walter still there?"

"Sure. He's eager to say hi, too, aren't you, Walter?"

Walter apparently managed to contain his enthusiasm, since I didn't hear a reply. Louie said, "He's just shy."

"Get rid of him," I said. "Give him the whole seven hundred. I'll give it to you, and some more, when I get there."

"Fine with me," Louie said. "The older I get, the stricter I am about who gets in. If life is really getting shorter, and it's silly to pretend it isn't, maybe we should circle the wagons, you know? Put out sentries, be picky about who sits around the fire with us."

"That's positively poetic."

"Well, the inspiration just got up to go to the bathroom. Has to wash his hands before he'll pick up a teacup."

"Lean close and breathe all over him," I said. "See you in a few."

On this side of the hill, the rain was more of a mist. The valley presented itself as an abstract painting, just formless smears of colored light stretching all the way to the dark hulks of the Santa Susana and San Gabriel mountains to the north. The mountains themselves were now invisible but their foothills were bordered by the farthest and dimmest margin of light. Below me and to my right were Glendale and North Hollywood, where I had caught my one horrified glimpse of Althea Beckwell-Stoddard, and *that* brought to mind the thought that cats are, by nature, nocturnal and this would be party time. Yet again I fought down the urge to report the killing. People in my position don't call in information about murders, not in an era where cops have access to the highest of high-tech. *Sooner or later*, I thought. A client's parent, a boyfriend, an unlucky UPS guy, *someone* would push that door the rest of the way open.

My phone rang again, and this time the screen announced *Ronnie*.

"I'm so sorry," I said. "This has been—"

"I haven't even accused you of anything yet. Anyway, I've had a great time. Here's a life-coaching tip: go to amusement parks when it's raining. I owned the place."

"I'm on my way to the Du-par's on Ventura to see Louie. You want to meet me there?"

"Du-par's? No, thanks. I totally ate my way through the day, one awful piece of fried junk after another, and I feel like my inside is bigger than my outside. Also, I have to confess that I didn't sleep very well at Ratville, so my plan is to take a shower and some heartburn medicine, watch something undemanding on the drive-in theater screen they put in this big, quiet, mouse-free room, digest for a while, and then pass out. Maybe order a bottle of wine."

"What's the bed situation?"

"Twin queens. If I don't wake up and say hello when you come in, do me a favor and sleep in the empty one. I'll make it up to you in the morning."

"Oh, boy," I said, passing Jake's driveway yet again. "Pepsodent love."

"I'll turn the covers down for you."

"And if you *do* say hello?"

"Well, then," she said. "It'll depend on you."

Louie was steaming. I could spot it from the doorway. The look he gave me nearly cut me in half.

I was most of the way to him when someone touched my arm. I looked down at a panorama of tattoos and said, "Hi, Glinda."

"You're with Pie Guy over there?" she said.

"I will be. How's the transubstantiation coming?"

"Piece of cake. It's all in the wrist, like everything else. Be nice to him. His date ran out on him, that guy with all the flakes on his face? Mr. Flakey went out to the parking lot for something and left your buddy sitting there, and after a few minutes he got up to see what had happened, and when he came back in he looked like a lighted match. He's been snarling at everybody ever since."

"I'll smooth him out."

"The management thanks you. Coffee?"

"Can you leave the pot again?"

"Shhhh," she said. "People will talk."

She headed toward the counter and I did a brief scan of the territory. Mostly families eating an early dinner, and other than the children whose parents had dragged them in, there was no one below the age of fifty: the Du-par's demographic, shading older on a daily basis. No cops for the moment, although that would change. Like a lot of all-night operations, Du-par's gives the cops a hundred-percent discount in exchange for the occasional drive-by and a pledge to respond within a couple of minutes to an emergency call.

I was tired and wrung out, still carrying the shock of those cats exploding out at me, the sight and smell of Althea on the floor, and also the unexpected revelation of Irwin Dressler's sudden mortality. *And* a prolonged case of the jitters that had been curled defensively inside me—just waiting for a chance to take charge again—since the moment I smelled the baby powder in that pitch-black hallway. This had not been a relaxing couple of days.

Louie was doing his best to stare a hole in the table, so I had an unobserved moment. I used it to draw a few big breaths, blow them out, and contract and release my shoulders a couple of times. I could feel Glinda watching me from behind the counter, so I nodded her way, inhaled again, and slid into the booth.

"So," I said. "He left without saying goodbye?"

"I could kill him," Louie said. "I gave him the money, like a schmuck, and after I finished reading Miss Daisy's will, which is more like a *won't*, I asked for the old guy's, and he slapped his forehead and said he'd left it in the car. *Silly me*, he said. *Be right back*, he said. Five minutes later I go out and his car is gone, and about two minutes after *that* he calls to say that the second will is gonna cost a thousand bucks, thank you very much. Said he knew we could get another copy tomorrow, and if that fit in with our schedule, we should feel free to do it. Son of a bitch."

I said, "I thought he was afraid of you."

Louie rubbed his face with both hands. "I *knew* you'd say that. If someone had bet me fifty K that I couldn't predict what you'd say, I woulda taken the bet in a second."

"Well," I said, "it doesn't lessen my respect for you, that you can't scare someone who hasn't even gotten his law degree yet, someone who's afraid to drink coffee, someone who—"

"But nobody offered me the bet," Louie said, continuing what he clearly saw as a monologue. "If they had, I'd be a rich man. I wouldn't be sitting here getting abused, I'd be on my way to the Ritz-Carlton for a fancy rubdown and one of those things where they put warm rocks all over you."

"Did you get that address?"

"What address? Oh, you mean the guy—"

He stopped talking because Glinda had materialized beside the table, a cup of coffee in one hand and a plate containing a bonus-size piece of pie in the other. "Here," she said, putting the pie in front of Louie. "On the house."

"Kind is it?" Louie asked squinting at it as though he expected a tiny hand, holding a gun, to emerge from it.

"Blackbird," Glinda said. "First, you take your four-and-twenty—"

"Yeah, yeah, yeah," Louie said. "That's nice, thanks to everybody. So what is it?"

Glinda exhaled in a meaningful manner. "What color is the filling?"

"Blue?"

"That's a clue," Glinda said. She looked over at me, crossed her eyes, and said, "Get anything else for you?"

"Cheeseburger," I said. "Lots of Dijon mustard, some onion, and I don't care how it's cooked."

"Wouldn't matter if you did." To Louie, she said, "More coffee, hon?"

"I'm good," Louie said. "Thanks again for the pie."

When Glinda was gone, I said, "The address that goes with the phone number I gave you the last time we were sitting here."

"Oh, yeah, sure, sure." He leaned to one side so he could get to his wallet, pulled it out, and tore off the top page on the little pad. "Not exactly in the nabe."

"I don't care. Gives me a chance to drive in the rain." I pocketed the paper, sat back and picked up my coffee. "So, how are you going to get Old Horton's will?"

"I'm gonna *pay* him, whaddya think? Nine-thirty tonight. Walter and a couple friends, which apparently he's got, will be in a movie theater. I'm supposed to send someone to meet him in the lobby, right by the popcorn, and make the switch, money in an envelope, the will *not* in an envelope. Then my guy leaves, and Walter and his buddy come out with like a thousand other people when the movie is over. I hope it's a shit movie, something with Robert De Niro playing a wise, good-hearted father-in-law. With a beard."

"Not a bad pass-off plan," I said. "Movie theater is a nice touch."

"I have to admit, he's got skills. I can't believe I fell for

the *I'll get it from the car* dodge, but he seemed so wit-
less."

"He'll make a good lawyer. By the time the other side
has figured out he's not an idiot he'll have the case in his
pocket."

"It's embarrassing. The extra thousand is on me."

"No, it isn't. Add it to my bill." I raised my cup and
waved it around and got a nod from Glinda. "And don't
argue about it. I would have fallen for it, too."

"You think?" He picked up his fork, interested in his
pie for the first time.

"Come on. He looks like someone who stands outside
the restrooms for a couple of minutes, trying to figure out
which is which."

"So," Louie said with his mouth full, "What's next."

"I'm going to drop in on the person at this address." I
tapped my shirt pocket. "I think he can tell me something
about what happened in Horton House during the last
few months before Miss Daisy kicked it. If it's what I think
it was, I hope he's not too old for me to hit."

"Yeah? You haven't read her will yet. I don't think she
inspired much loyalty."

"Well, then," I said, "let's have a look at Miss Daisy's
will."

27
Additional Layers of Toxic Waste

It was a pretty crappy photocopy, considering how much it had cost. Some civil servant was obviously trying to save the tax dollars spent on toner.

But it was legible, and as Louie had said, it was more a won't then a will. And Miss Daisy's personality was stamped into every sentence.

This is what it said:

Will of Daisy Laurel Horton

I, Daisy Laurel Horton, a resident of Los Angeles County California, being of sound mind and deteriorating body on this fifth day of January, 2017, do hereby revoke all prior wills and codicils made by me (often under duress from people I loathe) and declare this to be my only and final Will.

Article One
Family Information

I am a member of a scattered, worthless, and mercifully small family that consists, for the purposes of this Will, of two great-great cousins on the paternal side, **Duane Peter Horton** and

Andrea Horton Phelps. They have endless children, spouses, in-laws, cousins, and other parasites, but it should be understood that any reference to "cousins" in this document refers solely to **Duane Peter Horton** and **Andrea Horton Phelps.** It is entirely their responsibility to determine how to share their dual inheritance as it is outlined below.

In the event that one of them should predecease me, all bequests are to be left to the survivor. If they both predecease me, my instructions about the ultimate disposition of the structure known as Horton House, outlined in the paragraphs below, shall be followed.

Article Two
Disposition of Tangible Personal Property

The term *tangible personal property* refers to **the structure known as Horton House and the double lot on which it sits,** located at 13217 Windsor Street, Los Angeles, CA 93146 **and to all the contents of that house, large and small, without exception**. My direction is that **the house and all its contents, without exception**, shall be bulldozed, intact and unexplored, within a month of my death, and that after said house and contents have been leveled they shall be fed into one or more tree-chipping machines to create debris of a substantially uniform size. This debris shall be taken to the toxic waste site run by **Waste Disposal Inc.** in Santa Fe Springs, California, with whom I have contracted for its disposal and a subsequent commitment that it will be promptly covered by additional layers of toxic waste. A notarized copy of the pre-paid contract for this disposal is appended to this Will.

The double-lot on which the structure sits, which is worth an estimated $220,000 as of the date of this document, shall be divided equally between my cousins, to be used or disposed of as they see fit.

Article Three
Disposal of Financial Reserves

The term *financial reserves* refers to **several bank accounts and financial instruments,** which are to be apportioned as hereby directed.

The **two savings accounts** in my name at Western Vista Bank totaling approximately $291,000, the **money market account** in my name at First Security Bank of Los Angeles totaling approximately $610,000, and the **checking account** at that same bank, containing perhaps $8,500, shall be divided equally between my cousins. If I had been healthier, I would have spent all of it. Bank addresses and account numbers are appended to this document.

A number of fully mature United States Treasury Bonds with a cash value of approximately $75,000 is hereby bequeathed to **Paulette Codwallader Creighton,** and by her acceptance of this inheritance Ms. Creighton shall be understood specifically to have relinquished all claims **to any other property, personal or otherwise, or assets of any kind in the residue of this estate.** The details of the Treasury Bond account are appended to this document.

Article Four
Conditions of this Will

1. Trespass in Horton House

All my heirs have been legally and unambiguously informed that access to the structure called Horton House, which I own solely, is forbidden to them whether I am living or dead. If any or all of them should be caught attempting to enter it and to take or otherwise claim even the least of its contents, they forfeit all right of inheritance as outlined above. In the case of such a breach, all proceeds from the sale of the property on which the house sits will be bequeathed instead to The Shure-Shot BB Company of Eddington, Illinois, which makes high-quality air-guns that, I am told, rural children use to kill birds. Birds are a great nuisance.

Additionally, any heir who attends the demolition of Horton House and attempts to remove any item, no matter how insignificant, either before or after the house has been leveled, or while its remains are being chipped, similarly forfeits all legacies contained herein. They are, however, welcome to ransack the chipped remains in the toxic waste site, if they can gain admittance to it.

2. Legal Challenges to this Document

Any legatee who challenges or attempts to challenge any aspect or detail of this Will shall forfeit all right of inheritance to all legacies herein. Those legacies will be bequeathed instead to The Shure-Shot BB Company.

Article Five
Executor

Joseph G. Loeb, of the law firm of Loeb and Hart, shall be charged with administering the terms of this Will. Mr. Loeb's contact information is attached to this document and he is, I am reliably informed, no one to fuck around with.

The thing was signed, witnessed by no one whose name I recognized, and stamped a bunch of times. Miss Daisy's handwriting looked like the agitated scribble of a seismograph, running downhill at about a thirty-degree angle relative to the line on which she'd been supposed to sign. Writing, reviewing, and signing it might have accounted for her sloppiness—the sheer venom it contained must have demanded most of the little physical energy she had—or it might have been intentional, a final, editorial *up yours* to the world she was leaving. One way or the other, however, there was no sense that the sheer force of her malice had been diminished or mellowed as she contemplated a world without her in it. Her eyesight, maybe, her hearing, maybe, but the loathing with which she regarded the world, or at least the parts of it that were unfortunate enough to rub up against her, was defiantly intact.

Who the hell was Paulette Codwallader Creighton? The others, I could understand; they were Hortons, but Ms. Creighton, despite the middle name, was not listed among the cousins. Then I felt like slapping my head. Of *course*, I knew who she was, at least on one level, and now I could almost see how she fit in.

"You know what it is?" Louie said.

"No," I said. "What is it?"

"Only thing she cares about in the whole world is totaling that house and every fucking thing in it, all the way down to the mice. Only reason she left that money to those people was to give them something to lose if they tried to save the place, or steal stuff out of it, or whatever. She's trying to protect something that's in this house, even from the grave."

"A lot's already been stolen," I said. "The paintings,

most of the furniture—all of it pretty good, too, probably. That's what I've got to talk to this guy about." I touched my shirt pocket again, and my phone buzzed, indicating another text. Without looking at it, I said, "The woman you sent to UCLA is doing a hell of a job. What time is the library likely to close down?"

"Nine, nine-thirty," Louie said. "Why don't you answer her text and ask her yourself?"

I said, "Good thinking," and pulled out my phone. But what was on the screen wasn't a text. What was on my screen was a view of my entry hall at the edgwood, and someone was just stepping out of camera range.

28
The One Thing That Doesn't Fit In

Within a few seconds I was on Louie's side of the booth and we were crowding each other, practically cheek to cheek, for a better view of the screen. At the moment, no one was visible although the front door was ajar by a few inches. I wasn't even aware of Glinda refilling my cup until she said, "Glad to see you guys are getting along." Then she was leaning down next to me, squinting at the screen and saying, "Hey. Where's that?"

"My place," I said.

"Nice. You leave your door open all the time like that?"

"Someone just opened it."

"Maybe you should call the—Yikes, that's a serious nose. Friend of yours?"

"Not even remotely," I said. Without the big 1968 Afro wig, he was a skinny, hawk-nosed, thin-lipped guy in his damaged late forties who looked like he could bite things in half without using his teeth and couldn't remember the last time he'd laughed. He pulled the door toward him a few inches, sighted through the opening, and then, slowly and obviously quietly, closed the door. Then, for good measure, he put an eye to the peephole.

"You know," Glinda said, "we *own* the cops around

here. I could probably have a squad car there in about six minutes."

"It's in Koreatown," I said.

"Okay, twelve minutes. Maybe ten."

I thought about it for a moment. Cops in my house. My emergency cash was no longer there, since it was in the trunk of the car, and most of the stolen stuff at the edgwood had been swiped so long ago it wouldn't be on anybody's hot list. But suppose the cops answered the call and caught Mr. Nose, and then I showed up. Where would that conversation take us? It's not like you can say to the cops, "Can I have a word in private with my burglar?" We'd all wind up downtown and someone down there would have heard my name in the past few years. Not being arrested isn't the same thing as not being suspected. It was hard to tell where the chain reaction might end up.

I said, "No, thanks. I'll call security in the building, though. Maybe."

She turned to look at me, so close her nose almost brushed my cheek, and then she straightened up. When I turned to her, she wasn't exactly smiling, but she wasn't exactly not smiling, either. She said, "Got it. No cops." She put a hand on her hip. "Property reallocation, huh?"

"It's a living," I said. "Louie, could you text the woman in the library for me? Tell her I want her to jump ahead to when Codwallader is in London and give me as much of it as she can. She can skip everything until then."

Glinda said, "Ah, there's your cheeseburger," and headed for the counter and the pass-through window.

"London, huh?" Louie said, texting. He was a lot better with his thumbs on the phone's keypad than I was.

"Whoa," he said, looking down at the screen on my phone. "Who's that?"

And there she was, at last. She was in her late forties or early fifties, older than I had thought, square-jawed and broad-shouldered, with blondish hair in a short, business-like Hillary Clinton bob, minus the symmetrical curl that softened the haircut on Clinton. Her hairline was lower than Sean Hannity's—she could almost have combed her eyebrows back to close the gap—and the low forehead, combined with the long, clearly defined jaw, made her look like her features had all been placed a little too high in her face, painted on by some neophyte with astigmatism. Without the orange bangs she had worn, the fatty pros-thesis that had softened her jaw, and the 1950s glasses, I never would have recognized her if I hadn't known who she was. She had the solid, curve-free frame of someone who was packing aggressive muscle, and when she walked her shoulders tick-tocked from side to side like a metro-nome.

Louie fired off his text, watched the woman on my screen, and said. "Bad hip. That's how Alice walked before she had her replacement."

"Her hips are going to be the least of her problems when I'm done with her," I said. "Have you got anybody in one of your cars down near K-Town?"

"I got no cars out, period," he said. "I know a couple people who live down there, though."

"Any of them know how to do a tail?"

"I don't have people fill out forms."

"Well, hell," I said. "What good are they?"

At the moment, no one was on the screen. She'd gone toward the living room, and he was on the other side of the entry hall, to the right, from the camera's perspective, where the kitchen, pantry, library, and bedrooms were. I said, "I wish I could pan this damn camera."

Some stuff flew across the screen, too fast for me to see what it was. The blur was followed by a cushion from the couch and then the vase into which Ronnie had put the carnations, which broke into a thousand pieces and splashed water all over the hall. Within a second, Mr. Nose was hurrying across the hall, hands out, palms down, pushing them repeatedly toward the floor. Message: *Shut the fuck up*. Eight or ten seconds later he came back, went to the door, and peered through the peephole to see whether the noise had drawn any curiosity or, perhaps, a do-gooder. He obviously knew nothing about the clientele at the edgwood, most of whom wouldn't open their doors if a circus were parading down the corridor, elephants and all.

"How'd they get in?" Louie said. "You got all those Koreans with the muscles."

"Same way I'd get in. The guards are in the lobby. Mr. Nose there jumped three, four feet in the air, grabbed the lowest extension of the fire escape, and pulled it down, and then they climbed up to my floor and came in through the window that we're supposed to go out through."

"Not locked?"

"These are not actually buildings people break into," I said. "If you don't know what they're like inside you'd figure nobody who lives there has anything worth stealing, and if you *do* know what they're like inside, then you also know they've got more guns per square yard than the White House."

"Well, they seem to be in there, anyway."

I looked at my watch. "Rush hour is pretty much over,"

I said, "but there's still the rain to slow me down. They'll probably be gone by the time I—"

I broke off because Mr. Nose had trotted by again, holding something—a drawer from the dresser in the bedroom—and as he neared the camera his eyes, just for a tenth of a second, darted up to the camera and back again. She came into view from the living room and took the drawer from him and they talked for a few seconds. It was one of Ronnie's drawers, and it pissed me off to see them handling it, even though I knew there was nothing in it that they'd want or, for that matter, that she'd miss.

"They've spotted the camera," Louie said. He leaned closer in, lowering his voice as though he was afraid they might hear. "Probly figured out you're watching. They're taking their time because they're betting you're coming and they can take you."

"Yeah. That's what I think, too." We watched them talk for a moment or so. Their body language said nothing about their relationship except that the thrill, if there had ever been one, was long gone, probably without leaving an imprint on the sheets; they could have been cousins, a couple who had been living in each other's pockets for twenty years, members of a long-lived business partnership, or simply people who were profoundly indifferent to each other.

"'Scuse," Glinda said, and I lifted my hands so she could slide the burger onto the mat. "They dangerous?" she said, leaning down to look at the screen.

"Very," I said.

"Must be somebody in property reallocation you could call," she said. "Get him to take care of them."

I said, "Maybe you're in the wrong business."

"No shit, Sherlock," she said, and turned to go back to the counter.

"Okay," Louie said, looking at his phone on the table. "She says she'll skip to the part where he's in England."

I was watching Glinda, hearing again what she'd said. "What?"

"Where'd you go?" Louie said. "What I said was—"

"Yeah, yeah, sorry, I heard you. I was thinking about old man Horton's books. One of them was an autographed first edition of *The Adventures of Sherlock Holmes*. He had a lot of very nice nineteenth-century first editions, but only one of them was signed to him by the author. You know, Herbie used to say, 'When you see *one thing that doesn't fit in with everything else*, it's probably the most important thing.'" I focused on my burger.

"Is that right?" Louie said. He didn't sound like the words had changed his life. "So," he said, "what are you going to do about them?"

"What *can* I do? I go there and shoot them, it'll be a situation. I go there and they shoot me, it'll be a worse situation. So," I said, "I'm going to chew and swallow. My mother always said, 'The food you don't eat nice is the food that you'll see twice.' And I'm going to find something to read. Then, if they're still waiting for me, I'm going to scare the shit out of them."

It took all of two minutes on the Project Gutenberg site to find and open *The Adventures of Sherlock Holmes*. To make sure it was the same twelve stories, I looked for "Miss Violent," but Gutenberg's type wasn't taken from the First Edition, so the page numbers were different. I did remember the name of the first tale in Horton's book, "A

Scandal in Bohemia," and it was right up front where it should have been. With no idea what I was looking for, I read the first couple of stories as I ate. By the time I was halfway through the second, "The Red-Headed League," I had decided that I'd much rather sit next to Watson than Holmes on an airplane, and that, in fact, I'd try to arrange it so someone I really disliked, someone who loved the sound of his own voice, sat next to Holmes. He'd be lucky to get through a sentence fragment before Holmes over-rode him. Beside me, Louie nervously fidgeted his way through yet another piece of pie. Every now and then he'd tap my arm as a prompt, and I'd abandon Holmes temporarily and go back to Anime's app. The second or third time, I thought they'd gone because no one crossed the screen during the two minutes we watched, but the next time I looked, about ten minutes later, Mr. Nose sauntered past in the direction of the library, yawning. When he was most of the way across, he turned and said something over his shoulder, so she was obviously in the living room.

"Pretty relaxed," Louie said.

"I think they're exhausted," I said. "Probably almost as tired as I am." I squeezed my eyes shut and widened them, and started to skim the third story, which was called "A Case of Identity."

"You're just going to sit here and read?"

I put the phone aside. "Why? Are you feeling left out? Is there something you need to share?"

"I don't know," Louie said. "They're in your house, not mine. I thought you were going to scare them off or something."

I picked up the phone again. "I changed my mind. This way, I know where they are."

"And they know *you* know. At least they probably figure you do, since that's what the camera is for, and all."

"Then they'll leave, eventually, when I don't arrive and
they start to feel silly. But in the meantime, I don't have to
think about what they're up to. Anyway, I think I know
where they'll be later tonight."

"Yeah, where?"

I did an imitation of being totally absorbed in my reading.

"How would you scare them, anyway?"

"I'm told there's an alarm," I said, "a really deafening
WHOOP WHOOP WHOOP, that I can trigger from here."

"You and me and three, four guys," he said, "we could
go wait at the bottom of that fire escape and you could set
that thing off."

"And somebody gets killed," I said. "No. I plan to be
completely and solely in charge of who gets killed."

That earned me a dubious-looking squint. "Yeah, how?"

"Strategy," I said. "Hey, it's almost nine. A time your
guy or girl is supposed to swap the thousand for the old
man's will. Are you supposed to be there?"

"Walter said no."

"Do you want to go home or something?"

"No."

"More pie?"

"Don't even say the word," Louie said. "Tell you what,
though. Why don't you get up and go back to your side of
the booth before the rumors start."

"Oh, come on," I said. "You're much too old for me."

"Hey, I'm not that much—"

"No," I said, "but you *look* older."

"What a guy," Louie said. "Low blow to aim at someone who's going gray, don't you think?"

"I haven't seen any gray."

"Bullshit. I saw you sneaking looks at my hair in that other restaurant."

"I wasn't sneaking—"

"It's not like it's *subtle*," Louie said. He used the hand with the fork in it to trace a vertical line down the side of his ponytail. "See? Silver threads among the gold. And a few weeks ago I decided to start a beard, one of those neat little triangular ones, like a jazz—"

"A goatee."

"I know what it's *called*," he said. "Whadya think, I never had a beard before? But four, five days in, I had to shave it. Two white stripes went from the corners of my mouth straight down to my jaw. Looked like I drooled bleach."

I said, "That's *really* interesting."

"Oh, fuck you. So I look older. So what?"

I said, "Exactly. That's what I *said*, you look older."

I went back to my reading.

"Cheap victory," he said. "So what's the book?"

"Sherlock Holmes."

"Wow," he said. "Great shit."

"You like Sherlock Holmes? Victorian England, all of that? Want me to tell you some stuff about Victorian silverware?"

"Naaahhh."

"It's interesting. By silverware standards, anyway."

"Yeah, well, to you, I'm sure it is. But if you go back to your side of the booth before you tell me, I can promise, it'll be boring on *my* side."

"Have it your way."

"Thing about Sherlock Holmes," Louie said, absolutely

refusing to let me end the conversation, "outa all the private eyes I ever read about, he's the only one ever lets a crook go. Got him dead to rights and let him walk."

"Really," I said to be polite. "Why would he do that?"

"'Cause he thinks the crook, underneath his crookness, is basically a good guy who just made a mistake. So old Sherlock lets him walk and start his life over. Says, like, you're not really a bad dude, you shouldn't be in jail. Not quite like that, but words to that effect. In longer sentences. You ever read a book where a detective does that?"

"I don't read genre fiction," I lied.

"Oh, pardon *me*. So what's Sherlock Holmes?"

"It's the *one thing that doesn't fit*, as Herbie used to say. So it's probably important."

"Got it," Louie said. "But you know, if you were listening to me, you would have realized that Old Sherlock letting the crook go doesn't fit, either. But, no, you're probably right, I should shut up."

I said, "Which story is that in?"

"I don't know. They all run together." He looked at his watch. "So," he said, "what're you gonna do now?"

"Read this thing. Wait for the next text from your girl at UCLA. Eventually, I'm going to go barge in on a guy named Eduardo."

Louie turned his fork so the tines pointed to his left and used the edge to scour the blue stickiness on his plate. "Who's he?" He licked the fork.

"He worked for Miss Daisy. For a long time."

"Not long enough to make it into her will."

Starting to read the same sentence for the fourth time, I said, "I have a feeling he wrote himself in, on an informal basis."

He said, "Are they still there?"

I stifled a sigh, exited Sherlock Holmes's London, and brought up Anime's app. They weren't in sight, but the entrance hall was still there, and I derived some comfort from that.

"Well, at least they haven't blown the place up," Louie said. His phone rang. "Yeah? Yeah, at the popcorn counter. You got people with you, like I said? No, they gotta be out of sight, but where they can see *you*. Get it in gear. Have them buy a ticket and then hang around outside till you come out, then they should go in and buy some popcorn, okay?"

I found my car keys in my pocket, took one last look at my hallway—still empty—and put my phone in my pocket. I'd just thought of another errand I needed to do before I went to see Eduardo. I waved at Glinda.

"Just in case he tries to stiff you, that's all," Louie said into the phone. "If he doesn't give you the will, or if it doesn't look like a will by a guy named Horton, you signal your guys and get the money back right then and there." He looked up at me as I asked Glinda for the check. "It'll be easy," he said. "And have one of your guys stay there and follow him, wherever he goes. Call me when you've got the will. Hang on." He took the phone away from his mouth. "Where you going?"

"Got a couple of errands to run."

"But the will—"

"When you've got it, call me. You can read it to me." I made a little circular gesture to take in the table. "I've got all this."

"'Kay," he said. "See you." Into the phone, he said, "Not *you*, bonehead," and I got up and went to pay my bill.

29
Islands in a Stream

After six or seven years of drought, the rain was doing its
best to make up for all that lost time on a single evening,
as though it suddenly realized there had been a lot of par-
ties to which it hadn't been invited. Even at double-time
my wipers were pushing rills of water ahead of them, and
visibility was so bad I got off the freeway at the first exit
and splashed a wet zigzag to the residential streets south
of Ventura Boulevard, narrow enough and empty enough
and well enough lighted to let me relax at the wheel.

Three blocks away, I called Eaglet.

"*Now* what?" she said. She sounded aggrieved.

"Am I interrupting something?" I steered around a
puddle where, for years, there had been a gaping pothole.

"We're playing charades. I'm up."

"Well, give them three guesses each and then come out
and meet me."

"Men," she said. "Threatened whenever women have a
good time without them."

"Bring your gun."

She said, "I don't want to leave. I'm having fun for the
first time in—"

"I don't need you," I said. "I just need your—" The

phone buzzed to announce a call. I said, "Call you back," and then I said to Louie, "Do you have it?"

"Sure. I'm looking at it now. Not real complicated."

I glanced up to realize I'd allowed the car to drift to the right and I was inches away from sideswiping a big steel-gray Lincoln. "Hang on," I said, "I need to get to the curb."

"That's okay. I'll keep reading. Well, well."

"Well, well, what?" I asked.

"Are you at the curb?"

"Not yet. Give me a couple of seconds." I came to a stop in front of a driveway, figuring I was a member of a very small minority who were crazy enough to leave home in this downpour. "Okay," I said, "What's the Readers Digest version?"

Louie said, "Sorry?"

"The overview. Skip everything except who gets what."

"Okay. Um, um, um, *here* we are. He leaves about two million three, lot of money in those days, plus the house and a horse ranch in Hollywood, if you can imagine a horse ranch in Hollywood, to his daughter, Daisy Laurel Horton. She also gets his library and his pictures and his furniture and pretty much anything else that wasn't nailed down. He says, and this is a quote, *I know it will not begin to heal the breach, but we will have eternity to find each other and be reconciled.* Guess he knows something I don't. Umm, there's a hundred thousand for someone named Benjamin Rommel, who's described as 'brother of my beloved, departed wife,' and—here's an interesting one—twenty-five K and a sealed letter, it says here, to Vesper Lucius Codwallader of Kansas City—"

"His father," I said. "I'd love to read that letter. They hated each other."

"And then there are eight bequests of five thou each to some guys, locations unknown, the will says, who are described as 'people to whom I did a wrong.' He gives the states he thinks they'll be in, if they're still alive, and leaves another five K to the executor of the will to pay one or more private detectives to track them down. He lists scars for a couple of them, another, he says, is missing two fingers, one was partly scalped—which I'll try never to think about again—these are, you know, like identifying characteristics: *You're looking for a guy named Butch who's missing half his scalp.* Jeez, what a bunch. They got first names like, well, Butch, and Lefty, Kid, Russian Bill, Curly Bill, Laughing Bill—lotta Bills—Burping Sam, and Cassius. Wonder how Cassius got into the gang. Also ten thousand to the widow of someone named Hermann Wendt."

"Is that it?"

"No, no, take a deep breath, would you? Couple thou to the Policeman's Protective League, a hundred K to the American Spiritualist Society, and—ho, ho, here we are."

"What?" I said.

"You know, you take life too quick. You gotta learn to slow down and savor the moment, especially a moment like—"

"Louie," I said, "I'm warning you."

"So, like I said, here we are: a little annuity, a hundred fifty K to be paid at the rate of seventy-five hundred a year for twenty years to someone he calls his 'dear companion,' Ramona Dillingham. And for her daughter, Adelaide, an additional fifty thou flat when she turns eighteen, and a doll, described as the *Triste* doll from the French firm of Jumeau, complete with its wardrobe."

I said, "Bullseye. Adelaide was his illegitimate daughter."

"How do you know?"

"Because Adelaide was his mother's name. He loved his mother and hated his father."

"So this is about a doll?"

"This is about someone being stiffed on a will, someone whom the maker of the will loved and the rest of the family loathed, someone to whom he left something extremely valuable, *inside* that damned doll. He gave it that way so his family wouldn't try to keep it away from the kid they obviously saw as his bastard. But the mistress, the kid's mother, knew what it really was, knew what was in it, and when she didn't get it, she started a chain of absolutely pure, livid hatred over being cheated out of something astonishing, and it's been passed down for a couple of generations. I'm ninety percent sure that the Bride of Plastic Man—sorry, Paulette Codwallader Creighton—is Adelaide's granddaughter." According to Miss Daisy's will, anyway.

"Works for me," Louie said. "How do you think Horton's family found whatever was in the doll?"

"It's only a guess," I said, "but I think Miss Daisy, who was only twelve or thirteen when her father died, was a little girl who liked to play with dolls, and she found this one tucked away somewhere. What's in it has got to be a jewel of some kind."

"This reminds me of something," Louie said. "If I can think of it, I'll call you back."

When she came out she was carrying her big purse and an umbrella. She was also being trailed by Rina. Halfway down the walk, Eaglet turned and gestured Rina back to the house, but Rina came up beside her and took the umbrella, a move that I thought boded well for her future as a chess player. Eaglet looked at me and did a *what can I do* shrug, and I waved them both forward.

"*Hi*, Dad," Rina said, really pouring it on. She'd been a little too interested lately in life on my side of the law.

I said, "Do I know you? Whoever you are, you're getting wet."

Rina said to Eaglet, "We try not to notice these little memory lapses. Sometimes he puts his shoes in the freezer."

To Eaglet, I said, "Let's swap." I held up my Glock, wrapped in the towel I keep to wipe the inside of the windows.

"What could *that* be?" Rina said.

Eaglet took it, ostentatiously turning her back on Rina, who reciprocated by pulling the umbrella back. Eaglet backed up and Rina literally put her chin on Eaglet's shoulder, watching wide-eyed as Eaglet pulled out her own gun, wrapped in toilet paper. When Rina saw it, she said, "A*ha*."

I said, "Fully equipped?"

"Of course," Eaglet said. "I'm working, remember?"

"Who was doing the charade?" I asked.

"Eaglet was," Rina said. "It was *The Old Man and the Sea* but we were pretending not to get it."

"You were not," Eaglet said. "That wasn't even what it was." To me, she said, "Why do you want mine?"

"It goes with my shirt."

"Not to my eye, it doesn't." She leaned forward, and

Rina thoughtfully moved the umbrella to cover her. "Hey, did you know you've got a spot on—"

"Yes," I said, "and it feels like people have been pointing it out to me since the redwoods were saplings, maybe twelve hundred years ago." I took the gun, bigger than I'd expected. "Is this thing clean?"

Eaglet gave me the look I'd probably get if I'd asked an astrophysicist whether he'd passed eighth-grade algebra. "Of course it is," she said. "And if you're planning to use it the way I think you are, I'm counting on its being even cleaner and at the bottom of a deep, deep well by the time the sun comes up. And that's going to add a bunch to your bill."

I tried to ignore the intensity of Rina's interest in the exchange. "If I'm right about tonight," I said, "which I figure is about a forty, forty-five percent probability, money's not going to be a problem."

"Really?" Rina said. "Can I have a pony?" She handed the umbrella to Eaglet, leaned in, letting the rain stream down on her, and kissed my cheek. Then she took a handful of my hair and gave it an attention-focusing yank. "You be careful, okay? And I want to hear about this when it's over."

Eduardo's house was a tiny, bare-bones bungalow in the Silverlake area, maybe eight hundred square feet, worth maybe $3,500 when it was sold for the first time. Now it was the sole survivor of a once-extensive lower middle-class neighborhood, and its new neighbors were aspiration on acid, built from property line to property line, a collision of mismatched architectural motifs as vulgar as a row of gold teeth. If Eduardo owned the place and he hadn't been borrowing against it for decades, he was sitting on a small fortune.

With my graduate degree in burglars' architecture, it took me all of thirty seconds to assemble the floor plan. Front door dead center, living room to the right, from where I was sitting across the street, dining room to the left, kitchen behind the dining room, two tiny bedrooms with bath behind the living room and entry area. Your basic working family's home, circa 1935.

No lights on in front. I got out, getting drenched instantly, and splashed up the driveway. No lights on in back, either. I called his number and got a ring and then voicemail, so I hung up and went to the front door and rang the bell. *Nada*. Dripping wet, I headed back to the car.

As I sat there—reassuring myself that I was in no danger of nodding off and keeping my eyes amphetamine-wide to make certain it was true—the phone buzzed again. I'd stopped paying attention to it, since it went off every time Bride of Plastic Man and Mr. Nose entered the camera's field of vision. I gave it a look: nobody. There were more lights on now, so either they were still there or they'd left and hadn't given any thought to my electric bill. Then it buzzed *again*, and I was looking at a text. It said, CLOSING TIME. HERE'S LONDON.

Another attachment. Settling in but not getting *too* comfortable, I opened it up.

I skimmed through the ocean voyage, the landing, his first impressions of this new Old World until I began to see, as he wandered London, that he was paying special attention to certain people, and that the thing they had in common was that they wore serious jewelry.

```
It is as though they consider thievery unthink-
able in the peaceful and plentiful world they
```

occupy. Perhaps this confidence is a testimonial
to the long subjugation of the lower classes,
but women wear in public jewels that would be
locked in safes in the more volatile land of
my birth. In a single afternoon on the Strand it
is possible to see jewelry enough to support a
family for years.

   I will not conceal my interest from the reader.
It was as though I were a miner who had accidentally uncovered a rich vein where he expected
nothing. Opening it up, he finds it only leads to
greater riches and deeper, purer deposits. The
effect upon me of the proximity of so much easily
portable wealth made it difficult at times for me
to recall that I had come here in large part to
change my life.

Self-portrait of a man in conflict: He was simultaneously giving himself a hand-slapping moral lecture even
as he staked out the street, keeping an eye on the traffic's
flow to see where the jewels came from and where they
went. He got near enough to the women with the best
jewels to overhear their conversations, and to his surprise, many of them spoke American English.

Then things got *really* schizophrenic. On the one
hand, he accompanied an English acquaintance to a
meeting of a society of Spiritualists, and then to many
others. They seemed to have shaken him profoundly,
although not *so* profoundly that he stopped following
the best jewelry he saw. He soon found himself focusing on Americans, for an almost triumphantly practical
reason.

I realized I would be more capable of breach-
ing the layers of protection between me and the
jewels of visitors than I would those of the English. The English, I was certain, would keep their
best baubles in homes, large and well-secured
establishments with extensive staff who knew the
family and its acquaintances by sight, whereas
the visitors would likely be housed in hotels.
Hotels may have little to recommend them to the
home-loving man, but to one such as I was at
the time, they possessed a single great advantage: in a hotel, there is no such thing as a
stranger. In time, I myself took up residence
in a hotel nearby the Strand, which I shall not
name. It catered to the richer Americans and was
quite dear, but I am almost ashamed to say that
I had in mind a strategy of relative simplicity
that, if carried out successfully, would add
substantial weight to my purse.

Whenever Horton wasn't scoping out the scene for
a jewel heist, he was going to spiritualist meetings with
his friend, whose name was Alfred—Alfie—Warwick.
And what he glimpsed occasionally in those meetings, as
though on the other side of a door just barely cracked
open, was suddenly revealed in mind-staggering detail
when the door was yanked off its hinges by the blinding
light of revelation. This happened not through meetings,
but when Alfie gave him a book and a magazine.

Neither was new; both were ten or twelve years old,
creased and dog-eared with repeated reading use, but Horton said Alfie handled them as though they were fragile

and unique. Horton was, Alfie said in all apparent serious-
ness, to read the book first and then the magazine, which
contained a letter to the editor that Alfie believed Horton
would find useful.

It took him days, spent mainly jewel-shopping on the
sidewalks and mapping the stones' destinations, but eventually he settled into his room's easy chair and opened the
book.

> I am ashamed to say that I had not read widely
> since I turned my back on Miss Greening's
> schoolhouse, but her instruction to question the
> trustworthiness of the author came immediately
> to mind. And, I must confess, there seemed at
> first to be a great deal to question. The book's
> author, F.W.H. Myers, was unknown to me, and
> its title, Human Personality and Its Survival
> of Bodily Death, seemed at first glance to be
> chosen almost intentionally to encourage doubt.
> I had heard this issue discussed endlessly, if
> seldom directly, in the meetings to which my
> friend took me. But they spoke to each other
> in a shared vocabulary such as those that are
> always developed by specialist, whether they are
> outlaws or plumbers, and many of the words they
> used, as well as the assumptions behind them,
> were unknown to me. But seeing the words on a
> page, their hard black outlines as pronounced
> as the border of a country against the white-
> ness of the paper, suggested a kind of metaphor:
> that black and white, light and darkness, life
> and death, were absolute and opposite entities

rather than the far ends of some sort of spectrum. This was, unfortunately, exactly opposite
the view the author was attempting to put forth.
I confess that it was a labor for me to battle
my doubt as I read the pages. Many times I put
it down and returned to my plan to steal a jewel
that would support me for life . . .

Well, of *course*, it's a jewel. It's *always* been a jewel.
That had been my first thought, from the moment the
Bride of Plastic Man—sorry, Paulette—told me that
my target was a doll. What else of great value is small
enough to be hidden inside a doll? I'd been thrown off
by the rectangular shape of the space cut into the doll's
back, but suddenly it was so obvious to me that I battled
an impulse to call myself names. Out loud. The jewel had
been in a box.

. . . and yet the book called me back. Time and
again it beckoned me to the table in the corner
of my hotel room where I had laid it down, I
thought, forever. But now I found myself reading
it at morning's first light, ordering my meals
delivered so they did not interrupt the flow,
rising from my bed in the darkest hours of the
night, drawn unerringly to it as though by some
magnetic force.

In the face of all we have been taught, the
author wrote that the conscious self, the thing
we think of as "I" and which we believe to be
mortal is, instead "largely an illusion, the rest
of the personality being separable from it and

superior to it, and connected directly to the soul." When seen in this way, Dr. Myers said, human beings are not sent alone into the universe, as to a prison, for the limited duration of a lifespan and then sentenced to individual extinction. Instead, they are, rather, "like islands in a stream; and this is proved in the way that certain human beings are able to release themselves from the confines of ordinary thought and establish contact between the islands, and build up connections with personalities who have survived the physical destruction of the brain."

<u>Personalities who have survived the destruction of the brain.</u> The dead, in short, are not only still among us, but can also listen—and even speak.

This vision of a world in which the dead remain with us, and one in which, later, we will remain with the living, was impossible for me to believe, but it was also impossible to reject. The great cruel joke of the world is and always has been death. All our lives, all our struggles, for nothing, for ashes, for an eternity spent in the damp, chill earth, a banquet for undiscriminating worms, the good being devoured alongside the bad. But what if that terrible fate is a deception? What if that iron door never actually closes? What if the islands in the stream are actually one and are never extinguished? What if dark and light are simply opposite ends of some unimaginable rainbow?

What if someday I could speak my heart to my

```
mother? What if somewhere there still exists
the spirit of Hermann Wendt, whom all called
The Kraut, and whom I shot to death in an ill-
planned attempt to steal his gold as he carried
it into Virginia City? Until he pulled his gun
I hadn't known he was armed, but that was no
balm to my soul; I had accosted him to do him
wrong. What if, in this new order of things, I
could drop to my knees and plead for pardon from
Hermann Wendt?
```

It went on in this vein for quite a few pages. He couldn't believe but he couldn't *not* believe, either. And in the meantime, an American woman living on the third floor of the hotel in which he was staying owned a sapphire of at least thirty carats that she wore as a kind of pendant. The stone had been cut in a peculiar way that rounded its top, rather than the more conventional approach of incising facets into it, so that it didn't sparkle but instead *glowed* like some impossibly clear, impossibly deep pool. Horton had already struck up a speaking acquaintance with the woman, whose raw Texas accent had been a surprise, and he had successfully picked the locks on enough of the hotel's unoccupied rooms to know he could open hers in less than half a minute. As the days went by and his purse, as he put it, began to shrink, he oscillated between the book, on the one hand, with its taunting, unverifiable vision of infinite life, where sins could be undone, and on the other, the hard certainty that he could take the stone easily and that he would not have to steal again for years to come. Finally, in agony that he had read nothing to assure him that this new world of enduring spirit was somehow *verifiable*, he laid the book aside and picked up the newspaper.

It had about it the smell of a document that has for a long, long time been someplace damp. The ink was blurred with handling and faded with time, and the margins were fingerprinted by those who had read it while the ink was still new and not fully set. The publication, printed on a coarse and flimsy paper, was a kind of magazine; it was called "Light: A Journal of Psychical, Occult, and Mystical Research," published by a group that proclaimed itself to be the Spiritualist Alliance, several of whose meetings I had attended. My friend had circled a letter to the editor on the third page that said, in part:

"I believe that it has been found a useful practice among revivalists for each member to give the assembled congregation a description of the manner in which they attained the often vague result known as 'finding salvation.' Among Spiritualists there is really a good deal to be said for such a practice, for the first steps of the inquirer after truth are along such a lonely and treacherous path that it must always be of interest to him to hear how some other wanderer has stumbled along it, uncertain whether he was following a fixed star or a will-o'-the-wisp, until at last his feet came upon firmer ground and he knew that all was well."

This letter, which I read over and over, spoke to me as though its writer had seen straight through me to all the doubt at my core. Certainty, he was saying, WAS POSSIBLE. I looked to the end of the letter and saw, for the first time in my life, the name of the man who had written it: A. Conan Doyle, M.D.

30
The Stink of People

A car, its headlights bringing the rain into sharp relief, pulled past me and into the driveway of Eduardo's little bungalow. It was an old Chevy, the finish here and there patched with primer, and I could hear the springs squeal as it took the little bounce up from the street.

I was out of my car and walking before he had his door open. He must have seen me in the rearview mirror, but he climbed out as though he was all alone in the world, without so much as a glance over his shoulder. When he'd completely unfolded himself, he was about three inches taller than I, which made him about six-three, and broad-shouldered, with a bristling shock of short-cut white hair. Without turning, he said, "Who are you?"

I said, "I called you."

"Back up," he said. "I need to close the door." Only a soft "s" on the verb "close," rather than the "z" in the common American pronunciation, suggested that he wasn't a lifelong English speaker. I took a step back, and he slammed the door and fit a key into the lock, and when he turned to face me, I saw a face as sharply lined as a crumpled piece of paper, dark eyes set deep in a nest of wrinkles, and, a bit lower down, a snub-nosed little belly gun of some kind pointed at the center of my gut.

"Hello," I said, raising my hands.

"Who are you? What do you want?"

"I want your side of what happened at Horton House."

"*My* side," he said scornfully. "There is no *my* side and *your* side. Just sadness and slow dying."

"What happened to all—" I put my hands halfway down. "Before I go any further, let's get one thing straight. I'm not on *anyone's* side. I don't want to punish anyone or give anyone an award. I just want to know what happened—"

"To?" he said.

The question took me off-balance. "Okay, for starters, all the stuff that was in the house."

"Of course," he said. "Furniture is always more interesting than people." He put the gun in his belt, where it looked right at home. "I don't want to be rude and the rain is falling on me, too, so we'll postpone *why* you are asking until we're inside, where it's dry. Come with me."

I followed him through the slanting rain and over a badly tended lawn, to the front door. "Just out of curiosity," I said, "if you haven't done anything wrong, why the gun?"

"Look at this estreet," he said, the little *eh* preceding "street" also a Hispanic verbal tag. "The gun is for realtors. Every day, every night, there's some asshole with a business card who wants to knock down my house and build one of *those*." He lifted his chin in the direction of the starter mansion across the way. "You know what I call them?"

"No. What do you call them?"

He stuck a key into the lock and turned it. "Man-eating houses," he said. "They eat the people who think they own them and then they chew them up to make them easier for the bank to swallow when it takes everything back. You've heard the *pendejos* on the radio who talk about *flipping houses*?"

"Sure."

"You notice they never say *flipping homes*. Never."

"Hadn't thought of it," I said as he pushed the door open. The scent of good wood rolled out at us. "And I probably know why. 'Homes' says *people*. 'Houses' says *money*."

"Maybe I'll let you live," he said, and then he laughed. It was a two-syllable laugh, but it relaxed me a little. "When the realtors knock on the door, I just lift my shirt and they go away fast." He reached around the door and the hall was bathed in light.

The wonderful fragrance came from a gorgeous, palace-quality, three-drawer cedar table, obviously Chinese, probably early nineteenth or late eighteenth century. Small but concentrated, deeply lacquered in a dark red, and highly polished, it had the characteristic that many old, beautiful things suggest, of being more *present*, more *there*, than anything else in the room, as though their physical mass were enhanced by the sheer weight of time. He saw me staring at it, nodded, and said, "Come in here," and turned left. Just ahead of me, he flicked on the overhead light to reveal a small dining room that might have been a curated space in a furniture museum: in the center, a gleam of darkness, an oval ebony table for eight, inlaid with mother-of-pearl, and ringed by matching chairs. Ebony, now endangered, is not only one of the hardest woods in the world—hard enough to be paired with ivory in piano keyboards intended for decades of use—but also one of the heaviest, so moving this dining room set must have been an ordeal.

Crowded as the room was, against the wall to my far left stood a tall hutch with a china cabinet, almost certainly British, from the early nineteenth century, that looked like it had been dusted for decades by people carefully blowing on it, and polished with kind words; it had been supernaturally well cared for. From where I stood, I couldn't see a scratch or a ding of any kind.

"I was going to sell it," Eduardo said. "I was *supposed* to sell all of it, that's what Rosa and Henry did. But some of it was too beautiful to let it go. The old man, whatever Miss Daisy said about him, he had a good eye for things."

"What *did* she say about him?"

"Why do you care?"

Well, he had to ask sooner or later. But the question was much easier to ask than to answer. "It's complicated," I said. "A couple of nights ago a friend of mine, a young woman, was killed. She had been interested in the house and the—the animosity between Miss Daisy and the heirs, the not so long ago. She wanted to go in and take a look."

"Many people would."

"But she *did*. And she was killed. Shot."

Eduardo looked into my eyes long enough to make me uncomfortable. "You coming here," he said, "will it put me in danger?"

"Not any more than you already were. Someone wants something that's in that house. But if I can figure out who killed my friend, I'm going to . . . fix things so that none of us will be in danger."

He nodded slowly and said, "You do not seem like someone who could make a threat like that."

"I know," I said. "And thanks for the compliment. So, what did Miss Daisy say about her father?"

"Mostly, that he could not keep it in his pants."

"She was talking about the mistress?"

"The mistress has been dead a long time. The mistress's daughter was poison to her. The *world* was poison to her, and I think it began with her father. She hated easily, but she hated her father most."

"You and Rosa and Henry were at the house, you said."

"We were all that was left, at the end," he said. "Miss Collins finally died. Miss Daisy said she died so she couldn't be kicked out of the house. With Miss Collins gone, Miss Daisy just pushed everybody else away. *Wanters*, she called them. Want, want, want. At the end it was just us and the doctors."

"More than one doctor?"

"She didn't like them, either. She didn't like anybody."

"Except you."

He looked around the room and let a sigh escape. "I wouldn't say she liked us. Why don't we sit down?"

"Where?"

He ran a finger over the back of one of the ebony chairs. "I never sit in here," he said, "Isn't that stupid, to have these things in my life and not to use them? Please." He turned away from me and I followed him across the narrow hallway with its thin, worn carpet. "Here," he said. "We can sit in here."

The living room was small and over-furnished: two plumped-up sofas where there was room for one, tables here and there with bric-a-brac on them—a plaster bird house, votive candles in painted glass cylinders, a miniature of the Eiffel Tower, tarnished enough to be sterling, bouquets of too-colorful plastic flowers, plus a scrum of miscellaneous items: car keys, reading glasses, change, folded bits of paper, the kind of stuff that people take out of their pockets and drop just anywhere. There was nothing to suggest that anyone else lived here.

He sat on one couch and waved me to the other. The sofas were from Sofas R Us or someplace like that, but the matching tables were very fine, possibly Amish. When I'd been seated, he leaned back and regarded me for a moment or two, and then he said, "So. Your friend who was killed—did she have something to do with the heirs?"

"No."

"Because they cannot have these things."

"I know," I said. "I've read her will."

"I signed it," he said. "I was a—a witness. You must have seen my name. I wrote it very large."

"Well, I saw it, but I have to confess that I didn't look at the witnesses' signatures, just hers."

He gave me the kind of level look that can be produced only by a totally honest person and the occasional psychopath who can make himself believe he's a totally honest person. "Why would you be reading her will? Do you represent *her*?"

"Who?" I asked.

"No, no, no, no," Eduardo said. "You can stop bullshitting me right now or you can go back out into the rain."

I said, "*She*, if you're talking about her father's illegitimate granddaughter, sent my friend. She believed there was something in the house that belonged to her."

"What?"

I took a deep breath. "A doll."

He sat back and put his hands flat on his thighs like someone who was about to lean forward. "The house is full of dolls."

"So I saw."

"You were in the house?"

"After my friend died."

"We didn't take any dolls," Eduardo said. "We—we were *loyal* to Miss Daisy, but we knew about that woman, heard about her endlessly, and, I suppose you could say, we felt for her. She came there once and forced her way in. She said that Miss Daisy had stolen something from her, something Miss Daisy's father had wanted to give the woman's mother or grandmother. As you said, a doll. You have never heard such screaming. We knew Miss Daisy better than most people, and there was nothing about her that made us believe she *hadn't* stolen whatever it was. Even if she didn't want it, she would have kept it. It was who she was."

I said, "I've gotten that impression."

He nodded a couple of times, just sort of sealing the pact that we both knew she had been a nightmare. "What we took—wait, stay here." He got up, rubbing at the small of his back, and left the room. I sat there, feeling a kind of empty-tank lassitude steal over me. This had been a long and unpleasant quest, crowded with miserable people, both living and dead. Eduardo seemed to be the only decent human being I'd met who had escaped the black hole of Horton House.

"Here," he said, coming back in. "Read this."

It was a typewritten document, dated almost two years

earlier, on the stationery of a lawyer, the guy named Loeb whom Miss Daisy had put in charge of her will. It said, in essence, that she was formally making a present of the furnishings and artwork in Horton House, without reservation or exceptions, to Eduardo Chavez, Rosa Reyes, and Enrique Gutierrez, aka Henry, in recognition of the faithful care they had taken of her during her prolonged illness. The three of them, in short, were free to take anything and everything, with the single exception of the items in Miss Daisy's room while she remained alive. After she passed, they were welcome to all that, too. Questions could be directed to the legal office where the notarized deed was on file.

"She didn't really do it for us," Eduardo said. "She was certain that the family would descend on the house while she was still warm, that's what she liked to say, *still warm*, and pick the place clean. This way, it would already be clean when they got there."

"*Did* you take the things from her room after she was gone?"

"I didn't," he said. He was looking straight into my eyes. "And I don't believe Henry and Rosa did, either. None of us even wanted to go in there."

My phone rang: Louie. I rejected it and said, "Just out of curiosity, how'd you divide stuff up?"

A very small smile; he'd been hoping I'd ask. "Mostly, we wanted different things. If more than one of us wanted something, we put out names into a hat. And it went on that way. It was very agreeable. And we traded a little, too."

"Whose idea was the cheap furniture?"

"Ours. We still needed places to sit and eat. And Miss Daisy, when Rosa told her about it, she laughed and said her relatives would probably fight over that, too." He shook his head. "Miss Daisy, she had so much hate."

"There were three of you," I said, "but when I was in the house, I only saw one bedroom behind the kitchen. Who stayed there?"

"We did," he said. "Rosa and Henry, they were together, you know? Now, they're married. So they slept there together two nights and I slept there alone one night, and we did that over and over. Taking turns." He pinched at the cloth of his trousers, paying attention to what he was doing, and I had the sense that he was about to confess something and was avoiding my eyes. He said, "I didn't like to sleep there. We were not alone."

I said, "I've never believed in ghosts, but Horton House is different. Who was it?"

"Two of them," he said. "The old man and Miss Collins, after she was gone."

"Miss Collins," I said. "The second bedroom upstairs?"

He nodded. "She was very old, so old you could see her veins through her skin. She was Miss Daisy's nursemaid, brought into the house, she told us, when she was nineteen and just arrived from Ireland. She said the old man asked her to stay when it was clear that Miss Daisy was not— was never going to be like other people, and that it had been arranged that Miss Collins would be paid as long as she stayed, even after he was dead, until Miss Daisy turned twenty-one. When he *did* die, two of the old man's relatives came in to take care of things until Miss Daisy came of age and threw them out. But she kept Miss Collins, although I think it was mostly to torment her. Miss Collins didn't know anyone else in America. She had no money to go back to Ireland. This had been her only job, and Miss Daisy told her that she wouldn't get a reference if she tried to leave. If anyone ever asked for one, Miss Daisy said she'd tell them that Miss Collins was a thief. Miss Collins told me all of this. She had no one to talk to, and I liked her. By the time I was hired, fifty years ago, she was already too old to get another job, and there was no one in America who would take her in. So she stayed. Every month or two Miss Daisy would kick her out, and Miss Collins would sleep on the front porch until Miss Daisy wanted her back again. She died eight or nine years ago, and Miss Daisy surprised all of us. She wept for days. She wouldn't let us touch Miss Collins's room. It's exactly the way it was the night she died."

"And you think Miss Collins haunted the house?"

"She and the old man. Sometimes in the dark I would see the old man, like a thick shadow, going up the last few stairs, right in front of his big picture, the one that hung there. He never did anything except that. He was never anywhere else. Miss Collins, we never saw Miss Collins, we just *felt* her, all three of us did. Just suddenly sadness was in the room, blown in like fog, nothing but sadness. Rosa would say, 'Hello, Miss Collins. Please sit down,' and some of the time that would make it go away."

I said, "It's the saddest place I've ever been."

"It will not be a bad thing to knock it down. They should dig a hole there and fill it with water and salt and let it sit for years. Except it would breed horrible mosquitoes."

"Tell me," I said. "Why all the baby powder? When I first went in, I almost choked on it."

He nodded. "Miss Daisy. She said other people stank. The stink of people made her sick."

We sat with that one for a moment, and then I said, "Only two more questions."

"Up to you. You go away, I will just watch television."

"The bed she was in. It was filthy, it was lopsided, it was—it was terrible. Why?"

"She wouldn't allow us to change it, although once in a while we did. We carried her to the toilet when she called us, but sometimes she didn't bother. We tried changing it when she was in there several times, but she went crazy when she saw it. She accused us of trying to steal from her."

"Do you know what she was hiding?"

He continued to meet my eyes.

"Is that the last question?"

"No, but I'd like an answer if you have one."

"We didn't know. She *gave* us everything in the house, and we knew we could have the things in her room, too, when she was gone. So we left it alone. And, yes, when she was gone, Rosa and Henry looked. We found nothing."

I said, "Her door had been kicked in. She'd propped a chair against it."

"I did that," he said. "Several weeks before she died. We smelled something burning, Rosa smelled it first, and we all thought the same thing: she is burning down the house. I knocked on the door, I banged on it. She called out for me to go away. I had to kick in the door. It was just some stuff, clothes and things, she was burning in the fireplace. She had crawled across the room—"

He stopped because I had stood up. I blinked down at him, as surprised as he was. I said, "I should be going."

"Do you want to see the old man?"

"At this point," I said, "I'm actually afraid to ask what you mean."

"His picture." He got up, too. "In here."

I don't know exactly what I'd expected: perhaps a blunt-featured, broad-shouldered bruiser just a step or two up from the professional wrestling ring, but Edgar Francis Codwallader, aka Henry Wallace Horton, Jr., wasn't it. He was thin-faced and parsimonious-looking, with crooked, projecting teeth, and one eye conspicuously higher than the other, a feature he'd shared with another spindly desperado, Billy the Kid. It was hard to find in his face the student of whom Miss Greening had been so fond or the guy who read and liked all those fat English novels. If I'd had to choose from among the living someone he reminded me of, I probably would have gone with the flaking nascent lawyer, Walter.

I sat in the car, working things through, trying for alternative courses of action, and not looking forward to the rest of the evening. I was about to reopen Horton's book when the phone rang again, and again it was Louie.

"Sorry," I said. "I've been talking to one of the ghosts of Horton House."

Louie said, "The jewel. It's a big blue something."

"I know," I said. "A sapphire. Or, at least that's what he seemed to be focusing on in his—wait a minute. How do *you* know?"

"Because I'm looking at it, whadya think?"

"Hold it, hold it. Looking at what?"

"At the *story* I was talking about, where Sherlock lets the crook off. What the guy stole was some kind of jewel that was blue. See? *The one thing that doesn't seem to fit—*"

"What's the story?"

"The umm, hold on a minute, it's a word I gotta look at if I'm gonna say it. It's the, umm, hold on, hold on, here we are, 'The Adventure of the Blue Carbuncle.' I thought a carbuncle was something you had an operation to get rid of."

"It is, it's like boils or a whole bunch of boils, all together."

Louie said, "Ouch."

"But it used to mean a red stone, a ruby or a garnet, usually."

"This one's blue."

"A ruby and a sapphire are essentially the same mineral, corundum, so a blue carbuncle would be a sapphire. No, wait." I closed my eyes and let the unsorted stuff in my mental dryer tumble around until the right thing fell past the window. "Jewelers also used 'carbuncle' to describe a stone that had been carved but not faceted, one where the shape was rounded. *Jesus.*"

"Jesus what?"

"That's actually *it*. The rounded top, it really *is* the rock he's planning to steal. In his book."

"It's a Christmas story," Louie said.

"I don't know what time of year it is in the period he's writing about in his memoir, when he spotted the jewel. He doesn't say anything about the season. Doesn't feel cold." I was paging through the old man's journal on my phone. "August, he arrived in August and he doesn't date things, but I'd guess this is October by now, late October at the latest."

"Want to know the trick?"

"There's a trick?"

"Yeah, the way the guy hides the rock in the story, he feeds it to a goose and then, when the coast is clear, the idea is to terminate the goose and take the rock out of its crop or craw or something that a goose has."

"He's living in a *hotel*," I said. "Pretty fancy hotel, too. I doubt he had a goose."

"I'll tell you," Louie said, "this is one of the dumbest conversations I ever had. But still, you're looking for a sapphire, too, huh? Can't be a coincidence, can it?"

"I'm not looking for it," I said. "I'm ninety percent sure I know where it is."

It was a little after eleven, and it seemed appropriate to arrive around midnight, so I had some time to spend with the old man's book, and bang, there it was. He managed to meet Doyle at a gathering of the Eternal Life Society or whatever the hell it was, even got to talk to him for a while. Found out, he says—sounding amazed—that Doyle wrote mystery stories of some kind. I lost track of time while I was reading, and when I looked up I realized it was later than I thought, so I did a three-point turn to put Eduardo's place behind me and headed, with no pleasant expectations, down the well-worn path to Horton House.

On my first drive-by it was obvious that there had been a couple of changes.

For one thing, someone had clearly felt there was a

shortage of darkness, because the streetlight in front was out and there was a scattering of glass or plastic on the sidewalk beneath it. The hedge was so high that the missing light wouldn't make much difference on the other side of its thick green border, but the approach via the sidewalk was now considerably less public than it had been before.

Second, the place was now surrounded by a chain link fence. It was eight feet high, which was a break because standard chain link goes all the way up to twelve feet, and above eight or nine feet it sways quite a bit beneath a climber's weight. It's not actually the sway that's the problem, although it *causes* the problem. No fencing surface I can think of gives a climber more foot- and hand-holds than chain link; it absolutely *begs* to be climbed. The problem is that swaying on a fence made of metal links fastened to metal poles is *noisy*. The trick to climbing it, if you're interested, is to do it *straddling a pole* with the pole separating your right and left appendages. The pole absorbs and tames most of the fence's movement, making it the quietest place to climb. It also gives you a nice, stiff two or three feet at the top when it's time to throw a leg over to the other side.

I went back to the car to put on my new shoes. The old ones were soaked through. I'd come full circle on the fast food wheel by stopping at a McDonald's a few miles away, and while my food was being custom-cooked or salted or, at least, bagged up, I'd ducked into the restroom and put on a completely new set of clothes, all black, never worn before; there's always one in my trunk. They'd been put into a plastic bag and stapled closed by the clerk from whom I bought them, and since then they'd been waiting for the next job. I'd still never actually touched the outside of the garments because I'd worn food service gloves to open the bag and put everything on. I put the gloves on again, just before getting out of the car. DNA is everywhere, but there's no need to make it any easier than it has to be.

When I closed the car door, my feet warm and dry for the moment, I found that the rain had temporarily exhausted its spite, tapering off to a mist, drilled by the occasional sprinkle for comic relief. I hiked a block from my car and walked past the house, which was so dark it almost seemed to thicken the night surrounding it, a giant drop of black ink spreading in water. One pass confirmed something I'd been certain of, which was that Horton House backed up against an alley. Many of LA's older places are built to face a street and turn their backs on an alley, providing a rear entrance for tradespeople, servants, and others not deemed worthy of the front door. Cops don't patrol the alleys as often as they do the streets.

There was only one light in the alley, on a high pole halfway between the cross streets at the end of the block. The houses that had their backs to me were all dark. I picked the second pole in, checked the angle of Eaglet's gun in the cargo pocket of my new black pants, pulled on the food service gloves, and started to climb. When I reached the top, before I committed myself to swinging a leg over to the other side, I stopped, breathed silently as I counted off two minutes, and listened.

I could hear the occasional car up on Pico. I could hear a cloud-muffled plane on the long downward diagonal to LAX. I could just barely hear a laugh track from some sitcom—a bunch of people, some of them undoubtedly dead, reacting uproariously to a joke they'd never heard; the

dead live merrily on in sitcom laugh tracks. The hilarity
was probably leaking into the night through a half-open
window two or three houses away. I could hear something
that sounded like the tack-tack of a dog's nails on a hardwood floor, then three dogs, then a mess of dogs, and then
it was raining hard enough to drown out any noise I might
have made topping the fence, so I was over it and shelter-
ing beside the dark slab of Horton House within a few
seconds. The house chose that moment to emit a basso
profundo creak, and I have to confess that I took several
quick steps back into the rain.

And from that perspective, I registered a darker gloom,
a hard-edged gloom, in the yard to the house's left.

It was massive and angular, and I like to think the part
of my brain that makes deductions figured out what it was
before the attention hog in my conscious mind—which
likes to take credit for everything—could put a name to
it. It was a bulldozer. Or, rather it was *the* bulldozer, the
forty-ton, steel-and-rubber manifestation of Miss Daisy's
willpower, potent even in death. Beyond it, its highest point
going all ghosty in the mist, was a crane, from which dangled a very large, very heavy-looking wrecking ball. The
bulldozer was low and squat, the crane-and-wrecking-ball
setup thin and vertical. It was easy to see how they would
work as a team, the Laurel and Hardy of destruction.

For a moment, I was deeply, *deeply* tempted to blow
off everything I'd come here to do, and instead hotwire
the bulldozer and drive it straight through Mr. Horton's
fucking house of pain. Shatter the covered windows, open
the whole thing to the rain and the sky, bring down that
stairway, liberate the ghosts, and go home.

But prudence, mixed with greed and an urgent, buzzing

desire for revenge, won the battle. Even if I could hotwire
the bulldozer, it would be noisy business in a quiet neighborhood at midnight. And I couldn't do it later, because
I would be leaving in a hurry. Back to the original plan.
Such as it was.

With several deep breaths to get me centered again, I
sidled along the wall until I was just beside the kitchen
window. I took a couple of steps back and then put three
or four feet between me and the wall so I would be visible only to someone who was within a few feet of the
door to the dining room, looking through the window
at a very sharp angle. I squinted through the rain. The
window on the left, from this perspective, seemed to be
raised about the same four inches I'd seen last time. No
mud on the sill. No one was visible through the window,
so I covered the distance to it, put my ear to the opening,
and waited.

I could just barely hear the rain on the second-story
roof, at the very edge of audible, but nothing else from
inside, so I went at double-time around to the front door,
inserted the key, waited for the barrage of handgun fire
that didn't come, and went in.

My old friend the elephant's foot was right where I'd
left it, creepy as ever. The sweetness of baby powder still
corrupted the air, underpinned by the scent of damp. The
rain was louder in here, and the house gave out a couple
of creaks as the wet wood swelled with moisture, but there
were no other sounds. For now, as near as I could tell, I was
alone. If you didn't count the old man and Miss Collins.

If I *was* alone, then either they'd come in last night,
after blowing the street lamp, probably with a silenced
gun, or they hadn't. I doubted that they'd risk coming in

after making the necessary noise to put out the lamp, but I supposed they could have come back hours later. If not, if they'd put it off until tonight, the chainlink fence was probably going to be a surprise.

I reached into the other cargo pocket on my nice, wet, new pants, and skipped over the big flashlight in favor of my little dim yellow one. Walking close to the walls, I soft-footed it down the hall and into the living room and then across it to check the bookcase. I had left two books lying on their spines so they'd protrude, and both were as I had arranged them. The books gave me a little *woo-hoo*, but they weren't why I was here.

It wasn't until I'd had turned back toward the hallway, in my mind already climbing the stairs, when I remembered that the very first time I'd been here, I'd rattled around like a clown for forty minutes or more while someone—not someone, *Lumia*—had patiently waited for a chance to stick a gun in my ear. It would have been an understatement to say that these past couple of days had tangled me in a snarl of emotions, but the thought of Lumia cut through them like a straight razor, straightened my spine, and simplified my life. There were only two things to do here, and both depended on my not being a bonehead. So I went up onto the balls of my feet, hugged the walls, and headed for the little alcove at the base of the stairs that contained the door to the basement.

At the bottom of the stairs, I stopped. The stairway might have been designed specifically for an ambush; the curve to the right meant that you were six steps up and committed before you could see all of the second-floor landing. What I heard up there was a steady rhythm track of dripping water and a random series of low notes contributed by the house. Try as I might, I couldn't identify any of the sounds that people make: steps, the squeak of heels on wood, breathing, whispers, nothing. So I turned my attention to the basement, pressing my ear against the door, which was cold enough to surprise me. It wasn't until then that I registered that I could see my breath. This rain was towing some weather behind it.

I passed an unpleasant two minutes in the basement, which looked like the place where the world's first spider scuttled into eight-legged existence, got big enough to move the furniture around, multiplied, and then moved on to terrorize the world, probably via the old coal scoop in the east wall. As much as I disliked Horton House, when I emerged from the basement, the first floor looked almost homey by contrast. The rain was drumming down now, and it got louder as I slowly took the stairs in the approved but silly-looking burglar manner. At the top I paused and listened yet *again*, and turned left and down the hall into Miss Daisy's room, straight past the broken chair and the sagging bed, to kneel in front of the fireplace. It took less than half a minute to feel the hard lump in the center and a somewhat longer time to peel the partially burned clothes away. She'd wrapped it tightly. A half-burned twist of old clothes, in plain sight, was a great place to hide a fortune. If she'd had her way it would have stayed there until the wrecking ball pulverized the chimney and the bulldozer crumpled the house into a motley heap of brick and glass and wood, ready to be broken up and covered in hazardous waste. Say what you like about Miss Daisy, she was a supreme hater.

When the flashlight picked it out, my heart almost stopped. It was an oval, rounded on top, more than three inches long. The chain it had dangled from was yellow, yellow gold. The blue that the stone threw onto the palm of my hand was enough to make me lose sense of time. Great stones, and this was the by far greatest I'd ever held in my hand, bring out the absolute worst in people. Even disregarding her apparent hatred of her father and his bastard daughter, I could almost understand Miss Daisy's deathbed refusal to give it to the mistress' granddaughter. She meant it to be hers until, and after, death.

A muted thumping sound made me aware that my heart was pounding. I took ten or twelve deep, even breaths to get it under control. I needed to be able to listen. Unless I was wrong, and they'd been here the previous night, there was no alternative; they were coming. Tomorrow, the house wouldn't be standing.

When I'd coaxed my heartbeat back into silent mode, I got up, put the sapphire in my pocket, took it out, put it in a different pocket, took it out, put it in the pocket of my T-shirt, and finally remembered that my new black shirt had not only a pocket, but a pocket with a *snap* on it. In it went, and the snap was satisfyingly loud. I tugged at the flap just to make sure, and it held.

Since I'd been distracted for God only knew how long, I did the listening routine for sixty seconds and then left Miss Daisy's room for what I hoped would be the last time. I eased the door shut between me and the worst of the baby-powder scent, and went into the nursery. Picking up the chair beside the cradle, I toted it out into the hallway, and set it down squarely at the top of the stairs, dead center in front of the darker patch of wallpaper that marked the place where the old man's portrait had hung. Then I went to the door of Miss Collins's room and looked in.

Her glasses and her book were where they'd prob-ably been when she passed away, if Miss Daisy's help had obeyed her command that the room should remain as it was. Listening over the sounds I was making, I went to the table to see what the book was and slowed when I saw that the table had two tiers, the lower one about eighteen inches below the upper. On it, deeply dusty, was a rusting metal box that, somehow, I had missed. I figured what the hell, and opened it. Before I talked to Eduardo, I hadn't known she existed. She was the newest member of the cast, so to speak, and I was curious.

A bunch of yellowing letters, or, rather, handwritten *copies* of letters, all from her to people in Ireland, pains-takingly transcribed before being sent so she'd know what she'd said. They were full of badly disguised yearning, a kind of tentative affection, and loneliness, all tamped down in favor of bright, unconvincing lies about how happy she was, how many wonderful things she had seen, and how well she was being treated. Very few letters in return, and those stiff, factual, unloving, and, it seemed to me, uninterested except for repeated requests for money. However she felt about the people she had left behind, there hadn't been much reciprocation. Still, she had kept their letters bound with a narrow scarlet ribbon, neatly tied but frayed around the knot with repeated reopening.

At the bottom of the box was a creased and faded photo of a girl of nineteen or twenty. She was stiffly seated beside something that was meant to pass as a marble pil-lar, a purported fragment of some classic ruin. Behind her was a very flat-looking backdrop, the kind of semi-mythical photographer's landscape that seems to call for a centaur or two. The young woman was stiff with terror at the camera, her eyes wide and her mouth curved in a smile that was all muscle. At the bottom, in a precise hand in once-dark ink, were the words, *On the verge of my great adventure.*

Something very heavy shifted around in my chest. I was found myself closing the box extremely carefully, and replacing it on its shelf as though the slightest jar would break it. I stood there looking down at it, feeling too big and too coarse to be in the same room with the photograph, too heavy, too earthbound, too indifferent. Miss Collins had endured more than enough indifference.

I was seized again with the urge to go out, get that bulldozer chugging, back up for a running start, and see whether I couldn't drive it straight into the living room in a single try.

Instead, I backed out of Miss Collins's room, went to the chair at the top of the stairs, and sat in the dark. Waited in the dark.

32
The Wild West

He'd met Conan Doyle five times.

The man whose letter in the magazine had so encouraged me was still young although already losing his hair, with a long, narrow face that seemed, to me, full of curiosity, a face meant to sniff out secrets. His features, delicate and regular, were all but overpowered by an elegantly waxed moustache, a "dude moustache," we would have called it out west. Its points looked sharp as needles. They curved up at the ends, almost touching his earlobes. His eyes were very calm. I only saw them spark three of four times, once, early in our acquaintance at something I had said, and I desired to provoke that reaction again, so I told him a good many things. Some of them I counterfeited, but only one more time did I see my words go home.

Dr. Conan Doyle took an interest in me, I believe, because I stood out as rougher and less polished than the others in the meetings, "more rooted in this world," he said, and because I

was American. There was an American he admired
shamelessly, a New York detective named William Burns, and Dr. Conan Doyle asked me eagerly
whether I knew of him, perhaps had even met him.
In his youth, he said, Burns befriended a forger
and counterfeiter who told exciting tales of his
brushes with the Secret Service, perhaps seeking
an apprentice. In the end, however, it was the
Service Burns chose, rather than following in
his friend's lawless footsteps, and he quickly
became famous for his skill at finding and identifying clues that no one else could discern.
Dr. Conan Doyle could talk about this man until
someone changed the subject, which I must say
the English do much more pleasantly than we
Americans.

But I believe the real reason he took the
remarkable step of befriending me was that I
was a denizen of what he called "the Wild West."
Several years earlier, in 1887, Buffalo Bill
Cody, that great fraud, had come to London with
his "Wild West" show, with its staged gunfights,
its tired, ailing Indians, and the one real wonder he could present, the female sharp shooter
Annie Oakley. Miss Oakley, who had never fired a
shot in anger and never went farther west than
Ohio, was married to another false gun fighter,
Frank Butler, who had been a dog trainer and
a glass blower before he began to compete in
shooting contests. Westerners they were not,
desperadoes they were not, but Miss Oakley could
undoubtedly shoot.

> Dr. Conan Doyle was bewitched. He thought it
> all real. The smell of gunpowder and the dust
> kicked up by the horses kindled a flame in his
> heart for the West. He had read many books about
> it since seeing Buffalo Bill, but I was the first
> westerner he had met, and this was a topic on
> which I could hold forth for some time. I told
> him about the little towns and the desperadoes,
> the slow end of the Indians, their land gone,
> alcohol their new anesthetic and poison. I told
> him about the exploits and misadventures of men,
> most of them fools, I had known. And in the end,
> with deep misgivings, I told him about myself.

The chair got harder and the house got colder by the minute. I forced a shiver to release some nervous energy, and said, "Brrrrrrrrr." A cliché, but it helped a little. The cold factor and the hard-chair factor were, of course, amplified by the *creep factor* with which Horton House was so richly endowed. So much unhappiness, betrayal, greed, illness, death, so much—no other word for it—*darkness*. As I sat there, distracting myself with Codwallader's, or rather, Horton's, adventures in London, It seemed to me at times that I could feel the old man's eyes fixed on my back from the pale patch of wallpaper where his portrait had hung for a century. At that point, thirty or forty minutes in, I wouldn't have been completely surprised to see him materialize like a heavy cloud on the stairs and walk straight through me, to gaze at the missing picture, an afterlife repetition of something he had probably done thousands of times while he was alive. Generally speaking, when you commission an enormous portrait it's of someone you admire, an ancestor or something. It's not often of oneself. Seemed to me he must have spent a lot of time looking at it. Why else did he want it?

Twelve forty-one. I allowed a bit of doubt to seep in. Perhaps I was wrong. Perhaps—on the last day this house would be standing, the last night before it was reduced to rubble, and guarded rubble at that—*perhaps* she wouldn't make one last, despairing pass at finding her treasure. She'd spent tens of thousands of dollars, money from some other area of her life, to find it. She'd killed two people and invaded my home in her attempt to find it. Maybe she'd finally admit defeat. Blow it off.

Or maybe she'd been here *last* night. It seemed to me that it would have been stupid to shoot out that streetlight and then do a little breaking and entering. The noise and the sudden loss of the light might have been heard or even seen. If I were she, and if I were careful, I would have done it the night before I broke in, relying on the city of Los Angeles's almost mythical slowness in responding to such things. But who knows? Maybe she wasn't as careful as I thought she was.

And then, of course, she'd been at my place not too long ago. So even if she *had* visited Horton House the previous evening, she was still on the hunt.

As little as I liked being here, I decided to give it until three. I owed at *least* that much to Lumia.

Just to move around and warm up a bit, I got up and walked the short hallway: portrait to sitting room, portrait to sitting room, three times. On the third pass I went into the sitting room and picked up the two best of the African American dolls, not for their value but because they had individual faces, which was seldom the case with these things. One of them had an air of secret amusement I especially liked, and it made me wish I had met the person, almost certainly a woman, who had painted it.

The rain had lightened. As I sat down again at the head of the stairs with my dolls in my lap and the pale patch behind me, I decided to stay until four. Or maybe five. I paged ahead in the old man's apology or justification or memoir, whichever it was, until I once again saw Conan Doyle's name.

My list of crimes, while they had seemed to me when I committed them to be grave offenses against mankind, did not, when I shared them with Dr. Conan Doyle, evoke censure or condemnation. He gave them the same attention he had probably given to Buffalo Bill. All went well as long as the stories lasted, but they soon grew scarcer and, quite obviously, less diverting to their audience. However short my criminal career had been, it was clear that I was unlikely to exhaust my store of tales before I exhausted Dr. Conan Doyle's interest. He had begun to listen dutifully, a terrible experience for the one who is telling the stories. I was not an accomplished storyteller, for one thing; and for another, all my tales shared a fault that is fatal to certain kinds of fiction: we both knew the ending. I was, after all, unharmed and present, in the flesh. One evening, at a cafe to which we had repaired when the meeting ended, feeling desperate at his diminished interest in my history and not wanting to lose the pleasure of his company, I plucked up my courage and told him about Hermann Wendt, the man whom I had killed in order to steal his gold.

I must confess, however, that I softened the tale. I said I had wounded Wendt and that he had recovered but had died soon after, of natural causes. The doctor let the silence between us grow until I could feel my face heat up, which was a revelation: I thought my days of blushing were long past. Then he asked me what, if I could see that man again, I would do.

At once, I was weeping. I told him of my wish to kneel before Wendt and beg his pardon and his blessing when I had joined him in the spirit world. I confided that the brutality of my life was the thing that made me most wish to survive its ending, in the hope that I could, in that other dimension, undo the things I had done in this one. Dr. Doyle was a man who kept his distance physically, but he reached across the table and put his hand on my shoulder and engaged my eyes with his own. He said that with sincere penance my soul would be unmarked—the soul was, he said, for all its heavenly origin, harder than diamond and endlessly bright—and that he knew I could shrug off my old ways and embrace the soul's natural path of light. He would not judge me harshly, he promised. Our friendship was not imperiled.

The forgiven criminal, I thought.

After I had recovered myself from a most unmanly

display of emotion, he asked me to tell him the details of my latest crime which, I swore to him, would be my last. Dr. Conan Doyle listened as I unspooled the story of the carbuncle, expressing special interest in the jewel itself. He praised the cut I had described to him, saying he found it more elegant and less vulgar than the hard sparkle of faceted stones. When I had finished the tale, he once again sat silent for long moments. I felt a sinking fear that, despite his earlier assurances, I had crossed a line from which there was no retreat, that he would disown me and sever our friendship.

Imagine my surprise when instead, he said, with that brightening of his eyes I had seen only on one previous occasion, "Let us look at a related problem. Suppose you had to conceal the stone. Let us imagine that you knew that the crime would be investigated by a fearsome antagonist, a detective as brilliant as . . ."

He stopped, and for a moment I was certain he would name his own creation, Mr. Holmes, who was then being talked about with great enthusiasm in London, but instead, he said, ". . . as brilliant as your countryman Mr. Burns. Where would you secure the jewel?"

I had, in fact, hidden the carbuncle by folding it into a piece of paper and using a dab of Hiltpeter's very sturdy mucilage to secure the little packet to the bottom of the closet door in my hotel room. It is extraordinary how seldom people look at the bottom of a door. The packet

cleared the carpet easily, and I was certain it
was safe there, although I did check daily to
make sure the mucilage's seal remained intact.

But I hesitated to reveal my arrangement, for
two reasons. The first, I am ashamed to say, was
that I was reluctant for anyone else, even my new
friend, to know where it was. Secrets can best be
kept, I have learned, if they are known only to
a single person. The second reason was that, in
casting about for another method of hiding ill-
gotten spoils, I remembered instead the story of
Clovis Menger, which had provoked laughter even
when I told it one evening to a group of desperate men sitting around a campfire that they all
knew could well have been their last. Indeed,
they laughed so hard and so loudly that their
leader brandished his guns to threaten them into
silence.

Even though it depended for its humor on a
kind of subject matter seldom discussed among
the cultured residents of London, the tale did
have to do with hiding stolen treasure. Thus,
with some misgivings, I told Doctor Conan Doyle
how Clovis, a common burglar and pig farmer, had
been warned one day that the sheriff was even then
swearing in a posse to arrest him for the theft
from the Swandale First Bank of more than eight
pounds of gold nuggets. This quantity of gold,
then selling at almost $21.00 per ounce, was
worth nearly $2700, in the west an unimaginable
fortune for all but the very rich.

Despite its grandiose name, Swandale was a

decrepit wooden building with a lock I could have picked with a dining fork. Clovis had apparently been spotted entering the bank, even at three in the morning, by some ne'er-do-well in the saloon across the way, and the drunkard had peached on him the very next morning in hope of a reward.

Clovis gave his friend thirty dollars, a great wad of money in that place at that time, and waited until he was sure the informer was gone and had not doubled back to see what he would do. Then he ran into the house, got the canvas bag of gold, and carried it to the pig pen. There he began to feed the pigs one at a time, and as each of them opened wide, Clovis inserted the metal cleaning rod from his six-gun vertically between the pig's jaws, thereby propping its mouth open while he forced nuggets down its throat. He finished the unorthodox meal by pouring a bucket of water into the pig's open mouth, compelling it to choose between swallowing and drowning. When he had fed all seven pigs, the gold was gone.

By the time the posse arrived, Clovis was sitting on his horse at an overlook that concealed him and gave him a good view of his property, the very one he had feared the informant might use to spy on him. After giving the posse time enough to search his house and the grounds, Clovis rode down to the homestead and demanded to know what the posse's members were doing on his property. The sheriff blustered, as sheriffs will, but without the gold he had no case against Clovis except the testimony of a well-known sot. He had no alternative but to abandon the field of battle.

When I had got this far in the story, I paused, and Doctor Conan Doyle cleared his throat and said, "Ingenious, but obviously one problem remained."

"Actually," I said, delighted by his expression of interest, "more than one." And I told him how, late that night, a group of masked men, several of whom Clovis recognized from the posse and one of whom was the informant, surrounded the cabin with much shooting of guns and how, when Clovis came out, they manhandled him to the pig pen, where he was securely tied to the fence. Then the masked men set a circle of fires around the pen and retired to their warmth. While Clovis shivered and listened to the laughter grow louder as the levels dropped in the bottles of rum and brandy the men had taken from his house, watchmen were set, with military precision, two at a time to stand on either side of the pig pen. Not, as Clovis first thought, to keep an eye on him. Rather, they were keeping an eye on the pigs.

It was the longest, weariest, and foulest night of Clovis's life. Every time a pig obeyed the command of nature, Clovis's rope was adjusted to allow him to reach the new set of droppings. Pig sewage is uniquely malodorous. The men laughed, holding their noses, as Clovis, as they put it, prospected for gold. When he had searched each deposit thoroughly, using his bare hands, he dropped his discoveries into a bucket of water,

which was then swirled around and tossed onto the
ground so the men could handle the nuggets without being soiled. Time, as many have observed,
has the elastic quality of slowing for misery;
to Clovis, that night and most of the following day seemed to take years. When, at last,
the men rode off, taking Clovis's gold with them,
they left behind in the pigpen a rough sign that
said 'CLOVIS MENGER'S GOLD MINE.' Clovis left it
there until he disappeared, several days later.
His travel was funded, people speculated, by one
or two pigs with especially slow constitutions.

I was surprised, as I told the tale, by how
avidly Dr. Conan Doyle followed it. When it was
finished, he picked up his glass of wine and drank.
"The plan was good," he said. "But it required a
more sophisticated digestive system." Not until
I received the book he sent to me in America
and read it did I realize that I had given him
a story, the one in which Holmes, in the spirit
of Christmas, uniquely forgives the thief he has
apprehended through his rigorous logic.

As I sat in the dark and I considered Conan Doyle's
remarkable, perhaps even schizophrenic, ability to
embrace both logic and spiritualism, I realized that at
some point in my reading I'd taken the stone from my
pocket and had been turning it over in my fingers as I followed Horton's story. I'd been doing it long enough that
it had warmed to the touch. And my fingers had found
something somewhere, some kind of irregularity, but—
My train of thought was derailed as I registered two

things almost simultaneously: first, that the rain had stopped; and second, that I was hearing a metallic sound, just audible, from outdoors. The fence was being climbed.

I got up, turned off the phone, and put it into one of my cargo pockets. Then I pulled out the other things I needed, sat the dolls on the floor beside the chair, and took my seat again. I turned out the little penlight, pocketed it, and waited, still turning the stone between my fingers, like a worry bead. In the fifth or sixth of a series of slow, quiet breaths, there was a sensation of something almost physically clicking into place and I realized what I had felt. I extracted the penlight again and turned it on to verify my suspicion. Then I returned the penlight and the jewel to my shirt pocket and focused on breathing. I was no longer cold. For what seemed like the first time since I first entered Horton House, it wasn't creaking.

I may have laughed.

They certainly weren't burglars. They fumbled getting the key into the lock so many times that I could have come in through the kitchen window, stopped in the hallway to listen, gone to the bookshelves, chosen a book, and carried it upstairs without accelerating my heart rate by the time they'd defeated the lock. Then, opening the door, they banged it into the wall. One of them said, "Sssshhhhhh," and I realized that I was saying it, too, although much more softly. Then the woman said, quietly but not really a whisper, "Do you think you can close it without slamming it?"

He said, "Oh, fuck off." So they were as cranky as I was. The door closed, just loudly enough for him to make the perpetual male point. There was some purposeful creaking as they went down the hall. The spill from an unfocused flashlight splashed on the wall beside the stairs.

"Hey," he said, "lookit the books." He creaked and groaned his way across the living room below.

"Who cares?" she said. "Wow, last time I was here this dump had furniture in it."

"That's very interesting," he said. "Some of these books are really old. *Shit!*"

"What? And come on over here. If it's anywhere, it's up—"

"These fucking pictures," he said. "Got fucking *spooks* in them."

"The old guy believed in, like, everything," she said. "Told my grandmother they'd be together forever in the afterlife, which he thought would be great, like Florida for dead people. She told my mother she'd had plenty of him already. Let's get upstairs. We made too much noise getting in."

"What a fucking *dump*," he said.

"It was nice twenty years ago. 'Course, that was in the daytime. Come *on*."

Her flashlight picked out the lower stairs, and I saw her hand on the banister. "If you don't *mind*," she said, "can we please get on with it? And don't aim that thing at me, you're blinding me."

He must have turned his flashlight off because the light level dropped, and then he appeared, nose first, on the first step after the stairs curved right, up toward me. Then she was beside him, and as she began to bring her flashlight up to point it at the second floor, I turned on mine, which was a zillion-watt cop special, and got them right in the eyes.

"*Jesus*," he said, backing away with his hands over his eyes. "I can't see shit."

"Both of you," I said, "stay exactly where you are, and I mean *exactly*. You, too, Paulette." Her jaw dropped. "Let go of that flashlight now, and I'm not kidding, if either of you moves, I'll shoot you."

He moved, in the form of a quick backward step down, and I shot him, low in the right leg, to the accompaniment of a discreetly muffled *phut* from Eaglet's silencer. It was a tricky shot, but Eaglet had a great gun. He went down screaming and grabbing at his leg, falling back a step to collapse on the landing, and I said to her, "Shut him up or I'll shoot him again."

She turned partly away and kicked him, and he shut up, although he whimpered a little. When she pivoted back, she had a gun in her hand. She fired twice at the light, but it was in my left hand and I had my arm fully extended from my body, so she missed me by a couple of feet. I fired twice into the stair above the one she was standing on, which got her attention.

"Next one's through the heart," I said. "Lower them both, the gun and the flashlight. Put them three steps up. *Don't climb the stairs,* just turn off the flashlight, lean forward, and put them down. I can kill both of you and be out of here in sixty seconds, leave you for the bulldozer."

She did it, lining them up perfectly parallel and then put a hand to her forehead, trying to cut the glare and catch sight of me. I wiggled the light back and forth and said, "Uh-uh. You already know who I am."

She said, "Cocksucker."

"Get your friend's gun," I said, "and put it on the same step, next to yours."

They had a brief tug of war until I fired another shot into the wall just above their heads, and then he yielded it.

"Put it right there," I said to her when she hesitated. "This is just going to take a minute," I said. "How did you get involved with Allan Frame?"

"*That's* your question?"

"It's my first. And my easiest, and I want an answer now."

"He was, you know, *friends* with my mother, like a lot of other guys. I was supposed to call him *Uncle Allan*."

"You spent a lot of money on this project—"

"No kidding, you asshole."

"Where did it come from?"

She looked up at me, and I gave her the light again, and she put up a hand to block it and said, "*Damn* you. Uncle Allan put it up. My mother never stopped talking about—about . . ." She glanced down at the fallen man and shook her head as though it was *his* fault he was lying there bleeding.

"What did Uncle Allan want?"

"Half," she said nastily. "Just half. Because he loved my mother and me *so much*."

"Too bad. Next question. When you picked up Lumia, who was driving?"

"I was," she said, and he said, "She was."

"So you, Mister Nose—wait, what's your name?"

"Phil."

"Not Eddie."

"Phil," he said again.

"So you, Phil, that makes you the one who shot Lumia."

"No," Phil said immediately, "I didn't."

"Then this is how I'm supposed to see it?" I said. "Sweet little Paulette here is driving, facing forward because that's where they put the controls and the window and everything, and you're in the front seat next to her and facing back, but *she's* the one who pulls the gun, turns her head a hundred eighty degrees, takes her foot off the pedal, and fires the shot?"

Paulette said, "I should have met someone like you."

I said to Phil, "And I suppose you killed that awful agent, too."

"No, I did," she said. "It was my turn, and she never saw Phil. But he *was* the one who shot your little friend."

"Why?" I said.

Her forehead wrinkled. "Why what?"

"Why shoot Lumia?"

"She'd *seen* us," Paulette said as though it were the simplest thing in the world. She didn't shrug, but the gesture was in her tone. "The stone was going to be the beginning of a new life. I couldn't leave people all over the place who knew about us. It was all—even with only half, everything was going to be *new*."

Phil groaned, and she said, "Shut up."

"Well," I said, "here's the issue. You two killed a friend of mine. He pulled the trigger, but who cares? You just told me that you would have shot her, too. What I *should* do, you know, in the interest of symmetry, is kill you both."

"*It was mine,*" she said. "That old bitch stole it from me. It was mine, it was my mother's, it was my *grand-mother's*. It didn't belong to *her*. It was rightfully mine."

"Okay," I said. I turned the light aside. "Tell me when you can see me."

She said, "What?"

"Let me know when you can see me clearly."

She squeezed her eyes shut, opened her mouth wide, relaxed her face, and looked up at me. "Okay," she said.

I said, "Catch," and threw the stone, underhand, to her. She fielded it neatly, looked down at it, and took an inadvertent step back that sent her tumbling down the stair behind her. Fortunately for her, she landed mainly on Phil, who let out a high puppy's yip of pain.

She was still on top of him, but I don't think she even knew he was there. She held the stone up to the splash of light from where my beam was hitting the wall. Her breath was coming short and fast and choppy, and then she began to weep, a harsh, rusty sound. In between sniffles, she said, "Where did—where did—"

I said, "Do you know anything about the Mohs Scale?"

She was blinking at me as though I'd begun to talk in tongues. "The—the what?" Her eyes went back to the jewel. She rubbed it against her cheek.

"It was invented early in the nineteenth century by a guy named Friedrich Mohs. It measures the hardness of minerals."

She said, "So *what*?"

"He used a method that's elegant in its simplicity. What it came down to was what you could use to put a scratch into what. For example, everybody knows you can scratch glass with a diamond." She was moving, putting her weight on Phil, who protested wordlessly as she rose, her eyes on mine. He was bleeding quite a lot. I said, "That's because glass has a hardness of about five or five and a half on the Mohs scale, depending on what kind of glass it is, and diamond is ranked at ten, making it the hardest of all naturally occurring minerals."

She said again, "So what," but she had already seen where it was going.

"So sapphire is ranked nine. There's almost nothing you can scratch sapphire with, except a diamond, and even then it takes a lot of strength. Turn the stone over."

She did, and all her breath escaped in a hiss.

"That's a pretty deep scratch," I said. "What you're holding is glass."

She put the hand with the stone on the banister, and it slipped from her fingers and fell with a clatter to the uncarpeted floor below the stairs. She said, "He left her a *fake*? Why would he—I mean, why—"

"I doubt it," I said. "My guess is that Miss Daisy sold it the moment she came of age, but she had this thing made first. That way, if you ever got hold of it legally, she could claim she knew nothing about it, not even that anything was in the doll, and if you somehow got in and stole it, either while she was living or after she died, it would be a terrific *fuck you*. And you know what else? She even hid it, pretty well, so you'd have the thrill of finding it, giving you even further to fall when you learned it was duff. That's the kind of hate you don't see much of these days. A parting gesture with some real weight behind it."

She had her eyes closed, and I went slowly down the stairs and took the guns she'd put there. I said to Phil, "You going to be able to walk?"

He swore at me, the words fairly vile but with no inflection at all. He had his eyes closed. I said, "Good to hear it. Listen, what I *want* to do is kill you both, but—and I don't expect you to understand this—there's a kind of chain of mercy here, and I don't think I want to break it. Also it would be nice if one of the last things that happens in this fucking awful house is an act of mercy. So instead of killing you, I'm going upstairs for a moment and then I'm coming back down and leaving. One more time, Phil. Do you think you can get over the fence?"

Phil said, "Fuck you."

"That's what I thought," I said. I went upstairs and grabbed the two rag dolls. Then I crossed the hall to Miss Collins's room and took the photograph from her box of letters. I suppose I hoped her ghost would follow the picture so it wouldn't be adrift when the house was no more. I tucked into my cargo pants everything but my gun and the flashlight, and went to the head of the stairs. Neither of them seemed to have moved.

"You need to get out of here," I said to Paulette. "That shot you fired was loud, and he's losing blood. I should volunteer to help you with him, but mercy goes only so far." I navigated around them on the stairs as though they were contaminated. When I was most of the way to the front door, a 20,000-volt spike of spite seized me, and I said, "Paulette?"

"What?"

"Miss Daisy really *got* you, didn't she? She played you like a harmonica, from the very beginning, and you behaved like a good little puppet. Something to sleep on, if you can sleep. Oh, and don't forget your nice piece of glass. You're going to make Uncle Allan *so* happy"

It was 2:46 A.M., according to the phone, when it rang, and it was going to take me one more minute of mechanical mindless driving, before I'd pull into the edgewood's driveway, numb, self-loathing, and exhausted. Even though it said CRIME BOSS, I let it go. After four rings it shut down, but then it started up again, so I said something unpleasant and picked it up. Tuffy said, "Mr. Dressler says you don't have to worry about Allan F."

"Allan F?" I said. My mind was empty. "Oh, right, Allan F."

In the background I heard Dressler saying, "Tell him what I said. It was pretty good."

"Mr. Dressler says to tell you that Allan F. just won a lottery he didn't know he'd entered."

"Good," I said. I blew out a quart of air, hearing it on the earpiece of the phone. "Tell him I said so. Bye."

"Wait," Tuffy said. "He—"

Dressler said, "Gimme that phone." Then he said, "Hello?"

I said, "I'm driving."

"So stop driving, schmuck. Have you stopped yet?"

"Sure," I said, still driving. "Thanks for—"

"You sound kinda down. Are you kinda down? 'Cause, listen, I was right. I got a little something. Doc Fleiss called the people who run the imaging center, what we used to call an X-ray, but with nuclear power or something, and they came in and made it work, and I got a little thing there. Doc says don't worry, but, you know, it's not *his* little thing, but he says there's miracles with that kinda thing these days."

I had pulled over. "What specific kind of little—"

"You know what kind. Since I told you about it, I figured I should also tell you the doc said it'll maybe be okay. Maybe. And if it isn't, it isn't. But right now, I'm standing up straight and talking to you in my fancy phone, and Allan F., he's on the other side of the curtain. Listen, come by sometime when you don't need a favor. I got some more wine I'd like you to tell me about."

He hung up. I sat there for a minute or two and then put the car back in gear. Only a minute more, and I'd be home.

33
Twenty Minutes

I threw the deadbolt and put the chain on the door. Then I flipped on the hallway light and looked at the broken glass sparkling on the marble floor of the entry hall, at the scattering of dead flowers, the eviscerated couch cushions, the warm-colored fragments of old Native American pottery given to me by a talented pot thief named Hubic Schuze. The water had dried, leaving a ghosty little outline of where it had been, a miniature dry lake bed.

I have no idea how much later it was, but the living room windows were going pale and I was on my knees with a damp cloth, rubbing at the minerals in the water's outline when my phone rang.

"Where *are* you?" Ronnie said. "I got up to pee and you weren't here. It's getting *light* out."

"I'm home," I said. "But I'm not fit company for anyone."

"Don't be silly," she said. "I'm not company, I'm the one you dance with."

"It's been . . ." I said. "It's been darker than I want to think about."

"I'll be there—" she began, but I cut her off.

"No. Really. Do yourself a favor and give me some time to—"

"I will," she said. "I'll give you until I get there. Twenty minutes, I'll be there in twenty minutes."

And she was. She was there before the sun came up.

Afterword

If ever a belief was born at the right time, it was spiritualism. It emerged from a world in which lives were much shorter than they are today and where infant mortality was high. By the time most people were in their mid-twenties, they had mourned loved ones—parents, children, brothers or sisters, friends, spouses, lovers. Death, it seemed to many of them, was in the last room they had left and would be waiting in the next room they entered.

Smallpox and flu repeatedly swept the world. In the last half of the nineteenth century wars and skirmishes broke out like brushfires in Europe, the New World, and Asia, global stress fractures that made new widows and orphans, killed entire families, wiped out towns.

Where had all those people gone? Were they lost forever to the living?

Spiritualism said no. It said it so often and so pervasively that spiritualist societies were formed, books were written, and mediums proliferated, offering brief chats with the departed, for a price. Spirit photography flourished, reuniting in somewhat vague black and white the mourner and the mournee.

And then 1918 brought the greatest cataclysms of all.

World War One killed almost eighteen million people, the Spanish Flu epidemic killed another 50 to 100 million, and suddenly, everyone was bereaved. The ranks of the spiritualists expanded exponentially. Mediums became so prevalent and (from one perspective) so flagrant that Scientific American offered a $5,000 prize to the medium whose tricks it could not detect.

The spiritualists and the anti-spiritualists coalesced behind two warring and very well-known men, once good friends, who would seem to have been on the wrong sides. Opposing spiritualism—even helping to evaluate the mediums who competed for the Scientific American prize—was the magician Harry Houdini, then at the apogee of his fame. Championing the mediums and the world of the spiritualists was the medical doctor Arthur Conan Doyle, better known as the creator of literature's most supremely rational detective, Sherlock Holmes.

The Conan Doyle in this book is accurate in that he was enamored of the American West as a result of attending Buffalo Bill's touring show; he was fascinated by the New York detective who was one inspiration for the sleuth of Baker Street; and he was a fervent spiritualist. Had he met Mr. Codwallader, he might well have been sufficiently interested in him to encourage a closer acquaintance and even listen to his stories. Truth really is stranger than fiction.

And on a very different note, RIP Du-par's. The restaurant in which Junior meets Louie, Glinda, and the scrofulous Walter was recently evicted after serving pretty good food at reasonable prices, twenty-four hours a day, for seventy years. The landlords, who were making tens of thousands a month in rent, demanded an increase the restaurant couldn't meet, thus supporting Louie the Lost's contention that "The whole fucking world economy has turned into a giant sponge that the only reason it exists is to squeeze all the money there is up to the One Percent. That's why these rents are going up. It's like, whatever river you're on, the water flows into Lake Fatso and stays there." From the shores of Lake Fatso, the landlords decided to lease the space to a chain makeup store.

Just what LA needs: more makeup.

Lots of great music went into this book: Lucius, Aimee Mann, Alabama Shakes, Anderson East, Alt-J, Aretha Franklin, Arcade Fire, Arctic Monkeys, Ashley Monroe—and that's mostly just the As. Also, a lot of Bartok and Eric Satie, plus Mozart's transcendentally beautiful clarinet quartet, Beethoven's world-refreshing violin concerto in D, and the gorgeous first violin concerto by Bruch.

As always, if you want to suggest some music or otherwise enrich my life, write me at http://www.timothyhallinan. com/contact.php